# A HANDBOOK OF AMERICAN MUSIC AND MUSICIANS

Da Capo Press Music Reprint Series

GENERAL EDITOR

FREDERICK FREEDMAN

VASSAR COLLEGE

# A HANDBOOK OF AMERICAN MUSIC AND MUSICIANS

*Containing Biographies of American Musicians
and Histories of the Principal Musical
Institutions, Firms and Societies*

Edited by F. O. Jones

𝄞 DA CAPO PRESS • NEW YORK • 1971

A Da Capo Press Reprint Edition

This Da Capo Press edition of
*A Handbook of American Music and Musicians*
is an unabridged republication of the first
edition published in Canaseraga, New York,
in 1886.

Library of Congress Catalog Card Number 76-155355

SBN 306-70163-4

Published by Da Capo Press, Inc.
A Subsidiary of Plenum Publishing Corporation
227 West 17th Street, New York, N. Y. 10011
All Rights Reserved

Manufactured in the United States of America

# A HANDBOOK OF AMERICAN MUSIC AND MUSICIANS

A

# HANDBOOK

OF

## AMERICAN

## MUSIC AND MUSICIANS,

CONTAINING

BIOGRAPHIES OF AMERICAN MUSICIANS,

AND

Histories of the Principal Musical Institutions, Firms
and Societies.

———

EDITED BY

## F. O. JONES.

———

CANASERAGA, N. Y.:
PUBLISHED BY F. O. JONES.
1886.

# PREFACE.

I deem it my first duty to apologize to my friends who have waited so long and so patiently for my "Dictionary of American and Foreign Music and Musicians," (commenced in 1878), which they had every reason to expect, from announcements made by myself, would be published ere this. Indeed, it was my own expectation at one time that it would be published three years ago, but the little matter of finding a publisher was one not easily accomplished. The merit of the work was universally conceded, and three firms were only dissuaded from undertaking it by its size, (about 700 octavo pages like these). Last autumn I determined to publish it myself, and made every arrangement to that effect. At the very last moment, however, for good and sufficient reasons, I substituted this little volume in its place, and sincerely hope it may prove useful to a degree far in excess of its size.

The present volume contains everything relative to American music, musicians (both native and foreign born), and musical subjects, which had been prepared for the larger work. None of the biographies or articles have been amplified or even changed. In every case has it been endeavored to give exact dates and facts, and to correct any errors which may have previously existed. Much of the information was derived from first sources by correspondence. If in any particular it is incorrect, I will be glad to receive notice of the fact from those who know such to be the case. It will also give me pleasure to receive a copy of every publication making any allusion to or criticism of my work, whether adverse or commendatory.

Undoubtedly some worthy subjects have received no attention in these pages. This may be due to a limited reputation, to failure to gain the necessary information, even after the most persistent efforts, or to an oversight. Whatever deficiency exists in this respect will, if possible, be remedied in a second edition. Lengthy articles are not always indicative of merit, nor short ones indicative of the reverse. In many cases, lack of information has made the article correspondingly brief. A thousand and one considerations and elements, of which the casual reader may never dream, enter into the preparation of a work like this.

In conclusion, I wish to tender my hearty thanks to the following well-known musical writers, and to all others who have in any manner assisted me in my arduous task : Karl Merz, Wooster, Ohio; C. H. Brittan, Chicago; Wm. M. Thoms, New York; Wm. D. Tuthill, New York; E. M. Bowman, St. Louis; E. Eugene Davis, Cincinnati; P. J. Smith, Brooklyn.

I trust that at no very far distant day my larger and complete work may appear.

THE AUTHOR.

CANASERAGA, (Allegany Co.,) N. Y., *February* 15, 1886.

# HANDBOOK

OF

# American Music and Musicians.

## A.

**Abbott,** EMMA, was born in 1850, at Chicago, where her father was a music teacher. From the first she exhibited a great love of music, and was almost constantly singing in her childish way. In 1854 her father removed to Peoria, Ill., where he had barely pupils enough to keep the wolf from the door. Miss Emma began to learn the guitar, on which she soon attained so much skill as to attract attention. This fact and her constantly increasing vocal powers led her father to think of bringing her out at a public concert with her brother, George, which he did with success. At that time she was nine years old. Encouraged by this venture, they visited and gave hundreds of concerts in other towns. At sixteen, in order to keep the family from want, Emma taught district school. She then started on a concert tour in Illinois, unaccompanied by any one. At Joliet she joined a Chicago opera troupe, but when the troupe broke up she found herself at Grand Haven, Mich., without any money. With great courage, however, she gave concerts and gradually worked her way to New York City, where she managed to hear Parepa-Rosa. But she failed to gain any recognition in that grea metropolis, and, utterly discouraged, borrowed money to return West. She then tried giving concerts in Chicago and Milwaukee, but without success. Finally, after a tour of some of the small towns, she arrived at Toledo, Ohio, and gave a concert in the parlors of the Oliver House, which proved a failure. At this critical juncture she met Clara Louise Kellogg, who was so well pleased with her voice that she sent her to New York. This was in 1870, and for two years she studied hard, meanwhile singing in Dr. Chapin's Fifth Avenue Church. In May, 1872, having previously furnished with the necessary means by a few of her friends, she went to Milan, and studied for some time under the best masters there. She then went to Paris and studied under Wartel, with whom she remained several years. After completing her education she was offered numerous good engagements in Europe. In 1880 she returned to her native country, and was well received. She has since sung in many of the principal cities here.

**Academy of Music,** NEW YORK. This is not an institution of learning, but a large building used for concerts and dramatic representations. It was opened Oct. 2, 1854, with a production of "Norma," Grisi and Mario in the chief *rôles*. In 1866 it was destroyed by fire, but re-opened in February; 1867. The ACADEMY OF MUSIC, *Philadelphia*, which is almost equally as noted as that at New York, was opened with Mme. Gazzaniga, Sig. Brignoli, and Sig. Amadio, in "Il Trovatore," Feb. 26, 1857. It is said to be one of the finest arranged theatres in the world.

**Adams,** CHARLES R., tenor singer, was born at Charlestown, Mass., about 1848, and early showed great musical talent. He studied with Mme. Arnoult, a French vocal teacher at Boston, and subsequently with Prof. Mulder, a French gentleman, whom he accompanied to Europe. At Vienna he became a pupil of Barhiere, and made such a brilliant record that he was engaged as first tenor at the Royal Opera House, Berlin, where he remained three years. The ensuing nine years were spent as first tenor at the Imperial Opera House, Vienna. Meanwhile he continued his studies under the best teachers of Europe, and sang in opera two seasons at Covent Garden, London; one season at La Scala, Milan, and one at the Royal Opera, Madrid, besides appearing at various theatres throughout Germany. As an exponent of Wagnerian music he was much admired, rendering the *rôles* in "Lohengrin" and "Tannhäuser" in a manner equaled by few artists. Since returning to this country he has sung one season in German opera with Mme. Pappenheim and one season in Italian opera with the Strakosch company. In 1879 he settled in Boston, where he is still (Jan., 1886) located, all his time aside from professional engagements being taken up in teaching. Mr. Adams is not only a fine singer but a good actor, his impersonation of *Raoul* in "Les Huguenots" and *Don Jose* in "Carmen" being especially excellent.

**Adams,** DR. F. W. A violin maker, born at Montpelier, Vermont, in 1787. Early in life he turned his attention to the making of violins, contending that the ancient Cremonas might be equaled, providing the right kind of wood in the right condition was used. He chiefly employed pine and maple, taken from old and thoroughly seasoned trees. During his life he completed one hundred and forty instruments, which brought large prices. Frequently he would refuse to sell at any price. His violins became known far and wide for the power and sweetness of their tone. He died in 1859.

**Albani,** MARIE LOUISE EMMA CECILIE, one of America's most noted singers, was born in 1851, at Chambly, near Montreal.*

* Moore's Encyclopædia of Music, page 5 of the Appendix, gives the year of her birth as 1850, and the place as Plattsburg, N. Y., with which most American writers agree. It appears that the family, after leaving Montreal, first removed to Plattsburg, where a stay of considerable length was made, and from there to Albany. This may account for the conflicting statements.

Her father, Joseph La Jeunesse, was a French Canadian, and her mother a Scotch lady. As her father was a music teacher, she was brought up in a musical atmosphere. When she was five years of age the family removed to Montreal, and she entered the school of the convent of the Sacre Cœur, where she remained some years. In 1864 the family went to Albany, and while studying Emma sang in the choir of the Catholic Cathedral. Her fine voice soon began to attract attention, and her father was urged to take her to Europe that her voice might be suitably cultivated. The necessary funds were raised by a concert, and in 1868 she left with her father for Europe. At Paris she studied for eight months with Duprez, and then proceeded to Milan, where she studied for some time with Lamperti. She made her *début* at Messina, in "La Sonnambula," having previously adopted the stage name of *Albani* in memory of the city where her musical career really began. Afterwards she sang at Pergola and Florence, and made her first appearance at London, at Covent Garden, April 2, 1872. She was well received and soon became a great favorite there. The same year she visited Paris and sang in the Italian Opera. Returning to Milan she continued her studies under her former master. In 1873 she again sang at London, at St. Petersburg, and during the winter of 1873-74 made a flying visit to this country. She was married to Ernst Gye, who is lessee of Covent Garden, Aug. 6, 1878, and makes it her home at London. Her voice is a light soprano, sympathetic in quality, and especially effective in the upper register. Her principal *rôles*, which indicate great versatility of talent, are *Amina* in "Sonnambula," *Margherita* in "Faust," *Mignon, Ophelia, Elsa* in "Lohengrin," *Lucia, Linda, Gilda* in "Rigoletto," and *Elizabetta* in "Tannhäuser."

**Allen,** CHESTER G., known as a teacher, composer and musical writer, was born Feb. 15, 1838, at Westford, Otsego Co., N. Y. He edited or compiled several collections of music, for schools and churches, containing many pieces of his own composing, some of which are well esteemed. For some time he was editor of the "New York Musical Gazette," now defunct. At one time he was also teacher of music in the public schools of

Cleveland, Ohio. He died at Cooperstown, N. Y., Oct. 18, 1878.

**American Art Journal** (The) NEW YORK. A twenty-page weekly publication devoted to reviews and criticisms of music, art, literature and the music trades. It was founded in 1863, by Henry C. Watson, who was for a long time its editor and proprietor. At present (Jan., 1886) it is edited by Wm. M. Thoms.

**American College of Musicians.** See COLLEGE OF MUSICIANS, AMERICAN.

**American Harmony.** 1.—A collection of hymn tunes compiled and published by Daniel Bailey of Newburyport, Mass. It was issued in two volumes, the first of which appeared in 1769 and the second in 1771. The first volume contains "A new and correct Introduction to the Grounds of Musik, Rudimental, Practical and Technical." Both volumes were made up from collections which had been published in England.

2.—A similar collection was published in 1792, at Charlestown, Mass., by Oliver Holden. In the preface the author says: "the whole entirely new," and styles himself "a teacher of music in Charlestown," though a carpenter by trade. Some of the tunes, which were harmonized in three and four parts, were undoubtedly of his own composing.

3.—A third collection bearing the same name was published at Philadelphia, in 1801, by Nehemiah Shumway. It contained 220 pages, and included a singers' manual.

**Amodio,** ALESSANDRO, born at Naples, in 1831, was a fine baritone singer. At a very early age he was taught music, learning the flute. Becoming enamored of the stage and failing to obtain his parents' consent to adopt it as a profession, he ran away from home and appeared at various places, earning considerable reputation. In 1855 he came to this country in company with the La Grange opera troupe, and traveled throughout the States. He afterwards went to Cuba and sang in the Tacon Theatre, Havana, and to Venezuela. Starting to return to New York, he was taken with a fever and died on the sea near Havana, in June, 1861.

**Amodio,** FREDRICO, brother of the preceding, was born at Naples in 1833. He also possessed a fine baritone voice, and achieved some reputation as a singer in his native coun-try. He went to South America, and was with his brother when he died, after which he came to this country, arriving here in 1861. The Amodio family comprised six sons and two daughters.

**Anschutz,** CARL, born in Germany about 1830, came to this country in 1857. He soon became prominently identified with its musical interests, taking a leading position among our musicians. He was largely engaged in conducting operas, and in 1861 was connected with the Academy of Music and the National Musical Institute, in New York. Mr. Anschutz came to the United States at a period when music was developing into a fresh, vigorous life, and did much to aid its growth, for which he will long be remembered. This excellent man died at his residence in Boston, January 23, 1870. The disease which hastened his end was cancer of the throat, and for four months previous to his death he lived entirely on fluids. Only the day before he died he bit his wife's finger to indicate his great hunger.

**Apollino.** A machine or instrument which could produce the sounds of twenty-eight different musical instruments, comprising a whole orchestra. It contained 25 flageolets, 25 clarinets, 25 imitations of birds, 4 bugles, 8 French horns, and other instruments in proportion, which could be played singly or all together. A Mr. Plimpton was the inventor, and it was first exhibited at New York and Boston, in 1820. It was only one of the numerous attempts to combine many instruments into one, made about the same time. Its name was changed to *Plimptonia* and subsequently to *Plimptonichord*, after its inventor. One man assisted by a boy could run it.

**Appy,** HENRI, was born at Hague, in 1828. He was the oldest son of John Appy, who held the position of solo violinist to King William I. of Holland, and inherited all his father's musical talents. Early in life he went on concert tours through various countries. He was appointed solo violinist to William II. of Holland, in 1848, and in 1850 gave concerts with Mlle. Bertha Johannsen. In 1851 he came to this country, and soon after made a tour of the States in company with Mme. Biscaccianti. He assisted at the Jenny Lind farewell concerts. In 1875 he was residing in Rochester, N. Y., as a teacher and conductor.

**Arbuckle,** MATTHEW, cornet player, was born at Lochside, near Glasgow, Scotland, in 1826. At the age of thirteen he entered the band of an English regiment, which he accompanied to China during the first "opium war" and to India during the Sikh war. On his return to England he studied under Wallace and Suckling, making very rapid progress. Soon after he came to the United States, and was for many years the leading cornet soloist of Gilmore's band. In 1869 he greatly distinguished himself at the great Peace Jubilee, playing the trumpet part while Mme. Parepa-Rosa sang the vocal part in "Let the bright Seraphim." He also won honors at the second Jubilee in 1872, as well as at the Centennial Exhibition in 1876, where he played for thirty consecutive days. During the summer season he usually played at Coney Island. In August, 1880, he became band-master of the Ninth Regiment band, a position that he ably filled until his death, which occurred (from pneumonia) at his residence in New York, May 23, 1883. He left a wife, a son and a daughter. The latter, Miss Lizzie Arbuckle, is a promising soprano.

**Arcadian Symphony.** A work in E minor, by George F. Bristow, originally intended as the introduction of a cantata entitled "The Pioneers; or, Westward Ho!" Performed by the Philarmonic Society, New York, Feb. 14, 1874. The libretto of the cantata was written by Henry C. Watson, for William Vincent Wallace, who had sketched out some of the music at the time of his death.

**Archer,** FREDERIC, was born June 16, 1838, at Oxford, England. Strange to relate, he at first exhibited a positive dislike for music, and it was not until he was eight years of age that this dislike suddenly gave way to an intense love for sweet sounds. His father, an excellent musician, now taught him the elements of music, and in the short space of a few months he was able to play almost any piece within the scope of his fingers at sight. In 1847 he became a member of the choir of Margaret Chapel (now All Saints' Church), London, where he not only attracted attention by his fine voice but by frequently assist-

ing the organist. He returned to Oxford in 1852. Some years later he made a tour in Europe. On his return he was appointed organist of the Panopticon, now the Alhambra theatre. In 1859 he married Miss Harriet Rothschild (related to the celebrated financiers of that name), who was his pupil, and for several years thereafter was engaged in conducting and giving organ recitals. He became organist and choirmaster of Christ Church, London, in 1864, and organist of Alexandria Palace in 1873. During his stay there he gave no less than 2000 organ recitals, but did not repeat a program. In 1877 he assumed the entire musical direction of the Palace. Notwithstanding the additional labors thus imposed, he found time to make visits to Glasgow as conductor, giving occasional recitals. In 1880 he organized an English opera company and gave performances in various cities and towns with good success. He came to this country in 1881 and has since resided in New York.

Mr. Archer's compositions are quite numerous and highly esteemed. Besides his organ pieces and arrangements, he has written two operas, some orchestral works, and considerable church, vocal, and piano music. As an organist he has complete control of his instrument and a wonderful faculty of sight playing.

**Archers, The;** or, THE MOUNTAINEERS OF SWITZERLAND. Probably the first American opera ever composed. The words are by William Dunlop; the music by Benjamin Carr. First produced at the John Street Theatre, New York, April 18, 1796. The opera is founded on the story of William Tell.

**Arnheim.** One of the few tunes which have survived from the days of the New England psalm singer, being still much used. It was composed by Samuel Holyoke when he was but fourteen years old (1785), and was the last tune he sang before his death in 1816. In all probability it was first published in his collection of sacred music, "Harmonia Americana," which appeared in 1791. See HARMONIA AMERICANA; also, HOLYOKE, SAMUEL.

**Arnhem,** MLLE., whose real name is KATE LARIMER JAMES, is the daughter of Judge James of Council Bluffs, Iowa. She was born there about 1862. Her mother was a Van Arnhem, born in Holland, and this name she adopted upon going upon the stage. Early in 1880 she went to Paris and became a pupil of Mme. La Grange. During her studies she memorized fifteen operas. She then went to London and studied ballad singing with Randegger. In 1881 she sang for Wilhelmj during his tour, and was frequently heard in the *salons* of ex-Queen Isabella of Spain at Paris. In the Spring of 1882 she appeared in the *rôle* of *Marguerite* at the Mechanics' Building, Boston, under Strakosch's management. Since then she has filled operatic engagements in Europe and this country. Her voice is a pleasing one, and her enunciation clear and distinct.

**Aronson,** RUDOLPH, was born in 1856, at New York City. At an early age he studied music under Leopold Meyer, then at Berlin, and finally at the Paris Conservatoire under Emile Durand, where he became well versed in harmony, counterpoint, and instrumentation. After returning to New York he became prominently connected with musical affairs there. He has for several years conducted an orchestra of fifty performers, and given concerts after the manner of Strauss, Arban and Gung'l. Metropolitan Concert Hall and The Casino were his projections and in a large measure due to his efforts. His compositions are quite numerous. Among the most popular are "Sweet Sixteen," a waltz written expressly for the celebrated cornet soloist, J. Levy; "The Marche Triomphale;" "Fête au Village," a fantasie;" "Mazurka Melodique," "Dwothy Waltz," and "Jockey Galop." He is at present (Jan., 1883) engaged on an operetta, "Captain Kidd," to be produced in the spring.

**Arthur,** ALFRED, was born Oct. 8, 1844, near Pittsburgh, Pa. When he was quite young his parents removed to Mansfield, O., where he began the study of music. From 1861 to 1864 he served in the army, the latter two years in the capacity of leader of the Eighth Brigade Band, under the command of General Hayes. At the close of the war he went to Boston to perfect his musical education, studying at the Boston School of Music and under private teachers, among whom was Julius Eichberg. In 1870 he settled in Cleveland, Ohio, as leader of the Germania Orchestra and chorister of Trinity Church. The latter position he soon resigned to accept a similar one at the Euclid Avenue Baptist Church, where he remained seven years, when he became leader of the Bach Choir at the Woodland Avenue Presbyterian Church, of which he still (Jan., 1884) has charge. He is also conductor of THE CLEVELAND VOCAL SOCIETY and other musical organizations, and had charge of the Cleveland May Festival forces in 1880 and 1882. Mr. Arthur has been very successful as a vocal teacher as well as a conductor. Among his more noted pupils are Mrs. Berdie Hale-Britton and Miss Dora Henninges. His compositions are not very numerous. Of the larger and more important are the operas of "The Water Carrier," first produced at Cleveland during the winter of 1872-73; "Cavaliers and Roundheads," and "Adeline."

# B.

**Bach Society, The,** CLEVELAND, O., was formed about 1878. The chorus consists of some eighty voices, with a string band of twelve pieces and an organ. The third annual concert was given Dec. 7, 1882. Though young, the society is an important factor in the musical affairs of the city. It forms the choir of the Woodland Avenue Presbyterian Church, and is one of the best models of chorus choirs in the United States. At present (Jan., 1884) Alfred Arthur is conductor, Miss F. J. Hopkins organist and J. H. Amme orchestral leader.

**Bærmann,** CARL, was born in Bavaria, in 1839. He descended from a very eminent musical family and began his studies in the Conservatorium at Munich in 1850. In 1857 he spent several months with Liszt. For some time after this he quietly devoted himself to teaching, marrying Beatrice von Dessauer in 1864. Upon the formation of the Royal School of Music at Munich, in 1867, he was appointed a professor of piano playing. In 1876 he was made royal professor by the King of Bavaria. Some time since he came to this country and made his *début* as a pianist at a concert of the Philharmonic Society, Boston, playing Beethoven's fourth concerto. He is at present (1883) a resident of Boston.

**Bailey,** THOMAS and DANIEL, were publishers and composers of music at Newburyport, Mass. Thomas republished a portion of a work by Wm. Tansur (English) in 1755, entitled "A Complete Melody, in Three Parts." It contained about one-third as much as the English work. In 1764 Daniel Bailey and John W. Gilman, an engraver of Exeter, N. H., published a small work entitled "A New and Complete Introduction to the Grounds and Rules of Music, in Two Parts." In the first part was an introduction to the art of singing by note, taken from a work by Thomas Walter, A. M., and in the second part a new and correct introduction to the grounds of music, rudimental and practical, taken from Wm. Tansur's "Royal Melody."

The work contained in all thirty-four tunes, arranged in three parts, for soprano, bass and tenor. Three editions were issued, apparently from the same plates but with different title pages and introductions, one for Bulkly Emerson and one for Mr. Bailey, at Newburyport, and one for Mascholl Williams, at Salem, Mass. Mr. Bailey's edition contained fourteen additional tunes. In 1769 Daniel Bailey published a work entitled "Universal Harmony," selected from Tansur's "Psalmody" and "Psalmody Evangelica" by Thomas Williams. The tunes in this were also in three parts. The Baileys are said to have published other works containing church tunes (always largely selected from English works), but no satisfactory trace of them can be found.

**Baker,** BENJAMIN FRANKLIN. Born at Wenham, Mass., July 10, 1811. When a young man he removed to Salem, and in 1831 commenced teaching music. In 1833 he traveled throughout the country as a member of a concert company. After this he studied with John Paddon, Boston, where, in 1839, he became musical director of Dr. Channing's church, a position which he retained eight years. In 1841 he began holding what were termed musical conventions, and soon after was appointed vice-president of the Handel and Haydn Society of Boston, holding the office six years. Commencing with 1842, he for six years was superintendent of musical instruction in grammar schools of the city. He subsequently became editor of the "Boston Musical Journal," and principal of the Boston Music School, which was incorporated in 1857. Since that time Mr. Baker has resided in Boston, devoting most of his time to teaching, in which he has been very successful, consequently his works are comparatively few. Among them are the "Burning Ship," "Storm King," and several other secular cantatas. He has also written a treatise on thorough-bass and harmony, which is published by O. Ditson & Co., of Boston, in 1 vol. 8vo. 112 pp. 1870.

**Balatka,** HANS, was born at Hoffnungs-thal, Moravia, Austria, March 5, 1827. He began his musical studies as choir-boy in the Olmütz cathedral. When sixteen years old, his parents being in comfortable circumstances, he was sent to Vienna to study law. However, he continued his musical studies under Proct and Sechter, and made such progress that in a year he was able to give some concerts. The Revolution of 1848 drove him, as it did many others, to seek some other country, and after a short time spent in Dresden and Hamburg he sailed for New York, where he arrived in June, 1849. Without making more than a temporary stop, he proceeded on to Milwaukee, Wis. There he organized in the same year the Milwaukee Musikverein (musical society) and became its first conductor, a position which he retained ten years (See MILWAUKEE MUSIKVEREIN). About 1860 he was invited to Chicago to bring out Mozart's "Requiem," and since then that city has been his home. His activity is unceasing. He has held position as leader of various English and German societies, and has often conducted the German Sængerfests. In 1869 he produced the "Creation" at Chicago, with Mme. Parepa-Rosa as soloist, and in 1870 the "Messiah," besides repeating the "Creation" with Nilsson as soloist. Mr. Balatka is a good composer, and an excellent performer on the double-bass, violoncello, violin, guitar, and piano. His composition "The Power of Song" gained for him the silver goblet offered as a prize by the Sængerbund held at Cincinnati in 1856. He has written besides several concertos, arias, songs, etc.

**Barus,** CARL, was born Oct. 12, 1823, at Schuegast, Prussian Silesia. In 1838 he went to Brieg, where he took lessons of Förster the organist and of Cantor Fischer. Three years later he was at Breslau, studying harmony under E. Richter and the organ under A. Hesse. He came to this country in 1849, landing at New York, but soon went to Saginaw, Mich., where he engaged in farming. The love of music was too strong, however, and he soon relinquished this and went to Cincinnati, where he was organist of the St. Philomena Church and later of St. Patrick's. For over twenty years he also officiated at the Jewish Temple. He has been director at various times of the principal musical societies of the city. The following meetings of the North American Sængerbund were conducted by him: The sixth, at Canton, O., 1854; the thirteenth, at Columbus, O., 1865; the fifteenth, at Indianapolis, Ind., 1867; the twentieth, at Louisville, Ky., 1877; and the twenty-first, at Cincinnati, 1879. At the meetings of the Indiana Sængerbund he conducted in 1858-59-60-68. During his long residence at Cincinnati, Mr. Barus did much towards its musical prosperity by his indefatigable labors. He is now located at Indianapolis, Ind. Of his numerous compositions none have as yet been published.

**Bassford,** WILLIAM K., was born in New York, April 23, 1839, and early gave unmistakable evidence of his musical talents. His first teacher in harmony and composition was Samuel Jackson, an excellent musician and for some time organist of St. Bartholomew's Church, New York. While still young he traveled quite extensively with a concert troupe as pianist. Not liking this mode of living and finding that it deprived him of the time necessary for study, he abandoned it and settled in New York as teacher and composer, and is still (Dec., 1885) located there. He has been very successful as a piano teacher, and some of his pupils have become brilliant players. But he is, perhaps, best known by his songs, of which a large number have been issued. His piano compositions are mostly *salon* and characteristic pieces. Among them are "Devotion," "Young Maiden and Flowers," "Meditation," "Morning Song," "Tranquility," and "Hunter's Song," all displaying more or less talent and ability. His sacred music consists of a mass in E flat and some other church pieces. He has written a two-act opera, "Cassilda," which is founded on a Spanish subject and contains some fine numbers. He was also engaged by Mme. Wallace to complete the opera of "Estrella," left unfinished by Vincent Wallace.

**Baumbach,** ADOLPH, was born in Germany, but when, we have been unable to ascertain, though probably about 1830. He came to this country when a young man, and was located in Boston as early as 1855. Afterwards, about 1863, he went to Chicago, where he resided during the rest of his life.

He was a teacher of the piano and organ, a good player, and composed considerable music, especially teaching pieces for the piano. He was also the compiler of a popular collection for quartet choirs. His death occurred some time in 1880, at Chicago.

**Baxter,** LYDIA, was born Sept. 2, 1809, at Petersburg, Rensselaer Co., N. Y. She is known as a poetess of considerable grace and beauty. Many of her hymns for the church and Sunday school have become very popular. Her well-known hymn, "Gates Ajar," has been sung in every Christian land, and is one of the jewels of hymnology. She died in New York, June 23, 1874.

**Bay State Psalm Book.** A collection of psalms and hymns, edited by several Puritan clergymen. It was published at Cambridge, Mass., in 1640, and was the second book produced by the American Colonies. Some changes were made and a second edition issued in 1646. An edition, revised and greatly improved by a number of New England ministers, among whom were Welde, Eliot of Roxbury, and Mather of Dorchester, appeared in 1691. The work was printed in clear, new type, imported expressly for the purpose, by Stephen Daye, and in all passed through more than seventy editions. It was republished in London, England, in 1737, and in Scotland in 1738. It would appear that Henry Dunster had charge of the musical portion of the collection, which was sometimes known as the "New England Version."

**Beckel,** JAMES C., a popular American composer, was born in Philadelphia, Dec. 20, 1811, his father being a German. When only 13 years old he was able to take his father's place as organist at one of the churches in the city. For eighteen years he was organist in a P. E. church of Germantown (now a part of Philadelphia). In 1847 he became organist of the Clinton street Emanuel church (Presbyterian), a position which he held until 1858. In 1875 he was tendered the position again, which he now (1883) holds. At various times during his long career he has been organist of many of the principal churches of his native city, always acquitting himself with great credit.

Mr. Beckel has written a great number of compositions, both sacred and secular, many of which remain in manuscript. Among his more important works are the cantatas of the "Pilgrim's Progress," "The Nativity," and "Ruth." The "Psalter" is a choice collection of music for the church. His latest work is a method for the organ, published by Lee & Walker, which is being received with great favor. O. Ditson & Co., of Boston, and Lee & Walker of Philadelphia, are the principal publishers of his music. Although Mr. Beckel is well advanced in years, he is still active, and will probably live to accomplish considerable more in the musical line.

**Beethoven's Conservatory of Music,** ST. LOUIS, MO. This institution was founded in the fall of 1871, by a few gentlemen desirous of cultivating a taste for music in that city. Five months later, it was bought of them by August Waldauer and Herman Lawitzky, who respectively had charge of the violin and the piano departments. Under this excellent directorship the opening season was attended with success. The faculty comprised some of the best resident musicians, and the Conservatory soon became popular. Since the death of Mr. Lawitzky, which occurred in 1874, it has been under the sole management of Mr. Waldauer, who has maintained its previous good reputation. There have been engaged as teachers at various times, De Compi, Tamburello, Goldbeck, Hanchett, and others equally well known. A series of *soirées* and concerts are given by the pupils during each season, and a number who were thus first introduced to the public are now acknowledged artists.

**Belshazzar.** An "American opera" in five acts. Music by James A. Butterfield. First produced in 1871, since when it has been given more than 350 times in different parts of the country, under the direction of the composer.

**Bergmann,** KARL, well known in this country as a violoncellist and conductor, was born in 1821, at Ebersbach, Saxony, and came to the United States with the Germania orchestra in 1850. In 1857 he removed to New York, where he became conductor of the Philharmonic Society, the Arion, and occupied a leading place in musical affairs. Toward the end of life he became very despondent, and was eventually forsaken by nearly all his former friends. He died in a

German hospital, New York, Aug. 10, 1876. Among his compositions are some orchestral pieces.

**Berge,** WILLIAM. An organist, pianist, teacher, and composer, native of Germany, who came to this country in 1846, and from that time chiefly resided at New York. He was noted for the number of his arrangements, transcriptions, etc., and for his abilities as a performer. His death occurred at New York, in March, 1883.

**Bethune,** THOMAS GREEN. See BLIND TOM.

**Bergner,** FREDERIC, violoncellist, was born at Donaüschingen, Baden, Germany, in 1827, and studied with C. L. Böhm and Kalliwoda. In 1849 he came to the United States, and settled in New York, which has since been his home. For several years he was violoncellist of the "Eisfeld Quartet," and afterwards of the "Mason-Thomas Quartet Soirées." He is at present member and one of the directors of the Philharmonic Society. As a player he possesses a fine *technique*, and is noted for the full, round, pure tone which he produces.

**Bial,** RUDOLF, was born Aug. 26, 1834, at Habelschwerdt, Silesia. His musical education was obtained at Breslau, and when only fifteen years old he became first violinist of the orchestra at the stadt theatre. For many years he labored in the opera at Berlin, and was instrumental in bringing out several first class artists there, among them Adelina Patti. In 1879 he came to this country, taking charge of the orchestra at Koster & Bial's, New York, and to his efficiency and good judgment much of the success of the concerts is due. In 1880 he became conductor at the Thalia theatre, and reorganized the orchestra there. During the summer of 1881 he gave a series of concerts at Metropolitan hall, which were very popular. Mr. Bial was an excellent conductor, and understood as few do how to prepare and make attractive a concert program. He died in New York, Nov. 23, 1881.

**Biddle,** HORACE P., was born in 1811, near Logan, Ohio, his father being one of the pioneers of the West. His early education was a limited one, but by close application and dilligence he has since become well versed not only in the various arts and sciences, but in Latin, French and German. He decided to follow the profession of law, and in 1839 was admitted to practice at the bar. Between this time and 1874 he was elected to various offices. In the latter named year he became judge of the Supreme Court of Indiana, and now resides at Logansport. Though not a professional musician, Mr. Biddle has devoted much of his leisure time to cultivating the art, and written numerous essays on musical subjects.

**Biglow & Main,** NEW YORK CITY. A music publishing firm, well-known in the United States, formed Feb. 15, 1868, by L. H. Biglow and Sylvester Main, as successors to William B. Bradbury. Mr. Main died Oct. 5, 1873, and the business has since been carried on by the surviving partner, L. H. Biglow, under the old name. The firm does not publish sheet music, but confines itself exclusively to books of music, largely of sacred music. They are in part publishers of the "Gospel Hymns," by Bliss and Sankey, and have issued many popular collections of music. They are very successful, and have sold the almost incredible number of 18,000,-000 copies of their various publications. Since the agitation of the "Tonic Sol-fa" question, they have become the principal publishers of this system in America.

**Billings,** WILLIAM, is the first native-born American composer who can justly lay claim to the title. Previous to his time the Colonies had no music, except a few old tunes imported from England. He was born at Boston, Oct. 7, 1746. His early education was very limited. While still young he showed his inclination for music, a knowledge of which he picked up by degrees, for music was then little cared for and far still less understood. Being entirely self-taught, his knowledge was both limited and very imperfect. Counterpoint was something he had no idea of, and he could have known but very little if anything about harmony, as his earlier pieces transgress the fundamental rules. Accent and rhythm were also disregarded. But we must remember the time when Billings lived and the circumstances under which he wrote. Though incorrectly constructed, his pieces give evidence of considerable musical genius, and form a pleasing contrast to the old English tunes then in use, being full of life and vigor. Later in life he wrote more correctly, while his pieces lost nothing in freshness. So popular did his music become, it was sung to the exclusion of almost everything else, consequently he had many weak imitators. He wrote six works or collections of music, the first of which was "The New England Psalm Singer," published Oct. 7, 1770. This was followed by " The Singing Master's Assistant, " an abridgement of his first work, published in 1778; " Music in Miniature," published in 1779, and containing 74 tunes, 31 of which were given to the public for the first time ; " The Psalm Singer's Amusement," published in 1781 ; "The Suffolk Harmony," published in 1786, and " The Continental Harmony," published in 1794. These, with some anthems, " Except the Lord build the house," " Mourn, mourn, ye saints," " The Lord is risen from the dead," "Jesus Christ is risen from the dead," etc., comprise all of his music that has been published. In the collections named above the tunes were, with few exceptions, his own. Some of them still live, " Aurora " and " Majesty " being frequently sung at the present day.

Billings may justly be considered as the founder of American church music, and though his efforts appear humble in comparison with those of the present day, with him dawned an era which has ever grown brighter and which has not yet had its fulfillment. He died in Boston, Sept. 26, 1800.

**Biscaccianti,** SIGNORA, (whose maiden name was Ostinelli), was born at Boston, Mass., in 1825. Her father, Louis Ostinelli, an Italian, resided for many years in Boston, where he was leader of the principal orchestras, and her mother was a New York lady. She early manifested a love for music, possessing a wonderful voice. A subscription was raised, and in 1843 she, in company with her father, went to Italy for the purpose of studying. She was brought to the notice of Pasta, from whom she received instruction for some time, and subsequently was a pupil of Vaccai, Nani, and Lamperti. In May, 1847 (previous to which she had been married), she made her *début* at the Carcano theatre, Milan, in " Ernani." She returned home in the summer of the same year, and sang in many of the principal cities here with great success. Afterward she made a trip to Europe, where she was well received. In 1853 or 1854 she was in California, and subsequently sang in various parts of the coun-

try. Her later history we have been unable to learn, except that she is now a resident of Rome.

**Bishop,** ANNA, born in 1814, wife of Sir H. R. Bishop, whom she married in 1832, was educated at the Royal Academy of Music, London, and made her first appearance in that city, July 5, 1839. She soon after went on a tour through the principal countries of Europe, which extended down to 1843. From this time until 1846 she remained in Italy, and was at one time prima donna at the San Carlo, Naples. After her stay in Italy she returned to England, but in 1847 came to this country, remaining here until 1855, when she sailed for Australia. She then again made a brief visit to England, and in 1859 came to this country for the second time. Her stay was prolonged to 1866 (with a brief visit to Mexico and Cuba), when she sailed for the Sandwich Islands, visited China, India, Australia, Egypt and England, arriving in the United States again about 1869. During all her wanderings down to 1855 she was accompanied by Bochsa, the eminent harpist, with whom she ran away from her husband. Her success in this country, though nothing phenomenal, has been uniform and decided. To recount all her wanderings or give anything like a complete history of her life would fill volumes. No singer that ever lived traveled so much or sang before so many people. She visited nearly every country on the globe, and the most of them repeatedly. In 1858 she married Martin Schultz, an American gentleman, and made it her permanent home at New York. She died there March 18, 1884, from a stroke of apoplexy. Her last public appearance was at a concert in New York city in the spring of 1883. Her voice was remarkably well preserved for one so far advanced in years and she retained some of her youthful appearance. No doubt if her biography were written it would prove very interesting.

**Blake,** CHARLES D., a popular American composer, was born at Walpole, Mass., in 1847. At the age of seven years he commenced the study of music, and at ten produced his first composition, after which his progress was very rapid. He has been a pupil of J. K. Paine, J. C. D. Parker, Ryder, and Pond. Mr. Blake aims only at producing music for the masses, in which he has been successful to an unusual degree. His compositions number about three thousand, a large part of which are for the piano, but including many songs. He has also written some larger works, one of which is the "Light-Keeper's Daughter" (libretto by Geo. M. Vickers), produced for the first time at the American Casino, Boston, June 12, 1882. He is at present (1884) a resident of Boston, where he is connected with the music publishing house of White, Smith & Co.

**Blake,** GEORGE E., was born in 1775. He commenced publishing music at Philadelphia, in 1802, and was the oldest music publisher in America. He died in Philadelphia, Feb. 24, 1871, at the great age of ninety-six.

**Blind Tom,** as he is generally known, whose real name is THOMAS GREEN BETHUNE, was born near Columbus, Ga., May 25, 1849. He was blind from his birth, but as a compensation therefor nature seems to have endowed him with wonderful musical abilities. Being by birth a slave, he was as such purchased by Perry H. Oliver, in 1850. When not more than five years old he had already become quite familiar with the piano, and in 1858 made his first public appearance as a player. Since that time he has made repeated concert tours in this country, visiting the principal cities and towns and always drawing good houses, and even visited Europe, where he attracted considerable attention. He is now (December, 1882) again making a tour of the States. Blind Tom can not be classed as a musician in a strict sense of the word, having never been educated as such, and consequently his few compositions are of no value. Yet his musical talents are indisputable, and that he is in some respects a player of exceptionable ability is also equally true. In fact, his seems to be one of nature's eccentric bestowals of genius with which we sometimes meet, but difficult to be explained or accounted for.

**Bliss,** PHILIP PAUL, was born in Clearfield County, Pa., July 9, 1838. He was very fond of music, and when a young man taught snging schools. Later, he held conventions, etc., for Root & Cady, in various parts of the West. During the latter part of his life he was connected with Moody and Sankey, and sang in the gospel meetings of Maj. D. W. Whittle. He only calls for notice here as being the composer of several remarkably popular religious tunes, of which it is but necessary to specify "Hold the Fort," "Only an Armor Bearer," "Pull for the Shore," "Rescue the Perishing," etc. He perished in the terrible accident at Ashtabula, Ohio, Dec. 29, 1876.

**Boise,** OTIS B., was born Aug. 13, 1845, at Oberlin, Ohio, where his father was a physician. Music had a special charm for him from an early age, and when fourteen years old he became organist of St. Paul's church, Cleveland. He in 1861 went to Leipsic, studying theory and composition there under Hauptmann, Richter, Moscheles, Menzel and others. After a stay of three years in Leipsic, he went to Berlin, where he studied with Kullak. Arduous labor, however, told upon him, and he was taken with a sickness which nearly terminated his life. Upon recovery, in 1864, he returned home and became organist at Euclid Avenue Presbyterian Church, Cleveland. In 1870 he removed to New York, where he held a similiar position in Dr. Hall's church and taught in a conservatory. On account of declining health he in 1876 again went to Europe and visited Leipsic, where a motet of his elicited favorable comments. The year 1877 was spent at Weisbaden, and there he made the acquaintance of Raff. In 1878 he returned to New York. Jan. 30, 1879, he gave a concert at Chickering Hall, the program of which was entirely made up from his own works—certainly a bold step for a composer so young. His compositions consist of a psalm for chorus and orchestra, symphonies, concertos, overtures, smaller instrumental pieces, etc.

**Bonawitz,** JOHANN HEINRICH, was born Dec. 4, 1839, at Durkheim, Germany, and at an early age entered the Conservatorium at Liege, where he remained until he was about thirteen years old. In 1852 the family removed to the United States, and soon located at Philadelphia. Young Bonawitz played at a concert of the Philadelphia Musical Fund Society, in the winter of 1854-5, creating great enthusiasm. He was a great admirer of Mozart's music, and would save up all his money to purchase the works of that great master. In this way his ambition to become a composer was stimulated, and he wrote a sonata and an overture (played by the orchestra of the Walnut Street Theatre), though at that time he was sadly deficient in knowledge of composition. In 1861 he went to Europe, first visiting England and then proceeding to Germany, everywhere meeting with great success as a pianist. He took up his residence at Weisbaden in 1862, where he remained four years. In the autumn of 1866 he gave a farewell concert and departed for Paris. There he both taught and studied, becoming much in demand on account of his abilities as a player. While in Paris he wrote his opera of "The Bride of Messina." In 1873 he returned to this country and settled at Philadelphia. Soon after, "The Bride of Messina" was brought out at the Academy of Music and met with a favorable reception. For some time he traveled for Decker Bros., New York, giving concerts on their pianos. In 1875 he was appointed conductor of music at the Centennial, but refused to act. Some unpleasantness arising, he in 1877 went to Europe for the second time and located at Vienna, where he still remains, devoting himself to teaching and composition. During the winter of 1879-80 he made a concert tour of Germany. He has written a second opera, "Ostrolenka" (1873 or 1874), which has not yet been performed.

**Boston.** Boston is noted for its musical culture, and some of its principal musical societies and institutions are here given. Its leading musical manufacturers and publishers are noticed in their alphabetical order.

BOSTON CONSERVATORY OF MUSIC. This institution, one of the leading ones of its kind in America, was established in 1867, by Julius Eichberg, who is still (Jan., 1886) its director. Thorough instruction in all branches of music is given by experienced teachers, and the advantages for rapid and sure progress on the part of the pupil are as great as can anywhere be found. The Conservatory has had a powerful influence in raising the standard of musical taste, not only through the 15,000 pupils who have passed through its courses and are scattered all over the country, but through the numerous public concerts given, which are always of high order.

The violin school, which is under the personal direction of Mr. Eichberg, deserves especial notice. By common consent it is regarded as having no equal in America and scarcely surpassed in Europe. The artistic and highly refined performances of its pupils give evidence of rare musical ability and training skill in its director and have won the highest praise. Mr. Eichberg has done much toward removing the prejudice existing in this country against the violin as a suitable musical instrument for ladies. The Eichberg String Quartet, composed entirely of Mr. Eichberg's pupils, recently returned from Europe, where it was accorded a flattering reception for its masterly interpretations of the best works. No one is so well qualified as Mr. Eichberg for the work he has in hand, and his success will mark an era in the musical history of this country.

BOSTON UNIVERSITY. There is connected with this University a College of Music, of which Dr. Eben Tourjéè is dean. Students having completed the course of study of any conservatory are admitted, after passing a satisfactory examination, to the study of the higher branches. Three years are generally necessary to complete this course, and the student may at the close receive the degree of Bachelor of Music, provided he is a graduate of any college of art, or if not, by passing an examination in the following branches: English composition, history, and literature, a modern language (French, German, or Italian), Latin (or a second modern language), and mathematics. After obtaining this degree, that of Doctor of Music may be obtained by pursuing an additional four years' course of study, and passing examinations in arithmetic, grammar, geography, modern history, elements of physics, elements of chemistry, ancient history and geography. In both cases the candidate is required to present satisfactory vouchers for his good moral character.

BOSTON ACADEMY OF MUSIC. A society formed in 1833, in Boston, having for its object the advancement of music in general, but more especially of sacred music. It was under the direction of Dr. Lowell Mason and George James Webb, two of the pioneer musicians of this country. Dr. George F. Root was also at one time prominently connected with it. The following was its program, a formidable one, surely, but none the less worthy of adoption:

1.—To establish schools of vocal music and juvenile classes.

2.—To establish similar classes for adults.

3.—To form a class for instruction in the methods of teaching music, which may be composed of teachers, parents, and all other persons desiring to qualify themselves for teaching vocal music.

4.—To form an association of choristers and leading members of choirs, for the purpose of improvement in conducting and performing sacred music in churches.

5.—To establish a course of popular lectures on the nature and object of church music, and style of composition and execution appropriate to it, with experimental illustrations by the performance of a select choir.

6.—To establish a course of scientific lectures.

7.—To establish exhibition concerts.

8.—To introduce vocal music in schools.

9.—To publish circulars and essays.

The influence of the Academy was felt all over the United States, and at one time it was considered an authority in everything relating to music. In 1847 it ceased to exist, giving way to the more recent societies of Boston, but not until it had performed an important mission.

BOSTON MUSIC HALL. A building erected in 1852 for musical purposes. The main hall is 130 feet long, 78 feet wide, and 65 feet high, with two balconies. The seats are so placed that every person can easily see and hear. Doors at short intervals lead from the floor and balconies to means of exit, so that the hall, which holds 3,000 people, can be emptied in a very few minutes if necessary. The building contains besides the hall numerous other rooms which may be used for any desired purpose.

BOYLSTON CLUB. This musical society, composed exclusively of gentlemen, was originated in February, 1872. During the ensuing season several pleasant evening entertainments were given, but it was not until Feb. 21, 1873, that the first real concert occurred. The second season, which was opened with a public rehearsal at Parker Memorial Hall, Nov. 28, 1873, proved a prosperous one, and soon the Club took its place among the recognized and influential musical organizations of Boston. In 1875 Carlyle Petersilea became its pianist, a post which he still retains. In 1876 it was voted to invite the ladies to assist at the concerts, but the membership is still exclusively male. Eben Phinney was its first director, but was soon succeeded by J. B. Sharland. Mr. Sharland resigned his position in 1875, when George L. Osgood became director, a capacity in which he still (Jan., 1883) acts. Under his able leadership the Club not only continued to prosper but improved its high musical standard, so largely due to the efforts of Mr. Sharland. The performances of the Club are of the highest order, and the programs comprise the best works, such as Mendelssohn's "Athalie," Schumann's "Pilgrimage of the Rose," Bach's "Motet in B flat," Brahm's "Choral Hymn," David's "Désert," and Paine's "Realms of Fancy."

APOLLO CLUB. This society was formed in July, 1871. Its object is the cultivation and performance of music for male voices only. The number of regular or active members was at first fifty, which has gradually increased to seventy-five, with five hundred "associate" (those who are subject to an annual assessment but take no part in the performances) members. In March, 1873, the Club was incorporated under a special act of the Massachusetts Legislature. Weekly rehearsals have been held from the first, and up to 1882 seventy-four concerts had been given, under the care of its efficient conductor, B. J. Lang. Among the works brought out (always with full orchestral accompaniment where existing) are Mendelssohn's "Antigone," "Œdipus at Colonus," and "A Vintage Song;" Schumann's "The Luck of Edenhall" and "Forester's Chorus;" Beethoven's "Chorus of Dervishes;" Bruch's "Scenes from the Frithjof-Saga" and "A roman Song of Triumph;" Raff's "The Warder Song;" Rubenstein's "Morning;" Buck's "The Nun of Nidaros" and "King Olaf's Christmas;" Whiting's "The March of the Monks of Bangor;" Paine's "Œdipus Tyrannus;" Chadwick's "The Viking's Last Voyage;" etc. The officers of the society consist of a president, vice-president, secretary, treasurer, and librarian, who constitute the board of directors; besides which there is a committee of three on music, and a committee of four on voices.

CECILIA, The. This society of mixed voices was originated in 1874 by the Harvard Musical Association, and was designed to assist at its concerts. There was no regular organization and it remained under the patronage of the Harvard Association until the spring of 1876. At that time a separation took place, and the Cecilia was remodeled and placed on a permanent footing of its own. The number of active members was fixed at 125 and the number of associate members (those subject to assessments but taking no part in the musical exercises) at 250. The concerts of the society were held in Tremont Temple until that building was destroyed by fire in 1879, when they were temporarily held in the Music Hall, and the number of active members increased to 150. B. J. Lang has from the first been its conductor, and under his direction it has given many important works.

EUTERPE (The). This society, though young, has a strong board of officers and occupies a prominent position. It was organized Dec. 13, 1878, and gave its first concert on the 15th of January following. Its object is the encouragement of chamber music and the production of the best compositions in this line. The number of members is 150, and all money received is expended on the concerts, after allowing for the necessary running expenses. Connected with the society are some of Boston's most prominent musicians, among whom are C. C. Perkins (president), B. J. Lang (vice-president), W. F. Apthorp (treasurer), Julius Eichberg, John Orth, S. B. Whitney, J. C. D. Parker, etc. F. H. Jenks is (Dec., 1882) secretary.

HANDEL AND HAYDN SOCIETY. The largest and most noted musical association of the United States. It was founded March 30, 1815. At that time sixteen gentlemen came together in response to an invitation dated several days before, and signed by Gottlieb Graupner, Thomas S. Webb and Asa Peabody. A second meeting was held a fortnight later, at which a set of rules was adopted and Matthew S. Parker elected secretary; but it was not until the third meeting, April 20, 1815, that the board of government was completed by the election of Thomas S. Webb, president; Amasa Winchester, vice-president; Nathaniel Tucker, treasurer, and nine trustees.

The Society, whose avowed object was the cultivation and improvement of sacred music and the introduction of the works of eminent composers, was thus perfected in form, but as yet had showed no signs of life. Early in September, 1815, there was talk of a public exhibition, which took place the following

Christmas night, before an audience of 1000. The chorus numbered about 100 performers, and the orchestra a dozen, which, with an organ, executed the accompaniments. The program included selections from "Messiah," "Creation," and other of Handel's works. An enthusiastic reception was tendered this performance.

February 9, 1816, the State legislature granted a special charter, in which the aim of the Society was recognized, and a new set of rules was adopted, calculated to strengthen the association. It was not until the seventeenth concert, Dec. 25, 1818, that an oratorio entire was performed, which was the "Messiah." Six festivals, resembling those of Birmingham (Eng.), have been held, the first occurring in 1857. In May, 1865, the fiftieth anniversary of the Society was held. Since 1868, triennial festivals have regularly been held.

Many of the works of the masters have been produced for the first time in this country by the Society, at whose concerts numbers of the most renowned singers, both native and foreign, have appeared. Until 1847 the president performed the duties of a conductor, but in that year they were assumed by Charles E. Horn. In 1850, C. C. Perkins, also president, assumed the conductorship. Since then the conductors have been J. E. Goodson, 1851; G. J. Webb, 1852; Carl Bergmann, 1852; Carl Zerrahn, Aug. 24, 1854, who is still conductor. The organists have been S. Stockwell, S. P. Taylor, S. A. Cooper, J. B. Taylor, Miss Sarah Hewett, Charles Zeuner, A. N. Hayter, G. F. Hayter, F. F. Mueller, J. C. D. Parker. B. J. Lang, elected Sept. 15, 1859, is the present organist. Rehearsals are regularly held Saturday evenings, from October to April. Up to 1878, 610 concerts had been given.

The Society is composed of about 300 members, active and retired. Its influence on the musical affairs of this country has been very marked.

The choral force is about 600 strong. A membership fee of $5 is charged.

The following is a list of the principal works performed by the Society up to 1881:

| First Time. | No. Times. | Work. | Composer. |
|---|---|---|---|
| 1818, Dec. 25 | 74 | Messiah, . . . | Handel. |
| 1819, Feb. 16 | 62 | Creation, . . . | Haydn. |
| 1819, Apr. 1 | 3 | Dettingen Te Deum, . . | Handel. |
| 1821, Feb. 6 | 4 | The Intercession, . . | King. |
| 1829, Jan. 18 | 11 | Mass (B flat major), . . | Haydn. |
| 1829, Apr. 12 | 1 | Mass (C major), . . | Mozart. |
| 1829, Dec. 13 | 2 | Mass (F major), . . | Bühler. |
| 1830, Nov. 21 | 7 | The Storm, . . | Haydn. |
| 1831, Mar. 27 | 1 | Te Deum (C major), . . | Haydn. |
| 1832, Feb. 26 | 2 | Ode to Washington, . . | Horn. |
| 1833, Mar. 24 | 9 | Christ on the Mount of Olives, . | Beethoven. |
| 1836, Feb. 28 | 57 | David, . . . | Neukomm. |
| 1836, Oct. 2 | 1 | The Remission of Sin, . . | Horn. |
| 1837, Oct. 1 | 4 | Hymn of the Night . . | Neukomm. |
| 1838, Nov. 4 | 2 | The Power of Song, . . | Romberg. |
| 1840, Oct. 4 | 7 | Mount Sinai, . . . | Neukomm. |
| 1841, Nov. 14 | 7 | The Transient and the Eternal, . | Romberg. |
| 1842, Mar. 20 | 9 | The Last Judgment, . | Spohr. |
| 1843, Jan. 22 | 12 | St. Paul, . . . . | Mendelssohn. |
| 1843, Feb. 26 | 27 | Stabat Mater, . . | Rossini. |
| 1845, Jan. 26 | 33 | Samson, . . . . | Handel. |
| 1845, Dec. 21 | 45 | Moses in Egypt, . , | Rossini. |
| 1847, Dec. 5 | 16 | Judas Maccabæus, . . | Handel. |
| 1848, Feb. 13 | 46 | Elijah, . . . | Mendelssohn. |
| 1849, Dec. 16 | 7 | The Martyrs, . . . | Donizetti. |
| 1853, Feb. 6 | 4 | Engedi, . . . | Beethoven. |
| 1853, Apr. 2 | 6 | Ninth Symphony (Choral), . | Beethoven. |
| 1855, Nov. 18 | 4 | Solomon, . . . | Handel. |
| 1857, Jan. 18 | 3 | Requiem Mass, . . | Mozart. |
| 1857, Feb. 15 | 4 | Eli, . . . . . | Costa. |
| 1858, Apr. 10 | 18 | Hymn of Praise, . . | Mendelssohn. |
| 1859, Feb. 13 | 6 | Israel in Egypt, . . | Handel. |
| 1863, Nov. 28 | 2 | Ode on St. Cecilia's Day, . . | Handel. |
| 1863, Nov. 28 | 5 | Overture, " Ein' feste Burg," . | Nicolai. |
| 1866, May 13 | 2 | Psalm 42, . . . | Mendelssohn. |
| 1867, Feb. 17 | 1 | Jephtha, . . . | Handel. |
| 1868, May 5 | 1 | Psalm 95, . . . | Mendelssohn. |
| 1869, Mar. 27 | 2 | Naaman, . . . | Costa. |
| 1871, May 13 | 1 | The Woman of Samaria, . . | Bennett. |
| 1874, May 7 | 1 | Christus, . . . | Mendelssohn. |
| 1874, May 7 | 3 | Hear my Prayer, . . | Mendelssohn. |
| 1874, May 7 | 2 | Psalm 46, . . | Buck. |
| 1874, May 8 | 5 | Passion music (St. Matthew), . | Bach. |
| 1874, May 9 | 1 | St. Peter, . . . . | Paine. |
| 1875, Apr. 28 | 1 | Seasons, . . . | Haydn. |
| 1876, Apr. 16 | 2 | Joshua, . . . . | Handel. |
| 1877, May 17 | 2 | Christmas Oratorio Parts I, II. . | Bach. |
| 1877, May 17 | 1 | Song of Victory, . . | Hiller. |
| 1877, May 17 | 1 | Psalm 18, . . . | Marcello. |
| 1877, May 17 | 3 | Redemption Hymn, . . | Parker. |
| 1877, May 17 | 2 | Noël, . . . . | Saint–Saëns. |
| 1878, May 5 | 3 | Requiem Mass, . . | Verdi. |
| 1879, Feb. 9 | 2 | Flight into Egypt, . . | Berlioz. |
| 1879, Nov. 23 | 1 | Prodigal Son, . . | Sullivan. |
| 1880, May 6 | 1 | Psalm 43, . . . | Mendelssohn. |
| 1880, May 7 | 1 | Le Déluge, . . . | Saint–Saëns. |

HARVARD MUSICAL ASSOCIATION. One of the most important and leading musical societies of the United States. It was formed Aug. 30, 1837, from a social and musical club comprising undergraduates in Harvard University, which dated back to 1808 and was known as the "Pierian Sodality." The objects of the society were to improve the musical taste in the college, to provide a way for a professorship of music there, and to collect a library of music and its literature, all of which have been faithfully carried out.

Fourteen series of concerts have been given (they were discontinued in 1880), comprising from six to ten concerts each, beginning in 1865. They have been, with a few exceptions, under the efficient leadership of Carl Zerrahn. The programs have comprised standard orchestral works and vocal and instrumental solos of the best class. These concerts have not only been an important factor in raising the standard of musical taste in Boston, but their influence has been felt in other parts of the country. Of the original members of the society only three are now living. They are John S. Dwight, president; Henry W. Pickering, vice-president, and Henry Gassett. Mr. Dwight was the founder and editor of "Dwight's Journal of Music" (which see), and is well known all over the United States as a clear, forcible writer on music.

The library of the Association comprises 2500 volumes, and is constantly receiving additions. It is now one of the largest and best in this country. Great care is exercised in making selections and that the sets be complete.

MENDELSSOHN QUINTET CLUB, one of Boston's oldest musical organizations, was formed in 1849 by August Fries. The original members were August Fries, 1st violin; Herr Gerloff, 2nd violin; Theodore Lehmann, 1st viola; Oscar Greiner, 2nd viola; and Wulf Fries, violoncello. The immediate cause of its formation was the performance of Mendelssohn's Quintet in A, at the house of John Bigelow, a great lover of classical chamber music. For many years the Club held a leading position and was very influential in promoting a taste for good music. It still exists, though the members are somewhat scattered, but has in a measure been superseded by the Beethoven Quartet Club, a more recent organization consisting of C. N. Allen, Gustav Dannreuther, H. Hemdel, and Wulf Fries. August Fries was for ten years the leader, at the end of which time he was succeeded by William Schultze.

NEW ENGLAND CONSERVATORY OF MUSIC. This institution, one of the largest and best of its kind in this country, was incorporated under its present name by an act of the Legislature of Massachusetts, passed March 18th and approved by the Governor, William Claflin, March 19th, 1870. Its origin, however, dates back to 1853, when the present director organized a sort of musical school at Providence, R. I. In 1859 this was enlarged, and in 1864 chartered under the name of Providence Conservatory of Music. It was removed to Boston, in February, 1867, when it became a conservatory in the present sense of the word, and in 1870 was incorporated as previously stated.

The Conservatory is conducted on the most approved plan, and embodies the best features of the European institutions. The various branches taught are piano, organ, violin, flute, all orchestral and band instruments, notation, formation and cultivation of the voice, solo singing in English, German and Italian, sight singing, part singing, dramatic action, lyric art and opera, *ensemble* playing, harmony, counterpoint, fugue, art of teaching vocal music in public schools, tuning and acoustics, art of conducting, normal instruction, church music, oratorio and chorus practice, the languages, science of music, etc. The corps of professors and teachers numbers nearly one hundred, among whom are W. F. Apthorp, Gustav Dannreuther, L. C. Elson, S. A. Emery, Wulf Fries, B. J. Lang, J. C. D. Parker, J. H. Wheeler, S. B. Whitney, Carl Zerrahn, and others equally well known.

Up to 1882, the Conservatory had occupied rooms in the Music Hall building, Boston, but in that year it was found necessary to obtain larger accommodations. Accordingly, through the generous loans and gifts of the people of the city, the large and handsome building with grounds, known as St. James Hotel, located on Newton and St. James streets and fronting on Franklin Square, was purchased as its permanent home. The building is of brick and granite, 185 by 210 feet and seven stories high, has every possible modern convenience, and is without doubt the finest conservatory building in the world. The total cost will reach about $700,000. There are accommodations for 550 lady students (the ladies only being allowed to board in the building), besides class rooms for 3,000 pupils, and a large hall, which is to be used for the Conservatory concerts, etc. The building was first opened as a conservatory Sep. 14th, 1882.

The director of the Conservatory is Dr. Eben Tourjée. The board of trustees consists of the following gentlemen: Henry Baldwin, A. I. Benyon, L. A. Chase, W. R. Clark, D. D., G. R. Eager, L. T. Jefts, E. Tourjée, A. S. Weed, L. Whitney, and Carl Zerrahn. There is besides an advisory board, composed of about twenty-five of the leading men, literary, musical and business, of Boston and vicinity. The number of students during the three terms of the year averages upwards of 900, and the expense for each student ranges from $350 to $480 per year, or one-third of that for a single term. A museum somewhat similar to that at South Kensington has been formed at the Conservatory, and already contains quite a large number of specimens of ancient musical instruments, etc. It is to be earnestly hoped that the managers will give special attention to increasing this collection by every possible means.

PHILHARMONIC SOCIETY. This Society is comparatively young. In 1879 the Boston Philharmonic Orchestra was organized for the purpose of giving performances of a higher order than had previously been done. At the end of two seasons, however, it was found that the scheme would not support itself. It was then proposed by several gentlemen that a society be organized to bear the financial burdens, while the orchestra continued to carry out its aims. This was done, and the third season proved a successful one. The orchestra is one of the best in the United States, and the Society has already produced some important works, among which are Raff's symphony, "Im Sommer," and Rheinberger's "Wallenstein" symphony. The following have been the conductors: Bernhard Listemann (1879), Dr. Louis Maas (1880), and Carl Zerrahn (1881-82). The officers for 1881-82 were Dr. Angell, president; Rev. Dr. J. T. Duryea, vice-president; and Oliver Ames, treasurer; besides which there are a clerk, three auditors, and a board of twenty-three directors.

There was in Boston an early Philharmonic Society. It was organized in 1810, by Gottlieb Graupner, a German, and some of his friends. A large proportion of the members were amateurs, and the meetings, which were held Saturday evenings, had more characteristics of social gatherings than anything else, although Haydn's symphonies and other orchestral works were practiced. Concerts were given at intervals, the last one taking place Nov. 24, 1824, soon after which the Society ceased to exist. The band consisted of only about sixteen pieces—violins, a viola, a violoncello (bass-viol), a double-bass, a flute, a clarinet, a bassoon, a French horn, a trumpet and timpani.

**Bowman,** EDWARD MORRIS, organist, was born in the town of Barnard, Vermont, in 1848. He began the study of the piano when ten years old at Ludlow Academy, and continued it at Canton, N. Y., under a Miss Brown, and later under A. G. Faville, a teacher of some repute. From the latter he also gained some knowledge of theory and organ playing. In 1862 the family removed to Minneapolis, Minn., where he became organist of Holy Trinity P. E. Church and began giving music lessons. He went to New York in 1866 and studied the piano with Wm. Mason and the organ and theory with John P. Morgan, and was for several months organist of Old Trinity Church, (Dr. Dix). In August, 1867, he located in St. Louis, Mo., where in 1870 he married. From 1872 to 1874 he sojourned in Europe in company with his wife, an artist of some ability. The most of this time was spent in Berlin, with Franz Bendel (piano), Haupt (organ), and Weitzmann (theory and composition) as teachers. Part of 1873 was spent in studying registration with Batiste at Paris. Returning to St. Louis in 1874 he became organist of the Second Presbyterian Church (Dr. Nicoll's), and in 1879 was called to a similar post at the Second Baptist Church (Dr. Boyd's), which he still (May, 1883) holds. Mr. Bowman passed, in 1881, the examination of the Board of Examiners (consisting of Turpin, Gladstone, Stephens, Arnold, Gadsby, and Hopkins) of the London Royal College of Organists, and was congratulated and dined by the board on being the first American to do so. In July, 1882, he was also elected president of the Music Teachers' National Association. He is one of our best organists and a thorough musician. Some time since he published "Bowman's Weitzmann's Manual of Musical Theory," a very excellent work.

**Bradbury,** WILLIAM B., one of the pioneer American musicians, to whom we owe much, was born at York, Maine, in 1816. He descended from a good family, his grandfather being an old revolutionary soldier who was highly esteemed. Both his father and his mother had a local reputation as musicians, his father being a choir leader and singing master. Young Bradbury thus inherited a taste for music which early manifested itself. He was employed on his father's farm, but spent all his spare time in dilligently practicing on such musical instruments as came within his reach, becoming quite proficient on some of them.

In 1830 his parents removed to Boston, where he saw and heard for the first time a piano and organ, as well as various other instruments. The effect was to lead him to devote his life to the service of music. Accordingly he took lessons upon the organ, and as early as 1834 had achieved some reputation as an organist. He commenced his career as a teacher in New York, in 1840, and as a composer about the same time, meeting with the trials and discouragements which usually fall to the lot of a young and unknown musician.

In 1847 Mr. Bradbury and his family went to Europe, traveling in Germany and Switzerland. At Leipsic he studied for some time under the best masters, gaining a deeper insight into music. After his return home, in 1849, he devoted his entire time to teaching, composing, and editing various collections of music. He was also called to various parts of the country to conduct musical conventions, then just beginning to be held. In 1854 he, in conjunction with his brother, E. G. Bradbury, commenced the business of manufacturing pianos, and the Bradbury instruments were at one time quite popular. The business is now carried on by Freeborn G. Smith.

Mr. Bradbury was one of the great trio (the other two being Dr. Lowell Mason and Dr. George F. Root) to which church and vocal music in this country owe so much. His music, though not classical, is far from being puerile, and was exactly fitted to the needs of the time. He was unceasingly active, having edited more than twenty collections of music, a large part of which was his own. His most popular collection was "The Jubilee," published in 1858, which attained a sale of over 200,000 copies. Of his other collections we have space to mention only a few, viz : " The Young Choir " (1841), " The School Singer "

(1843), " Social Singing Glee Book " (1844), "Psalmodist" (1844), "Young Melodist" (1845), "The Choralist" (1847), "Musical Gems for School and Home " (1849), " Mendelssohn Collection" (1849), "Sabbath-School Melodies " (1850), " Alpine Glee Singer " (1850), " Metropolitan Glee Book " (1852), " Psalmista " (1851), " The Shawm " (1853), " New York Glee and Chorus Book" (1855), " Sabbath-School Choir " (1856), and " The Jubilee " (1858). He also composed several cantatas, one of which is " Esther," produced in 1856, and assisted in composing others.

Mr. Bradbury died at his residence, Montclair, N. J., Jan. 8, 1868, leaving a widow, four daughters, two of whom are married, and a son. He will always occupy a prominent place in American musical history.

**Brainard,** SILAS, was born Feb. 14, 1814, at Lempster, N. H. In 1834 he removed with his parents to Cleveland, Ohio, and became a leading member of a musical society organized there in the following year, arranging music for the orchestra and chorus. He gained some notoriety as a flutist in his youth. In 1836 he established a music store in Cleveland, and in 1845 began the extremely hazardous business of publishing music, founding the present extensive house of S. Brainard's Sons (See BRAINARD'S SON'S, S.). He was the author of several musical instruction books. He died at his home in Cleveland, April 8, 1871, leaving two sons, Charles S. and Henry M. Brainard, who now conduct their father's business as publisher.

**Brainard's Sons, S.** This music-publishing firm, ranking among the foremost in the United States and one of the most extensive ones in the West, was founded at Cleveland, Ohio, in 1836, by Silas Brainard, a native of New Hampshire. At that early day, it was considered a particularly hazardous venture, but by careful management combined with the rapid development of the country, the business was successful and soon became established on a sound footing. The subsequent career of the firm has been one of steady progress to its present high position, necessitating several removals to larger buildings. In 1876 the business was removed to the new building on Euclid Avenue, erected expressly for the purpose, within the walls of which its various branches are conveniently located. The firm has, in addition, an electrotype foundry and bindery. Nearly 20,000 pieces of sheet-music are published by them, besides many music-books, and they deal largely in the leading makes of all kinds of musical instruments. They have a branch house in Chicago and numerous agencies throughout the country.

In 1871, Mr. Silas Brainard, the founder of the firm, passed away, and waș succeeded by his two sons, Charles S. and Henry M. Brainard, who had long been associated with him. They have since carried on the business under the firm name as given above.

**Brainard's Musical World.** A 32-page musical monthly established in 1863 and published by the above firm. It is one of the leading journals of music in America, being ably conducted and devoted to the advancement of the art in all its branches. Karl Merz became its editor in 1868, a position which he still (Jan., 1886) holds.

**Brandt,** HERMANN, was born at Hamburg, Germany, in 1842, and in 1864 became a violin pupil of Ferdinand David. Having appeared with success in various German cities, he in 1868 was appointed *concertmeister* of the German Theatre, Prague. He came to this country in 1873 as chief violinist of the Thomas orchestra, but settled in New York after that organization disbanded. He is now *concertmeister* of the Philharmonic Society.

**Brandeis,** FREDERIK, was born at Vienna in 1835, and studied the piano under Fischhof and Czerny and composition under Rufinatscha. In 1848 he came to the United States and settled at New York, where he has since resided, much esteemed as a teacher and composer. He has written a considerable number of piano compositions and songs. Among his larger pieces are an "andante" for small orchestra; "The Ring," ballade for solos, chorus and piano; and a sonata for the piano.

**Bride of Messina.** An opera by Jean Henri Bonawitz. Produced for the first time at the Academy of Music, Philadelphia, April 22, 1874, when it met with a good reception. It has since been produced in many of the other principal cities and towns.

**Brignoli,** PASQUILINO. An Italian tenor singer of some eminence who came to this country in 1855, and who was well known here, having sung in nearly every city of importance. During the season of 1882-83 he traveled throughout the West with the Kellogg-Brignoli Concert Company. He died at the Everett House, New York, Thursday afternoon, Oct. 30, 1884, attended by only two or three faithful friends.

**Brinkerhoff,** CLARA M., (*née* ROLPH), well known as a concert and oratorio *prima donna*, was born in London, England, about 1830. Her parents, Mr. and Mrs. John A. Rolph, who were highly cultivated people, removed to this country when she was little more than an infant. For seven years, beginning at the age of five, her vocal studies were conducted by her mother, according to the old Italian method. Upon the death of her mother, at the end of that time, she was placed under the care of Mr. Derwort, a German musician, with whom she remained some time. She subsequently studied with Mme. Arnault, and also with George and Eliza Loder in English and oratorio music. In her sixteenth year she made her *début* under the direction of Henry Meiggs at a concert given in Apollo Hall, on Broadway, with decided success. Dec. 25, 1848, she was married to Mr. C. E. L. Brinkerhoff, but did not forsake her profession. She has sung much in concerts in New York city, and in various States of the Union. In 1861 she visited Europe and was the recipient of many flattering favors in Paris and London. Mme. Brinkerhoff's voice is a rich soprano of nearly three octaves range, full and clear in quality. She resides in New York City, and much of her time is devoted to teaching. She has composed a number of songs, of which "Claritta" and "One Flag or no Flag" have gained some popularity. She has also written a romance called "Alva Vine; Art Versus Duty."

**Bristow,** GEORGE FREDERICK, one of America's representative musicians, was born in Brooklyn, N. Y., Dec. 19, 1825. At the age of five years he regularly began the study of music under a competent master, and when thirteen became second leader of violins in an orchestra. A year later his first composition was published. In 1836 he received his first professional appointment as violinist in the orchestra of the Olympic Theatre, then led by

George Loder. Upon the organization of the New York Philharmonic Society, in 1842, he entered the orchestra as violinist, a position which he has retained down to the present time, February, 1883. His first overture was performed by the Philharmonic Society while he was yet in his seventeenth year. His concert overture (op. 3) was also performed by the Society, and attracted considerable attention. It was followed in 1845 by a symphony in E flat. He in 1849 wrote the orchestral score to " Eleutheria," a cantata by G. H. Curtis, which was performed at the Tabernacle. During the brilliant career of Jenny Lind in this country he held the position of *concertmeister* under Sir Jules Benedict, and was engaged in the same capacity by Jullien, for whom he wrote a symphony in D minor, receiving therefor $200, which was considered a large price in those days for a production by an American composer. It was a work of more than ordinary merit, and proved a profitable investment for Mr. Jullien. Bristow's romantic opera, " Rip Van Winkle," was produced at Niblo's Garden, New York, Sept. 27, 1855, by the Pyne-Harrison English Opera Company. Such was its success that it ran for thirty consecutive nights. The libretto is by J. H. Wainright. The work is of more than ordinary merit, containing many fine and powerful numbers, and deserves to be revived by some *impresario*. It was translated into Italian, new scenery, costumes, etc., were prepared, and it was just about to be reproduced under the direction of Max Maretzek, with Clara Louise Kellogg as the heroine, when the New York Academy of Music was destroyed by fire in 1865. It has not yet been published in complete form. Some time after the production of " Rip Van Winkle," Mr. Bristow wrote his first oratorio, " Praise to God." It was thrice performed, and greatly added to its composer's reputation. The third performance was given by the New York Harmonic Society (of which Mr. Bristow was leader) at the Brooklyn Academy of Music, and netted over $2,000, the composer receiving only $25 for his services. Mr. Bristow's second oratorio, " Daniel," was first performed under his own direction at Steinway Hall, Dec. 30, 1867, by the Mendelssohn Union. Mme. Parepa-Rosa assumed the leading *rôle*, and the orchestral and choral forces were in excellent training. The work

aroused unusual interest, and was very favorably received. As compared with his previous works it shows greater maturity, depth, and earnestness and certainly entitles Mr. Bristow to rank as the foremost of American oratorical composers. His Arcadian symphony was performed by the Philharmonic Society at the Academy of Music, New York, Feb. 14, 1874. It was written as the introduction to the cantata of "The Pioneer ; or, Westward Ho ! " which was begun by William Vincent Wallace and which Mr. Bristow is engaged in completing. When produced it will undoubtedly greatly enhance his reputation.

Mr. Bristow's talents are varied as well as of the highest order. He is an accomplished organist, an excellent orchestral conductor, a good choral drill master, an experienced teacher, and a fine violinist. For half of a lifetime he has taught music in the public schools of New York, and in this capacity he has exercised an untold influence for good. His life has been a simple and uneventful one. He appears but little in society, and his home for many years has been a cottage in Morrisania. The usual methods of gaining fame and popularity are despised by him, but he is most highly esteemed both as a gentleman and a musician. All of his works are written with much care and are frequently subject to repeated revisions before being presented to the public. Many of them exhibit a purity of form, nobility, inspiration, and masterly treatment which will render them in a measure classics, and perpetuate the name of their composer. The total number of Mr. Bristow's works is above 60, the most of which remain in manuscript. A complete list is as follows:

| Op. | Name. |
|---|---|
| 1. | Quartet, in F. 1st and 2nd violins, viola, and 'cello. |
| 2. | Quartet, in G minor. 1st and 2nd violins, viola, and 'cello. |
| 3. | Concert Overture, in E flat. Grand orchestra. |
| 4. | La Belle Amerique, nocturne. Piano. |
| 5. | Duo, " La fille du Regiment," 4 hands. Piano. |
| 6. | Waltz, in E flat. Piano. |
| 7. | La toile du noir, nocturne. Piano. |
| 8. | La Serenade, nocturne. Piano. |
| 9. | La pensée, nocturne. Piano. |
| 10. | Symphonie, in E flat. Orchestra. |
| 11. | La Belle du joir, nocturne. Piano. |
| 12. | Sonale, in G. Violin and piano. |

13. Fantasie (violin); "Cracovienne," violin and piano.
14. "Innocence," nocturne. Piano.
15. Sentence, in E flat, "The Lord is in His holy temple."
16. Waltz, in E flat. Piano.
17. "Zampa." Solo violin and orchestra.
18. Polonaise, in E flat. Piano.
19. Morning service, in E flat. Organ accompt.
20. "La Belle nuit," nocturne. Piano.
21. "Life on the ocean wave," variation. Piano.
22. "Rip Van Winkle," opera.
23. Sentence, in E. Organ accompt.
24. Symphonie, in D minor. Orchestra.
25. Friendship, nocturne in E. Piano.
26. Symphonie, in F sharp minor. Orchestra.
27. Blue Bell, nocturne. Piano.
28. Pot-pourri. Organ.
29. Waltz, in E flat. Piano.
30. Overture, "Winter's Tale." Orchestra.
31. Canzonet, "The Abode of Music." Piano accompt.
32. Oratorio, "Praise to God." Solos, chorus, and orchestra.
33. Overture, "Columbus." Orchestra.
34. Burial service. Organ accompt.
35. Waltz, in E. Piano.
36. Evening service, in D.
37. "Canary Bird." Piano solo.
38. "Eroica." Piano solo.
39. Easter anthem, in E flat, "Christ our Passover.
40. Sentence, "The Lord in his holy temple."
41. Epigram, in A flat. Piano.
42. Oratorio, "Daniel." Solos, chorus, and orchestra.
43. "Rain Drops." Piano solo.
44. Collection of Psalmody, Chants, etc.
45. Six organ pieces.
46. Piano piece, in A flat.
47. Overture, "Great Republic." Orchestra.
48. Ascription. Voice and organ.
49. Cantata, "The Pioneer." Solos, chorus, and orchestra.
50. Symphonie, "Arcadian." Orchestra.
51. Morning service, in B flat.
52. "No More," cantata. Solos, chorus, and orchestra.
53. Chromatic Fantasie and Fugue, by Bach, instrumented for the orchestra.
54. Morning service, in C.
55. La Militaire. Piano solo.
56. Evening service, in G.
57. Impromptu, in B minor. Piano.
58. Morning service, in F.
59. Piano piece, in G flat.
60. Military March.
61. Piano piece, in F.
62. Saltarello, in A flat minor. Piano.
63. Mass, in C. Solos, chorus and organ.

This list does not include many unfinished sketches. Mr. Bristow is at present engaged in composing two operas, two oratorios, and a symphony, which, we doubt not, will surpass any of his previous works.

**Brooklyn.** See NEW YORK AND BROOKLYN.

**Buckley,** FREDERICK, was born in England early in the present century, and came to this country some time about 1840. He, with his father, James Buckley, and his two brothers, George S. and R. Bishop, formed the famous Buckley Minstrels. He was a fine solo violinist, but will be chiefly remembered as the composer of a number of popular songs. Among them may be mentioned, "I'd Choose to be a Daisy," "Come in and Shut the Door," "I am Dreaming, Sadly Dreaming," "Mother, O Sing me to Rest," "Gentle Annie Ray," "For Thee and Only Thee," "Softly Falls the Moonlight," "She is Waiting for Me There," "My Home is on the Sea," "Angry Words are Lightly Spoken," and "Our Union Right or Wrong." He died at his residence, East Canton Street, Boston, in October, 1864.

**Buck,** DUDLEY, one of America's most prominent musicians, was born March 10, 1839, at Hartford, Conn., where his father was a prosperous merchant. A love and aptitude for music showed itself at an early age, but as he was designed for a business career, it was not encouraged. He was, however, allowed to attend singing school, and when twelve years of age learned to play upon a flute which he had borrowed of one of his acquaintances. On his next birthday his father, in order to gratify what he considered as merely a youthful desire, presented him with a flute. About two years later his father also presented him with a melodeon. He now dilligently applied himself to study, and soon became able to play some of the accompaniments to Haydn's and Mozart's masses, though he had no teacher. When sixteen years of age he received a piano, and for a short period had a teacher in the person of W. J. Babcock. About the same time he was appointed deputy organist at St. John's Church in his native city, a post which he held some time. His father now saw that nature had intended him for a musician, and wisely concluded to give him a good musical education. In the summer of 1858 he left home for Europe. He first went to Leipsic, where he studied the piano under Plaidy and Moscheles, instrumentation under Julius Rietz, and theory and composition under Hauptmann and Richter, both at the Conservatorium and in private. Among his fellow pupils at the Conservatorium were S. B. Mills, A. S. Sullivan, J. F. Barnet, Walter Bach, Carl Rosa, Madeline Schiller, Edward Dannreuther, etc. After remaining a year and a half at Leipsic, he went to Dresden and placed himself under Johann Schneider, for the especial study of Bach's works. It so happened that soon after Rietz was called to Dresden, which gave him an opportunity to continue his studies with his former master. Having spent three years in Germany, he proceeded to Paris, where he became acquainted with French music and musicians. In 1862 he returned to the United States, and in deference to the wishes of his parents settled at Hartford, accepting the post of organist at Park Church. About this time he commenced his career as a composer, signing his compositions with "Dudley Buck, Jr." He was, however, little satisfied with his position at Hartford, and longed for more cultivated musical society and extended opportunities. After the death of his parents he removed to Chicago, where he accepted the post of organist at St. James' Church and engaged in teaching. The great Chicago fire of October, 1871, destroyed his home and many of his compositions which were in manuscript. Soon after the fire he returned, with his wife and child, to Boston. There he was appointed organist at St. Paul's, and subsequently of the Music Hall Association, which included charge of the great Music Hall organ. After remaining for three years in Boston, he again removed, this time to New York. He speedily acquired a high position as an organist and teacher, which he has since fully maintained. At present (1883) he is organist of the Church of the Holy Trinity, Brooklyn.

Mr. Buck is one of our most talented and thorough musicians, and his music is of a high order, possessing qualities which make it of more than ordinarily lasting value. We have been unable to obtain a complete list of his works, but among some of the larger and more important ones are "The Golden Legend," a prize cantata, first performed at the Cincinnati May Festival in 1880 (See GOLDEN LEGEND); "Don Munio," a cantata; a Centennial cantata, written for and first produced at the Centennial of 1876, the original copy of which has been deposited in the archives of the Connecticut Historical Society, an Easter Cantata, published by S. Brainard's Sons; "Forty-Sixth Psalm," for solos, chorus, and orchestra, performed by the Handel and Haydn Society of Boston; "Buck's Motet Collection," in two volumes; several organ sonatas; a symphonic overture on Scott's "Marmion," performed by the Brooklyn Philharmonic Society; six songs for male voices; "Illustrations in Choir Accompaniment, with Hints in Registration," etc.

**Bull,** OLOUS BORNEMANN, one of the most renowned violinists of the present century, was born at Bergen, Norway, Feb. 5, 1810, and was the eldest of ten children. His susceptibilty to the charms of music became plainly evident when he was a mere infant, and so strong did the passion grow that when five years old his uncle presented him with a yellow violin. At first he had no teacher but afterwards received some instruction from a certain Paulsen. It was his own inherent genius that taught him most, however, and when he had arrived at the age of eight he was able to take part in his uncle's quartet. A year later he led the violins in the orchestra of the theatre. In 1822 he for a short time received lessons from Lundholm, a Swedish violinist. At this period his mother taught him the 24 caprices of Paganini, which he faithfully practiced. He was sent to the University at Christiania in 1828, after having been under a private tutor for a number of years, but he made poor work with his lessons. Music was the only thing which had any attraction for him, and it must have been a great joy to him when he was appointed conductor of the Philharmonic and Dramatic Societies. In May, 1829, he visited Cassel to hear Spohr, but was coldly received by that great violinist. However, he spent several happy months at Göttingen before returning to his native place. It now became his absorbing idea to go to Paris, and in August, 1831, he arrived in that city. This is the commencement of a period of privation and suffering, to which he had hitherto been a stranger. The terrors of the Revolution had hardly passed and everything was at fever heat. He had brought sufficient money to carry him through the winter, but being robbed by a fellow boarder he was left in extremely reduced circumstances. At this juncture an incident of strange character happened. One morning at breakfast he was met by a middle-aged gentleman who seemed to take a kindly interest in him. Upon the advice of this stranger he was induced to try his luck at gambling. As he had no money of his own, he borrowed five francs and in the evening repaired to the establishment indicated. Placing his money on the red as directed he let it remain there. Once, twice, thrice, again and again it wins, until 800 francs are his. His feelings may better be imagined than described. Suddenly a small white hand grasps the money, but the Norwegian was too quick. A calm, clear voice near by commands the woman to release her hold and Ole to take his money. Turning about he recognizes his friend of the morning, whom he afterwards learned was none other than Vidocq, the famous Parisian chief of police. His wants were thus relieved, but it was only temporarily, and he at one time became so despondent as to think of suicide. He tried for various positions without success. Finally, in April, 1832, he gave his first concert, under the patronage of the Duke of Montebello. This was the opening of his career as an artist. Soon after he made a tour of Switzerland and Italy, remaining some time in the latter country. In Bologna occurred his encounter with Malibran, when he was dragged from bed at night to satisfy the clamorings of an audience she had disappointed. He visited Pisa, Leghorn, Lucca, Rome, and other cities, everywhere meeting with great success, and it was not until May, 1835, that he returned to Paris. In the summer of 1836 he was married to Félicie Villeminot, daughter of one of his former landladies. The match was a happy one, and she died in Norway in 1862, having borne him one son. After his marriage he traveled in France, England (he had appeared in London previous to that event), Germany, and Russia, returning to his old home in Norway. In 1838 he started on his second continental tour, during which he became a firm friend of Liszt.

By this time "Ole's" reputation as a *virtuoso* of the first order was fully established in Europe. Acting upon the advice of Fanny Elssler, he determined to visit America. He arrived in Boston, by the way of Amsterdam and London, in November, 1843, but immediately went to New York, where he gave his first concert November 23. During the month of December he gave concerts in New York, Philadelphia, Baltimore, Washington, Richmond and Petersburg. From the latter place he went to Mobile, New Orleans, and other southern cities. During his travel in the South he met with many adventures, only one of which we will relate. On one occasion he took passage on a Mississippi steamboat which had on board a lot of rough western men. He was invited to drink, but politely refused. Anyone who is acquainted with the customs of those men knows that to refuse to drink is a deadly insult, and it soon became evident that the matter could only be settled by a test of strength. Ole, to avoid what might have been unpleasant circumstances, offered to meet any man of the company in wrestling. A big fellow was chosen, who stepped forward and grasped the violinist around the waist, but was immediately thrown over his head and lay senseless on the deck amid the laughter of his companions. This same man subsequently called an editor to account for some adverse criticism on "Ole's" playing. After visiting Cuba, he made another tour of the United States, including Canada also. Dec. 3, 1845, he left for Paris, where his family awaited him. During the next two years he visited various cities in France and Spain, and even made a trip to Algiers. In January, 1852, he again came to this country, landing at New York. He visited the principal cities and was received with even more than his old cordiality. During this visit he purchased a large tract of land in Potter county, Pennsylvania, for a Norwegian colony, but the title was defective and he lost nearly the whole of it. This was not the only misfortune which befell him, for in one way and another it involved him in numerous lawsuits. Then came a fever which greatly impaired his health, and it was not until 1857 that he returned to Europe for the second time. From 1863 to 1867 he gave concerts in Germany, Poland, Russia, and other countries. In December of the latter year he came to the United States for the third time. The visit lasted until April, 1870. In the autumn of that year he married his second wife, a lady of Madison, Wis., who still survives him. The event was solemnized in Norway. Thenceforth his time was mainly

divided between this and his native country. At length his health began to fail and it became such a serious matter that some time was spent at the famous German baths, Wiesbaden. No permanent improvement resulted. It was decided that he should remain here during the winter of 1879-80, and he took a residence at Cambridge, Mass., where some of his friends celebrated his seventieth birthday, Feb. 5, 1880. In the spring he sailed for his old home in Norway, but rapidly grew weaker, and died there Aug. 19, 1880, greatly esteemed and lamented. No one could help liking both the artist and the man. Thoroughly unselfish, he often gave not only his services but large sums of money for charitable purposes.

There is a "Memoir" of Bull, edited by Sara C. Bull, his wife, and published by Houghton, Mifflin & Co., Boston, in 1 vol., 1883. It deals in a pleasing manner with the life of the great violinist and contains an appendix illustrating his methods of holding his instrument. When playing he always stood upright and his fingers rested on the fingerboard at an acute angle. He can hardly be called the representative of any school of violinists, though, perhaps, his style was more largely founded on the Italian than any other. He was, in fact, both individual and original, and in many respects unlike anyone who preceded him. His playing was distinguished for animation, feeling, and ease of execution. He was emphatically a master in his own sphere of playing, and possessed the rare faculty of quickly putting his audiences *en rapport* with himself. Even his appearance on the stage was generally a signal for applause. To these qualities is due the wonderful success of his tours and the fact that he never failed of having a good house wherever he went. Greater artists than he may have lived, but it may safely be asserted that none have had in such a wonderful degree the gift of appealing to and arousing the feelings of the masses.

**Butterfield,** JAMES A., was born in Great Berkhampsted, England, May 18, 1837. When only four years of age he could play easy tunes on the violin by note. At the age of eight he performed the 1st violin part of Handel's "Hallelujah Chorus" before Stephen Glover, to that musician's great delight. His fine voice gained him several requests to become a choir-boy of Westminster Abbey, but to this proposal his parents would not listen. He early became a member of the Philharmonic Society of his native town, and once, though but ten years old, directed a performance of the "Messiah" in absence of the conductor. Later, he was a pupil of John Hullah for some time.

In 1855 he came to the United States, but after three years returned to England and resumed his musical studies. He soon came back to this country, however, and was appointed principal of a musical academy in the South. Being forced to come North by the outbreak of the Rebellion, he located in Indianapolis, Ind., as a teacher of music. After residing in Indianapolis for six years and a half, he removed to Chicago, where he took a prominent position as teacher and conductor. He was at one period director of the Chicago Oratorio Society, and had charge of the chorus of the Chicago Jubilee in 1873. Quite recently, on account of ill health, he decided to come East, and located in Norwich, Conn., where he now (March, 1885) resides. Of his four operas "Belshazzar" is the most important and most popular, and has often been produced throughout the country. A complete list of his works is as follows:

Seventy songs, written between 1859 and 1873, of which "When you and I were young, Maggie," sold to the extent of 250,000 copies; "The Star of the West," a text book for schools (1863); "Butterfield's Anthems" (1869); Butterfield's Collection," consisting of sacred music (1870); "Belshazzar," an opera in five acts, for solos, chorus, and orchestra, given under the composer's direction more than 350 times (1871); "Ruth, the Gleaner," an opera in five acts, for solos, chorus, and orchestra, performed under the author's direction 39 times (1875); "The Requisite," for singing schools and conventions (1878); "The Race for a Wife," a comedy in three acts, (1879); "Window Glass," a comedy in two acts given three times (1880); "Butterfield's System of Vocal Training and Music Readers for Children," in three books.

# C.

**Calliope.** A musical instrument, the tones of which are produced by steam instead of wind. It has a cylinder, along the top of which are valve chambers connected with whistles tuned according to the diatonic scale. The instrument may be played from a keyboard similar to that of an organ, or the cylinder can be set to certain tunes and made to revolve as in barrel organs. It was invented by I. C. Stoddard of Worcester, Mass. The tones may be heard five miles or more, and at a distance are quite pleasing.

**Candidus,** WILLIAM, was born in 1845, at Philadelphia, of German parents. He received a good general education, to which was added an excellent musical training. He played the piano and organ, and became a baritone singer in a German musical society of Philadelphia. His mother was a good singer and helped to form his taste. He followed the trade of his father, that of a piano keyboard maker. Being called to New York by the Steinways, he there had an opportunity to hear nearly all of the great artists. He made his first operatic appearance as *Max* in "Freischütz," with such success as to lead him to devote himself to the stage. Accordingly he went to Germany and studied for some time, making his professional *début* at Weimar in "Stradella." He was offered and accepted an engagement at the Royal Opera, Hanover, and afterwards at the Hamburg opera. In 1865 he had married the widowed daughter of the late Henry Steinway, but just after leaving Hanover his wife died. This caused him to give up the stage, but he devoted himself more closely than ever to his art. He went to Italy and studied under Rouchette at Milan. After this he appeared in the principal cities of West Germany, and was well received. During a portion of 1879 and 1880 he sang at Her Majesty's, London, and in the autumn of 1880 accepted an engagement at Frankfort-on-the-Main, where he still (1883) remains, making occasional visits to this country. In June, 1881, he sang at the Chicago Sængerfest, and at the New York, Cincinnati, and Chicago May Festivals of 1882.

**Cappa,** CARLO ALBERTO, one of the most celebrated of American bandmasters, was born at Allessandria, in the kingdom of Sardinia, Dec. 9, 1834. His father was a major in the Sardinian army, and fought under Napoleon in the great campaign against Russia. At the age of ten years he entered the Royal Academy at Asti (to which only soldiers' sons are admitted) and remained there five years. He then enlisted in the band of the Sixth Lancers and was present at the battle of Novara in 1849. He remained in the army six years, and then enlisted in the U. S. Navy, shipping on board the frigate Congress at Genoa. The cruise lasted two years. On Feb. 22, 1858, he arrived at New York. As a member of Ned Kendall's band he visited the principal American cities. Later, he became a member of Shelton's band, and in 1860 entered the 7th Regiment band, of which he was elected bandmaster in 1881. For seven years, beginning with 1869, he was first trombone player in Thomas' orchestra. As conductor of the concerts in Central Park, at Coney Island, Brighton Beach, and other places, he has given great satisfaction and won a substantial reputation.

**Carlberg,** GOTTHOLD, was born June 13, 1838, at Berlin, where his father was a merchant. Almost from infancy he was used to hearing *matinée* performances of chamber music (held in the *salon* of Leon de St. Lubrin, violinist, who lived in the same house) in which Liszt, Mendelssohn, Schulhoff, Rice, and other eminent musicians took part. At he age of four years he began the study of the piano under the organist Thiele. When nine he left school and entered the gymnasium. He was intended for a physician by his father, but never relinquished the study of music, and at fifteen began to take harmony lessons of Dr. A. B. Marx. On arriving at the age of eighteen his father gave up his long cherished desire and allowed the young man to follow the bent of his nature. Soon after he went to Paris, and from there to London. In 1857 he came to New York, where he finally succeeded in obtaining the post of musical editor of the "Staats Zeitung." Becoming acquainted with Carl Anschütz, he continued his musical studies with that gentleman, and received his first initiation into the art of conducting. In 1861 he was compelled to return to Europe and enter the ranks of the Prussian army, being a Prussian subject. After eight months of service he was released on account of sickness, and became editor of the "Neu Berliner Musikzeitung." In 1863 he organized an orchestra, called "Carlbergscher Orchesterverein," with which he gave over 150 concerts. He left Berlin in November, 1864, and proceeded to Vienna, where he studied the voice under Lugi Salvi and H. M. Wolf. He was persuaded to organize an orchestra for the purpose of giving classical concerts, but the scheme proved a failure. The ensuing three years were spent in Brunn as leader of the philharmonic concerts and teacher of singing. In 1869 he returned to Vienna, and wrote two works, "Ueber Gesangkunst und Kunstgesang," a treatise on the culture of the voice, and "Die Kunst Saenger zu Werden." During the season of 1870 he was engaged as director of the opera at Trieste, after which he made a tour of Northern Italy. Returning to Vienna again in June, he was engaged by Strauss for a season at Warsaw, Poland. From there he in June, 1871, went to St. Petersburg in the capacity of conductor. Not long after he came to the United States for the second time having been engaged by Prince George Galitzin to conduct a series of Russian concerts here. These proved a failure, and he was engaged by Max Maretzek. For the next few years he was teacher, writer and conductor, and engaged in various enterprises. In 1877 he became editor of the "Music Trade Review," New York, which was discontinued about the beginning of 1880. During the season of 1878-79 he gave a series of symphony concerts at Chickering Hall, wielding the *bâton* over Thomas' orchestra. Mr. Carlberg died at New York, April 27, 1881, just a few days before he intended to set sail for Germany. His death was caused by overwork.

**Carreno,** TERESA, the well-known pianist, was born at Caraccas, Venezuela, South America, Dec. 22, 1853. She descended from a distinguished Spanish family. When only two years old she could sing operatic airs, and at the age of seven had mastered Thalberg's fantasia on "Norma." Her earliest lessons were received from her father. Subsequently for a short time she received lessons of Julius Hoheni, a German professor. In the latter part of 1862, being only nine years of age, she appeared in New York, where she had an interview with Gottschalk and played with him on the piano a four-hand piece. In a short time she had learned his "Jerusalem" and "Bananier" so as to be able to play them without the score, he kindly giving her some advice concerning the rendering of the pieces. After appearing in New York she went to Boston, and at both places created a great sensation on account of her remarkable playing for one so young. Since that time she has traveled extensively, giving concerts in various parts of the country and elsewhere. She has written a few piano pieces of fair order.

**Carter,** HENRY, was born at London, England, in 1837, and commenced his career as an organist in that city. Early in life he went to Canada, and at the age of seventeen became organist of the English Cathedral of Quebec, where he established the first Canadian oratorio society and successfully gave eight oratorios. Upon the erection of the organ in the Music Hall, Boston, he removed there and became one of the regular performers on the instrument, and also chorister of the Church of the Advent. He subsequently removed to Providence, R. I., and in 1873 to New York, his weekly recitals on the large organ in Trinity church bringing him much into notice. In 1880 he accepted a position as professor of the piano, voice, organ, and lecturer on music, in the College of Music, Cincinnati. This he resigned early in 1883 to take charge of the music of Plymouth Church, Brooklyn.

**Cary,** ANNA LOUISE, one of America's most celebrated contralto singers, was born in 1844,* at Wayne, Kennebec Co., Maine, where her father was a physician. The family consisted of six children, of whom Anna was the youngest. She led a life of song almost from infancy, and when fifteen years of age was sent to Boston, where her elder brother lived, to study music. Lyman W. Wheeler

---

*The year of her birth is variously given as 1840, 1842, 1844, and 1846.

was her principal teacher, but she also took lessons of several other Boston teachers. During her six years residence in Boston she sang in the churches of Dr. Stowe (Bedford Street), Dr. Lowell, and Dr. Huntington. At the end of this time she very naturally turned her attention toward Europe as the only place where a singer could gain a finished education. A benefit concert furnished her with means, and she proceeded to Milan, where she placed herself under Corsi. In Dec., 1867, having made rapid progress, she was induced to go with an Italian opera company to Copenhagen, where she made her *début* on the stage. The trip did not prove very successful, and she returned to Baden-Baden, Germany, and continued her studies under Mme. Viardot-Garcia. From there she went to Hamburg, where she met with success. She then accepted an engagement with M. Strakosch to sing in Stockholm during the season of 1868. The summer of 1869 was spent at Paris, and a brilliant engagement at Brussels followed. Shortly after she was engaged for three years by Strakosch. In the spring of 1870 she sang at Drury Lane, London, and Sept. 19 of the same year made her first appearance in New York, singing with Nilsson. After this she sang throughout the country at the principal cities, and created the greatest enthusiasm. In 1875 she was in St. Petersburg, where she caused a *furore* by her singing. She returned to the United States in 1876. In June, 1880, she went to England, where she remained some time. She sang at the Cincinnati May Festival of 1882, and has appeared at various other places since her return. Quite recently (1882) she was married to a Mr. Raymond. Her voice is rich, deep and sweet, and well managed. Mrs. Ada Cary-Sturgis, a sister of Anna, who also possesses a fine contralto voice, has lately appeared in concerts with much success.

**Centennial Cantata.** A cantata written to celebrate the 100th anniversary (1876) of our existence as a nation. The music is by Dudley Buck. It was performed at the opening of the great Centennial Exhibition, Philadelphia, May 10, 1876. The autograph is preserved in the archives of the Connecticut Historical Society. The *Centennial March*, also rendered at the opening of the Exhibition, was composed by Richard Wagner, for which he received $5000.

**Chadwick**, GEORGE W., was born Nov. 13, 1854, at Lowell, Mass., but in 1860 his parents removed to Lawrence. His first instruction in music was received from his elder brother, whom he succeeded as organist at one of the local churches. After leaving school he entered the office of his father, who was an insurance agent and desired that his son should follow the same business, but after remaining there three years he gave it up and adopted music as a profession. This was in 1875. In the following year he went to Olivet, Mich., where he had charge of the musical department of the college. Despite the remonstrances of his father, in 1877 he departed for Europe, going to Germany, where he studied for two years under Jadassohn and Reinecke. The former, according to his own expression, was almost a father to him, and gave him more than usual encouragement. In July, 1879, he left Leipsic, and after traveling some in Germany, settled at Munich, where he studied theory and organ playing with Rheinberger for nearly a year.

Previous to going to Germany, Mr. Chadwick had written many songs and piano pieces, two trios for strings, and two overtures. While at Leipsic he wrote his two quartets for strings and the overture to "Rip Van Winkle," all of which were publicly performed with good success. His greatest work, the symphony in C, was projected or begun while he was at Munich, and finished after his return home, which occurred early in 1880. It was first performed from manuscript at the Harvard Musical Association symphony concerts this year (1882). His overture to "Rip Van Winkle" was also performed at the Handel and Haydn Festival in May, 1880. Some of his other works have been performed at various times.

Mr. Chadwick is at present (June, 1883) a resident of Boston, where he is organist of Park Street Church. His time is devoted to teaching, composing, and conducting, but it is to the latter two branches that he gives his greatest energies. Having given such early and substantial evidences of his talents, his future course will be watched with great interest.

**Chautauqua Musical Reading Club.** An organization having for its object the assistance of such persons as desire to pursue a course of reading and study in the science and history of music. The plan of operation is similar to that of the Chautauqua Literary and Scientific Circle. Members are admitted upon answering certain questions and paying an annual fee of either 75 cents or $1.50. The course of reading, which covers a period of four years and may be pursued at home, is divided into two portions, scientific and literary. Forty minutes each day will suffice to complete the course in the required time. The affairs of the Club are regulated by a board of counsellors consisting of George F. Root, H. R. Palmer, E. E. Ayres, W. F. Sherwin, and C. C. Case. Prof. E. E. Ayres, Richmond, Va., is secretary. Books are furnished at reduced prices. The course of reading for the first year (1883-84—the year commencing with October and ending with June) includes the following works: Palmer's Theory of Music, Richter's Fundamental Harmonies, The Great German Composers (Ferris), Musical Forms (Pauer), Life of Bach (Shuttleworth), Life of Handel (Schœlcher), Music of the Bible (Hutchinson), Old Hundredth Psalm Tune, History of Music, vols. 1 and 2 (Ritter), Readings from Burney and Hawkins and in ancient Greek and Roman music, The Soprano, Money and Music, and Curiosities of Music (Elson).

**Chicago.** Chicago can not, strictly speaking, at this stage of its history be called a musical city. It is great in commercial activity and has much wealth, but it is quite moderate in its support of the arts. Opera and star companies are very well patronized, but our home organizations have to struggle for life. Music has not become a necessity here, as in the older cities of the country. We have but three or four important musical societies, and they are generally burdened by debt.

THE APOLLO CLUB was founded directly after the big fire in October, 1871, by S. G. Pratt and George B. Lyon. It first existed as a male chorus. Its first conductor was Mr. S. G. Pratt, followed by Mr. Dohn, who in turn gave way to Mr. Tomlins, the present director. Under the latter gentleman it became a mixed chorus, and numbers some 150 voices. It has given three regular concerts each year since its organization, and now annually performs at Christmas time Handel's oratorio of the "Messiah."

THE BEETHOVEN SOCIETY. This Society was organized by Carl Wolfsohn some ten years ago (1873), and has continued ever since under his direction. It is a mixed chorus, and brings out the important modern works, in three concerts each year. The best productions of Max Bruch, Hofmann, Gade, Mendelssohn, Beethoven, Verdi, and Wagner, have been given.

THE MOZART SOCIETY. This Society consists of a select chorus of about forty male voices. It has had two conductors, Mr. Hans Balatka, and the present director, Mr. Bartlett. Three concerts are given every year, and the larger works for male voices brought forward. Mr. E. G. Newhall, the secretary, has accomplished much in giving it an important place among our home societies.

THE FESTIVAL CHORUS was organized under the direction of Theodore Thomas, assisted by Mr. Tomlins. It consists of 600 voices, and large festivals are to be given by it every two years, the first of which was held in May, 1882. (See MAY FESTIVALS). The cost of the Festival was very large—over $60,000—and was not fully met by the sale of tickets. A fund has to be raised each year of the Festival to secure Mr. Thomas and the committee against loss.

THE PHILHARMONIC SOCIETY, under the direction of Mr. Liesegang, gives three concerts each year. It consists of some fifty men, and includes all of the best orchestral players in the city. The concerts are mostly devoted to symphonies, although other works are given.

GERMAN SOCIETIES. There are one or two German singing societies in the city, but at present none that give public concerts.

SUMMER-NIGHT CONCERTS. Every summer, Theodore Thomas with an orchestra of fifty musicians gives six weeks of nightly concerts in the Exposition building, which are well supported.

THE HERSHEY SCHOOL OF MUSICAL ART. This school was founded some seven years since by Mrs. Sara B. Hershey (now Mrs. Eddy), assisted by H. Clarence Eddy. Up to date (April, 1883), there have been some 405 concerts given, including 125 organ recitals by

Mr. Eddy, who is an accomplished organist. This school, although the result of private enterprise, has its own concert hall, containing a $6000 pipe organ, and is well arranged to hold a first-class position as a musical institution. It has a regular four years' course, and a " post-graduate" course following.

CHICAGO COLLEGE OF MUSIC. This institution is under the direction of Dr. F. Ziegfeld, and is a private enterprise. It has been in existence over twelve years, and has a regular course of study.

PRIVATE INSTRUCTION. There is a large number of first-class teachers in the city, and the greater percentage of musical instruction is given by them.

MUSIC HOUSES AND MUSIC HALLS. Chicago enjoys a large music trade, and some $3,500,-000 worth of business in that line is done each year—mostly with the Western States. There are a number of music halls, the most important of which is *Central Music Hall*. This beautiful hall will hold 3000 people, and was built through the energy of the late George B. Carpenter.                    C. H. BRITTAN.

## Chicago College of Music.

This institution, one of the leading of its kind in Chicago, was founded in 1867, by the present president, Dr. F. Ziegfeld. It had scarcely earned a permanent position among similar institutions and a growing reputation when the great fire of October, 1871, occurred, which destroyed the College rooms, library and other property. In a few weeks, however, new rooms were secured and the school re-opened. It now (1886) occupies a magnificent building on the corner of State and Randolph streets. There is also a branch of the College located on West Adams street for the accommodation of patrons residing in West Chicago. The College is incorporated under the name given above, and is governed by a board of eleven directors. The faculty numbers nearly twenty-five, and includes some of the most widely-known teachers in the West. Dr. Ziegfeld has from the first devoted all his energies to the College, and its success is largely due to his superior ability as an educator and manager. The course of study embraces every department of music and the principal modern languages. Students may receive the degree of Doctor of Music after complying with the necessary conditions.

**Chickering,** JONAS, was born April 5, 1797, at New Ipswich, N. H. His education was limited to that afforded by the common school. At the age of seventeen years he was apprenticed to a cabinet maker in his native town. Two years after, he volunteered to both tune and repair a certain piano (and, by the way, the only one) in the place. Proving successful, he seems to have turned his thoughts towards the manufacture of pianos, and accordingly in 1818, being of age, he went to Boston and entered the establishment of a Mr. Osborn to learn the trade. In 1823 he founded the present extensive house of Chickering & Sons (See CHICKERING & SONS) by setting up in business for himself. He then gradually introduced the improvements which have made his name famous and his pianos among the best manufactured. Mr. Chickering was a member of many musical societies, liberally patronized the arts, and held several offices of importance. He died at Boston, Dec. 9, 1853.

**Chickering & Sons,** BOSTON and NEW YORK. This celebrated American piano manufacturing firm was established at Boston, April 15, 1823, by Jonas Chickering (For some particulars of his life, see preceding article). At that early time the piano had not reached its present high state of development, and piano making in the United States was in its infancy. Considerable impetus was given to the business by a Scotchman named Stewart, who induced Jonas Chickering to enter into partnership with him. Before his advent, however, American energy and skill had awakened to a partial realization of the great future before them in the production of pianos. Two years later, Stewart returned to Europe, leaving Mr. Chickering alone. This was previous to the year 1823, in which the firm of Chickering was established, and its success is entirely due to the man whose name it bears.

In 1837, Mr. Chickering produced the first square piano with an iron frame complete except the wrest-pin block, and in 1840 the first full iron frame for a grand piano ever made. Three years later, he invented and patented an improvement of great importance at that time. On the upper side or top of the plate, covering the head-block, he introduced a cast-iron flange, which was drilled for each string to pass through, thus giving a firm upward tendency to the strings and at the same time forming a transverse strengthening bar. Grand pianos of this construction were sent to the first Great International Exhibition held in London, in 1851, where they created a profound sensation and were awarded a prize medal. This method of construction was discontinued in the year 1856, and the present method of casting a solid iron flange on the under side of the iron frame into which the "agraffes" are screwed, was adopted. In 1845 the circular scale as used in square pianos was invented and tested by Mr. Chickering, whose ceaseless activity was constantly directed toward the improvement of his instruments. The number of patents granted the house is very large, and its history is inseparably connected with the history of piano making in America.

In 1853, Mr. Chickering died, since when the business has been successfully carried on by his sons, under the old firm name. Once, in December, 1852, the firm suffered a heavy loss by fire, but immediately rebuilt on a much more extensive scale. Their pianos, of which they have manufactured 70,000, are favorably known all over the world, and to their excellence is largely due the fact that American pianos lead all other makes.

**China.** One of the early American hymn tunes, at one time very popular, and still sung. It was composed by Timothy Swan, and probably first published in his collection of church music, FEDERAL HARMONY, which appeared in 1785, he being at that time twenty-eight years of age. It was originally set to the words, "Why do we mourn for dying friends," by Dr. Watts, and is rarely ever employed but with them.

**Chorister's Companion.** A collection of sacred music edited and published by Simeon Jocelyn, of New Haven, Conn., in 1788. His name is not attached to any of the pieces which it contains, but it is supposed that some of them were of his composition. A supplement to the work was published in 1793.

**Christian Harmony.** 1.—A collection of sacred music published at Exeter, N. H., in 1805, by Jeremiah Ingalls. It contained 200 pages and a good amount of music, but seems not to have been a financial success.

2. A work issued in 1794 (according to John W. Moore) by Andrew Law, a native of Cheshire, Conn. It numbered 64 pages, and was engraved in a kind of patent notes of which Mr. Law was the inventor.

**Church Co., The John,** CINCINNATI, OHIO. This music-publishing firm, one of the most prominent in the United States, was established in 1854, by John Church. At that time the West, musically speaking, was just beginning to show signs of growth. To this fact and to excellent management the remarkable success of the firm is no doubt due. Along with the publication of music, an extensive business is carried on in the line of general musical merchandise. The firm publishes many popular and standard works. Among these are "The New Musical Curriculum," by Dr. George F. Root, a piano instructor of more than ordinary merit; "The School of Singing," by F. W. Root, an excellent work; "Palmer's Theory of Music," by Dr. H. R. Palmer, a very concise and handy little volume; and the "Graded Singer" series for day schools. With the above must also be included the "Gospel Hymns" series, of which the firm is part publisher. The latter work has sold to the extent of millions of copies, and is known in every civilized land. Wise and judicious management during the past quarter of a century or more has been conducive to the rapid growth and solid financial reputation of the firm, which, while achieving its own deserved success, has done much by its broad and liberal policy toward elevating and extending the musical taste of Cincinnati and the section of country tributary to it.

**Church's Musical Visitor.** A 32-page monthly magazine, published by the foregoing firm. It is devoted to the interests of music in general. Dr. Root is one of its chief contributors. Since the organization of the Chautauqua Musical Reading Club it has been designated as the official organ of that society.

**Cincinnati.** The prominence this city has been honored with as an art center is founded on the realities of a magnificent music hall, one of the largest and most complete organs in the world, an unsurpassed chorus of six hundred and fifty members, and the homes of nearly three hundred thousand music-loving people. This perfected state of art elements was not an instantaneous transition from an entirely absent condition, but represents the outgrowth of a gradual development since 1797, when the first musical organ was the formation of a band, under the leadership of Gen. Wilkinson, at Fort Washington. This was soon succeeded by another in the management of local influences, and was directed by Mr. Albert Ratel. His achievements were of a sufficient incentive momentum that in 1820 a musical academy was founded and placed under the superintendence of Prof. J. W. Hoffman. Principally in the course of instruction was attention devoted to band music and band instruments, such as clarinet, oboe, horns, etc. During this period the first singing society was organized and called the HAYDN SOCIETY OF CINCINNATI. The production of Haydn's oratorio, "Creation," marked the greatest artistic accomplishment. The concert was given May 25, 1823. Mr. Charles Fox continued its leader until their forces were usurped by the first German Gesang-Verein, in 1830. The following year a band of about thirty Saxons was brought to this country, and, finding in Cincinnati the most liberal appreciation, they determined to reside here. Now, with the foreign artists and local musicians, a force requisite to render symphonies was organized, and a series of concerts planned. For a space covering six years these entertainments were successfully conducted, under the leadership of Mr. Michael Brand. The generous donations of several wealthy citizens afforded means for securing the Theodore Thomas orchestra. This undertaking was augmented by the erection of the fine Music Hall and great organ, and the formation of the grand chorus.

THE WELSH SINGING SOCIETY. Since its organization in the fall of 1871, this chorus has been one of the most active. The object of its organization was to promote a more friendly intercourse among the Welsh singers of the city. The success attending its first meetings was so rapidly augmented that the works selected for their study were only the best which have ever been written, such as Mendelssohn's "St. Paul," Handel's "Messiah," etc. The Society meets every Wednesday evening in the Welsh church, situated between Sixth and Seventh streets, on the west side of College. It has been among the most successful competitors in the great Welsh musical festivals held throughout the state. Its accurate and animated rendering of Dr. Joseph Parry's "Blodwen," at the last Festival, which was held at Columbus, secured them the three prizes offered and contended for by about thirty five different societies. Mr. Ebenezer Bowen, its efficient leader, was its founder, and has ever since remained its commander-in-chief, although at different periods it has given performances under the direction of visiting conductors. The chorus numbers about one hundred selected voices, which is the main support of their concerts, the accompaniment being the piano and the organ.

THE ORPHEUS. This society can be called the Wagnerian society of Cincinnati, although, of late, it has drifted far from Wagner's compositions as the principal selections for its study. Its organization occurred on the 4th of April, 1868. Prof. Carl Barus was elected conductor and remained its leader until 1881. Under his direction, Wagner's "Flying Dutchman" and "Lohengrin" and many selections from his other works were rehearsed and produced. It has rendered a large number of Bach's works, including the Passion Music according to St. Matthew, the cantata of "Ein' Feste Burg," "Actus Tragicus," and "Tantum Ergo;" Beethoven's "Missa Solennis," and "Christus am Oelberge" (Mount of Olives); Cherubini's "Medée" and "La Primavera;" Gluck's "Orpheus;" Handel's "Messiah" and "Dettingen Te Deum;" and Mozart's "Requiem." It has produced, aside from these, many works by other composers. Its first public appearance was made in Hérold's "Zampa" and Lortzing's "Der Wildschütz." The society supported for four years an amateur orchestra, which at one time numbered forty-five musicians. They gave several very successful orchestral concerts, rendering Beethoven's first and second symphonies, aside from many overtures and much dance music. The society gives four grand concerts every season, and forms one of the principal features of the May Festival chorus. Its meetings are held every Tuesday and Friday evenings and Sunday afternoons. Mr. Arthur Mees is the present conductor, with Mr. Louis Ergott as assistant. The society also forms one of the supports of the National Sängerfests, and numbers sixty male and fifty female voices upon its active member list. On several occasions it has been victorious in gaining the first prizes for the most artistic performances at the Sängerfests. Sufficient funds have been secured to purchase a hall, which is located at Twelfth and Walnut streets.

DRAMATIC FESTIVAL ASSOCIATION (The) assumed the notable characteristics of the May Festivals, and under such glowing auspices presented six of Shakspeare's greatest plays in a manner never excelled in this country before, the list consisting of "Julius Cæsar," "The Haunchback," "Much Ado About Nothing," "Othello," "Hamlet," and "Romeo and Juliet." The entire work throughout proved a most brilliant success, and upon such results a second festival is being arranged for. The casts will include the most prominent actors in Europe or America. The casts of the late festival included only such performers as have for years been playing as individual stars, such as John McCullough, Lawrence Barrett, Miss Mary Anderson, Mlle. Rhea, Clara Morris, James E. Murdock, N. C. Goodwin, John Ellsler, and others equally celebrated. Mr. R. E. J. Miles was appointed dramatic director, and Mr. Michael Brand musical director. The festival was held in the Music Hall, beginning April 30th, and closing May 5th, 1883. The tickets were disposed of by auction to the highest bidder for the choice of seats. The receipts amounted to $94,908.40, and the expenses to about $50,000.

THE CINCINNATI MÆNNERCHOR was made a society, May 24, 1857, by the uniting of the Liedertafel, Germania, and Sängerbund. The organization elected Mr. A. Paulsen, president, and W. Klausmeyer, director. The first concert which served to attract public attention was given in Wood's Theatre, May 18, 1858, the net proceeds amounting to $166.50. Mr. Carl Barus was appointed conductor in September of the same year, and under his efficient efforts "Czar and Zimmermann," "Stradella," "Freischütz," and "Oberon," were produced. The study of this elevated class of compositions necessitated the addition of lady members, and the constitution was amended to that effect, June 19, 1860. In 1864, Mr. A. Nembach became conductor, and under his direction the operas of "Zampa" and "Der Freischütz were given. A discussion arose between the active and passive members, at this time, the question being as to whether or not operas should longer be rendered, and resulted in the active members withdrawing and forming a new society, under the name of "Orpheus." For the old society, Mr. H. G. Andres accepted the leadership, but resigned in 1869, and Mr. H. Gerold was chosen in his stead. The society remained under his charge until 1873, when he was in turn succeeded by Mr. Otto Singer, who has since been conductor. Mr. Henry Curth is its president, and it is in a very flourishing condition. Plans and specifications for a new hall, to be personal property, have been prepared, and soon a building costing $100,000 will be completed. Meetings are held every Wednesday and Sunday evenings in Eureck Hall, where concerts are given once in four weeks. The membership is divided into one hundred active and two hundred passive constituents. The object of the society is a more liberal culture in the study of classical music.

MAY FESTIVALS. These are now a settled feature, but one, it must be remembered, which is the outgrowth of plans and enterprises of years ago. Many and varied elements have combined to bring the festival to its present standing. It may properly be said to have had its origin in the German festivals held in Cincinnati as early as 1849. While the Sängerfest degenerated greatly from its original purpose, it undoubtedly led the way to the noble efforts which characterize our May Festivals. In 1870, nearly twenty years later, in the same city, the second festival was held, in which nearly two thousand singers participated, and from which went out an influence very powerful in establishing the May Festivals. When, two years later (1872), the project of holding a national festival of singers and instrumentalists of the United States, at Cincinnati, was suggested to Mr. Thomas, a man of marvelous faculty in executing things of magnitude, he thought it possible, and readily undertook the work of carrying out the suggestion. This resulted in the first May Festival, held in 1873. A guarantee fund sufficient to meet all expenditures, should it be necessary, having been raised, the plans for the first festival were acted upon, and resulted in such a grand triumph that they have become a world-noted institution. This was under the direction of Mr. Thomas, who still holds the position of chief director. The chorus consisted of several societies, mostly from Cincinnati, and numbered 1250. The impossibility of securing adequate preparation and dicipline in foreign societies and the impracticability of their attendance away from home at a festival of a week's duration, was seen at once and consequently abandoned at subsequent festivals. A single manual organ of fourteen stops was used as an accompaniment to the chorus. The orchestra numbered 108, and included Mr. Thomas' celebrated orchestra, aided by Cincinnati musicians and members of the New York Philharmonic Society. The festival was well attended and so well received that a request, signed by prominent citizens, for another festival was presented at the last concert. It was then determined to give the festival of 1875. To better conduct the business management, the Cincinnati Biennial Musical Festival Association was incorporated in 1874, under whose care the succeeding festivals have been given. Immediately the study of the music began, and in the fall of 1874 the chorus proper was organized under Mr. Singer, who, fortunately, then came to make his home in Cincinnati. Weekly part rehearsals and monthly mass rehearsals were held, though afterward changed to weekly mass rehearsals for men and women. The chorus was splendidly prepared and numbered nearly 600. The orchestra, composed of the same elements as that of the first festival, numbered 101. The soloists were Mrs. H. H. Smith and Miss Whinnery, sopranos; Miss Annie Louise Cary and Miss Emma Cranch, contraltos; Messrs. Winch and Alex. Bischoff, tenors; and Messrs. F. Remmertz and M. W. Whitney, basses. The choral works performed were "Elijah," the 9th Symphony, Brahm's "Triumphal Hymn" (op. 55), scenes from Wagner's "Lohengrin," Bach's "Magnificat" in D, and Liszt's cantata of "Prometheus." The great success of this festival led to the movement, so generously headed by Mr. Springer, which gave to Cincinnati the finest music hall and organ in America. A space of three years elapsed between the second and the third festival, which took place in 1878, this being necessary on account of the non-completion of the hall.

The chorus and orchestra were composed of the same elements as the preceding ones, and respectively numbered 650 and 101. The soloists were Mme. Pappenheim and Mrs. Osgood, sopranos; the contraltos the same as in 1875, with the addition of Miss Rollwagen; Messrs. Charles Adams and Fritsch, tenors; Messrs. Whitney and Remmertz, basses; Sig. G. Tagliapietra, baritone; and G. E. Whiting, organist. The program included the "Eroica" Symphony, and the following choral works: "Messiah," 9th Symphony, scenes from Gluck's "Alceste," a "Festival Ode" by Otto Singer, Liszt's "Missa Solennis," and Berlioz's dramatic symphony "Romeo and Juliet." In all respects this was a grand success, and from the beginning the business management has been in keeping with the high artistic direction. The first festival came within a trifling sum of clearing its expenses, the second left a surplus, and the third, after contributing to the debt which remained upon the organ, left the sum of $10,000 as a capital for future festivals. The success was partly due to the enthusiasm created here by the movement to build the Music Hall and the curiosity abroad to see the new structure and hear the new organ. Starting with a plan which looked to the coöperation of all large cities of the West, they have gradually withdrawn from all resources but their own, and the fourth festival was given in 1880, with a chorus of Cincinnati singers, as large as that of 1878, who displayed their proficiency in the mastery of the great Beethoven mass. The chorus was superior in quality and tone to that of any other. No pains were spared in the preparation for this festival. The program was undoubtedly in advance of any preceding one, the soloists the best the country could afford, and the orchestra in numbers the largest and in material incomparably the finest ever heard in this country, and not to be surpassed by any in the world. With all this, the festival of 1880 could be nothing less than a grand success. This brings us down to the fifth and last festival, held in 1882. Since the last festival, the chorus had been organized into a permanent body with Mr. Arthur Mees as director. Never before did it receive such long or more faithful and competent training. During two years, rehearsals, together with reviews under Mr. Thomas' personal direction, were held without intermission. It numbered a little over 600. The orchestra numbered 165 artists, though essentially the same as that for the festival of 1880. It was at this festival that Miss Cary, identified with them from the beginning, took leave of the public for private life. Taken altogether, it is believed that no musical festival was ever held with better equipment or more artistic excellence and popular success than that of 1882. It may truly be said that the May Festivals have been the most potent medium of art encouragement which this city and country have ever known. A high aim and a lofty purpose were constantly kept in view, and with each recurring event this aim and purpose became clearer and the method adopted for their attainment more direct. As a rule, the works which require large numbers of performers have been given at night, while in the afternoon consideration has been had for the natural desire for variety and pieces which could not, without discord, be consorted with the works performed at night. This has always been done, however, without lowering the artistic standard fixed as the key-note of the festivals. (See also the heading MAY FESTIVALS).          * * *

CINCINNATI CONSERVATORY OF MUSIC. This institution was established in 1867, by the present directress, Miss Clara Bauer. It is modeled after the famous Conservatorium at Stuttgart. There is attached to it a boarding department for the benefit of the young ladies attending. All the branches of music are taught, and also elocution and modern languages. Instruction is imparted by a corps of twenty teachers, among whom are Michael Brand, E. Eugene Davis, and others well known.

CINCINNATI MUSIC SCHOOL. This institution was inaugurated in September, 1880, by George Schneider, B., W. Foley and Arthur Mees, who were connected with the College of Music previous to that time. It has remained under the management of those gentlemen, all eminent musicians and teachers. Miss Emma Cranch, well known as a vocalist, has had charge of the vocal department from the first. The usual branches of music are taught. A special feature of the School is that every pupil receives private instruction. Particular opportunities are offered those wishing to become teachers or pursuing select studies.

**Clarke,** HUGH A., was born in Canada, in the year 1839. His knowledge of music, aside from that gained by his own unaided study, was imparted by his father, J. P. Clarke, Mus. Doc., Oxon. Col., and professor of music in Upper Canada University. In 1859 he went to Philadelphia, where he gradually acquired a reputation both as teacher and composer. In 1875 he was elected professor of music in the University of Pennsylvania, located at Philadelphia, a position which he still (March, 1884) holds. He has taught a number of eminent pupils, among whom is Wm. W. Gilchrist. His works consist of some songs and piano pieces, a method for the piano and one for the organ, and " Harmony on the Inductive Method," published by Lee & Walker.

**Clarke,** WILLIAM HORATIO, organist, was born at Newton, Mass., a suburb of Boston, in 1840, and came of a musical family. At the age of seven years he began to play upon different musical instruments, but the organ was his favorite, which he assiduously studied under competent teachers. In 1856 he was elected organist of the Congregational Church of South Dedham (now Norwood), in 1857 of Rev. Dr. Alvin Lamson's Church in Dedham, and in 1859 of the Berkely Street Church in Boston. This latter position he resigned in 1866 to accept a similar one in Woburn, Mass. (where he had previously married). In 1872, after returning from Europe, he was engaged as superintendent of musical instruction in the public schools of Dayton, Ohio. From there he removed in 1874 to Indianapolis, Ind., and in 1878 to Boston. In June, 1880, he accepted the position of organist of the Jarvis Street Baptist Church, Toronto, Canada. Four years later he accepted a call from the Plymouth Church of Indianapolis, Ind., and he is still (January, 1886) located in that city. His first instruction book for the organ was issued in 1865. It was followed by " Clarke's New Method for Reed Organs," of which nearly 100,000 copies have been sold. He has put forth other works, chief among which is the " Harmonic School for the Organ." He has also composed much church and organ music. As an organist he ranks among the foremost in this country.

**Cleveland Conservatory of Music,** CLEVELAND, OHIO. This institution was established in the summer of 1871, by J. Underner, Wm. Heydler and John Hart, who constituted the board of directors. These gentlemen having had several years' experience in Europe, the Conservatory was largely modeled on the European conservatory plan, the class system being the same as that used in the conservatories of Leipsic, Paris, etc. It has been successful in elevating the standard of musical taste, especially in the city of Cleveland, where it has accomplished and is still accomplishing an excellent work. Its pupils are drawn not only from towns near by, but from all parts of the country. The Conservatory remained under the management of the original board of directors until the death in August, 1881, of Mr. Heydler, after which it was for some time conducted by the remaining directors. The present (January, 1886) directors are F. Bassett and Chas. Heydler.

**Cleveland Vocal Society, The,** CLEVELAND, OHIO, was organized in 1873, with a chorus of 40 voices, which has gradually been enlarged to 90 voices. The orchestra consists of about 40 pieces. The Society was not incorporated until Sep. 11, 1882. Its object, as avowed in the articles of incorporation, is the "study, cultivation, and rendition of music, and to receive, hold, and apply for such uses and purposes any funds or property lawfully acquired by the corporation." The Cleveland May Festivals of 1880 and 1882 were held under the auspices of the Society, and with the net proceeds ($4000) a permanent fund was created. It is intended to hold another May Festival in 1884, and the forces are already at work rehearsing. The chorus will be about 300 strong. Three concerts are annually given by the Society to its honorary members, the first one of which occurred Dec. 14, 1882. The number of members is about 115. Alfred Arthur, who was also one of the founders, has been the conductor from the first, and to his energy and ability much of the success of the Society is due. The officers are as follows : T. P. Handy, president; Oscar J. Campbell, vice-president; Charles A. Cook, secretary ; and L. P. Hulburd, librarian; with a board of 17 trustees and various committees. Miss M. S. Wright acts as accompanist.

**Clough & Warren,** DETROIT, MICHIGAN. One of the leading American reed-organ manufacturing firms. It was founded in 1850 by Simmons & Clough, who for twenty years conducted the business in a quiet way. In 1870 the present firm was organized, Jesse H. Farwell being admitted as special partner. Mr. Clough brought with him the experience of more than a score of years, while Mr. Warren's executive ability well qualified him for the position of general manager of the works. Since 1870, the firm has rapidly come to the front and taken its present high position, which has been well earned by years of patient labor and inventive genius. The reputation of Clough & Warren is not only national but almost world-wide, their instruments being known and appreciated in every civilized country. The leading quality of their organs is the pure, full and correct intonation. An ingenious invention used in the larger makes is the "patent qualifying tubes," which consist of tubes of wood of certain fixed proportions, placed so as to operate in connection with the diapason and melodia reeds, each tube having an opening on the upper side at the lower end, through which the air (subsequently passing through the reeds) enters, and through which the sound escapes. The effect is to give a fulness and volume to the tone almost equal to that produced by pipe organs.

The firm has large and extensive buildings with expensive machinery and everything conveniently arranged. Employment is given to 150 men, whose monthly wages in the aggregate amount to about $6000.

**Coleman,** OBED M., was born Jan. 23, 1817, at Barnstable, Mass. It was not until he was sixteen years old, after a severe illness, that his inventive talents showed themselves. While living at New Bedford, Mass., he invented an automaton consisting of a lady minstrel playing on an accordeon and a singing bird. This he disposed of for $800 and then removed to Saratoga, N. Y. After this he made several improvements of the accordeon and invented his æolian attachment for the piano, which sold in this country for $110,000, it is said. He died April 5, 1845, in the prime of life.

**Collection of the Best Psalm Tunes.** A book of church music compiled and published by Josiah Flagg of Boston in

1764. It was of small, oblong form, containing about eighty pages, and engraved in round notes, and was the first book printed on paper manufactured in the Colonies. The title page ran as follows: "A collection of the best Psalm Tunes, in two, three and four parts; from the most approved authors, fitted to all measures, and approved by the best masters in Boston, New England; the greater part of them never before printed in America. Engraved by Paul Revere; printed and sold by him and Jos. Flagg." In the preface, the author says: "The Editor has endeavored, according to the best of his judgment, to extract the sweets out of a variety of fragrant flowers, has taken from every author he has seen, a few Tunes," etc. The work contains one hundred and sixteen tunes and two anthems. Hood, in his "History of Music in New England," supposes that some of them were by American composers, which may quite possibly have been the case.

**College of Music,** NEW YORK, was incorporated under the laws of the State of New York, in 1878, and is mainly due to the energy and devotion of its present director, Mr. Louis Alexander. The building is specially adapted for the purposes of the College, and there are conveniences for instructing 700 pupils. Four terms of ten weeks each (or 30 lessons) constitute the school year. Beginners are admitted upon the same terms as those more advanced. Instruction is imparted by a corps of about twenty professors, among whom are Theodore Thomas (vocal sight-reading), Rafael Joseffy (piano), Edward Mollenhauer and George Matzka (violin), Carl C. Müller (theory and harmony), and George F. Bristow (organ). A series of concerts, in which the more advanced pupils take part, are given each season, the object being the endowment of a Scholarship Fund for the support of promising but indigent students. A "bureau of artists' engagements" has also been established, of which professional students have the benefit without extra charge. Musical degrees are conferred at the discretion of the director and faculty. The officers are at present (May, 1883) as follows: President, Hon. A. S. Sullivan; director, Louis Alexander; secretary, George W. Clark; treasurer, Otto Rother.

**College of Music,** CINCINNATI, OHIO. This College, which was incorporated under the laws of the State of Ohio, in 1878, was organized, as stated in the act of incorporation, "To cultivate a taste for music, and for that purpose, to organize a school of instruction and practice in all branches of musical education; the establishment of an orchestra; the giving of concerts; the production and publication of musical works, and such other musical enterprises as shall be conducive to the ends above mentioned."

The College is the outgrowth of the May Festivals held in Cincinnati, in 1873 and 1875, and was suggested by Reuben R. Springer, a wealthy and influential citizen of that city. In 1875, Mr. Springer generously offered to give $125,000 toward the erection of a suitable building for a college of music, if the people would contribute another $125,000. After many difficulties and delays the needed amount was raised, and the erection of the building commenced. Meanwhile, the musical festival association decided to hold their third May Festival in 1877, and Mr. Springer, in his anxiety to see the building completed in time for that event, offered to give an additional $20,000, provided the citizens would raise $15,000 within 30 days, which was done. The building, however, could not be completed, and the festival association wisely decided to postpone the festival until the following year (1878), when it was held in the music hall of the building, and was in many respects the grandest one that has taken place.

The main hall of the building is 112 feet wide by 192 feet long, and will accommodate several thousand persons. The stage is 56 by 112 feet, and furnishes room for a chorus of nearly 600 voices. In front of the hall is a vestibule 46 by 112 feet, while on each side is a corridor, so that ingress or egress can easily be effected. Over the vestibule is a small hall 46 by 112 feet and 30 feet high. There is on each side of the Music Hall building, and forming wings thereto, a smaller building. These, also largely erected through the aid of Mr. Springer, are used for industrial exposition purposes. The whole mass of buildings has a frontage of 372 feet on Elm street and extends back to Plum street 293 feet, and is of a modernized gothic style of architecture.

The first session of the College began Oct. 14, 1878. Besides the usual three terms, there is a fourth term, held during the summer months, for the especial benefit of teachers and others who can not attend the other terms. Instruction is given in every branch of music and the languages, and upon every musical instrument. There is an academic department for advanced pupils. Graduates of this department receive diplomas. Certificates are conferred on such pupils as are enough advanced to become teachers in some branch. There is a perpetual fund, donated by Mr. Springer, the annual income of which is distributed in ten gold medals, among such pupils as have been in the College one year and have superior musical ability.

The College is under the control of a board of Trustees, consisting, at this date (1885), of P. R. Neff, president; W. McAlpin, vice-president; W. J. Mitchell, secretary; A. C. Edwards, treasurer; A. T. Goshorn, T. D. Lincoln, J. Balke, L. Markbreit, L. Anderson, I. B. Resor, R. H. Galbreath, P. H. Hartmann, H. S. Fechheimer, W. Worthington. The faculty consists of some thirty professors, many of whom are eminent specialists and have a national reputation.

**College of Musicians, American.** The preliminary steps regarding the establishment of the College of Musicians were taken at the meeting of the Music Teachers' National Association held at Providence, R. I., July 4, 5 and 6, 1883, by the adoption of the following resolutions, which succinctly and forcibly state the principles on which this organization was founded :

*Whereas*, On the one hand the pernicious and debasing influence of the incompetent, ill-prepared teacher of music has become a burden to the long suffering public, and a stumbling block to the best efforts of the profession ; and

*Whereas*, It seems eminently proper and equitable that some means should be devised of substantiating the prior claims of the competent, well prepared teacher to public and professional recognition, it is hereby

*Resolved*, That in order first to protect the public from incompetent teachers, and secondly to protect the teachers who have made an adequate preparation, it is the sense of the Music Teachers' National Association in convention assembled, that it is desirable to provide a system of examination for those desiring to practice the profession of teaching ; an examination which shall fairly and impartially draw the line between the incompetent and competent.

In accordance with the succeeding and final resolution of the above series, a committee composed of about one hundred and thirty representative musicians was formed to inquire into the feasibility of founding an association for the purpose above expressed, and, at a meeting held at Cleveland, July 1, by virtue of the power vested in them by the M. T. N. A., the members of this committee resolved themselves into the charter members of an association to be called "The American College of Musicians."

The officiary is as follows :

President, E. M. Bowman ; First Vice-President, H. Clarence Eddy ; Second Vice-President, S. B. Whitney ; Secretary and Treasurer, A. A. Stanley.

BOARD OF DIRECTORS : W. W. Gilchrist, Dr. Louis Maas, W. H. Sherwood, S. E. Jacobsohn, Chas. R. Adams, F. Grant Gleason and J. H. Wheeler.

BOARD OF EXAMINERS : *Pianoforte :—* Wm. H. Sherwood, Dr. Louis Maas, Dr. William Mason. *Rudimentary*, (Music Teachers for Public Schools) :—Arthur Mees, Julius Eichberg, John W. Tufts. *Organ :—*H. Clarence Eddy, S. B. Whitney, S. P. Warren. *Voice:* — Mme. Luisa Cappiani, Chas. R. Adams, J. H. Wheeler. *Orchestral Stringed Instruments:—*Henry Schradieck, S. E. Jacobsohn, Dr. L. Damrosch. *Musical Theory:—* E. M. Bowman, W. W. Gilchrist, F. Grant Gleason.

It was decided to institute three grades of examination, and to confer suitable degrees or certificates upon such as pass these examinations.

The first grade of examination will call for a comprehensive working knowledge of the resources of musical art (choral and orchestral), proficiency in musical history and acoustics, together with special powers as a composer, artist or teacher. Candidates passing this examination will receive a diploma and degree, Master of Musical Art.

The second grade of examination will call for special powers in the branch followed and a working knowledge of harmony and counterpoint. Analysis of musical forms, musical history, principles of acoustics, and the special history of the branch engaged in will also constitute a part of this examination. Candidates passing the second grade of examinations will be awarded a diploma and the degree, Fellow of the College of Musicians.

The third grade of examination will call for the special and general preparation needful for those conducting the earlier studies of the musical student. This will involve correct technical knowledge of the branch followed, the principles of teaching, rudiments of harmony and musical forms, and the outlines of musical history. Candidates passing this examination will be awarded a certificate of competency, and membership in the College of Musicians.

At the first annual meeting, held at New York, June 30, 1885, it was resolved that the College of Musicians should become incorporated. Action has since been taken to that effect, and the organization has secured a charter under the laws of the State of New York. Owing to the death of the lamented Dr. Leopold Damrosch, Mr. Joseph Mosenthal of New York was elected violin examiner, and Mr. W. F. Heath was appointed to fill the vacancy caused by the resignation of Mr. John W. Tufts. With these two exceptions the Board of Examiners remains as given above, and the Officiary also remains unchanged, with the exception of the secretary-treasurer. Mr. A. A. Stanley having resigned, Mr. Robert Bonner, of Providence, was elected to serve his unexpired term of office. The application for information regarding this society conclusively shows the great interest taken in this step by the public, and we feel confident that it will become an honor to the profession.        *   *   *

**Complete Melody.** A collection of church tunes compiled by Thomas Bailey of Newburyport, Mass., mainly from William Tansur's English collection, and published in 1755. It was in three parts, and seems to have met with a very encouraging sale.

**Conn,** C. G., ELKHART, INDIANA, is one of the most noted inventors and manufacturers of band instruments. His establishment is one of the very largest and most complete in the world, and his business has rapidly developed from a small beginning. In 1876, Mr. Conn invented the "elastic-face" mouthpiece, which met with a great demand. With a sagacity characteristic of Americans, he foresaw the opportunity which the manufacture of band instruments offered, and accordingly began a series of experiments in a small shop, employing only three men. The remarkable success with which he met soon compelled him to build a large factory. This was destroyed by fire, January 31, 1883, with all its contents. The loss of the tools, patterns and machinery, which it had taken him years to perfect and complete, was a severe blow to Mr. Conn. With undaunted energy, however, he immediately rebuilt and was soon running again as before. All parts of the instruments are made and finished at the factory. Upwards of 130 skilled workmen are employed. Mr. Conn's instruments are noted for a rich, powerful and sympathetic tone, freedom of action, correct intonation, both the open and valve tones being the same in quality and quantity, and ease with which they are blown. An important feature of his system is the tuning of instruments in sets, thus insuring, as far as possible, an *ensemble* which is perfect. In connection with the band instrument business, he publishes and keeps for sale all the latest and best band music. His activity and energy are ceaseless and constantly directed toward the improvement of his instruments. He is also manager of the local daily paper, and takes a prominent part in the affairs of the town.

**Conventions, Musical.** Musical conventions are purely American in origin. According to John W. Moore's "Encyclopædia of Music," in 1829 the idea of a musical convention was first suggested to the members of the New Hampshire Central Musical Society, at its session at Goffstown, and one was appointed to be held at Concord in the following September. It continued for two days. In 1830, another one was held at Pembroke, and in 1831, a third one at Goffstown. They all were under the direction of Mr. Henry E. Moore. In 1836, a convention was held in Boston, under the auspices of the Boston Academy of Music, and was conducted by Lowell Mason and George J. Webb. For nearly fifteen years an annual one was held at Boston. In 1842 or 1843, after the Boston session, the teachers went to Rochester. This was the first one held outside of Boston, except those already mentioned. Conventions grew in public favor and soon began to be held in other places. Those who first became popular in the work were Dr. George F. Root, Wm. B. Bradbury, Isaac B. Woodbury, Thomas Hastings, and Benj. F. Baker. Of these, all but the first and last named are dead. Among the leading convention conductors of the present time are Dr. Root, Dr. H. R. Palmer, L. O. Emerson, W. O. and H. S. Perkins, and several others. The aim of conventions is both social enjoyment and musical advancement, the latter always being paramount. The program generally consists of exercises in notation and reading at sight, the practice of glees, choruses, anthems, etc., interspersed with remarks, explanations and short lectures by the conductor. Individual performances by the members are always in order. A convention ordinarily lasts four days, commencing on Tuesday and ending on Friday. Three sessions are held each day; morning, afternoon and evening, making twelve in all, each one about two hours in duration. All those attending a convention from a distance are either entertained free at private houses or given the benefit of board at greatly reduced rates. The remuneration of a first-class conductor is generally $125 and expenses.

Musical conventions are well calculated to awaken a love and enthusiasm for music, and undoubtedly have been instrumental in promoting the progress of the art in this country. See INSTITUTES OF MUSIC, NORMAL.

**Converse,** CHARLES CROZAT, was born Oct. 7, 1834, at Warren, Mass. While he was yet young his parents removed to New York State, and he received a good education at the Elmira Academy. He had a great love for music, and desire for a better musical education led him to go to Germany, in 1855, where he was a pupil at the Leipsic Conservatorium, studying under Hauptmann and Richter, and Haupt at Berlin. While in Germany he wrote several compositions which were highly commended by the best musicians. In 1857 he returned home and was shortly after married. Notwithstanding his musical talents he decided to pursue law as a profession, and with that end in view entered the law department of the University of Albany, from which he graduaded as LL.B., in 1861. For some time thereafter he pursued his calling in the West, then removed to Brooklyn, and finally to Erie, Pa., about 1875, where he is still

located and where he is a partner in the Burdette Organ Co. He has written some large orchestral works, but is best known perhaps by his hymn tunes, "What a Friend we have in Jesus" having been sung all over the world. Many of his pieces appear under the name of "Karl Redan."

**Coronation.** One of the most popular church tunes ever composed. It was written by Oliver Holden (born 1765; died 1834), a resident of Charlestown, and was probably first published in his AMERICAN HARMONY, which appeared in 1792. It is generally sung to the hymn beginning "All hail the power of Jesus' name."

**Courtney,** WILLIAM, was born Dec. 7, 1844, at Monmouthshire, England. He early manifested a great love for music, and possessed a high soprano voice of great purity and fulness, which made his services often called for as a chorister boy. His voice changing into a beautiful tenor, he in 1869 went to London, where he placed himself under the care of Mr. Frank, husband of Louisa Pyne. He made such rapid progress that in the ensuing winter he was engaged by Madam Pyne as first tenor during her tour in Scotland and the English provinces. Returning to London, he sang for some time in concerts and oratorios and afterwards in the opera, having been engaged for two seasons at the English Opera, Crystal Palace. He was the original *Dependant* in Sullivan's "Trial by Jury," and created the tenor *rôle* in Cellier's "Nell Gwyne," Gallwick's "Donna Constanza," and several other operas.

In 1878, Mr. Courtney met and married, in London, Madam Louise-Gage, an American vocalist, and soon after proceeded with her to Italy, where he studied a year under Vannucini at Florence. He then came to this country and soon became well known. He has filled various festival engagements in Boston, Pittsburg, and New York, under Dr. Damrosch, and sung in "Messiah," "Judas Maccabæus," "Solomon," "Last Judgment," "Mount of Olives," and other oratorios, at the Handel and Haydn Society's concerts in Boston. He has also sang in oratorio and other engagements in the principal cities of the country. His success as a teacher leads him to devote much of his time to that branch of the profession.

**Cranch,** EMMA.  This singer is a native of Cincinnati, Ohio, and took her first vocal lessons from Mrs. Emma R. Dexter, to whom belongs the credit of having laid the foundation of that finished method which she subsequently acquired.  After leaving Mrs. Dexter, she studied alone one year, and then went to Milan, where, for eight months, she took lessons from San Giovanni.  Thence she went to Paris, where she studied with Signor Brignoli, the tenor; thence to London, where for a short time she was a pupil of Mrs. McFarren, wife of the English composer, George W. McFarren.  Returning home, she was engaged by Mr. Thomas to travel as soloist with his orchestra, and for the purpose of studying her concert selections thoroughly, she went to New York and placed herself under the tuition of Signor Errani.  She made the concert tours with the orchestra for eight months, part of which time she sang seven times a week.  In May, 1875, she sang at the second of the Cincinnati May Festivals.  She has been since that time one of the soloists at all our larger concerts and festivals, including the festival of 1878, and the Sængerfest of the North American Sængerbund, in 1879.  She went east in 1876 and for a year was the alto soloist in the choir of Plymouth Church, Brooklyn.  When the College of Music was established, she was engaged as one of the teachers of singing, her methods of instruction proving very successful.  She severed her connection with the College about a year ago, and since that time has been giving vocal instruction at the Cincinnati Musical School.  She sang at the Messiah performance of 1880, and at present belongs to the quartet of the Unitarian church of Cincinnati.      *   *   *

**Crouch,** FREDERICK NICHOLLS, an English composer, was born July 31, 1808, at London.  When nine years old he was able to play the bass in the orchestra of the Royal Coburg Theatre, and finally became attached to Her Majesty's Theatre as violoncellist.  Under the patronage of George IV, he entered the Royal Academy of Music upon its establishment in 1822, and after his graduation secured the post of principal violoncellist at Drury Lane.  For many years he was contributor of musical articles and reviews to various publications, and composed besides songs, among which is the celebrated KATHLEEN MAVOURNEEN, two operas, "The Fifth of November" and "Sir Roger de Coverly."  In 1849 he came to the United States with Max Maretzek, and after the disbandment of the company went to Maine, residing for a number of years at Portland.  From there he removed to Philadelphia, and thence to Washington, where he was for some time organist of St. Matthew's church.  At the outbreak of the war he was residing at Richmond, and was one of the first to enlist, serving in the Richmond Grays and the Richmond Howitzers.  Soon after its close he settled in Baltimore, where he is still (June, 1884) residing at an advanced age.  He has been out of employment for some time, and is now in destitute circumstances, greatly needing help.  He has written an autobiography, which, could it be published, would undoubtedly be an interesting addition to our musical literature.

**Cutler,** DR. HENRY STEPHEN, was born Oct. 7, 1825, at Boston, where he was organist for some time.  He then became organist of Trinity Church, New York, and subsequently of St. Ann's, Brooklyn, a position which he still holds.  He has written numerous compositions for the church, among which are a number of anthems, issued in book form under the title of "Trinity Anthems" (1866).  The "Trinity Psalter" (1863) was issued under his editorship.

# D.

**Damrosch,** DR. LEOPOLD, well-known as one of America's most able conductors, was born at Posen, Prussia, October 22, 1832, and was therefore in his fifty-third year. From his father, a merchant and a man of considerable culture, he undoubtedly inherited many of his fine tastes, that for music predominating over everything else. The displays of what was destined to be the ruling passion of his life began at the earliest age, and were probably not displeasing to his parents, but the thought of his becoming a professional musician was a repugnant one. At the age of nine years he regularly commenced the study of the violin unknown to them, practicing at the houses of friends. In deference to their wishes, after completing the usual course at the gymnasium, he entered the University at Berlin for the study of medicine, graduating with high honors as *medicina doctor*, after three years of close application. During all this time every leisure moment was devoted to music. Concert-meister Ries was his instructor in violin playing, and Dehn and Böhmer taught him theory and composition. Under them he acquired the foundation of that broad, deep culture which has ever characterized him.

Having complied with the desires of his parents, he felt at liberty to pursue his own inclinations, and appeared as solo violinist in various German cities. Such was his success that his reputation soon became a national one. Liszt was then in the height of his powers and had made Weimar a sort of Mecca to musical pilgrims. Thither in 1855 he directed his steps. The master was much pleased with his playing, and gave him the position of solo violinist in the Grand Duke's orchestra, a post which he very acceptably filled for some eighteen months. This period brought him into contact with many of the first musicians of the day, and was fruitful in inspirations and lasting impressions. The friendships thus formed have only been broken by death. That of Liszt was of the warmest character, and in token thereof the great pianist dedicated to him the second of his symphonic poems,

"Tasso." A similar compliment is said to have been conferred on only two other persons —Wagner and Berlioz. Wagner's friendship was not less sincere. The last token of esteem which he received from that master-composer was the famous *finale* to the first act of "Parsifal," in manuscript, which arrived only a short time before the latter's death. Still dearer memories must have bound him to Weimar, for it was there that he met and married his wife, a lady of considerable culture and musical attainments.

After leaving Weimar, Dr. Damrosch went to Breslau. It was there that he made his *début* as a conductor at the Philharmonic concerts. He continued in that capacity about a year, and then resigned it only to make a concert tour with von Bülow and Tausig. In 1861 he returned and organized a symphony society with an orchestra of eighty players. Twelve concerts were given each season, and the fame of them spread over all Europe. Nearly all the celebrated artists of the day appeared at them, among whom were Rubenstein, von Bülow, Tausig, Joachim, and Madame Viardot-Garcia. Both Liszt and Wagner personally assumed the *bâton* on various occasions. His labors, however, were not confined to the society of which he was conductor, but extended into various other fields.

Actuated in part, perhaps, by a desire to visit the United States, Dr. Damrosch in 1871 accepted a call from the Arion Society (a male chorus), of New York, to become its conductor. His first public appearance in this country was at Steinway Hall, May 6th of that year, in the triple character of conductor, composer, and violinist. He met with an enthusiastic reception, which must have been more than ordinarily gratifying to the stranger in a strange land. In 1873 he organized the Oratorio Society of New York with only twelve members. It was not until the third concert that the Society became anything like an assured fact. He organized in 1878 a second society, the Symphony Society of New York, the orchestra of which has become so noted.

These societies, with the Philharmonic, are the representative ones of the metropolis. The success of both, which have from the first been under his direction, is due in a large measure to his energy, ability, and wisdom. It was as their conductor that he was instrumental in first bringing before the public here many important works, of which may be mentioned Berlioz's "La Damnation de Faust" (entire) and "Grande Messe des Morts" (requiem); Wagner's "Siegfried" and "Götterdämmerung;" Rubenstein's "Tower of Babel;" Bruch's Symphony, No. 2; and Saint-Saën's Symphony, No. 2, in A Minor.

In 1880, Dr. Damrosch was honored with the degree of Doctor of Music by Columbia College, New York. In 1882 he had charge of the music at the New York May Festival. Its successful organization and termination was mostly due to his untiring efforts, and displayed to an unusual degree his faculty for organizing and controling musical forces.   In the fall of 1882 he made a tour of the principal Western cities with his orchestra, consisting of fifty-five trained instrumentalists. Mlle. Isadora-Martinez was vocal soloist.   Notwithstanding the difficulties which beset such an undertaking it was successfully accomplished. The programs were varied, but of high order. From this time up to his death he conducted various festivals in different parts of the country, besides attending to the regular work of his two societies. Last August he was tendered, and accepted, the position of conductor and *impresario* at the Metropolitan Opera House. and the same month he departed for Europe to engage a company. His labors were indeed multifarious and constantly increasing. His one great ambition to see German opera a success in New York was realized.

On Monday evening, February 9th, 1885, Dr. Damrosch conducted a performance of "Lohengrin" at the Metropolitan Opera House. He then appeared to be in his usual health and no one dreamed of the end being so near. The next evening he undertook to direct a rehearsal of the Oratorio Society in the Young Men's Christian Association building.   In the middle of the performance he was taken with a chill, and was compelled to lay down the *bâton*.   He was conveyed to his residence, No. 160 East Forty-sixth Street, and medical aid summoned. Next morning the physicians decided that it was a case of pneumonia, but even then no serious alarm was felt.   At eight o'clock Sunday morning, the 15th, a sudden change for the worse occurred, and it soon became evident that he was dying.   About two o'clock he sank into a sleep, and in fifteen minutes passed peacefully away without awaking.   He leaves a family of five children, all of whom, excepting the oldest son, who is organist of Plymouth Church, Brooklyn, were present at the time of his death. The youngest member of the family is a daughter of sixteen.   The funeral service was held at the Metropolitan Opera House on the Wednesday afternoon following his death.   An immense concourse of people made the occasion a very solemn one. Friends and strangers alike sadly paid their last respects.   Siegfried's funeral march from "Götterdämmerung" and several selections from oratorios were rendered.

The secret of Dr. Damrosch's success as a conductor lay not only in the precision and surety with which he wielded the *bâton*, but also in the fine artistic conception and feeling with which he interpreted the work under consideration, and the faculty he had of imparting this feeling to his forces.   Some conductors are coldly perfect, but in his conducting the artist-musician could at once be recognized.   Though his reputation is mainly that of a conductor, he was far from being unknown both as a violinist and a composer. His attachment for and study of the violin have previously been touched upon, and it will suffice to add here that though hardly to be considered a *virtuoso* in the sense of being a phenomenal performer, he exquisitely played that instrument.   So much of his time was taken up by other duties that his compositions are not numerous.   They consist of a biblical idyl or cantata, "Ruth and Naomi;" a festival overture and other orchestral pieces; various pieces for the violin, among which is a concerto; a collection of church music, "St. Cecelia;" a number of male choruses, and some songs.

Dr. Damrosch's fine qualities as a musician were well supplemented by those of a gentleman.   His kindly nature at once put you at ease in his society.   He was well read in literature, art, and science, and an excellent conversationalist.   Among America's musicians none stood higher and few have done more for the advancement of the art. To all human knowledge he seemed destined for long years of usefulness yet. Death has removed a star of the first magnitude from the musical firmament, whose place will not be easily filled. The name of Dr. Leopold Damrosch will live long in memory and occupy an imperishable place in history.

**Daniel,** JOHN, one of the oldest music teachers in America at the time of his death, was born in 1803, at Aberdeen, Scotland. His music lessons were commenced in the house in which Lord Byron was born, and with this poet as well as with Burns he became well acquainted. In 1840 he came to the United States and settled at New York, where he was highly esteemed as a teacher of vocal and instrumental music, numbering among his pupils many of the wealthier classes. His compositions are numerous and in almost every form. He died in New York, June 21, 1881.

**Daniel.** 1.—A sacred cantata written by Dr. Geo. F. Root, assisted by C. M. Cady and W. B. Bradbury. First produced in New York City, in 1853.

2. An oratorio by George F. Bristow, first produced at Steinway Hall, New York, Dec. 30, 1867, by the Mendelssohn Union, with Mme. Parepa-Rosa as chief vocalist. It is one of Mr. Bristow's greatest works.

**Danks,** HART P. This well-known and very successful song composer was born April 6, 1834, at New Haven, Conn. When he was eight years old his parents removed to Saratoga, N. Y. At an early age he showed the true bent of his nature, and was placed under the care of Dr. L. E. Whiting of Saratoga, who was an excellent amateur musician as well as a physician. His progress was so rapid that he was soon admitted to the choir of the First Presbyterian church over which Dr. Whiting presided. Some time after he accepted a similar position in the choir of the M. E. Church, About 1850 his parents removed again, this time to Chicago, where he was engaged as bass at the Clark street M. E. Church, his voice having changed. Soon after removing to Chicago he began to try his hand at composing, but his father, who had no idea of his following music as a profession, looked upon all this as foolishness, and put the young man to work at his own trade, that of a builder.

It was about this time that William B. Bradbury, then in the hight of his career, held a convention in the city, which young Danks attended. Plucking up courage he presented to that excellent musician a copy of his first hymn-tune, with a request that it be examined. Mr. Bradbury was so much pleased with it that he inserted it in his next book, the "Jubilee," under the name of "Lake Street." This decided Mr. Dank's future course, and he devoted himself to study and composition. His first song, "The Old Lane," was published by Higgins Brothers of Chicago, in 1856. It was followed in the same year by his second song, "Anna Lee," published by Ditson & Co. of Boston. In 1858 he married Miss Hattie R. Colahan of Cleveland, Ohio, making that city his residence until 1861, when he returned to Chicago, where, however, he remained only three years. At the expiration of that time he removed to New York City, where he has since resided.

Mr. Danks does not aspire to be ranked as a classical musician, but his music is of fair order, flowingly written, and well appreciated by the masses. Among his most popular songs are "Let the Angels in," "Roses underneath the Snow," "Nobody's Darling but Mine," "You are always young to me," "Little Bright-eyes, will you miss me," "Angel of Beauty," "Fly Back, O Years," etc. The most popular of all, however, was "Silver Threads Among the Gold," published in 1872, which sold to the extent of over 300,000 copies in this country alone, to say nothing of England. "Don't be angry with me, Darling," though published two years earlier, achieved a success almost as great. For six or seven years Mr. Danks has, under contract, furnished an English music publishing firm in London with songs. Though so successful as a song composer he has composed much church music, and edited several collections of anthems, etc. Among his works is also the operetta, "Pauline." Mr. Danks is still in the prime of life and his pen ever busy.

**Decker Brothers,** NEW YORK CITY. This firm of American piano manufacturers was established in 1862, by two brothers, David and John Jacob Decker. Both were thoroughly conversant with the business, having worked for years in the best manufactories of this country previous to setting up on their own hook. Their first attempt at piano making was on a small scale, the money saved by steady industry and economy while working for others being their only capital. This was sufficient to manufacture a few square pianos, which were made in the best manner. The aim of Messrs. Decker Brothers at first was the production of a few pianos for retail trade in New York and vicinity, but these meeting with a very favorable reception, the present large business of the firm was rapidly developed.

The youngest of the brothers, John Jacob Decker, is an expert in judging of the quality of piano materials. Early in life he was employed by Messrs. Raven & Bacon as superintendent of their manufactory. He had held this position scarcely three months when he was admitted into the firm as a partner. Here he continued eight years, when he withdrew to establish, in partnership with his brother, their present business.

Messrs. Decker Brothers, constantly aiming for improvement, have invented and patented several improvements, whereby the tone and finish of their pianos is materially bettered. Probably the most important one is the improved construction of the full iron plate, whereby the necessity of placing the string bearings on the plate is obviated. Thus a better and purer tone is secured. The strings are also hitched to the pins close to the wrest-plank.

As a proof of the high esteem in which the Decker Brothers' pianos are held, it may be stated that in the short space of twenty years their business has increased from almost nothing to the present large proportions, so that now they have a manufactory equal in point of size and convenience to the manufactories of many much older firms. To their already well-established reputation they are constantly adding by their improved methods of piano making.

**Decker & Son.** A firm of piano manufacturers, located in New York City, and founded in 1856, by the present senior member of the firm, Myron A. Decker. In that year he commenced business in Albany, N. Y., and in 1858 received an award of merit for his pianos at the state fair held at Syracuse. Not liking Albany, he removed to New York City, in 1860. There he continued in business alone

until the year 1865, his pianos being known as the Decker piano. In the last mentioned year, he associated himself with a partner. The partnership did not last long, however, and in 1868 the business was closed up. Nothing daunted by one failure, Mr. Decker started anew in the business, and in 1871 associated himself in partnership with a gentleman by the name of Barnes. Their pianos became known as the Decker & Barnes. The partnership proved mutually agreeable, and lasted until the winter of 1877, when Mr. Barnes lost his wife, and his health being poor he withdrew from the firm, leaving Mr. Decker alone. Mr. Decker continued the business alone until July, 1878, when he associated his son with himself, and the firm became Decker & Son. Their pianos now became known by that name, which they still bear.

**Dengremont** MAURICE, born in 1865, in Rio Janerio, Brazil, exhibited a wonderful precocity for the violin when a mere infant. He has already made several concert tours both in this country and Europe, astonishing everyone by his phenomenal powers of performance. His gifts and acquirements would seem to indicate that he is to be one of the most eminent of future violinists.

**Dictionaries of Music, American.** The number of American encyclopædias or dictionaries is very small. The largest and most important one is "Complete Encyclopædia of Music," by John W. Moore, 1 vol. 8 vo. of over 1000 pages; Boston, O. Ditson & Co., 1854. Much valuable matter is contained in the work, but it is somewhat inaccurate as regards the biographies of foreign musicians. The number of topics treated is large. So rapid, however, has been the progress of musical affairs, especially in this country, since the book was first published (some 30 years) that it is now considerably out of date. Were it revised and corrected to the present time, it would be a very valuable work indeed, and we understand that Mr. Moore has (1884) undertaken that task. He has in the meantime edited a "Dictionary of Musical Information," Boston, O. Ditson & Co., 1876, which is a neat little work. An exceedingly handy little dictionary is "Ludden's Pronouncing Dictionary of Musical Terms," 12 mo., New York, J. L. Peters, 1875, which contains nearly all musical terms from the principal languages, with their pronunciation and a short definition. A still more recent and a commendable little book is "Mathews' Dictionary of Music and Musicians," by W. S. B. Mathews, published by the author at Chicago, Ill., in 1 vol. 8vo., 1880.

**Ditson,** OLIVER, well-known as the founder and senior member of the music-publishing firm bearing his name, was born in 1812, and when twelve years of age entered the store of Samuel H. Parker, bookseller and stationer, as clerk. In 1834 he became one of the proprietors, under the firm name of Parker & Ditson, and in 1844 sole proprietor, Mr. Parker withdrawing. The publication of sheet music and music books was commenced in 1834. From almost nothing, under the care of Mr. Ditson, the business has increased to its present colossal proportions, always keeping abreast of the times. The firm consists of Oliver Ditson, John C. Haynes, and Charles H. Ditson. The senior member, though well advanced in years, is still active and exercises a general supervision of affairs.

**Ditson, Oliver & Co.,** BOSTON, MASS. This, with its branches, is one of the largest music-publishing houses in the United States, as well as in the world. It is also, with perhaps one exception, the oldest American house now doing business. Samuel H. Parker, bookseller and stationer, who kept a store in Boston, commenced selling music about the year 1820. In 1824 there entered his store as clerk a young man by the name of Oliver Ditson. Ten years later, or in 1834, he was admitted into partnership with Mr. Parker, and the firm became Parker & Ditson. The publication of sheet music, music books, etc., was now commenced, and from this time dates the foundation of the present house of Oliver Ditson & Co.

The firm continued as Parker & Ditson until 1844, when Mr. Parker withdrew. It now became simply Oliver Ditson, who was left alone, and who conducted the growing business with marked ability and success. He continued alone until 1856, when he admitted into partnership John C. Haynes, who had been in his employment from boyhood, and the firm became Oliver Ditson & Co., the present name of the house.

This is a brief history of the parent house. But Messrs. O. Ditson & Co., to accommodate their large business in various parts of the country, have established several branch houses. In 1867, they established C. H. Ditson & Co. in business in New York City, by the purchase of the catalogue and stock of Firth, Son & Co. Mr. Firth was formerly the senior partner of the firm of Firth, Hall & Pond, and later, Firth, Pond & Co (See POND, WM. A. & Co.) In 1876, they established in business J. E. Ditson & Co., in Philadelphia, by the purchase of the publications and stock of Lee & Walker. Lyon & Healy, Chicago, were also established in business by them about the year 1865. Some years ago, C. H. Ditson & Co., New York, purchased the catalogue and publications of J. L. Peters, of that city. Thus it will be seen that Ditson & Co. have gradually absorbed several other smaller music-publishing firms.

Messrs. Ditson & Co. largely publish both foreign and American music of all kinds. Their catalogue embraces a list of over 80,000 different pieces of sheet music, and more than 2000 music books, among which are the lives of all the great masters, works on the art and science of music, dictionaries, encyclopædias, etc. They deserve credit for rendering available to American readers many foreign works on music. They are the agents in this country for the English publications of Novello, Ewer & Co.

**Doctor of Alcantara, The.** An opera in two acts, by Julius Eichberg. Libretto by Benjamin E. Woolf. First produced at the Boston Museum, April 7, 1862. Its success was something remarkable. It has been sung in every part of the country, but still retains its popularity.

**Dobson,** GEORGE C., was born at Williamsburg, N. Y., in April, 1842. From boyhood he evidenced a great liking for the banjo, on which he has become an unrivaled performer. He has appeared at concerts in the principal cities of the country and has done much to popularize an instrument which had not been looked upon with much favor. He resides at Boston, where he owns and personally conducts a banjo manufactory. His numerous instruction books for the banjo are the best of their kind and the result of many years' experience as a teacher.

**Dressel,** OTTO, was born in 1826, at Andernach-on-the-Rhine, and after acquiring a good fundamental knowledge of music placed himself under Hiller at Cologne and then under Mendelssohn at Leipzig. In the autumn of 1852 he came to Boston, where he has ever since resided. His life has been an uneventful one, and perhaps his name is not so well known outside of Boston as that of many other musicians, but he has exercised a powerful influence for good on the musical tastes of that city, and to him is largely due the leading place which it now occupies. He is a highly refined and cultivated musician, and fully acquainted with the works of Mendelssohn, Schumann, Bach, Chopin, Beethoven, and other masters. He was the intimate friend of Robert Franz, and introduced the songs of that composer in this country. His own compositions consist of songs, piano pieces, quartets, etc., all of which bear the impress of a finished musician.

**Dwight,** JOHN SULLIVAN, one of the most widely known and oldest musical writers in America, was born May 13, 1813, at Boston, Mass. At an early age his love of music manifested itself. Having completed an elementary education at the public schools, he entered Harvard University, studying dilligently and graduating therefrom in 1832. While at the University he was a member of a musical society formed of students and called Pierian Sodality, which afterwards developed into the HARVARD MUSICAL ASSOCIATION. During this time he practiced on the clarinet, but finding the exertion too great, relinquished it for the flute. He also made the acquaintance of several of the works of Beethoven and Mozart by gradually picking out their beauties himself. After having graduated from the University he entered the school of divinity and studied for the ministry. Upon completing the theological course he was ordained as pastor of the Unitarian church at Northampton, Mass. The ministry, however, did not seem to be his sphere, and he left it after a few years to devote himself entirely to literary pursuits. It was about this time that he began to make himself known as a writer on various musical subjects.

Mr. Dwight was one of the founders of the Brook's Farm community, where he remained during the six years that the community flourished, contributing meanwhile to the *Dial* and the *Christian Examiner*, and striving in various ways to advance the cause of music. In the organization of the Harvard Musical Association, which occurred Aug. 30, 1837, he took a prominent part, and much is due to his wise counsels and suggestions. The Association grew rapidly and its headquarters were soon removed to Boston. At its annual dinners have been originated, discussed, and set on foot many important musical schemes, among them the building of the Music Hall and the series of symphony concerts. The first number of DWIGHT'S JOURNAL OF MUSIC, which has rendered its founder's name so familiar, was issued April 10, 1852. Its aim was solely the advancement of the art, and it was for a long time the only paper of its kind; in fact, it has always occupied a rather unique position. No better person than Mr. Dwight could have been selected for its editor, the great mass of whose valuable musical writings is to be found in it. For twelve or fifteen years it was published as a weekly and then changed to a bi-weekly. In 1881 it ceased to exist.

Mr. Dwight was probably the earliest musical writer in this country who can really be called such. His articles were always well written and to the point, and though on account of their high standard they often ran counter to the public taste, they carried with them a weight which compelled attention. When he commenced writing the appreciation of music was at a very low ebb. How much influence his pen has had in bringing about the present high state of musical culture in Boston, and thus to a greater or lesser extent that of the whole country, it would be impossible to fully ascertain, though very great. Whatever the public standard has been he has never lowered his own ideals, and it seems quite likely that, contrary to the case of most reformers, he will live to see them fulfilled. Besides his musical articles, he has written considerable on other subjects, and is the compiler of a collection of excellent translations of select minor poems from Goethe and Schiller, which forms one of the series of Ripley's " Specimens of Standard Foreign Literature."

Mr. Dwight is unmarried, having lost his wife many years ago. He lives in one of the Harvard Musical Association's rooms, and has charge of its library. It is plainly but comfortably furnished. Over the fire-place hangs an original painting of Gluck, made by Duplessis of Paris, and over a mantel a framed autograph letter of Beethoven, while in the middle of the room stands a grand piano. Here he spends many quiet hours, which he has fairly earned. As a token of the esteem in which he is held, he was tendered a benefit concert, Dec. 9, 1880, which was the most successful affair of the season and realized several thousand dollars.

**Dwight's Journal of Music,** BOS-TON, Mass., edited by John S. Dwight, was for a long time one of the leading musical journals of America. It was established by Mr. Dwight in 1852. Although Mr. Dwight is not a professional musician, his writings on music have exercised a powerful influence, and always on the side of truth and nobility. Through the columns of his journal he has always sought to advance the art. For six year he was editor, proprietor and publisher, when the publication was assumed by O. Ditson & Co. It was changed from a weekly to a fortnightly during the war. After an active and useful life of nearly 30 years, it ceased to exist in 1881.

# E.

**Eddy,** HIRAM CLARENCE, one of America's best organists, was born June 23, 1851, at Greenfield, Mass., and consequently is still a comparatively young man. From his earliest youth, however, he has devoted himself assiduously to music. He studied for some time with Dudley Buck, and in 1872 or 1873 went to Germany, where he placed himself under the direction of Haupt, at Berlin, with whom he remained two years. While at Berlin he was called upon to play at a court concert, and rendered Bach's Fantasia in C and Merkel's sonata in G minor in a manner to call forth hearty praise from the critics. He also made a tour through Germany, Austria, and Switzerland, meeting with great applause everywhere. On his way home he played with equal success in Holland, Belgium, France, and England, and made it a point to test all the great organs.

In 1875 he returned to his native country and located at Chicago, where he became director of the Hershey Music School, marrying its founder, Mrs. Sara B. Hershey, in 1879. He has regularly given organ recitals, completing in June, 1879, the 100th of the series, without repeating a single number. Besides these he has given recitals in many of the principal cities and towns of the country, uniformly with success. In addition to his duties as director of the Hershey School, he is at present (June, 1883) organist of the First Presbyterian Church, Chicago.

Mr. Eddy has a wonderful command of his instrument, and plays with an ease and grace that charms the hearer. His programs include classical and romantic music of every kind, and he seems equally skilled in rendering either. As a key to his wonderful power of playing it may be stated that while in Germany he for several months made it a point to play the six organ sonatas of Bach every day in addition to his regular studies. After one month's careful study he was enabled to master Thiele's "Theme and Variations in C," which he played before Haupt. His own compositions consist of canons, preludes and fugues, and some other organ music, all of high order. He translated and produced in this country Haupt's "Theory of Counterpoint and Fugue."

**Edwin and Angelina.** One of the early American attempts at operas. The libretto is by Dr. E. H. Smith, of Connecticut, and founded on Goldsmith's poem; the music by M. Pellesier, a French resident of New York. Produced in New York, Dec. 19, 1798.

**Eichberg,** JULIUS, one of America's representative musicians, was born June 13, 1824, at Düsseldorf, Germany. He came of a musical family, his father being an excellent musician, who early taught his son the rudiments of music. Young Eichberg was used to the violin from his earliest childhood, and at the age of seven years was able to play acceptably. It is related that one time being confined to his bed by illness his father brought him a piece of music paper, on which was written a melody, and requested him to sing it at sight, which was considered no unusual thing. Upon his failing, his father playfully remarked: "You will never be a musician; you are more fit for a cobbler," a prediction which has signally proved untrue. At the age of eight years he was sent to Mayence, where he became a pupil on the violin of F. W. Eichler, a noted violinist, but when this musician departed on a concert tour, he was placed under another teacher, a selfish, unprincipled man, by whom he was shamefully treated. From Mayence he returned to his native place and was once more under the care of his father. He also studied harmony of J. Rietz, afterwards director of the Gewandhaus concerts and *capellmeister* to the King of Saxony at Dresden. He was a member of the orchestra at Düsseldorf as one of the second violins. About this time he became acquainted with Schumann. Burgmüller was a frequent visitor at the Eichberg home. In 1843 or 1844 he entered the Brussels Conservatoire, under Fétis, studying there two years and perfecting himself in the theory of music. Upon graduating he took the first prize for violin playing and for composition. After a short rest he went to Geneva as the director of an opera troupe. His abilities were soon recognized, and he was appointed a professor in the conservatory there and had charge of the music in one of the churches. He remained in Geneva for eleven years.

In 1857 Mr. Eichberg came to this country with a view of benefiting his health and landed in New York City. For some time he taught and played there, but gaining no permanent position he in 1859 went to Boston, where he was engaged as director of music at the Museum. This position he retained seven years, and after a year's rest, in 1867 established the BOSTON CONSERVATORY OF MUSIC (See BOSTON), one of the best institutions of its kind in this country, of which he is still the head, and through which he has exercised a powerful influence on the musical tastes of the people. The violin school connected with the Conservatory is under his immediate care and is the best in America. He has done much to render the violin a popular instrument, and especially to remove the prejudice which has long existed toward it as being unsuited for the use of ladies.

Mr. Eichberg's works are quite numerous. The best known of them all in this country are the four operettas, "The Doctor of Alcantara," "The Rose of Tyrol," "Two Cadis," and "A Night in Rome." The first mentioned of these was first produced April 7, 1862, at the Museum, Boston, and had an extraordinary run. It has been played in all the principal towns and cities of the different States, and still retains its popularity. The other three were also successful, though not to the same degree. His other works are several books of violin studies, which have been adopted in various European conservatories; two volumes for use in the Boston public schools, of which he for many years had the musical charge; a set of piano pieces called "Lebensfruhling" and published at Leipsic; a set of string quartets; and numerous songs, etc.

**Eisfeld,** THEODORE, was born at Wolfenbüttel, Germany, in 1816. He was taught the violin by Karl Müller at Bremen and composition by Reissiger at Dresden. In 1848 he came to the United States, and located at New York. He returned to Europe for a visit, and on the passage back in 1858 was one of the few survivors of the steamer "Austria," which burnt in mid-ocean. He was conductor of the Philharmonic Society for many years and also of the Harmonic Society when first established. He was also leader of the Eisfeld quartet *soirées,* the first concert of which was given Feb. 18, 1851. Eisfeld held a high position in New York musical circles, and was greatly esteemed both as a man and as an artist. He returned to Europe in 1866, and died at Wiesbaden, Sep. 16, 1882.

**Electric Piano.** In 1851, Thomas, Davenport of Salisbury, Vermont, made an attempt to prolong the tones of a piano by the introduction of electricity, and with partial success. It does not appear, however, that his experiments resulted in anything practical.

Some years ago a piano was exhibited in Paris which had an ordinary keyboard, but the music was produced mechanically from perforated paper which passed between two cylinders of wood and over a third one of metal. Whenever the perforations came in the right place a small copper hammer passed through and established an electric current which operated the hammer that struck the strings. The experiment was interesting but of no real value.

**Elson,** LOUIS C., was born April 17, 1848, at Boston, Mass. He began the study of music in childhood, relinquishing it only for a short time while he was engaged in mercantile pursuits. Upon returning to his favorite art he studied with renewed dilligence under August Kreissmann, Gloggner-Castelli, and others. As a singer he was chiefly interested in German "lieder" or songs, and introduced many of them in this country by faithful translations. He has also translated, adapted, or arranged a large number of French, Italian, and English songs. In 1877 he began to make himself known in the field of musical literature by becoming assistant, editor of the *Vox Humana.* In 1879 he became sole editor. He was prominently identified with the *Musical Times and Trade Review* during its brilliant career, and is at present connected with the leading musical journals of America. His criticisms are widely read and appreciated. He has written some vocal and instrumental music, which is of fair order and shows a decided leaning toward the German style. His book, "Curiosities of Music," a history of music in a popular form, was published in 1880 by O. Ditson & Co., Boston. Besides his musical works and articles he has written several poems.

**Emerson,** LUTHER ORLANDO, was born Aug. 3, 1820, at Parsonsfield, Maine. His early life seems to have been devoted to other pursuits, for it was not until he was twenty-four years of age that he seriously set to work to study music. His first collection of music, the "Romberg Collection," designed for the church, was published in 1853. This was followed in 1857 by the Sunday school book, "Golden Wreath," of which 300,000 copies were sold. The success of this work led Mr. Emerson to devote himself largely to book-making, and resulted in "The Golden Harp" (1860), "The Sabbath Harmony" (1863), "The Harp of Judah" (1865), "Merry Chimes" (1866), followed by the "Jubilate," "Chorus Wreath," "Greeting" (glees), "Choral Tribute" (church music), "Glad Tidings" (Sunday school), "Sabbath Guest" (anthems), "Emerson's Singing School," "National Chorus Book," "Chants and Responses," "Episcopal Chants," "The Song Monarch" (singing schools), "The Standard," and "The Leader," the latter two being for the church. "Cheerful Voices," for the Sabbath school, was edited in conjunction with H. R. Palmer, and "The Hour of Singing," "The High School Choir," and "The American School Music Readers," in three volumes and graded for the use of public schools, in conjunction with W. S. Tilden. Besides these he has published some other collections.

Mr. Emerson, it will thus be seen, is a prolific composer of church and easy vocal music, considerable of which has come into general use. He is also well known as the conductor of musical conventions and institutes in every part of the country, in which sphere he is very successful, having a rare faculty of imparting instruction. He has done much to improve the standard of church music, and is a faithful, hard worker. Some few of his compositions have been published in sheet-music form and have become quite popular.

**Emery,** STEPHEN ALBERT, was born at Paris, Oxford Co., Maine, Oct. 4, 1841. His father, Hon. Stephen Emery, was an able lawyer and judge, and noted for his legal ability and general intelligence. Young Emery early exhibited more than ordinary love of music, and even composed some little piano pieces before he was able to read notes, his elder sister showing him how to write them down. After a common school education, he fitted for college, entering Colby University (then known as Waterville College) in the fall of 1859, but owing to ill health and a partial loss of eyesight, he was compelled to leave during the freshman year. He then, as a pastime, took up the study of the piano and harmony under the care of Henry L. Edwards of Portland, Me. Upon the advice of his teacher, he went, in the summer of 1862, to Leipsic, where for two years he continued his studies with Papperitz, Plaidy, E. F. Richter, and Hauptmann. After a short additional time in Dresden, under Spindler, he returned to the United States, remaining in Portland until after the great fire of 1866, when he removed to Boston. He was engaged as teacher of the piano and harmony at the opening of the New England Conservatory of Music, in 1867, and was afterwards appointed professor of harmony, theory, and composition, in the Boston University College of Music. Mr. Emery has written many piano pieces and songs. His "Foundation Studies in Pianoforte Playing," op. 35 (written for his own children), is a remarkably simple and easy course for beginners, while his "Elements of Harmony" is used throughout the country. His lectures and editorial contributions to the "Musical Herald" have exercised a decided influence in elevating the standard of musical taste.

**Errani,** ACHILLE, one of the most successful vocal teachers of this country, was born at Faenza, Central Italy, in 1824. When sixteen years of age he entered the Conservatorio of Milan, studying singing under Vaccai. He afterwards was a private pupil of that master for some time, and then came before the public as a leading tenor. For the next fifteen years he sang in the principal cities of Europe, and at the end of that time came to the United States, landing at New York. He made his first public appearance there in 1860, at the old Winter Garden, as *Edgardo* in "Lucia," with Maretzek as conductor. After visiting the principal cities of this country, Cuba, and Mexico, he left the stage and settled (1864) in New York as a teacher. Sig. Errani employs only the pure Italian method, and has met with great and well-deserved success. Among his pupils may be mentioned Minnie Hauck, Emma Thursby, Louise Durand, and Stella Bonheur. He is still (May, 1885) located at New York.

**Estey, Jacob & Co.** An American reed organ manufacturing firm located in Brattleboro, Vermont. The business was begun in 1846, by two gentlemen. Their "factory" was a room in a building owned by Jacob Estey. The instruments were, of course, rude and uncouth as compared with those of the present day, for the art was then in its infancy. After much urging, Mr. Estey reluctantly consented to take an interest in the business in lieu of rent for his room. It appears not to have been very profitable, for the originators lost all heart in it, and in 1852 the entire concern passed into the hands of Mr. Estey. At this time six men were employed in the establishment and its estimated total value was only $2700!

After the business passed into Mr. Estey's care, he succeeded in resuscitating and placing it upon a substantial basis. He was burned out in 1857, but rebuilt, only to be burned out again in 1864. During this time he had several partners, but the partnership in no case seems to have lasted long. In 1866, however, he took into partnership his son, Julius J. Estey, and his son-in-law, Levi K. Fuller, by which the present firm of J. Estey & Co. was formed. They suffered heavy losses by a flood in 1869, but nothing daunted they purchased sixty acres of land on which to erect new buildings. These are eight in number, one each for the various branches of the business, and are at a sufficient distance from one another to insure safety in case of fire.

The organs of Messrs Estey & Co. are well known in this country and also abroad, and rank among the leading makes. The firm does an immense business, amounting to over one million dollars annually, which evidences great prosperity and a good demand for their organs. The firm has very recently (December, 1885) begun the manufacture of upright pianos.

**Etude, The.** A musical periodical edited by Theodore Presser, and published at Philadelphia, Pa. It is more especially devoted to the wants and needs of teachers and students of the piano. From eight to twelve of its thirty pages are given to *études*, exercises, teaching pieces, etc. It has a list of eminent contributors, and its articles are clear, forcible and meritorious, making it one of the very best journals of its class published. Issued monthly at $1.50 per year. Circulation about 2500. Established in 1883.

**Euphoniad.** An instrument combining in itself the tones of an organ, clarinet, horn, bassoon, and violin, and invented by Peter L. and George Grosh, of Petersburg, Pa. It had a compass of 36 keys with semitones, and could be played with ease.

# F.

**Fairlamb,** J. REMINGTON, was born Jan. 23, 1839, at Philadelphia, Pa. His earliest musical instruction was received from his mother, but subsequently he studied with Charles Boyer, organist of St. Stephen's church. A quantity of Spohr's music happened to fall into his hands, including the mass in C minor, " The Last Judgment," and selections from the operas of "Faust" and "Jessonda," and in this he became greatly interested, studying it assiduously. His thirst for musical knowledge became so great that he eagerly devoured every work on harmony, composition, or theory, which he could obtain. When sixteen years of age he gave to the public his first composition, and about the same time became organist of a Methodist Episcopal Church in the city, performing the duties solely for practice and receiving no remuneration. A year later he accepted a similar position at the Tabernacle Baptist Church, which he held for three years, and then transferred his services to the Clinton Street Presbyterian Church. In 1859, being then not quite twenty-one years of age, he departed for Europe. His first destination was Paris, where he studied the piano under Pru.dent and Marmontel and the voice under M. Masset and Mme. Bockholtz-Falconi. From Paris he proceeded to Florence and there continued his vocal studies with Mabellini. Shortly after the beginning of the Civil War he returned home, but not finding things to his taste he resolved on a second visit to Europe. He sought and obtained the post of United States consul at Zurich, Switzerland. During his residence there he became acquainted with many prominent German musicians, among whom were Dr. A. B. Marx, Moscheles, Kullak, Dr. Kocher, and J. J. Abert. He composed and dedicated to King Karl of Wurtenburg a Te Deum for double chorus, orchestra, and organ, which was accepted, and in consequence he had the gold medal of art and science ("Die grosse goldene Medaille für Kunst und Wissenschaft") bestowed upon him. While residing at Zurich he also commenced work upon a grand opera, the libretto being German.

In 1865 he returned to the United States and temporarily located at Washington, where he was director of music at Epiphany Church. The following year he married and settled in Philadelphia, and resumed work on his opera, ranslating the libretto into English. The work was too large to gain a production, and in consequence he wrote a smaller work, "Treasured Tokens" (2 acts), which was produced at the Chestnut Street Theatre. In 1870 he removed to Washington, where for two years he was director of music at St. John's Episcopal Church. At the end of that time he accepted a call to the Assembly Presbyterian Church, a position which he was still holding in 1881. As a teacher he is highly esteemed and is very successful. His works consist of several Te Deums, a jubilate in C, numerous anthems for various occasions, and other church pieces, which are much sung throughout the country; his two operas, which have already been mentioned; and about sixty other compositions of various kinds, all of which are of high order.

**Federal Harmony.** A collection of sacred music, edited by Simeon Jocelyn of New Haven, Conn., and published at Boston, Mass., in 1793. A similar collection was made and issued by Timothy Swan in 1788.

**Fillmore,** JOHN C., pianist, teacher, and critic, was born Feb. 4, 1843, in Connecticut. He studied at Oberlin, and subsequently at Leipsic. For nine years he was professor of music at Ripon College, Wis., but now resides at Milwaukee in the same state, and is director of the Milwaukee School of Music. He is highly esteemed as a teacher and critic.

**Fischer, J. & C.** This well-known piano manufacturing firm, located in New York City, was established in 1840, by John W. and Charles S. Fischer. They learned the art of piano making from their father and their grandfather, Sig. Bernardo Fischer, who established himself in business in Naples, about the beginning of the present century. Previous to coming to America, they traveled all over Europe, visiting and working in the principal manufactories of that country, thus gaining a ripeness of knowledge and experience not otherwise attainable. Their wanderings terminated in New York, where they arrived in 1839, John at that time being 23 and Charles 21 years of age. Nunses & Clark, piano makers, dissolving business relations in that year, they entered into partnership with Wm. Nunses under the firm name of Nunses & Fischer. After a few years Nunses was bought out and retired, the two brothers conducting business under the present firm name, J. & C. Fischer. In 1873, John Fischer withdrew from the firm and returned to the ancestral estates at Naples, where he still lives. Charles S. Fischer, Jr., who is well known in New York as organist of some of the leading churches and an able musician, was until quite recently a member of the firm, but withdrew to enter the medical profession. The present firm is composed of Charles S. Fischer, Sr., Henry B. Fischer, Bernardo F. Fischer, Adolfo H. Fischer, and Frederick G. Fischer, though the old firm name is retained. Each member has a special department which he oversees, and hence the work is systematically and thoroughly carried on.

The Fischer pianos are well known and esteemed, as is evidenced by the annual sale of over 5000, and very justly ranks the firm among the leading piano manufacturing concerns of this country.

**Fisk Jubilee Singers.** This troupe, so well known all over the country, was organized in October, 1871, by George L. White, treasurer of Fisk University, Nashville, Tenn., from among the students. Seven of the company had been in slavery, and all of them were colored. The original members were as follows : Ella Sheppard, pianist and soprano; Jennie Jackson, soprano; Maggie Porter, soprano; Minnie Tate, contralto; Eliza Walker, contralto; Thomas Rutling, tenor; B. M. Holmes, tenor; I. P. Dickerson, bass; and Greene Evans, bass. Their object was to raise money sufficient to meet a financial crisis of the University. They had no definite plan of action, and the experiment of singing genuine negro songs before cultured northern audiences was a new one. It proved a great success, however, and

the songs, which rapidly became very popular, were embodied in book form. So successful was the company that they soon raised $20,000 for their college home, and then $100,000 for an endowment. Other large sums of money have been earned and received by them, which have gone to help the University. They have twice visited Europe and sung before the most cultured audiences with great and uniform success. Up to 1881, twenty-four different persons had been members of the company, twenty of whom had been in slavery. Their aims have always been pure and noble, and the good they have done for their race can hardly be estimated.

**Flower Queen, The.** A secular cantata, produced in New York City, in 1852. The words are by Fanny J. Crosby; the music by Dr. George F. Root. It has met with considerable success.

**Folio, The.** A monthly publication issued by White, Smith & Co., Boston, and devoted to music, drama and art. Each number contains 16 pages of vocal and instrumental music. Earl Marble is at present ( January, 1886) editor. Subscription price $1.60 per annum. Circulation about 15,000. Established in 1869.

**Formes,** KARL, bass singer, son of the sexton at Mühlheim on the Rhine, born Aug. 7, 1810. What musical instruction he had he seems to have obtained in the church choir; but he first attracted attention at the benefit of the cathedral fund at Cologne in 1841. So obvious was his talent that he was urged to go on the stage and made his *début* at Cologne as *Sarastro* in " Zauberflöte," Jan. 6, 1842, with the most marked success, ending in an engagement for three years. His next appearance was at Vienna. In 1849 he came to London, and sang first at Drury Lane in a German company as *Sarastro* on May 30. He made his appearance on the Italian stage at Covent Garden, March 16, 1850, as *Caspar* in " Il Franco Arciero" (" Der Freischütz "). At the Philharmonic he sang first on the following Monday, March 18. From that time for some years he was a regular visitor to London, and filled the parts of *Bertram, Marcel, Rocco, Leporello, Beltramo,* etc.—*Grove.*

In 1857 Formes came to this country, and made his first appearance here at the New York Academy of Music, Dec. 2d. Since that time he has led a rather irregular and wandering life, going wherever fancy propelled him. His voice is one of the most magnificent ones ever possessed by any man, excelling in volume, compass, and quality. He is fine appearing and has a decided talent for the stage. With industry he might have attained a position equaled by few. He is now (March, 1886) located at San Francisco as a teacher of singing.

**Forty-sixth Psalm.** 1.—For solos, chorus, and orchestra, by Dudley Buck. First performed by the Handel and Haydn Society of Boston, May 7, 1874.

2.—Also for solos, chorus, and orchestra, by William W. Gilchrist. The prize composition for the Cincinnati May Festival of 1882, where it was first performed. See GILCHRIST, WILLIAM W.

**Foster,** STEPHEN COLLINS, one of America's most noted song writers, was born July 4, 1826, at Lawrenceburg, Pa., now a part of the city of Pittsburgh. His father came from Virginia, was one of the earliest settlers of Western Pennsylvania, a prosperous merchant, and at one time mayor of Pittsburgh. Young Foster began his studies at an academy in Alleghany, Pa., entered a school at Athens in 1839, and in 1841 the Jefferson College at Cannonsburgh, where he finished his education. After this he was for some time book-keeper for his brother at Cincinnati, Ohio, spending his leisure moments in learning German, French, drawing, and painting.

His musical tastes early made themselves known. When seven years old he learned to play the flageolet, also the flute and the piano, though having no teacher. He had a good but rather weak voice, rarely ever using it, however. His first composition was a waltz arranged for three performers, composed while attending school at Athens and performed at one of the commencements there, which he called "Tioga Waltz." It was well received, and served to stimulate the young composer to other efforts. He soon began to try his hand at song writing, in which he afterwards became so proficient. Becoming acquainted with Henry Kleber, a musician of his native city, he formed an intimate friendship with that gentleman and joined his vocal society. Many of his compositions were submitted to Kleber for criticism, for whose opinions he entertained a high regard. Some time after this a minstrel troupe visited Pittsburgh, and happening to be present at one of their performances, he sought to have them take and introduce one of his songs. "Oh, Susanna" was accepted and sung with success. It was afterwards published by Peters of Cincinnati, the author receiving as his remuneration twenty-five copies.

Seeing his musical talents, he was advised by friends to go through a regular course of study in music, but he declined on the ground that it might injure his own originality and freshness, an error which young minds are sometimes liable to fall into. Later in life he learned to regret this decision, and became acquainted with and appreciated to a certain extent the works of some of the masters. The theme and inspiration of many of his songs may be explained by the fact that whenever opportunity offered he visited religious camp-meetings, especially those held by the negroes, listening to the music and ready to grasp any stray thought which might come along. "Hard times come again no more" was thus originated, and became exceedingly popular with the slaves.

In 1854 Foster married Miss Jennie McDowell, daughter of Dr. A. N. McDowell, a physician of Pittsburgh. To her many of his songs were addressed. The marriage promised to be a happy one, but all these promises were broken by the dissipated habits into which he fell. In 1860 he left his family and went to New York City. For some time he made his headquarters at an old grocery on the corner of Christie and Hester streets, in the neighborhood of the Bowery. His personal appearance and surroundings are thus described by a well-known musical writer:

"A figure slight and a little below medium stature, attired in a well-worn suit; his face was long and closely shaven; soft brown eyes and somewhat shaded by a lofty forehead, which was disfigured by the peak of a glazed cap that hung closely to his head, scarcely allowing his short brown hair to be seen. His appearance was at once so youthful and so aged that it was difficult to tell at a casual glance if he were 25 or 50. An anxious startled expression hovered over a face that was painful to witness. Looking at him thus, it was hard for me to believe that standing before me was the then most popular song writer in the country; but it was Foster indeed! He seemed as embarrassed as a girl in the presence of a stranger, and this diffidence never wore off. Whether it was a natural bashfulness or a voluntary reserve I cannot say; but even with those who knew him most intimately he was never familiar. His conversation, made up mostly of musical reminiscences, was always interesting. He lodged generally at a small hotel in the Bowery, but that small grocery he made his usual sitting room, and many an exquisite melody had its birth in that uncongenial place. A friend of mine, who knew Foster, said to me that many of the now popular melodies were first written upon the common kind of brown paper used to wrap up bundles."

Such a state of existence must have been a monotonous one and little fitted for musical inspiration. But the end was near. While staying at the American Hotel he was attacked by the fever and ague, of which, however, nothing much was thought. One morning while dressing himself he fainted and fell, cutting himself severely on a broken piece of crockery. After this he conversed but very little, though conscious. He was taken to Bellevue Hospital, where he remained until his death, Jan. 13, 1864. His last words were: "Oh, wait till to-morrow," in response to some question of an attendant who had come to dress his wounds. The remains were conveyed to Pittsburgh and interred there.

Foster occupies a distinctive place among our song writers. His songs are unlike anything before or since produced, in some respects, having a nature of their own; and though not scientifically written, they have a peculiar charm and appeal directly to the popular heart. To enumerate all of his songs would be useless, as they are more or less familiar in every musical household. The first one which he published was "Open the Lattice, Love," issued by Willig of Baltimore, in 1842. For some time he wrote gratuitously, but latterly he received royalty amounting to thousands of dollars. The "Old Folks at Home," (See that heading), perhaps his most popular production, he hoped would rival "Home, Sweet Home." It has sold to the extent of 500,000 copies. "My Old Kentucky Home" was almost equally successful. It

was placed in Bryant's "Library of Poetry and Song," but no credit given the author. Among his other most popular songs are "Marsa's in de Cold, Cold, Ground," "Old Dog Tray," "Willie, We Have Missed You," "Ellen Bayne," and "Come Where My Love Lies Dreaming." To the most of his songs he wrote the poetry as well as the music. Had he improved his talents by study and been free from the vice of intemperance, he would undoubtedly have produced songs equal in every respect to any in the world. But this was not his aim. As far as his aspirations carried him he left nothing to be desired.

Under the heading of OLD FOLKS AT HOME, some idea of how Foster was taken advantage of, during his residence in New York, is given. It is a fact not very generally known that though his songs were extraordinarily popular and brought large profits, he was uniformly compelled by the music publishers to accept next to nothing for them. With a bundle of manuscripts he would go from one to another, offering them at $50 each, which was indeed a paltry sum, but the crafty publishers well knew his destitute condition, and would actually starve him into accepting their price. To add to his misfortunes there were a number of so-called friends who were always ready to take advantage of his frank, generous nature. When his remains were removed from New York to Pittsburgh, they were transported free by the Pennsylvania Railroad Co. They now repose in the Allegheny Cemetery, and the place is marked by a plain marble slab, bearing this simple inscription:

Stephen C. Foster
of Pittsburgh,
Born July 4, 1826;
Died in New York,
January 13, 1864.

The more we study the nature of Foster the more we shall be drawn towards him. Few musicians have been gifted with so fine and sensitive a nature, but the very qualities which we most admire in him made him also an easy prey to habit and false friends. We have evidence that during the terrible struggle his soul kept its innate purity. If we will but remember our own faults and the weakness of human nature, we can easily forgive and overlook his one great failing.

**Franklin,** BENJAMIN, the eminent American philosopher and statesman, was born in 1706 at Boston. His only claim to notice in a work like this is as having been the inventor of the harmonica (See HARMONICA.) He had considerable musical faculty, as is evidenced by his letters on Scotch music and the defects of modern music. He died at Philadelphia, in 1790.

**Franosch,** ADOLPH, was born in 1830, at Cologne, and after serving in the German army was given a position in the custom house at his native place. His fine bass voice attracted attention, and through the assistance of an operatic manager he made his appearance on the stage. He then sang with success in Germany and Russia. In 1870 he came to this country with the Lichtmay company, and for several seasons thereafter sang at the Stadt Theatre in the Bowery, New York. For some time he was manager of the German opera troupe, and gave performances in St. Louis, Cincinnati, Louisville, and other places. He was then engaged for the Germania Theatre by A. Neuendorff, and was the original Gen. Kautschukoff in "Fatinitza." He died Aug. 4, 1880, at New York.

**Fries,** WULF, violoncellist, was born at Garbeck, a village of Holstein, Germany, Jan. 10, 1825. He began playing his favorite instrument when only nine years old, and at twelve had his first and only lessons from a local player. At the age of thirteen he made his *début*, though compelled to perform his solo on a very poor instrument. His father, being poor and unable to furnish him means for a first-class musical education, sent him to Plöen, a small city of Holstein, where he played under the direction of the "Stadt Musikus," but received no regular instruction. What he learned in the art of playing was chiefly through hearing the soloists who gave concerts while passing through the city. He received some lessons on the trombone from a fine trombonist, and was soon able to play solos on that instrument with good effect, but he afterwards gave it up and devoted himself exclusively to the violoncello. In September, 1847, he came to America and settled in Boston, which has since been and still is (May, 1885) his home. About 1849 he organized, assisted by his brother, August, three years his senior, the "Mendelssohn Quintet Club," the immediate occasion of which was the performance at a private house of Mendelssohn's Quintet in A. The original members of the Club, with which he was connected for twenty-three years, were August Fries, 1st violin; Herr Gerloff, 2d violin; Theodor Lehman, 1st viola; Oscar Greiner, 2d viola; and Wulf Fries, 'cello. August Fries was the leader for ten years, when his place was taken by William Schultze. Mr. Fries (Wulf) is now violoncellist of the "Beethoven Quartet Club." He is also professor of the violoncello at the Boston and New England conservatories of music, and an esteemed musician.

**Fry,** WILLIAM HENRY, an American composer, was born at Philadelphia, Pa., August 10, 1815 (1813?). In 1849 he went to Paris for the purpose of collecting musical specimens, acting meanwhile as correspondent for several papers. He returned in 1854 and became musical critic of the New York Tribune. In 1855 he undertook in a series of papers to prove that Italian music is superior to any other, but only succeeded in bringing abuse upon himself. He also delivered a course of lectures upon music, and illustrated them by practical performances. The chorus consisted of 100 singers, the orchestra of 80 performers, and the military band of 50 performers, besides which there were several Italian solo vocalists. The venture, however, did not pay, and resulted in a loss of several thousand dollars. Mr. Fry's principal works are a set of symphonies, performed by Jullien's orchestra when in New York; several cantatas, some songs, a Stabat Mater, eleven violin quartets, and two operas, "Leonora," first performed at the Academy of Music, New York, March 29, 1858, and "Notre Dame de Paris," first performed at the Academy of Music, Philadelphia, in April, 1864, both of which were well received. He died at Santa Cruz, Dec. 21, 1864. He was one of our most talented native-born musicians, and had his abilities been rightly directed would have won a world-wide reputation.

# G.

**Gemuender,** George, whose fame as a violin maker is world-wide, was born April 13, 1816, at Ingelfingen, Würtemburg. He learned the principles of his trade from his father, who was a manufacturer of bow instruments. His father thought, however, to make a schoolmaster of him, and for that purpose sent him to the seminary. He remained there only three weeks and was back again to his trade, and the business for which nature had fitted him. His father dying in 1835, when he was in his nineteenth year, he traveled, working at Pesth, Presburg, Vienna, Munich, and other places, and meeting with success. Finding no suitable place to establish himself in business, he through the kindness of a friend made an engagement with a musical instrument maker in Strasburg, but on arriving there found that the man manufactured only brass instruments. Disappointed, he was invited by the manufacturer, whose name was Roth, to make his house his home until he found employment. There he remained several weeks, and during the time formed the acquaintance of a gentleman who wrote for him a letter of introduction and sent it to Vuillaume, the celebrated violin maker of Paris. Receiving an invitation from Vuillaume he at once repaired to Paris. His wages at first were 30 sous per day, but at the end of three months they were increased to 40 sous. While at Vuillaume's he studied and worked industriously, and became acquainted with the peculiarities of the best violins. On returning from this country to Paris, in 1845, Ole Bull took his wonderful violin, "Caspar da Salo," to Vuillaume for repairs. The latter intrusted it to Gemünder, who made the repairs in such a satisfactory manner that Ole Bull sought an introduction to him.

In 1847, after having been four years at Vuillaume's, Gemünder received an invitation from his two brothers in this country to join them. Accordingly he left Paris and arrived at Springfield, Mass., in November of that year. In company with his brothers and other musicians he gave concerts, but these proving unsuccessful he borrowed twenty-five dollars from a friend and began to manufacture and repair violins at Boston. He determined to submit some of his instruments for inspection at the London exhibition of 1851, and sent a quartet of bow instruments in imitation of Stradivarius, a violin of the Joseph Guarnerius pattern, and one of the Nicolas Amati pattern. Not meeting with sufficient encouragement in Boston he removed to New York in 1851, and later learned that his instruments had received the first prize at the exhibition, where they were examined by Spohr, Thalberg, Vieuxtemps, and other eminent authorities. Later, his instruments were similarly successful at exhibitions in Paris and Vienna. To the Vienna exhibition of 1873 he sent only one violin, and that in competition for a prize offered for the best imitation. The violin was called "Kaiser" (Emperor), built after the pattern of Guarnerius, and so deceived the judges as to be declared genuine by them. The instrument was a center of attraction to all musicians, and received the highest commendations, but few were willing to admit that it was newly made.

The success of Mr. Gemünder has led many persons to claim that the wood of his violins is chemically prepared. It is well known that the tone of such instruments deteriorates after awhile, but this has not been the case with those made by him. He has also offered to submit any of his instruments to be tested, provided upon failure to find any chemicals the price of the instrument be paid him by the parties making the test. Mr. Gemünder certainly claims more than any other violin maker has yet dared to claim, viz.: To equal, and in some respects excel, the instruments made by the old Italian masters. He has repeatedly deceived the best judges, and the tone of his violins has been acknowledged equal if not superior to that of the best Italian instruments. The prejudice against a new instrument and the belief that the work of two or three centuries ago can not now be equaled are so firmly fixed in the minds of most people, that rather than admit Mr. Gemünder's claims they accuse him of chemically preparing the wood which he uses. There is no reason why it should be thought impossible to equal past achievements, though the attempt has often been made and resulted in failure. Perhaps a hundred years from now Mr. Gemünder's instruments will be considered "classical," and accorded their true worth.

Mr. Gemünder resides at Astoria, Long Island, and though at quite an advanced age still continues the manufacture of his instruments.

**Germania Orchestra.** A band of twenty-four musicians, which originally came from Germany. The unsettled state of affairs in Europe in 1847 made the members resolve to seek new fields of music. After obtaining letters of introduction from the English and American embassadors at Berlin, they proceeded to England, but met with a poor reception. Leaving England they sailed for the United States, arriving at New York, Sept. 28, 1848. They gave their first concert at the Astor-place opera house, on October 5th. At that time the musical tastes and culture of the country were of far lower order than now, and the concerts which they gave failed to pay expenses, though considered from an artistic standpoint they were successful. From New York the members proceeded to Philadelphia, where they gave their first concert Dec. 4, but met with no better success. After a desperate struggle they temporarily disbanded. Soon after, however, they were again called together to play at the presidential inauguration ball at Washington. They then went to Baltimore, where they first met with the success they deserved, though Gung'l was at that time occupying the city. Leaving Baltimore they proceeded to Boston, giving concerts at New Haven, Worcester, and other large towns on the way. At Boston they gave their first concert in Melodeon Hall, April 14, 1849, but met with little encouragement at first, though afterwards well patronized. They played at the Castle Garden concerts, New York, and in the summer at Newport, then beginning to come into prominence as a fashionable resort. During the winter of 1849-50 they were in Baltimore, and the ensuing summer undertook a tour of the United States and Canada, which proved successful.

The next winter they were again in Baltimore, made a Southern trip under the management of Strakosch, with Patti as soloist, gave thirty concerts with Jenny Lind, and in the summer played for the second time at Newport. The season of 1851-52 was spent in Boston and in making a tour with Ole Bull. During the next season they again gave concerts in Boston with Jaell, Camilla Urso, and other artists, and also in Philadelphia with Mme. Sontag. The summer of 1853 was spent in traveling throughout the West and other portions of the country. In 1853-54 they were in Boston for the third time, but did not meet with their previous success. The orchestra had previously been increased to thirty members, but only fourteen of the original ones remained. The engagement with P. T. Barnum that followed was a failure, and a growing dissatisfaction led to the dissolution of the Orchestra, September 13, 1854. Of its members a few have become well known, chief of whom is Carl Zerrahn. The leaders were Leuschow, Schultze, and Carl Bergmann. During its existence the orchestra was probably one of the most potent factors in advancing the musical tastes of this country.

There is in Boston an organization called "The Germania Band," originated about 1850, the original six members of which came from Saxony. Among them were Carl Eichler, the present leader, and Wulf Fries, the well-known violoncellist. It was soon turned into a serenade band, and has gradually grown to its present dimensions, including some fine artists. The "Germania Quartet" consists of four brass instruments from the "Band," with Rose Stewart as vocalist.

**Giffe,** WILLIAM T., was born June 28, 1848, at Portland, Ind. He is the author of several popular collections of music, among which are the "Western Anthem Book," "Song Clarion," "New Favorite," "Giffe's Male Quartet Book," "Helping Hand," "Brilliant," etc. He is also a good chorus and convention conductor. At present (1884) he is teacher and superintendent of music in the public schools of Logansport, Ind.

**Gilchrist,** WILLIAM WALLACE, who has lately become noted as a composer, was born in 1846, at Jersey City, N. J. When he was nine years of age his parents removed to Philadelphia, where he studied for three years under H. A. Clarke, professor of music in the University of Pennsylvania. In 1872 he went to Cincinnati, where he became organist at the New Jerusalem Church and teacher in the conservatory of Miss Bauer. In 1873, however, he returned to Philadelphia, and has since been located there, being at the present conductor of four musical societies and organist at Christ's Church, Germantown. He has gained several prizes from the Abt Society of Philadelphia for his compositions, and three prizes from the Mendelssohn Club, New York. In 1880 he contended for the Cincinnati May Festival prize, but was ranked as third. This year (1882) he carried away the prize, his composition being a setting of the 46th psalm, for solo, chorus, orchestra, and organ. The awarding committee consisted of Reinecke of Leipsic, Saint Saëns of Paris, and Thomas of New York. The prize composition is thus described by the composer himself:

"The composition has four principal divisions exclusive of an introduction each following the other without pause, and connected by a gradual decrescendo in the orchestra. The opening of the psalm seemed to me to indicate a strong outburst of praise or of thanksgiving for a deliverance from trials, which the introduction is intended to convey. But instead of commencing with a strong outburst I lead up to it from a very subdued beginning, working gradually to a climax at the entrance of the chorus on the words, 'God is our refuge and our strength.' The opening movement of the chorus becomes a little subdued very shortly as it takes up the words, 'A very present help in trouble,' which is followed again by an allegro con fuoco movement on the words, 'Therefore we will not fear though the earth be removed, though the mountains be carried into the midst of the sea.'' This movement leads into still another, a furioso movement on the words, 'Though the waters thereof roar, though the mountains shake with the swelling thereof.' This is followed by an elaborate coda in which all the themes of the preceding movement are worded together, and which brings the chorus to a close. The second division, in E major, is marked by an andante contemplative on the words, 'There is a river the streams whereof shall make glad the city of God.' This movement is intended to be one of tranquility, varied with occasional passionate outbursts on the words, 'God is in the midst of her; she shall not be moved.' A peculiar rythmical effect is sought by the alteration of 4-4 and 3-4 time, three bars of the first being answered by two bars of the second. This movement ends very tranquilly on the words, 'God shall help her and that right early,' and is immediately followed by an allegro molto, in B minor, on the words, 'The heathen raged, the kingdoms were moved; he uttered his voice, the earth melted.' In the middle of this chorus the soprano solo enters for the first time on the words, 'He that maketh wars to cease unto the end of the world; He breaketh the bow and cutteth the spear in sunder.' The chorus works up to a strong climax on the words, 'He burneth the chariot with fire,' which is suddenly interrupted by a decrescendo on the words, 'Be still, and know that I am God.' This leads to the third division, which is a return of the second division in E major, and which is played through almost entirely by the orchestra, the chorus merely meditating on the words last quoted. This leads to the final chorus, which is a fugue in E major, with alla breve time, on the words, 'And the Lord of Hosts is with us; the God of Jacob is our refuge,' towards the close of which a gloria patri is introduced, being woven in with fragments of the fugue to a strong climax. The whole composition finishes with an impetuous accelerando. My central idea was to make a choral and orchestral work, the solo, while requiring a good singer, being only secondary. The psalm seemed to me particularly adapted for musical composition, as being capable of a varied, even dramatic effect."

**Gilmore**, PATRICK SARSFIELD, well-known in this country as a conductor, was born Dec. 25, 1829, near Dublin, Ireland. Early in life he came to Canada with an English band, and afterward found his way to Salem, Mass., where he became leader of a brass band. In 1849 he went to Boston and acted as leader of numerous bands there. He organized Gilmore's band in 1859, and with it traveled all over the country, giving concerts in the principal cities. In 1864 he gave a grand festival in New Orleans, and was the prime mover and conductor of the Peace Jubilee at Boston, in 1869 and 1872 (See PEACE JUBILEES). Mr. Gilmore has repeatedly made tours of this country, employing the best vocal and instrumental soloists, and in 1878 visited the principal countries of Europe. He now resides at New York. His compositions are few.

**Gleason,** FREDERIC GRANT, was born Dec. 17, 1848, at Middletown, Conn. His love of music was inherited from both his father and mother, the former being an excellent amateur flutist, and the latter a good contralto singer and pianist. The bent of his nature was early manifested by his composing melodies and singing them to himself. When he was six years old his parents removed to Hartford, Conn., where he became a member of one of the church choirs. His desire to study music, however, did not meet with parental approval, as he had been selected for the ministry. At the age of sixteen years he assumed the *rôle* of a composer and wrote an oratorio, entitled, "The Captivity," the poem being by Goldsmith. This he had not fully completed before he relinquished it for a "Christmas oratorio," the words of which he selected from the Bible and from Montgomery's version of the psalms. Both of these works showed more than ordinary talent, but were crude, as their author was not acquainted with harmony and composition. His father could not longer refuse to gratify the son's musical tastes, and accordingly decided to educate him for a musician. He was placed under the care of Dudley Buck, with whom he studied piano and composition for some time. After this he was sent to Germany, and entered the Conservatorium at Leipsic, where he was taught the piano by Moscheles and harmony by Richter. At the same time he took private lessons from Plaidy and was instructed in composition by J. C. Lobe. Upon the death of Moscheles, in 1870, he went to Berlin, where he continued his piano studies under Oscar Raif, a pupil of Tausig, and his theoretical studies under Carl Frederic Weitzmann, now court musician to the Emperor of Russia and a pupil of Spohr and Hauptman. After staying for some time in Ber-

lin, Mr. Gleason returned home and visited his parents. Shortly after, however, he went to London, where he studied English music, and the piano under Oscar Berringer, also a pupil of Tausig. He then went again to Berlin and there for the second time took lessons in theory from Weitzman, studying the piano under Loeschorn and the organ under Haupt. It was during his second stay in Berlin that he prepared his work, "Gleason's Motet Collection," published by W. A. Pond & Co. of New York.

After remaining for some time in Germany, Mr. Gleason again returned home, and settled in Hartford, where his parents resided. He became organist of one of the churches in Hartford and also of the South Church in New Britain, Conn. Besides his teaching duties, he was busily engaged upon his opera, "Otho Visconti." The work has not yet been performed entire, but selections from it have frequently been given, the vorspiel and trios being especially liked. In 1876 he removed to Chicago, and became teacher of piano, organ, composition and instrumentation, in the Hershey Music School, a position which he still (1884) holds. In 1878 he was married to Miss Grace A. Hiltz, a Western lady who is well-known as a vocalist (See HILTZ-GLEASON). Gleason's principal works are as follows:

Op.  1.  Songs for the soprano voice.
"    2.  Organ sonata (C sharp minor).
"    3.  Barcarola.  Piano.
"    4.  Episcopal Church music.
"    5.  Songs for the alto voice.
"    6.  Episcopal Church music.
"    7.  "Otho Visconti," a grand romantic opera in three acts. Selections published by W. A. Pond & Co., N.Y.
"    8.  Piano pieces.
"    9.  Trio, No. 1 (C minor). Piano, violin and violoncello.
"   10.  Quartets for female voices.
"   11.  "Overture Triomphale." Organ.
"   12.  "God Our Deliverer," cantata. Solos, chorus, and orchestra.
"   13.  Trio, No. 2 (A major). Piano, violin, and violoncello.
"   14.  "Culprit Fay," cantata. Solos, chorus and orchestra. Words by Jos. Rodman Drake.
"   15.  Trio, No. 3 (D minor). Piano, violin, and violoncello.

This list does not include many small pieces, published and unpublished, having no opus number attached to them. Mr. Gleason is the joint editor with H. C. Eddy of "The Church and Concert Organist," a work of 127 pages, containing various compositions for the organ, original and selected, with pedalling, finger-ing, and registration marked. It was recently published by E. Schuberth & Co., New York, and has already reached a second edition. He has also for several years devoted all his leisure time to the composition, both words and music, of the grand romantic opera, "Montezuma." The scene is laid in Mexico, and the work deals with Mexican religious beliefs and customs. About one year yet will be required for its completion, but various selections have been given, which show that when completed it will take its place as the equal of any American operatic work ever produced. A number of terse, pungent articles which have appeared in different musical publications have made Mr. Gleason favorably known as a writer.

**Glenn,** HOPE, contralto singer, was born in the state of Pennsylvania, but the family removed to Iowa when she was very young. From 1867 to 1871 she studied at the Iowa State Normal Academy of Music, Iowa City, where she resided. She then studied at Chicago for two or three years. In 1875 she went to Europe and was introduced to Wartel by Marie Roze. With him she studied about a year, as she also did with Mme. Viardot-Garcia. After this she went to Milan and finished with Lamperti. Her operatic *début* was at Malta in 1879, as *Pierotto* in "Linda." She has sung much in England, mainly in concerts and oratorio. During the season of 1882-83 and that of 1883-84 she sang in the principal cities of this country, and was everywhere well received.

**Goldbeck,** ROBERT, pianist, composer, and teacher, was born at Potsdam, near Berlin, Prussia, April 19, 1839. He evinced striking musical talent when a boy, and attracted the attention of prominent persons in his native town, chiefly that of Alexander von Humboldt, through whose influence an introduction to the King of Prussia was managed, at a concert expressly arranged for this purpose. Goldbeck was, in consequence of this, sent to the great master of the piano, Henry Litolff (Brunswick), under whom he pursued the higher branches of piano playing and composition. His first teacher in piano and harmony was his uncle, the brother of his mother, Louis Köhler, the pupil of the Knight von Seyfried (in turn pupil and friend of Beethoven). Provided with letters from Humboldt for members of the highest circles of Parisian and London society, notably of the latter, the Duke of Devonshire, in honor of the rising young artist, threw open the famous picture gallery of Devonshire House, Piccadilly, there to have him appear in a concert. In 1861 Goldbeck came to New York, where he wrote the greater number of his larger compositions, such as his five symphonic pieces for piano and orchestra (repeatedly performed by the Philharmonic societies of New York and Brooklyn), two piano concertos with orchestra, his "Symphony Victoria," and a very large number of piano pieces and songs. Besides these he has written two trios for piano, violin, and 'cello; a quintet for piano and stringed instruments, and a number of quartets for voices, among which stands foremost the "Three Fishers," for male voices, a composition which has been repeatedly given by the most celebrated singing societies of New York, Boston, Philadelphia, Chicago, and Milwaukee. At present, Goldbeck resides in St. Louis, where he is the director of a prosperous College of Music, and from whence he issues the well-known "Musical Instructor" and "Musical Art," which have placed him in the front ranks of musical writers. He is an indefatigable worker in the cause of music, be it as a composer, teacher, pianist, or literary writer.—*From Brenner's "Handlexicon of Music."*

Mr. Goldbeck's stay in Paris covered a period of three years, during which time he made the acquaintance of Alexander Dumas, the Dutchess Geaune de Maille, Berlioz, Halévy, Pauseron, Henry Herz, and other celebrated personages, and became a great favorite in the highest circles of society. It was upon the advice of Countess Therese de Appongi of Hungary that he went to London, where he remained about eighteen months. After spending some time in New York, Boston, and other eastern cities, he proceeded to Chicago, where he took charge of the Chicago Conservatory of Music, and where he resided for seven years. During the great Chicago fire of October, 1871, he lost many of his manuscripts, and among them that of the "Symphony Victoria." Some seven or eight years ago he removed to St. Louis, where he was for some time one of the directors of the

Beethoven Conservatory. He also occupied the post of conductor of the St. Louis Harmonic Society. As a composer, especially of vocal music, he shows great ingenuity and originality, and is one of the few composers who have something like a style of their own. As a teacher he is unusually successful and his pupils are numbered by the thousands. His playing is distinguished for clearness of execution, great expression, and high spirit. Mr. Goldbeck recently (December, 1885) removed to New York City, where he is engaged in teaching, giving piano recitals, and conducting.

**Golden Legend.** A cantata composed by Dudley Buck. The libretto is formed of extracts from Longfellow's celebrated poem, "The Golden Legend." There are fourteen numbers, three of which are wholly instrumental. In general style the work, which is for solos, chorus and full orchestra, somewhat resembles those of Berlioz, and is essentially modern in every respect. It was written in competition for the prize of $1000 offered by the Cincinnati May Festival Association in 1879 for the best composition by a native born American composer, and was awarded the prize. Performed at the Festival in May, 1880.

**Gottschalk,** LOUIS MOREAU, one of the most popular and gifted of American pianists, was born May 8, 1829, at New Orleans, La. His father, Edward Gottschalk, came to this country from England, and his mother's name was Aimée Marie de Braslé. At an early age his musical talents began to manifest themselves, and when about four years old he was placed under the instruction of a Mr. Letellier, a French musician of New Orleans. When six years old he also began to study the violin under a Mr. Ely. His progress was very rapid, and about this time he was once permitted to play the organ in church. At the age of eight years he appeared in public as a player, and gave a concert for the benefit of a Mr. Miolan, a violinist at the French opera. In 1842 he was sent to Paris to complete his studies, where for a short time he took lessons of Charles Halle, but shortly after was placed under Camille Stamaty, and at the age of thirteen began to study harmony with M. Maledan. Shortly after this he assumed the rôle of a composer, his first pieces being two

ballads, called "Ossian," followed by "Danse des Ombres." In the summer of 1846 he went on a tour through the Vosges. During the winter of 1846 and 1847 he gave a series of concerts with Berlioz, at the Italian opera, which were very successful. In the summer of 1847 he made a tour of Switzerland. Returning to Paris in December, he gave many concerts. In 1849 he journeyed through France and Spain, everywhere meeting with a flattering reception. His stay in Spain was lengthened to two years, and it was not until the autumn of 1852 that he returned to Paris. Early in 1853 he arrived in New York, where he gave his first concert Feb. 11th, at Niblo's Garden, and was well received. His second concert occurred Feb. 17th, when he rendered many of his own compositions. Oct. 18, 1853, he made his first appearance in Boston, at the Music Hall, but was rather coldly received. At a second concert soon after he fared better. During the winter of 1853 and 1854 he gave concerts in the Middle States, and then went to New Orleans. In September he returned to New York and gave performances in Syracuse, Albany, and other cities of the State. The following November he went to Philadelphia, and shortly after to the West Indies, via New Orleans. His stay there was protracted to six years, during which time he gave concerts and conducted musical performances. In February, 1862, he returned to New York, and the time of the ensuing summer was spent in giving concerts in various parts of the country. His first appearance at Chicago was made April 14, 1862, when he was supported by Carlotta Patti, George Simpson, Morine, and Carl Bergmann. In 1864 he made a tour of Canada and part of the West, and in June, 1865, sailed for California. He then went to Chili, and gave concerts, etc., there and in other South American States. In May, 1869, he went to Rio de Janeiro, Brazil, and there prepared for a grand festival, which took place Nov. 26th, at the Opera House. The following day he was seized with a severe illness. On Dec. 8th he was taken to Tijuca, a plateau a short distance from the city, in hopes that the change would benefit him. There he died Dec. 18, 1869.

As a pianist Gottschalk was refined, graceful, and *suave*, to the last degree, though not incapable of imparting a force and depth of feeling to his playing. His compositions are full of the same characteristics, but devoid of any originality and little calculated to endure. Some of his many pieces are " Bannier," " Savane," and " Bamboula," 1844; " Mancenillier," " Chasse de jeune Henri," " Songe d'une Nuit d'Eté," and " La Morssonneuse Mazurka," 1847; " Carnival de Venise;" " Jerusalem ;" "Chant de Soldat," " Ricordati," and "Valse Poétique," 1857 ; "March Solennelle," "Minuit à Séville," and " Reflets du Passé," 1858; three insignificant pieces under the name of "Seven Octaves," 1859; "Mauchega" (étude), "Souvenir de la Havane," " Ardennes," " Jeunesse Masourka," "La Chute des Feuilles," and a duo, 1860; " Polonia," 1861; "O ma Charmante" (caprice), " Suis Moi " (caprice), and " Berceuse," 1862 ; several songs, 1863 ; "La Colombe," "Ojos Criollos," "Miserere du Trovatore," "Réponds" (duo), overture to William Tell, and songs, 1864; and a song and duo, " La Gallina," 1865. " Life and Letters of Gottschalk," by Octavia Hensel (Boston, O. Ditson & Co., 1870), is a romantic biography, pleasant to read but of little value to the historian. A sketch of his life and works has lately been prepared by his sister, Clara Gottschalk.

**Gould,** NATHANIEL DAYER, born at Chlemsford, Mass., in 1789, was one of the early American composers and teachers, a contemporary of Mason and Hastings. He was very successful as a teacher and conducted a great many singing schools. According to his own statement he had no less than fifty thousand pupils in these schools. The following are his works, all of which were published at Boston : " The Social Harmony" (1823), 152 pages, 4to ; " National Church Harmony" (1832); "Sacred Minstrel" (1840); "Companion for the Psalmist, containing original Music for Hymns of peculiar Character and Meter, and to most of which no Tunes are to be found in existing Publications" (1844); and "Church Music in America" (1853), 240 pages, 12 mo. The last is the most important, and while, as might be expected, there is considerable ambiguity and incorrectness, it is still of value. Gould died in 1864. John W. Moore, in his "Dictionary of Musical Information," says that his name

was originally Duren, but was changed in 1806 to secure the estate of an uncle.

**Grand Conservatory of Music,** NEW YORK CITY. The conservatory system proper did not take root in this country until 1859. Singing-schools, conventions, and institutes, were held prior to this, but while they undoubtedly prepared the way for conservatories, they were more or less imperfect and incomplete. In the year named, the National Conservatory of Music was founded by the elder of the Mollenhauer brothers and Lejeat. Though successful for awhile, a dispute arose among the teachers, which finally led to the secession of several of them and a large number of pupils. The seceding faction was taken in charge by Julius Schuberth, and gradually developed into what was later known as the New York Conservatory of Music. This institution prospered as long as Mr. Schuberth was connected with it, but upon his retiral it passed into the hands of those who were not musicians, and after considerable wrangling among the management and teachers, shared a fate similar to that of its parent.

After this, the conservatory system led a rather checkered career in New York. Up to the year 1873, the following conservatories were inaugurated, flourished and died : The American Conservatory, The European Conservatory, The Mason and Thomas Conservatory, Anschutz's Conservatory, The New York Normal Conservatory, and several others of less importance. The permanent artistic results were very small. In the spring of 1874 the present Grand Conservatory of Music was founded by Ernst Eberhard, who is an excellent musician and well qualified to take charge of such an institution. The success of the Conservatory, which is conducted on thoroughly artistic principles, was not only immediate but has been lasting. So rapidly has the number of pupils increased that larger accommodations were necessary, and in February of the present (1882) year, the Conservatory was removed to 46 West 23rd Street. The course of study at the Conservatory includes every branch of music. A staff of about thirty professors imparts instruction. Among them are Geo. C. Müller, G. Operti, Francesco Tamburello, William H. Walter, George W. Morgan, H. Maylath, and others equally well known. The institution is incorporated, and has a board of nine directors, with the following officers: E. Eberhard, president; Alf. R. Kirkus, vice-president; Wm. Dinsmore, secretary, and E. Core, treasurer.

A special feature of the Conservatory is the artists' class in virtuoso playing for advanced pianists, which has led to excellent results. A good library is connected with the institution, free to pupils, which contains many valuable and rare works, among them being several manuscripts of the 13th, 14th and 15th centuries. The Grand Conservatory Publishing Company issues in uniform style for the use of the Conservatory the principal studies of Bertini, Bülow, Chopin, Clementi, Tansig, Thalberg, Cramer, etc., as well as other works.

**Graupner,** GOTTLIEB, one of the first foreign musicians who came to America, was probably born about 1740. He was oboist in a Hanoverian regiment band, but after obtaining an honorable discharge (April 8, 1788) went to London, where he played in the orchestra of Solomon's concerts when Haydn brought out his twelve symphonies. "From London," in the words of J. S. Dwight, "he came to Prince Edward's Island; then spent some time in Charlestown, S. C., where he married, and came to Boston in 1798." He gathered around him some musical friends, and together they formed a "Philharmonic Society," which was the precursor of the Handel and Haydn Society. He also took an active part in the organization of the latter society, and was one of the three persons who signed the call, dated March 24, 1815. For some time he kept a small music store, and even engraved and published music for his pupils. "The Rudiments of the Art of Playing on the Pianoforte," a work of merit, was one which he edited. The date of his death we have been unable to ascertain. Mrs. Catherine Graupner was a prominent singer of her time. She died at Boston about July 1, 1821.

**Greatorex,** HENRY W., American psalmodist, was born in 1816, at Boston. He was for some time organist at Hartford, Conn. Among his several compilations is the "Greatorex Collection," published in 1851. Some of his music has come into general use. He died at Charleston, S. C., in 1858.

**Griswold,** GERTRUDE, a young but already celebrated *prima donna*, was born in 1861 at New York City, where her father was a wealthy ship-owner and importer. She was brought up with every advantage which money could procure, but reverses came, and her father, whose health had been destroyed by the blow, soon died. It was then that she thought of turning her fine voice to some practical account, and, accompanied by her mother, left New York for Paris. Fortunately she was able to obtain admission to the Conservatoire, where, under the care of Barbot and Obin, she bent all her energies toward preparing for the stage. Innumerable difficulties and discouragements lay in her way, not the least of which was the natural envy of the native students, but she bravely met them all. At last the time for her *début* came, which was effected at the Académie, Paris, June 6, 1881, in Ambroise Thomas' "Ophelia," which she had studied under the direction of the composer himself. Her success was unbounded, and at the close she was greeted with prolonged applause. Gounod, Thomas, and many others, congratulated her. According to the rules of the Conservatoire, the government is entitled to her services for two years, but at the end of that time she will be free to accept such engagements (she has already been offered several good ones) as she may desire. Gounod wrote the soprano part of his "Redemption" with especial reference to her voice, which is a pure, clear, sweet soprano of extended range. She can take D in *alt* with scarcely an effort, and surmounts the hardest technical difficulties with ease. Miss Griswold will undoubtedly soon become one of the greatest operatic singers of the world. Her first appearance in her native country will be watched for with unusual interest.

**Grounds and Rules of Music.** A singing book published by Rev. Thomas Walter of Roxbury, Mass., in the year 1721. The title page runs thus: "The Grounds and Rules of Musick explained. Or an Introduction to the Art of singing by Note: Fitted to the meanest Capacity. By Thomas Walter, A. M. Recommended by several Ministers. 'Let everything that hath truth praise the Lord,' Ps. 150, 6. Boston: Printed by Benjamin Mecon at the new Printing Office near the Town Hall: for Thomas Johnstone, in Brattle Street." The book was a small oblong volume, and the preface, which is dated "Boston, April 18, 1721," recommends that everyone sing with "*Grace in their Hearts*" that "*they may make Melody to the Lord*." Its tunes are arranged in three parts, and the music is barred. That the little volume met with a cordial reception is evidenced by the fact that it passed through many editions. The names of the "several Ministers" who recommended it are as follows:

Peter Thacher, Joseph Sewell, Thomas Prince, John Webb, William Cooper, Thomas Foxcroft, Samuel Checkley, Increase Mather, Cotton Mather, Nehemiah Walter, Joseph Belcher, Benjamin Wadsworth, Benjamin Coleman, Nathaniel Williams, Nathaniel Hunting.

In 1764, Daniel Bailey of Newburyport, Mass., published "A new and complete Introduction to the Grounds and Rules of Music, in two books." The first book is compiled from that of Walter, and the second from Wm. Tansur's "Royal Melody." The tunes are arranged in three parts.

# H.

**Hagen,** THEODORE, was born April 15, 1823, at Hamburg, Germany. He studied the piano under Jaquez Schmitt, and in 1841 went to Paris, where he was a pupil in harmony for two years of Kastner. Returning to Germany he gave concerts, in which he introduced some of his own compositions. About this time he began to be known as a musical writer, and contributed articles to many German publications, especially Schumann's "Neue Zeitschrift für Musik." He was employed as musical editor of a Hamburg daily paper, and soon after published his book, "Civilization and Music," which was followed in 1848 by his "Musical Novels." These were so successful as to be translated into French and English. In 1854 he came to this country, and having made the acquaintance of William Mason at Weimar, he was offered the editorship of "The Musical Gazette," a new publication about to be started by the Mason brothers. At the end of about six months it was consolidated with the "New York Musical Review and Gazette," of which he also became editor. In 1862 he became both editor and proprietor. He was little known as a practical musician, but as a writer he took a prominent place. He died at New York, Dec. 27, 1871.

**Hail, Columbia.** One of the most popular of American national songs. The words were written by Judge Joseph Hopkinson in 1798 for a friend of his. This friend was a singer at one of the theatres of Philadelphia (then capitol of the United States), and the piece was first sung at this theatre. Its success was instantaneous, and by common consent it became a national song. The melody is from the "President's March," then a very popular piece, but as to whom the composer was is not known. The melody as usually sung is here given with the words :

1.—Hail, Columbia, happy land !
Hail, ye heroes ! heaven-born band !
‖: Who fought and bled in freedom's cause :‖
And when the storm of war was gone,
Enjoyed the peace your valor won.
Let independence be our boast,
Ever mindful what it cost ;
Ever grateful for the prize,
Let its altar reach the skies.

2.—Immortal patriots ! rise once more,
Defend your rights, defend your shore ;
‖: Let no rude foe with impious hand :‖
Invade the shrine where sacred lies,
Of toil and blood the well-earned prize.
While offering peace, sincere and just,
In heaven we place a manly trust,
That truth and justice will prevail,
And every scheme of bondage fail.

3.—Sound, sound the trump of fame !
Let Washington's great name
‖: Ring through the world with great applause:‖
Let every clime to freedom dear
Listen with a joyful ear.
With equal skill, with god-like power,
He governs in the fearful hour
Of horrid war, or guides with ease
The happier times of honest peace.

4.—Behold the Chief who now commands,
Once more to serve his country stands.
‖: The rock on which the storm will beat :‖
But armed in virtue, firm and true,
His hopes are fixed on heaven and you.
When gloom obscured Columbia's day,
When hope was sinking in dismay,
His steady mind from changes free,
Resolved on death or Liberty.

Refrain :—Firm, united, let us be,
Rallying round our liberty ;
As a band of brothers joined,
Peace and safety we shall find.

**Hall,** GENERAL WILLIAM, was born May 13, 1796, at Tarrytown (then Sparta), N.Y. He was apprenticed to a musical instrument manufacturer in Albany, and in 1812 went to New York City, where in 1821 he commenced business in partnership with John Firth, an Englishman, under the firm name of Firth & Hall. In 1832 the firm became Firth, Hall & Pond, but in 1847 Gen. Hall withdrew and established a business in conjunction with his son, James F., under the name of Wm. Hall & Son. Gen. Hall was for some time president of the Sacred Music Society. He died May 3, 1874.

**Hamerik,** ASGER, was born April 8, 1843, at Copenhagen, Denmark. His father was professor in a university, and he, being designed for a similar position in life, was sent to college. His taste for music, however, was very strong, and he persistently studied it without the aid of a teacher. When fifteen years of age he wrote a cantata for solo voices, chorus, and orchestra, which was not without merit. Meanwhile he continued to attend school, and it was not until 1859 that his father consented to employ a music teacher for him. From this time his progress was very rapid. He was successively placed under Gade and Haberbier. In 1861 he went to London, and from there to Berlin, where he studied three winters under von Bülow. In the spring of 1863 he left Berlin for Paris, where he was fortunate enough to become the pupil (and only one) of Berlioz. After a stay of two years in the French capital, he returned to Copenhagen, and there brought out his first opera, "Tovelille," in five acts. In 1866 he again went to Paris, composed his opera of "Hjalmar and Ingeborg," and then in company with Berlioz spent the ensuing winter in Vienna. The following year (1867) he was one of the jury that awarded the musical prizes at the exhibition in Paris. He was also decorated with a gold medal for his "Hymne à la paix," written for solo, chorus, orchestra, two organs, thirteen harps, and four church bells. After this he visited Italy, and while there wrote his opera of "La Vendetta,' produced at Milan in 1870. At Vienna he wrote the opera of "The Traveler."

In the autumn of 1870 he came to the United States, and was engaged as director of the conservatory of music connected with the Peabody Institute, Baltimore, a position which he still (Jan., 1885) retains. Since coming here his principal compositions have been five Norse suites for orchestra. A complete list of his works is as follows : "Roland," op. 1; orchestral fantasia, op. 2; symphony in C minor, op. 3; a set of songs, op. 4*; cantata, op. 5; quintet in C minor, for piano, violins, viola, and violoncello, op. 6; overture in D minor, op. 7; fantasia, op. 8; fantasia, op. 9; "Le voile," op. 10*; Christmas cantata, op. 11; "Tovelille," an opera in five acts, op. 12; set of songs, op. 13*; Ave Maria, op. 14*; march, op. 15; "Hymn to Liberty," op. 16; "Hymne à la paix," op. 17*; "Hjalmar and Ingeborg," an opera in five acts, op. 18; Jewish trilogy in C minor for orchestra, op. 19*; "La Vendetta," opera, op. 20*, "The Traveler, op. 21*; first Norse suite, cp. 22*; second Norse suite, op. 23*; third Norse suite, op. 24*; fourth Norse suite, op. 25*; fifth Norse suite, op. 26*; Romance for violoncello, op. 27*; May-dance, op. 28*; Symphonie poétique, No. 1, in F major, op. 29*; Opera without words, op. 30*; Christain trilogy, for orchestra, chorus, baritone solo and organ, op. 31*; Symphonie tragique, No. 2, op. 32*; Symphonie lyrique, No. 3, op. 33* The numbers that are marked with an asterisk are those that have been published; the rest remain in manuscript.

Mr. Hamerik is a thorough musician, has a rare faculty of conducting, and is a fine composer. All of his works are pervaded by that element which is the characteristic of all Norse composers, and in this respect he closely resembles Gade. His summers are spent in visiting his old home and in traveling in Europe.

**Hanchett,** HENRY G., pianist, was born Aug. 29, 1853, at Syracuse, N. Y. When three years old he began to take music lessons of his parents, and at the age of six was placed under the care of Ernest Held, an excellent musician of his native city, with whom he studied nine years. Considerable of his time was occupied with childish amusements, but he became proficient enough to master Liszt's arrangement of Schuberts "Wanderer" and Beethoven's op. 7. Awaking to the necessity of study, he set himself to work with renewed dilligence. Upon proposing to become a professional musician he was opposed by his father, and received no more lessons for some time, but continued to practice. About 1870 he took some lessons in theory from A. J. Goodrich, by whom he was advised and encouraged. Unremitted application, however, brought its penalty, and in 1872 he was attacked by congestion of the brain, which produced intermittent blindness. Four years of absolute rest from study, plenty of exercise, and medical treatment cured him, but it was not until 1878 that he fully resumed study and practice. In 1879 he made his *début* as a player at Chickering Hall, New York City. About this time he received and accepted an offer to become a professor in the Beethoven Conservatory, St. Louis, with which institution he was connected a year or two. He is now (1885) located in New York. In 1881 he went to Germany and examined the methods of study there. While in Berlin he was asked by Dr. Kullak to fill a vacant post as professor of the piano at the Conservatorium. Mr. Hanchett is not only a fine pianist, but an unusually gifted musical writer and lecturer.

**Harmonia Americana.** A collection of church music published at Boston, in 1791, by Samuel Holyoke. The title-page reads; "Harmonia Americana, Containing a concise introduction to the grounds of Music, with a variety of airs suitable to Divine Worship, and the use of Musical Societies, consisting of three and four parts. Boston, Jan. 24, 1791." In the preface, the author condemns the "fuguing" pieces, which were then quite popular. At the time the book was published, Holyoke was but twenty years of age.

**Harmonica.** An instrument invented or rather perfected by Benjamin Franklin, who called it "Armonica." It consisted of a box or trough mounted on legs, through which ran a spindle having a wheel affixed at one end. On this spindle were arranged in regular order, according to their size, glass bells or basons. A treadle was connected with the wheel on the spindle, by which the glasses were made to revolve. The music was produced by applying the fingers to the edges of the glasses, which were kept damp by the water in the trough. The harmonica seems to have been quite fashionable during the latter part of the last and the early part of this century, especially in Europe. The first notable performer thereon was Miss Marianne Davis, for whom Hasse composed music. Another celebrated player, though blind, was Marianna Kirchgässner. So much in favor did the harmonica become, that several great musicians were induced to compose music for it. Mozart wrote an adagio and rondo in C for harmonica, flute, oboe, viola and violoncello. Beethoven also wrote a short piece for it for his friend Duncker, in 1814 or 1815. Attempts at something like the harmonica were made some time before Franklin brought out his instrument, and the capacity of glasses to produce music seems to have been known as early as the middle of the 17th century. It remained, however, for Franklin's practical mind to make a practical musical instrument from them. Attempts have been made to modify or improve the harmonica, but without success thus far.

**Hastings,** DR. THOMAS, was born Oct. 15, 1784, at Washington, Litchfield Co., Conn. In 1796 his parents removed to Oneida County, N. Y., and in 1819 he published "Musica Sacra; or Springfield and Utica Collections

United." He was assisted in the labor by Solomon Warriner of Utica. His "Dissertation on Musical Taste," which created a great deal of discussion, was published in 1822. In 1823 he removed from Albany to Utica, N. Y., where he became editor of a religious publication. He continued to act in this capacity nine years, writing many articles on sacred music. These gained him numerous requests to lecture. In 1832, upon the invitation of twelve New York churches, he removed to that city. From that time he devoted himself to the interests of church music. His works are "Spiritual Songs" (Utica, 1831); "The Christain Psalmodist" (1836), in the preparation of which he was assisted by Dr. William Patton;" "Manhattan Collection," 1837; "Sacred Lyre" (1840); a collection of juvenile and nursery songs, issued about the same time; "The Psalmodist" (1844) "The Choralist"(1847) "Mendelssohn Collection" (1847); "The Psalmista" (1851), these last four being edited in conjunction with Wm. B. Bradbury; and "Selah" (1856). Besides these he issued "Devotional Hymns and Poems," of his own writing, and "The Church Melodies," in which he was assisted by his son, Rev. T. S. Hastings, and edited two collections of hymns and tunes for the American Tract Society and the Presbyterian Board of Publication. During the latter part of life he wrote his "Forty Choirs," which had an extensive circulation, and revised his work on musical taste. His poetical abilities were considerable, and he wrote nearly six hundred hymns, many of which have come to be classed as standards in church poetry. He was also a fine tenor singer. His death occurred May 15, 1872, and was the ending of an eminently useful career.

**Hauck,** MINNIE, was born Nov. 16, 1852, at New York. Her father, as the name indicates, was a German, but her mother was an American lady. Her first public appearance was at a benefit concert in New Orleans in 1865. She studied with Sig. Errani at New York, and in 1868 made her *début* on the stage as *Amina* in "Sonnambula," under the care of Max Maretzek. After singing in the principal cities of this country she visited England and appeared at Covent Garden, Oct. 26, 1868, in the same *rôle*. Later, she sang in Paris, at the Grand Opera, Vienna, and subsequently at Moscow, Berlin and Brussels, everywhere with almost

phenomenal success. In March, 1876, she sang at the Hungarian National Theatre, Pesth, before Wagner, assuming the *rôles* of *Elsa* in "Lohengrin" and *Senta* in "The Flying Dutchman" to that composer's satisfaction. Meanwhile she filled an engagement of several years at the Imperial Opera, Vienna. In 1877 she sang at Berlin with such success that the Emperor of Germany conferred on her the title of "Imperial German Chamber Singer," an honor shared only by Patti and Lucca. Jan. 2, 1878, at Brussels, she created her celebrated *rôle* of *Carmen*, in which she has never been equaled. She returned to her native country in the autumn of the same year, and achieved great triumphs in the leading cities. In 1880 she sang again in London. The following year she was married to Ernst von Hesse-Wartegg, a literary gentleman of Vienna, we believe, but still retains her own name upon the stage. Her voice is a mezzo-soprano of great force and richness, and her use of it proclaims her to be a true artist. She sings with facility in Italian, German, French and Hungarian, and is well versed in literature and the fine arts.

**Hays,** WILLIAM SHAKSPEARE, one of America's most famous song writers, was born July 19, 1837, at Louisville, Ky. He evidenced his love of music when a boy by learning to play several musical instruments. In 1856 he began his career as a song writer. His first song of any consequence was "Evangeline," published by Silas Brainard, Cleveland, Ohio, which had a large sale. It was followed by others, among which were "Wandering Refugee," "Lone Grave by the Sea," "Drummer Boy of Shiloh," and "My Southern Sunny Home," all of which were more or less successful. Thus far Mr. Hays had written more for pleasure and amusement than anything else, and the publishers pocketed all the profits, which was no doubt very agreeable to them. During the war, however, he corresponded with several of the leading music publishing firms of the country to ascertain what inducement they would offer him. The replies were so discouraging that he resolved never to let another of his songs appear in print. Some time after this he met John L. Peters, music-publisher, Cincinnati, Ohio, (subsequently of New York), who offered him $25 each for one or two of his songs. An agreement was afterwards entered into where-by Mr. Peters published all of his songs. He continued to write for Mr. Peters for many years, though receiving tempting offers from other publishers.

The number of Mr. Hays' songs is something like 300. To the most of these he wrote the words as well as the music. Some of the more popular of his productions of which we have the name and number of copies sold are as follows : " Write me a Letter from Home " (350,000), " We Parted by the River Side " (300,000), " Driven from Home " (300,000), "Nora O'Neal "(250,000), "Shamus O'Brien" (200,000), " Mollie Darling" (150,000), "You've Been a Friend to Me " (60,000), " The Moon is out Tonight, Love " (60,000), "Katy McFerran " (60,000), " I'm Still a Friend to You " (50,000), " Mistress Jenks of Madison Square " (40,000). As these figures were made several years ago they have since been considerably increased—for some of the songs still have a fair sale. The total number of copies sold of all Mr. Hays' songs must be several millions. Their extraordinary popularity is due to charming melodies, easy and effective accompaniments, and a genuine feeling. They were written for the masses and by the masses appreciated. Mr. Hays has a wife and one child, and resides at Louisville, which has always been his home. He has for more than twenty-five years been engaged in editorial work, and is now connected with the Louisville *Courier-Journal.*

**Hayter,** A. U., was born Dec. 16, 1799, at Gillingham, England. He was instructed in music by Mr. Corfe, organist of Salisbury Cathedral, whom he afterwards succeeded, retaining the post several years. He then became organist of Hereford Cathedral. In 1835 he came to this country, and was appointed organist of Grace Church, New York. Soon after he went to Boston and became organist of Trinity Church, which position he held for a quarter of a century. From 1838 to 1849 he was also organist of the Handel and Haydn Society. In 1862 he received a stroke of paralysis from which he never fully recovered, and died at Boston, July 28, 1873. His son, GEORGE F. HAYTER, is an able musician, and was for some time organist of the Handel and Haydn Society.

**Heath,** W. F., was born at Corinth, Vt., June 11, 1843. Early in life all his spare time was devoted to the study of music. During the Civil War he was leader of an Illinois regimental band, which headed the procession at President Lincoln's funeral. He subsequently studied under the best teachers in Boston. After filling the positions of teacher of music in the normal school at Iowa City and in the public schools of Marengo, Iowa, he accepted a similar position at Fort Wayne, Ind., which he has filled for thirteen years. He has prepared several works for use in public schools, among which is "Heath's Common-School Music Readers." He was for three years secretary and treasurer of the Music Teachers' National Association.

**Henninges,** DORA, was born Aug. 2, 1860, at Cleveland, Ohio, where her father is a resident physician. She evidenced not only a great love of music but more than ordinary vocal powers at an early age. After some objections on the part of her father, she was permitted to commence studying for a singer. Her first lessons were received of Arthur Mees of her native city. She then successively studied under Sig. Villa and Sig. Steffanoin at Cincinnati, Max Maretzek of New York, and Mme. La Grange of Paris. During much of this time she sang at concerts and oratorios. She made her operatic *début* as *Lenora* in "Fidelio" at the Cincinnati Opera Festival. She has sung much both in the East and West and already gained considerable reputation. If her life is spared she will take a front rank among American singers. Her voice is a fine, clear mezzo-soprano.

**Henschel,** GEORG, was born Feb. 18, 1850, at Breslau. When twelve years old he appeared in public as a pianist, and in 1867 entered the Conservatorium at Leipsic, where he studied under Moscheles, Richter, and Götze. In 1870 he went to Berlin and placed himself under the care of Kiel, with whom he studied composition, and Schulze, with whom he studied the art of singing. His voice developed into a baritone of great force and richness. He speedily achieved such fame as a singer that his services were requested in various parts of Europe. In 1877 he went to England, where he met with great success and where he decided to locate. In 1880 he came to this country on a visit, and soon after married Miss

Lillian Bailey. He was offered various engagements in Boston, where he is still (November, 1882) staying, but whether he will make this country his future home or not is unknown. His compositions are quite numerous, and include a number of fine songs and orchestral pieces. He has also set the 130th psalm for solos, chorus, and orchestra (op. 30).

**Hill,** URIAH C., was born in Greenwich street, New York, about 1802. He learned the violin at an early age, and while a young man played in different orchestras. In 1836 he went to Germany and studied under Spohr at Cassel for some time. He was conductor of the Sacred-Music Society, New York, for some time, and the moving spirit in the formation of the Philharmonic Society in 1842. He invented a kind of piano (which he claimed would never get out of tune) in which small bells were substituted for wires. This he exhibited in New York and then in London. Afterwards, he resided in Cincinnati for several years. On his return East he settled at Patterson, N. J., and invested in real estate, but it proved an unfortunate venture. This with numerous other disappointments completely crushed him, and he took his own life in September, 1875. Hill was not a remarkable musician, but his enthusiasm and devotion gave him success where others of greater ability might have failed, and his sad end is to be greatly regretted.

**Hiltz-Gleason,** MRS. GRACE, was born about 1854, on the banks of the Kennebec, near Portland, Maine, and while still quite young was taken by her mother to Providence, R. I., to be educated. There she pursued her studies for nine years, and in 1872 went to Chicago, accompanied by her mother. For the study of singing she placed herself under the care of Mrs. Sara Hershey-Eddy, with whom she remained four years. She then went to Boston and received instruction from George L. Osgood, Charles R. Adams, Julius Jardan, and Georg Henschel. She continued her studies at Boston for nearly two years, and during a portion of the time sang in the Union Congregationalist Church, Providence, R. I., at a salary of $1,000 a year, also filling many concert engagements. In 1878 she was married to Frederic Grant Gleason, the well-known teacher and composer. After singing the soprano solo in Verdi's " Requiem," at

the Worcester Festival, she went to Paris to complete her studies, receiving lessons from Mme. Viardot-Garcia, Mme. La Grange, and Sig. Sbrilgia. She sang in public several times with good success. Proceeding to London she filled several engagements as a concert singer, and received a flattering offer to make a tour of the English provinces. This she was obliged to decline, as she had already been secured for the second Heimendahl Symphony Concert at Chicago, Dec. 19, 1882, where she made her re-appearance and was received with the warmest tokens of appreciation. Her voice is a pure, rich soprano, of great range and flexibility, and her enunciation nearly perfect. As an interpreter of Franz's, Schumann's, and Schubert's songs she has few equals in this country.

**Hoffman,** RICHARD H., was born in Manchester, England, May 24, 1831, and received his early musical instruction from his father, a pupil of Kalkbrenner and Hummel. Later, he studied under Pleyel, Moscheles, Rubinstein, Döhler, Thalberg, and Liszt. In 1847 he came to New York, where he made his *début* at the " Tabernacle," playing Thalberg's "Sonnambula" and De Meyer's "Semiramide" in a manner that called forth the praise of every one. Shortly after he played at a concert of the Philharmonic Society, and in 1848 undertook a concert tour with Burke the violinist, traveling all over this country and Canada. He was soloist of the first series of the Jenny Lind concerts. In 1854 he was elected honorary member of the Philharmonic Society, New York, and has frequently appeared at its concerts. After this he settled in New York as a teacher and composer and has been very successful. When von Bülow came to the United States in 1875 he again appeared in public and played several duos with him. In January, 1879, he performed Brahm's concert (op. 10) at Chickering Hall—the first time it was heard in this country. He rarely ever appears in public except at the Philharmonic concerts. Mr. Hoffman's works are quite numerous, and almost exclusively for the piano. Many of them are published in Germany and England, and have become very popular. As a player he has great command of his instrument, a remarkably brilliant but exquisitely clear execution, and a pure style, which charms all his hearers. As a teacher he is highly esteemed, not only for his abilities but also for his gentlemanly qualities. He is still (November, 1885) located in New York.

EDWARD, brother of the preceding, is the writer of many popular piano pieces, which have had a wide circulation.

**Hohnstock**, KARL, was born in 1828, in Brunswick, Germany. After giving concerts with good success in the principal European countries, he came to the United States in 1848, gave concerts in Boston and other cities, and finally settled in Philadelphia as pianist, violinist, and teacher. His sister, ADELAIDE, also born at Brunswick, accompanied him on his concert tours, and resided with him at Philadelphia until her death, which occurred in January, 1856. She was a fine pianist.

**Holden**, OLIVER, an American psalmodist, was born in 1765, probably at Charlestown, Mass., where he resided. He was a carpenter by trade, but devoted much of his time to music, and opened a book and music store. In 1793 he published his first collection, "The American Harmony," consisting of tunes arranged for three and four parts, the most of which were original. Soon after he published "Union Harmony, or a Universal Collection of Sacred Music," and in 1795 associated himself with Hans Gram and Samuel Holyoke. Together they produced " The Massachusetts Compiler." In 1797 he was engaged by Isaiah Thomas of Worcester, Mass., to edit the " Worcester Collection of Sacred Harmony," of which several editions were issued. During the latter part of his life he taught and composed very little, but retained his love for music. His tunes were very popular in their day, and some of them are still so. "Coronation" alone will perpetuate his name to the end of time. He died, according to "Moore's Encyclopædia of Music," at Charlestown in 1831, though some writers give 1834 as the date.

**Hook** (E. & G. G.) **& Hastings.**— This church (pipe) organ building firm of Boston is one of the leading ones in America, and ranks among the oldest and best in the world. It was founded by the brothers Hook in 1827. In 1855 Mr. F. H. Hastings was first engaged with them, and now succeeds them. Mr. George G. Hook died in 1880, aged 73 years, and his brother, Elias, the following year, aged 76. By exercising dilli-

gence and turning out only the best work, they built up a large trade, that now requires an extensive manufactory, which is fitted with every convenience for turning out large or small organs. Each department is under the supervision of an expert, who employs only the most skilled workmen. The firm possesses and applies all improvements of worth, being in constant communication with eminent foreign builders, and is an institution of which Americans may well be proud. Mr. Hastings, who now carries on the business, has been over thirty years an organ builder, and to his energy, enterprise and skill the establishment owes much of its rapid growth and prosperity. He became a partner of the Messrs. Hook in 1865, and from that time was the active manager. Up to the present time the old firm name (Hook & Hastings) has been retained, which has become so well known in this country and Europe. The manufactory is one of the objective points toward which music-loving persons visiting Boston gravitate, as visitors are always cordially welcomed.

Up to 1855, the Messrs. Hook had built 170 organs. Since then (March, 1886) this number has been increased to over 1,300. During the years 1882, 1883 and 1884, the number of instruments turned out was respectively 63, 67 and 53. Among those more celebrated, and which are equal to any in point of excellence and finish, are the following ones:

1. The organ in the Music Hall, Cincinnati, built in 1878, which is one of the very largest in this country as well as in the world. Its dimensions are: Width, 47 feet; depth, 30 feet; hight, 70 feet. It has 4 manuals, 96 stops, and 6,237 pipes, divided as follows:

|  | Stops. | Pipes. |
|---|---|---|
| Great organ, | 22 | 2,282 |
| Swell   " | 19 | 1,708 |
| Choir   " | 17 | 1,281 |
| Solo   " | 6 | 366 |
| Pedal   " | 16 | 600 |

and 14 mechanical stops. In addition, there are 12 pedal movements, a grand crescendo pedal, by which the performer may gradually bring into play the whole power of the instrument, and a carillon of 30 bells. Its cost was upwards of $32,000.

2. The organ in Tremont Temple, Boston, erected in 1880. It has 4 manuals, 65 stops, and 3,442 pipes, beside 10 pedal movements,

including a grand crescendo, like that in the Music Hall organ, Cincinnati. In size it is excelled by several organs in this country, but in artistic completeness and perfection it is second to none.

3. The Centennial organ, which was seen and admired by many who visited Philadelphia in 1876. Its dimensions are: Width, 32 feet; depth, 21 feet; hight, 40 feet. It has 4 manuals, 59 stops and 2,704 pipes.

4. The organ in the Cathedral of Holy Cross, Boston, which was erected in 1875. This is probably one of the largest church organs in this country. It has 3 manuals, 83 stops and 5,294 pipes, and is a marvel of workmanship.

**Hopkins,** JEROME, born April 4, 1836, at Burlington, Vt., early took up the study of music, and at the age of twelve years became organist. After awhile, he settled in New York, as pianist, composer, and teacher. He was for some time the editor of the "Philharmonic Journal." His works are numerous and comprise church pieces, songs, piano pieces, fugues, and orchestral and choral pieces.

**Holyoke,** SAMUEL, A. M., was born in 1771, at Boxford, Mass. His father, Dr. Holyoke, soon after removed to Salem, in the same state. In 1791 his first collection of music was issued, under the name of HARMONICA AMERICANA. It was printed at Boston, from type, by Isaiah Thomas and E. T. Andrews, and sold by subscription. All "fugue" tunes, then very popular, were omitted, as being little suited to public worship. In 1806 he published at Exeter, N. H., the first volume of the "Instrumental Assistant," a quarto of 80 pages, and in 1807, the second volume, 104 pages. The two volumes contain about 200 pieces arranged for various instruments. "The Columbian Repository of Sacred Harmony" appeared in 1809, a very voluminous work, containing 472 pages and 750 pieces of music. It was also published by subscription, the price per copy being three dollars. He was associated with O. Holden and Hans Gram in editing THE MASSACHUSETTS COMPILER (1795), and at the time of his death was preparing a third volume of instrumental music. He was extensively known as a teacher, and highly esteemed by all who knew him. His death took place at Concord, N. H., in the spring of 1816, being produced by congestion of the lungs. He ranks among the foremost of early American composers. His tune "Arnheim" is still sung.

**Howard,** FRANK, whose real name is DELOS GARDINER SPALDING, was born in 1833, at Athens, Pa. He was a self-taught performer on several instruments. He led a roving and rather irregular life for some time, but in 1853 settled in Chicago. His claim to mention is as the composer of over 100 songs, many of which have become quite popular, though not of very high order.

**Hutchinson Family.** A family of natural musicians, natives of Milford, New Hampshire, and well-known both in this country and England. Four of the brothers, born from 1818 to 1828, were noted as temperance and anti-slavery singers, from 1846 to 1858. After awhile they became separated, and are now represented by John and Asa with their families.

**Hutchings, Plaisted & Co.,** BOSTON. This firm, which has gained considerable reputation for its church organs, was founded in the fall of 1869, by the late Dr. J. H. Willcox, George S. Hutchings, Mark H. Plaisted, and G. V. Nordstrom. These four gentlemen were previously connected with the house of Hook & Hastings, Dr. Willcox as chief of the musical department, Mr. Hutchings as superintendent, and the other two as heads of different departments. The firm name was at first "J. H. Willcox & Co," which, upon the retirement of Dr. Willcox, in 1872, was changed to Hutchings, Plaisted & Co., the present name. In 1873 Mr. Nordstrom retired from the firm, and his place was filled by C. H. Preston. Mr. Preston dying in 1876, Mr. Hutchings and Mr. Plaisted are now the only members of the house. The firm has constructed upwards of 150 organs, mostly for use in this country. Instruments of their make may be found in the following places: Congregational Church, La Crosse, Wis.; First Baptist Church, Jackson, Mich.; Mechanic's Hall, Salem, Mass.; St. Peter's Church (Catholic), Philadelphia; Presbyterian Church, Wheeling, West Va.; Christ Church, Baltimore, Md.; Methodist Episcopal Church, Malden, Mass.; Baptist Church, Windsor, N. S.; Christ Church, Houston,

Texas ; Old South Church, Boston (64 regis- | registers). The business is now (January, ters) ; Hebrew Chapel, New Orleans ; All | 1886) carried on by Geo. S. Hutchings, as Saints Church, Worcester, Mass. ; and Church | successor to Hutchings, Plaisted & Co. of Immaculate Conception, Lowell, Mass. (52

# I.

**Ingalls,** JEREMIAH, American psalmo-dist, was born March 1, 1764, at Andover, Mass. He was mainly self-taught in music, and became a fair performer on the violon-cello. For many years he taught music in Massachusetts, New Hampshire and Vermont. In 1805 he published at Exeter, N. H., "The Christian Harmony," a volume of 200 pages. He married and settled at Newberry Vt., removed to Rochester, in 1810, and finally to Hancock, where he died April 6, 1828. Some of his church tunes are still in general use, those of "Kentucky" and "Northfield" being familiar to almost every church singer.

**Institute of Music, Normal.** An institution of purely American origin and character. Its aim is, primarily, the prepara-tion of persons desiring to teach music for that profession and the improvement of teach-ers already in the work, and, secondarily, the advancement of musical students in general in the science of music and the cultivation of musical taste and judgment. An Institute generally holds four weeks, during the sum-mer vacation, lessons in harmony, voice-cul-ture, composition, vocal practice, etc., being given daily. Instruction is imparted by a corps of from three to five teachers, each specialists in their own departments. A series of piano recitals is always given by some eminent pianist, the programs consisting of both classical and romantic music. Vocal recitals are also sometimes given. The price of membership in an Institute, which is gen-erally $10, places it within the reach of every-one. This is exclusive of board, which will cost from $4 to $6 per week. As it is held during the season of the year that teachers and students are most at leisure, it offers them a good opportunity for advancement in music. The first normal institute of music was pro-jected by Dr. George F. Root, and held in New York City in 1852. Its faculty consisted of Dr. Lowell Mason, Thomas Has-tings, Wm. B. Bradbury, and Dr. Root. For some years Dr. Root's was the only Normal Institute held. Other teachers, however, soon began to hold Institutes, largely modelled on the same plan, and they are now held in almost every part of the country. Among the best Institutes are those held by Dr. Root, Dr. H. R. Palmer, L. O. Emerson, H. S. and W. O. Perkins, etc. The importance of these Institutes as a factor in the cultivation and im-provement of musical taste is considerable.

# J.

**Jackson,** SAMUEL, was born in New York, Feb. 25, 1818. His father, James Jackson, an Englishman by birth, was an organ builder, and at the same trade he worked until of age. Meanwhile, he studied music with Moran, Thornton and Lozier, well-known teachers in their day, and was considered a precocious youth. He was, at different periods, organist of St. Bartholomew's, Church of the Ascension, and Christ Church. His career of forty-five years as organist terminated at the Anthon Memorial Church in 1875. As a teacher he was very successful. Of his pupils may be mentioned Wm. K. Bassford, the eminent song composer. For twenty-nine years he proof-read every piece of music issued by G. Schirmer, the music-publisher. He died at his home in Brooklyn, July 27, 1885, leaving a family of four children, two sons and two daughters. His compositions number several hundred (besides many arrangements from other composers) and mainly consist of church pieces and services and organ pieces. He also wrote a dictionary of musical terms. He was an organist of sterling qualities, a sound and acute theorist, and a conscientious and eminently successful teacher.

**Jacobsohn,** S. E., violinist, was born at Mitan, Russia, in 1839. His father dying when he was young, he was compelled to aid in supporting the family by playing the violin and other instruments at balls and parties. This state of things continued until he was fifteen years old, when, through the efforts of some friends, he was enabled to go to Riga, where he studied under Weller, making rapid progress. Four years later he was similarly enabled to go to Leipsic, where he entered the Conservatorium and had the benefit of David's instruction. He played at the Gewandhaus concerts and soon achieved a reputation that brought him invitations to play from various quarters. At the end of a year, however, he returned to Mitan and gave concerts in Western Russia with great success. About 1860 he accepted the position of *concertmeister* at Bremen, Germany, where he remained twelve years, meanwhile playing at the Gewandhaus and other concerts. In September, 1872, he came to this country and was engaged by Theodore Thomas as *concertmeister* and soloist in his orchestra. In this capacity he traveled all over the United States and was well received. In 1878 he was engaged as professor of the violin at the College of Music, Cincinnati, a position which he held some four years. Since leaving the College he has established a violin school of his own. Mr. Jacobsohn possesses a great command of his instrument, good taste, and an excellent style.

**Jardine, George & Son.** George Jardine, the head of this firm of church organ builders, located in New York City, was born at Dartford, England, Nov. 1, 1801. He learned his business with the famous London firm of Flight & Robson, who were then considered the first organ builders in England. Young George went to his work in a thorough and systematic manner, and having a natural taste for drawing, he studied architecture in all its various details under competent masters. Many of the most beautiful organ cases to be found in this country are the emanations of his active brain. He came to this country in 1837, bringing his wife and five children, and also his nephew, F. W. Jardine, now of Manchester, England, who, after learning the business of manufacturing organs with his uncle, returned to England and entered into partnership with Mr. Kirtland, in Manchester.

The year Mr. Jardine landed in New York was a time of great financial crisis. Instead of finding churches ready and anxious to purchase organs, he found it rather hard work to find bread for his family, and for the first two years after his arrival he was obliged to turn his hand to various other employments to keep the "wolf from the door." The opportunity to return to his business came at last. He succeeded in obtaining an order to build a small organ for the church of St. James, New York, which marked the beginning of his prosperous career. His workshop was originally in the attic of the house in which he lived, corner of Broadway and Grand street, with one or two workmen at most in his employ. Business increasing from year to year, his factory became more pretentious, until the present large building was erected, which furnishes employment for between 50 and 60 skilled workmen. In the year 1860, Mr. Jardine took into partnership his eldest son, E. G. Jardine, who, like his father, had early evinced a desire to become an organ builder, and was accordingly instructed in the art. Father and son both work at their art, and frequently travel to Europe, keeping themselves well posted on all the latest improvements made abroad.

The following is a partial list of the largest and finest organs built by Messrs. Jardine & Son:

Fifth Avenue Cathedral, New York, - 4
St. George's Church, " - 4
St. Paul's M. E. Church, " - 4
Holy Innocents " " - 4
Brooklyn Tabernacle, - - 4
Pittsburgh Cathedral, - - - - 4
Mobile Cathedral, - - - - 3
First Pres. Church, Philadelphia, - 3
St. John's M. E. Church, Brooklyn, - 3
Trinity Church, San Francisco, - 3
Christ Church, New Orleans, - - 3

**Jarvis,** CHARLES H., pianist, was born at Philadelphia, Dec. 20, 1837, and received his musical education from his father, an excellent musician. He has done much to raise the standard of music in his native city, and since 1862 has given an annual series of classical chamber concerts. He played Beethoven's concerto in G at a concert of the Philharmonic Society, New York, in 1869, and has appeared at various places as soloist.

**Jenks,** STEPHEN, American psalmodist, was born in 1772, at New Canaan, Conn. In 1805 he published "The Delights of Harmony," containing 96 pages of tunes, hymns, anthems, and set pieces, twenty-six of which were original and the rest selected. He afterwards removed to Thompson, Ohio, where he died in 1856. Some of his pieces are still in general use.

**Johnson,** A. N., was born at Middlebury, Vt., about 1825, and early in life went to Boston, where he became organist when eighteen years old. He commenced teaching and conducting conventions, in which capacity he has traveled all over the country. His works are numerous, the most important among which are his "methods" of thoroughbass and harmony. He is the composer of a quantity of church music, and a frequent contributor to various musical publications.

**Joseffy,** RAFAEL, pianist, was born in 1852, at Muskolcz, Hungary. He first studied under Moscheles at Leipsic and then under Thalberg. Diligent application combined with a great degree of natural talent ensured him rapid progress, and he soon began to astonish the people of Vienna with his wonderful playing. After finishing his studies he made a concert tour of Holland and Germany, and won both fame and applause, being everywhere well received. Two or three years ago (1879 or 1880) he came to this country, and has regularly appeared in the principal cities of the Union with great success. As a player he has a marvelous *technique*, noted not only for brilliancy but also for softness and elasticity.

# K.

**Karl,** THOMAS, tenor singer, was born in Ireland, in January, 1847, and educated in England, to which country he was taken at an early age. He commenced studying with the celebrated English basso, Henry Phillips, and by his advice went to Italy to prepare himself for a concert singer and teacher. He then spent several weeks in Paris, taking lessons of Delle Sedie, who urged him to go to Milan, which he did and studied for three years with San Giovanni. One day he was heard by the Italian composer, Enrico Petrella, who desired him to sing in a new opera, "La Contessa d'Amalfi," which he was just on the eve of producing. After much persuasion he was induced to do so, and met with a flattering reception. He had various offers of engagements, and sang in all the important theatres of Milan, from La Scala down. He came to the United States with the Carl Rosa company and appeared in the leading cities. Four seasons ago he joined the Boston Ideal Opera Company as principal tenor, with which organization he has since remained, excepting one season spent with the Emma Abbott Company. Mr. Karl has sung in England, Spain, Italy, Russia, and other European countries, with the most distinguished singers. Much of his time is spent in Boston or in traveling with his company, but he has a summer home at Rochester, N. Y., where he resides during the heated term.

**Kathleen Mavourneen.** One of the few songs which have attained a world-wide reputation. The words are by Mrs. Crawford, a London lady, and the music by F. Nicholls Crouch. It was composed not long after an unsuccessful and disastrous business venture, and during a period of retirement from the world. The composer himself thus gives an account of its inception : "The words had been sent me by Mrs. Crawford from London, and as I was riding one day in West England on the banks of the Tamar, thinking of the poem, the melody suddenly came to me. I was so infatuated with it that I sang it to a large audience in the assembly rooms at Ply-mouth, Devonshire, immediately that I had written it down, and within a week its fame had spread. Thus was my offspring begotten and so became a child of the world." The writer of this beautiful song, which has often been sung with great applause by noted singers, is now residing at Baltimore, Md., at a very advanced age and in destitute circumstances.

**Kellogg,** CLARA LOUISE, one of the most celebrated American *prima donnas*, was born of northern parents at Sumterville, South Carolina, in July, 1842. In 1856 the family removed to New York, where Clara received her musical education. Her *début* was made in 1861, as *Gilda* in "Rigoletto," at the New York Academy of Music. Nov. 2, 1867, she appeared at Her Majesty's Theatre, London, as *Margherita*, with such success as to be re-engaged for the next season. She returned home in 1868, and from that time until 1872 sang in the principal cities of the United States, being warmly received wherever she went. In 1872 (May 11) she again appeared in London at Drury Lane, as *Linda* and also as *Gilda*. In 1874 she organized an opera company, assuming general direction of the affairs herself, with which she successfully traveled throughout the Union. Since that time she has repeatedly visited the principal cities, always with success. Her voice is a high soprano of great clearness and purity, which she controls in an excellent manner. She is said to be acquainted with thirty-five operas, but her best *rôle* is that of *Margherita* in "Faust." Many interesting incidents might be gleaned from her career. It is related that upon one occasion when Miss Kellogg and Mme. Pauline Lucca were singing in St. Louis as rivals, the Germans espoused the cause of Lucca and the Americans that of Kellogg. The Germans took up a subscription and on the first night of Lucca's appearance presented her with a bouquet of flowers costing $35. On the following evening the friends of Miss Kellogg made her a present of a turret of rare roses, nearly eight feet high, which was laid at her feet during one of the performances and elicited overwhelming applause. The cost was $135. This excited the friends of Lucca, and they raised over $200, which they presented to the celebrated songstress in the shape of a laurel wreath lined with pure gold. But the Americans were not to be outdone, and presented their favorite with a gold medal and chain costing nearly $350. This ended the competition.

**Keller,** MATTHIAS, born March 20, 1813, at Ulm, Wurtemburg, was in early life a bandmaster, and in 1846 came to this country. He located in Philadelphia as a violinist, subsequently became conductor of the English opera in New York, and finally removed to Boston. His songs are numerous, but he is perhaps best known as the composer of the "American Hymn," performed at the Great Peace Jubilee of 1869 by a chorus of over 10,000 voices and an orchestra of 1100 performers.

**Key,** FRANCIS SCOTT, the author of the words to our national song, "The Star Spangled Banner," was born in Maryland in 1780. He was about thirty-four years of age when he wrote the hymn which will carry his name down to posterity. A volume of poems from his pen was published in 1857. He died in 1843. The remains repose in a cemetery near Washington, and the grave is marked by a plain marble slab bearing this inscription: "Francis Scott Key, born Aug. 9, 1780; died Jan. 11, 1843." By the side of this is another slab marked as follows: "Mary Taylor Key, born May 26, 1784; died May 18, 1859."

**Keyed violin.** An instrument exhibited in New York, in 1848, having five octaves of strings, stretched as in a piano. At right angles and within a minute distance of each string passes a horsehair bow. These bows are kept in motion by machinery worked by a pedal. On pressing the keys of the keyboard, which is the same as that of a piano or organ, bows are brought into contact with the corresponding strings, and sounds similar to those of a violin produced.

**Keynote, The.** A weekly publication devoted to the interests of music in general. Edited by Frederic Archer; published by John J. King. Each number contains 20 pages. Subscription price $4.00 per annum. Established in 1883.

**Kimball,** JACOB, one of the early American psalmodists, was born at Topsfield, Mass., in February, 1761. He was a lawyer by profession, but music proved the most enticing and he left his first love. In 1793 he published "Rural Harmony," the music of which was largely original. He taught music in various New England towns for many years, and wrote numerous church pieces. That he was not very successful in worldly affairs would seem from the fact that he became an inmate of the poor house at his native place, where he died Feb. 26, 1826.

**Kinkel,** CHARLES, the composer of many light, pleasing piano pieces, was born in the Rheinpfalz, Germany, in 1832. He was not specially educated in music, though he always evidenced a great love therefor. The Revolution of 1848 produced such an unsettled state of things in Germany that he resolved to leave, and the following year he arrived in the United States. On observing the opportunities for success in the musical profession, he entered the ranks, and for twenty years was professor of music at the Science Hill Female Academy, Shelbyville, Ky. His compositions are almost exclusively piano pieces, many of which are designed for teaching purposes. Among the more popular we may mention "Angel's Serenade," "Pearl and Daisy Polka," "Polymnia Polka," "Postillion d'Amour," "Mabel Mazurka," "Angel of Night," and "Lover's Serenade."

**Knabe, William & Co.** A firm of American piano manufacturers, located at Baltimore, Maryland. William Knabe, the founder of the house, was born at Kreutzberg, in the Duchy of Saxe Weimer, Germany, in 1803. Early in life he was apprenticed to a cabinet maker, and, later, to Langehan, a piano maker of Gotha, with whom he remained three years. After leaving Gotha he traveled throughout Germany, and finally came to this country and settled in Baltimore. He entered the service of Mr. Hartge, a piano manufacturer, with whom he stayed four years. At the expiration of that time he went into business for himself, and in 1839 took into partnership H. Gaehle. From this time the business rapidly and steadily increased, both being men of energy and skill. In 1855 the partnership was dissolved by the death of Mr. Gaehle, but the business was continued under the firm name of Wm. Knabe & Co. by Mr. Knabe. Five years later, or in 1860, the erection of the present large and commodious factory was begun, to accommodate the constantly increasing trade. Mr. Knabe died in 1864, and was succeeded by his two sons, William and Ernest, and his son-in-law, Charles Keidel, who constitute the present firm. The War of the Rebellion caused serious interruption to the business of the firm, and compelled them to seek new channels for their trade, which they did in the North and West. This eventually proved to be the most beneficial thing that could have happened to them, as it extended their trade all over the country and made their reputation a national one.

Messrs. Knabe & Co. are one of the leading piano manufacturing firms of the country, and their factory is one of the chief institutions of Baltimore. It is a massive structure five stories high, and is fitted with every possible convenience for turning out first-class work. The firm has a branch house in New York City and active agencies all over the world. There is a large demand for their instruments from Europe, and even from Japan. The Knabe piano possesses in all respects every requisite of a first-class instrument, and is used by artists and musicians everywhere.

**Kreissmann,** AUGUST, was born in 1823, at Frankenhausen, Saxony. He studied singing at Dresden, Vienna, and Milan, and about 1849 came to the United States, settling in Boston. For many years he was conductor of the famous "Orpheus Club," and was very successful as a teacher, numbering among his pupils some who are now excellent musicians. He was the pioneer of and contributed greatly to the popularity of German *lieder*, especially those of Franz. His singing was expressive and intelligent, and his voice, a tenor, full, sweet and sympathetic. On account of failing health, he returned to Germany in 1876, and died at Gera, March 12, 1879. He was of a kindly nature, and highly esteemed by all who knew him.

**Kunkel Brothers.** A music publishing and dealing firm located at St Louis, Mo., formed about 1868. It is one of the leading houses west of the Mississippi river. They have an extensive catalogue, mainly comprising piano music of the better class.

JACOB, the younger brother, was born Oct. 22, 1846, at Kleiniedesheim, Germany. He studied with his father and elder brother, Charles, and afterwards with Gottschalk. He was also a nominal pupil of Tausig. While very young he came to this country, and in 1868 located in St. Louis, where in conjunction with his brother he entered into the music dealing business and commenced the publication of "Kunkel's Musical Review." He was a pianist of extraordinary ability and in the rendering of poetical compositions had few equals. Tausig, to whom he went for lessons, said to him : "I can not take you as a pupil—I have nothing to teach you. You are a finished pianist of the first rank. You can come to me as a friend, and I am willing to make suggestions as to the interpretation of the works you may choose to play, but that is all." His compositions, mostly piano pieces, are quite numerous. He did at St. Louis, Oct. 16, 1882.

CHARLES, the elder brother, was born July 22, 1840, at Sippersfeld, in the Rheinpfalz. He came to the United States in 1849, when only nine years of age. His musical studies were pursued under the care of his father, a good musician, Thalberg and Gottschalk. In 1868 he removed with his brother to St. Louis, where they engaged in the music business and where he now (March, 1886) resides. He has written many piano pieces of more than ordinary merit, both under his own name and under *noms de plume*. As a pianist he ranked with his brother, with, perhaps, greater range of interpretation. His *duo* playing with his brother was unequaled, and was warmly commended by Anton Rubinstein when he visited St. Louis, in January, 1873. As a sight reader he has few equals either in this country or Europe.

**Kunkel's Musical Review.** A 48 to 60 page musical publication, full sheet-music size, issued by the foregoing firm. From 16 to 30 pages are devoted to musical articles, sketches, reviews, and criticisms, and 24 or more pages contain vocal and instrumental music. It is edited by I. D. Foulon, A. M., LL.B., and is published monthly. Established in 1878. Subscription price, $2.00 per annum. Circulation about 23,000.

# L.

**La Jeunesse.** The family name of Albani. See ALBANI, MARIE EMMA.

**Lang,** BENJAMIN JOHASON, was born in 1840, at Salem, Mass., and when only eleven years of age became organist of one of the churches of his native city. His first musical instruction was received from his father; he then studied under Alfred Jaell, Gustav Satter, and F. Hill, and subsequently went to Europe to study with Liszt. Since then he has several times been abroad for instruction and to obtain a thorough knowledge of foreign musical culture. During these trips he has occasionally given concerts in Berlin, Dresden, Vienna, and other places with good success. Mr. Lang has always resided at Boston, where he was appointed organist of the Handel and Haydn Society in 1859, conductor of the Apollo Club upon its organization in 1871, and leader of the Cecilia Society upon its organization in 1874, all of which posts he has ably filled and still retains. This, however, does not indicate his activity, for he occupies a leading place in Boston's musical affairs. His energy, ability and good sense have promoted and successfully carried through many musical undertakings. To him belongs the credit of having first produced in Boston many notable works, among which are Mendelssohn's "Lobgesang," "Walpurgis Nacht," "Athalia," "Loreley," and "Antigone;" Haydn's "Seasons;" Schumann's "Paradise and the Peri;" Berlioz's "Le Damnation de Faust;" and Beethoven's "Ruins of Athens." He is highly esteemed as a teacher, and of his many pupils over sixty are concert soloists. Though not a *virtuoso* in the strictest sense of the word, he is a fine player, and above all a thoroughly educated and sound musician. His calmness and presence of mind under all circumstances and surety of score reading has more than once saved a careless or nervous performer from disaster. These qualities make him one of the best conductors, and enabled him to successfully act in that capacity for the belligerent von Bülow and the meteoric Joseffy. Mr. Lang has for many years faithfully filled the position of organist at the leading Unitarian Church, Boston. His compositions are numerous and have frequently been performed in public, but thus far none of them have been published.

**Lavallée,** CALIXA, pianist and composer, was born at Vercheres, Dec. 28, 1842, and is of French extraction. His first lessons were received from his father, and such was his progress that at the age of ten years he made his first public appearance. At the age of fifteen, through the financial aid of some of his father's friends, he was sent to Paris, where he studied under Marmontel, Boieldieu and Bazin. While there he wrote a number of works, particularly a "Suite d'Orchestre," which gained a public performance. For several years he made Paris his home, meanwhile traveling all over Europe. He was recalled to his native country to found a conservatory of music, but the scheme proved a failure. While in Quebec, he was requested by the Government to write a cantata for the reception of the Princess Louise and the Marquis of Lorne, on their arrival in Canada. The work was composed and scored in one month, and rendered by a chorus of five hundred voices and an orchestra of 80 performers. It was very highly complimented, but Mr. Lavallée was kindly left to "pay the fiddler" himself. Not long after this, he removed to the United States, and has for some time been a resident of Boston.

Mr. Lavallée is a warm advocate of American music and musicians. At the meeting of the Music Teachers' National Association in Cleveland, in July, 1884, he gave a piano recital from American composers alone, which was well received. Through his efforts, the Association gave two concerts of American works, vocal and instrumental, at its last meeting (July, 1885) in New York. During the winter of 1884-5, he also gave two concerts in Boston, the music of which was purely American. He has also given a series of American concerts during the past winter. He is an active member of the M. T. N. A., and at present chairman of the program committee. As a pianist he ranks among the foremost in the country. His execution is brilliant, facile, graceful and clear; his *technique* wonderful, and his *répertoire* extensive. Among his works are two operas, one symphony, a book of piano studies, and many piano and vocal pieces. Most of them have been published in Europe, though a few have appeared in this country. An offertory, "Tu es Petrus," and an oratorio are his latest works. Mr. Lavallée is at present (January, 1886) connected with the Petersilea Academy of Music at Boston.

**Law,** ANDREW, one of the early American church composers, was born in 1748, at Cheshire, Conn. From whence his musical education was derived is not known, but he was probably largely self-taught. For many years he was a very successful teacher of music in New England and in the South, and seems to have been much in demand, having a good general education in addition to his knowledge of music. In 1782 he published at Cheshire a volume entitled "A Collection of the best and most approved Tunes and Anthems known to exist." A second volume followed, and both were subsequently combined under the name of "Christian Harmony." His first work was probably a "Musical Primer," published in 1780. In 1786 he published an "Original Collection of Music," at Baltimore, Md., and in 1792 the fourth edition of a work entitled "The Rudiments of Music," containing 76 pages. A copy of this work, formerly owned by Timothy Swan, is now in the library of the Harvard Musical Association. About the beginning of the century his "Art of Singing" was issued. It consisted of three departments, or rather three works combined under one head. The first was the "Musical Primer," the second the "Christian Harmony," and the third the "Musical Magazine." This was the first musical publication of America. Law died at Cheshire, Conn., in July, 1821. He was the composer of many church tunes, some of which are still known. Many of his works were printed in a notation of his own invention, in which the heads of the notes were square, diamond, quarter diamond, half diamond, etc., according to kind. A similar notation is used by some petty publishers at the present day.

**Leavitt,** W. J. D., was born at Boston, June 28, 1841, and commenced the study of music at an early age. After having studied for some time with such teachers as his native city then afforded, he went to Europe and finished his musical education under the best instructors there. After returning to this country, he was from 1865 to 1870 principal of the Oneida Conservatory, Oneida, N. Y. In 1870 he returned to Boston, where he is still located as an organist and teacher. Since 1875 he has had charge of the large organ in the Music Hall, Boston, and has given several hundred recitals upon it of classical and other music. Mr. Leavitt's works, which are highly esteemed, extend to op. 65. Among the more important are "The Coronation of David," op. 11; Instructions for the Organ, op. 29; "Mercedes," a grand opera, op. 44; Andante and Polonaise for orchestra, op. 46; "The Lord of the Sea," cantata, op. 48; "Camb'yses, or the Pearl of Persia," operatic cantata, op. 50; Organ Sonata, op. 51; "The Adventure Club," comic operetta for male voices, op. 55; and "Flowers and Lilies," comic operetta for male voices, op. 56. The balance of the works consist of a Bridal and Torchlight March for the organ, organ fantasies, piano *études*, three sets of quartets for male voices, numerous sacred pieces, songs, orchestral compositions, etc.

**Lee & Walker.** A music publishing firm of Philadelphia, Pa., which was founded in 1848, by Julius Lee and William Walker. The firm was successor to George Willig, who established himself in business in that city as early as 1794, Lee and Walker having been clerks in his store. Mr. Walker died in 1857, and the business was carried on by Mr. Lee under the same firm name, which had now become well known. Mr. Lee dying in 1875, the business was temporarily suspended, and in 1876 the stock and publications of the firm were bought by Ditson & Co., who established J. E. Ditson & Co. in business as successors. Meanwhile, Julius Lee Jr. and J. F. Morrison entered into partnership and continued the business under the old and well-known firm name, Lee & Walker. The firm has published many popular works, especially those by Sep. Winner ("Alice Hawthorne"), whose first song they issued about 1850. They confine themselves more to the publication of a light, popular class of music, rather than of the heavy, classical works; and in this line they have been very successful.

**Lennon, J. G.,** pianist, organist and conductor, was born at Lowell, Mass., about 1855. While still quite young, he studied with various Boston teachers, among whom were G. E. Whiting, Carlyle Petersilea and Dr. J. H. Willcox. In 1874, having held several positions as organist, he went to Europe for study, having Haupt and Loeschorn for teachers while at Berlin. At Paris he was a pupil of Edouard Batiste. On his return to Boston, Mr. Lennon became organist of St. Augustine Church. At present (March, 1886) he is organist and director of music at St. Peter's Church, which has a very fine organ built under his supervision. He is also conductor of the Boston Oratorio Society.

**Lenora.** A cantata for four solos, chorus, and orchestra. The poem is by Burger; the music by George E. Whiting. Composed since 1878. It still remains in manuscript, and has not yet been performed.

**Leonora.** An American opera by W. H. Fry. First produced at the Academy of Music, New York, March 29, 1858.

**Levy,** JULES, one of the most celebrated cornet soloists of the present time, was born about 1840. When only five years old he began to practice on the cornet; and is entirely self-taught, excepting a few lessons received to assist him in the proper formation of the lip. At the age of seventeen he became a member of the Grenadier Guard's Band, then under the direction of Godfrey, and in 1860 made his *début* at Floral Hall, near Covent Garden, London. From there he went to Crystal Palace, Sydenham, but was soon after engaged by Alfred Mellon for his promenade concerts at Covent Garden, playing also during the day at Crystal Palace. He remained with Mellon until 1864, when he went to Paris and was engaged as soloist. In the latter part of the year he first came to this country, accompanying Mme. Parepa-Rosa and being under the management of Mr. Bateman. On returning to Europe he filled various engagements in London and Paris, and in 1868 came to this country the second time, under the management of Parepa-Rosa herself. In 1870 he was engaged as solo cornetist in the Ninth Regiment Band. Six months after he left New York for Russia, accompanying the Grand Duke Alexis. He remained in Russia until 1873, when he went to England and played at Riviere's concerts, Covent Garden. In 1875 he came to the United States for the third time, since when, excepting a portion of 1876, 1877, and a portion of 1878, when he was in Australia, he has made his home here, and has been the most of the time under P. S. Gilmore's management. He is universally considered to be one of the leading cornet players of the world, having a good style and great facility of execution.

**Liberati,** ALESSANDRO, one of the most celebrated of living cornet *virtuosi*, was born at Frascati, a small town fourteen miles from Rome, July 7, 1847. At the age of twelve years he began to study cornet playing under the care of Nini. After filling various positions as soloist in Europe, he in 1872 came to America, landing in Boston in October of that year. Soon after he proceeded to Ottawa, Canada, where he became very popular and where he remained about three years. He accompanied the Detroit National Guard Band to the Centennial Exposition as leader. From Detroit he went to Boston, playing both there and in New York. He played at Chicago in 1880, at New Orleans in 1883, and at Louisville, Ky., in the same year. He has repeatedly appeared in the principal cities of the country, always with the greatest success. As a cornetist he has a wonderful execution, playing the most intricate music at sight. He has written numerous compositions for the cornet.

**Liebling,** EMIL, was born April 12, 1851, at Pless, near the Austrian frontier. He first studied under Adam Kong, a blind pianist, and then under Ehrlich of Berlin, whither his parents had removed. At the age of twelve years he appeared in public as a pianist at Liebig's Symphony Concerts, and played *duos* with his teacher. In 1867 he came to this country, and from that time until 1871 was a teacher of music in a seminary for ladies, in Kentucky. In the latter named year he went to Europe for study, but returned in 1872 and settled in Chicago. He again went abroad in 1874, studied with Kullak at Berlin during the ensuing winter, next went to Vienna and studied with Dachs and Kreun, and after six months went back to Berlin and resumed his studies under Kullak. In the spring of 1876 he went to Weimar and stayed with Liszt for a short time, after which he returned to his home in Chicago. While at Berlin he frequently appeared in public at concerts, and was highly praised by the critics for his finely developed *technique*, excellent touch, and true interpretation of works of the masters. In 1877 he gave concerts in Steinway Hall, New York, and in other principal cities of the country. He has also played with Thomas' orchestra, and taken two trips throughout the West with Wilhelmj, the violinist.

Mr. Liebling is one of the foremost American pianists. His *répertoire* contains a large number of classical pieces from Beethoven, Bach, Mozart, Handel, Haydn, etc. He is not only a *virtuoso* but a musician as well. His compositions include a nocturne ("First Meeting"), "Le Meteor," "Galop de Concert," "Gavott modern," "Valse de Concert," and some songs and other pieces, all of merit. At present (1885) he is still located in Chicago, where he is highly esteemed as a teacher and player.

**Listemann,** BERNHARD, was born in 1841, at Schlotheim, Thuringia, and early evinced a great love for the violin. So great was his progress thereon that when a small child he appeared in public at his native place, playing the Adagio of Spohr's 9th Concerto and David's variations on "The Little Drummer Boy." He went to Leipsic, where he studied under David for some time, and then accepted the position of *kammer-virtuos* to the reigning prince at Rudolstadt. This post he retained nine years, and also continued his studies under Joachim and Vieuxtemps at Leipsic. In 1867 he came to the United States, speedily took a leading position, and in 1871 was engaged by Theodore Thomas as a solo violinist. He afterwards held the same position in the orchestra of the Harvard Musical Association, and organized a concert company and a string quartet. In 1880, upon the formation of the Philharmonic Society, Boston, he became its first conductor. As a violinist he takes high rank, possessing all the qualities of a true artist. His works are not numerous. Besides a number of minor pieces, he has written a symphony in C minor, which remains in manuscript, and a school for the violin, published in Boston. He is at present located in Boston, and is *chef d' attaque* in the Symphony Orchestra.

**Litta,** MARIE, whose real name was MARIE VON ELSNER, was born June 1, 1856, at Bloomington, Ill., where her father was a musician. She sang in concerts almost from infancy, and when thirteen had attracted such attention that she was placed under John Underner of Cleveland, Ohio. After studying for some time under Mr. Underner she was enabled, through the liberality of her friends, to visit Paris, where she remained a year with Mme. Viardot-Garcia. She then made her *début* as *Isabella* in "Robert le Diable" at Drury Lane, London, May 20, 1876, under Col. Mapleson's management. Returning to Paris she continued her studies with Mme. La Grange. At the end of six months she made her first appearance in that city at the Grand Opéra in "Lucia di Lammermoor" with great success. Her American *début* was at McVicker's theatre, Chicago, Nov. 16, 1878, as *Lucia* in "Lammermoor." She sang for several years in various parts of the country, firmly establishing her reputation. But her career was destined to be short, for she died at her native place, in July, 1883, greatly lamented. With her death a brilliant and rising star ceased to shine.

**Lucas,** GEORGE W., was born April 12, 1800, at Glastenbury, Hartford Co., Conn. He studied music under Thomas Hastings at Albany and New York, and when sixteen years old commenced teaching in his native state. In 1828 he was elected honorary member of the Handel and Haydn Society at Boston, and in 1842 of the Sacred-Music Society of Montreal. In 1843 he was president of the National Musical Convention, which was held at Boston. He has traveled all over the United States and Canada as a lecturer and teacher of vocal music, numbering his pupils by the thousands. From 1820 to 1835 he was a resident of Northampton, Mass., from 1835 to 1837 of Charlestown, and from 1837 to 1844 of Troy, N. Y. After this he went West but returned to Northampton in 1852 or 1853. His subsequent history has not been learned.

**Ludden,** WILLIAM, was born in 1823, at Williamsburg, Mass. In 1840 he commenced the study of music with George James Webb and Dr. Lowell Mason at Boston. Two years later he located in Pittsfield in his native state as

a teacher of music, and in 1844 became professor of music in Williston Seminary. In
1846 he entered the freshman class in Yale
College, at the same time assuming the duties
of organist and chorister at Trinity Church,
New Haven, which he discharged for seven
years. The Beethoven Society, composed of
college students, chose him as their president
and conductor in 1847, and under his care the
public performances assumed a high order.
Among the works given was Félicien David's
"Le Désert," of which several repetitions
were demanded. After graduating in 1850 he
entered the medical department of the college,
meanwhile teaching music. In 1853 he went
to Paris and studied voice-culture under the
best masters, also completing his medical
studies. The following year he returned,
married Miss M. J. Blatchley, one of his former pupils, and devoted his time to giving vocal
lessons, which he made a specialty. After a
very successful period of teaching, the last
eight years of which were spent in Chicago,
he in 1870 removed to Savannah, Ga., and
with J. A. Bates formed the firm of Ludden &
Bates, music dealers, of which he is still
(1884) an active partner. During his
residence in Savannah he was editor of the
"Southern Musical Journal." In 1880 he removed to New York City, where he is still
located, devoting his time mainly to the preparation of musical works. Among those
already issued are "Thorough-Bass School,"
"Sacred Lyrics," "School for the Voice,"
etc., and more recently, "Ludden's Pronouncing Dictionary of Musical Terms" (12-
mo., 1876), a very complete and handy little
volume, "Standard Organ School," and others.

**Lyon & Healy.** The name of a musical firm located in Chicago, who commenced
business about the year 1865. They deal very
largely in band and orchestral instruments and
supplies, and in this respect they take a leading position among the various music houses
of the West.

**Lyons Musical Academy,** LYONS,
N. Y., is one of the oldest as well as best institutions of its kind in the United States. It
was founded in January, 1854, by L. H. Sherwood, father of the celebrated pianist and
composer, Wm. H. Sherwood, at the request
of numerous friends, who had observed his
special aptitude for teaching. The primary
object of the school is a thorough instruction
of its pupils in the different branches of music,
both theoretical and practical, especially of
those who desire to become teachers. Some
idea of the success which has attended it may
be inferred from the fact that its graduates and
*elves*, scattered all over the country, many of
whom fill positions of honor, are unusually
successful. A special and very excellent
feature of the school is the giving of daily
piano lessons to the students individually.
More than ordinary attention is also given to
the classes in theory, including harmony, and
the art of fingering; indeed, the Academy is
everywhere noted for its thorough and logical
methods. It is still under the excellent care
of its founder.

# M.

**Maas,** DR. LOUIS, well known both in this country and Europe as a pianist and composer, was born at Wiesbaden, Germany, June 21, 1852. His father, Theodor Maas, was a music teacher, and taught him the rudiments of the art. His youth was mostly spent in London, where the family resided from 1854, excepting a short period. He was placed in the King's College, from which he graduated when fifteen years of age. His musical talents, which were early manifested, now became so strong and so evident that the same year (1867) he was sent to the Conservatorium at Leipzig, where he had Reinecke and Papperitz for teachers. He remained there four years, making very rapid progress. During this time he made his *début* at a concert in the Ducal Theatre, Weimar. For three years he studied with Liszt during the summer, and filled concert engagements during the winter. By this time his reputation as a composer was becoming extended. A string quartet of his was highly praised by Liszt. In 1875 he was appointed professor of the piano at the Leipzig Conservatorium. He had over 300 pupils there, many of them Americans.

In November, 1880, he came to the United States, landing at New York. He soon went to Boston, where he has since resided. During the season of 1881–82 he conducted the concerts of the Philharmonic Society, Boston, in a brilliant and successful manner. He has since often appeared in the principal cities of this country and always with uniform success. Dr. Maas possesses a *technique* which is as nearly as possible perfect. In the most rapid passages, even though pianissimo, every note may be distinctly heard, and this clearness of touch is not lost in the forte passages. His playing is refined and delicate, but does not lack spirit and fire ; indeed, it is of sufficient breadth to include every class of composition, and justly ranks him among the foremost pianists of our times. His compositions are of high order, and consist of overtures, symphonies, string quartets, concertos, characteristic pieces, piano pieces, etc. His second (American) symphony, op. 15, is a work of importance. It consists of four divisions, 1. "Morning on the Prairies," 2. "The Chase" (Scherzo) presto, 3. "An Indian Legend," adagio-andante, 4. "Evening, Night, and Sunrise." It was suggested to him while crossing the great prairies of the West, and is dedicated to Ex-President Arthur. Rendered for the first time at the Music Hall, Boston, Dec. 14, 1883, with great success.

**Macy,** JAMES C., song writer, was born at New York City about 1840 and educated at Elmira, N. Y. For many years he has resided in the West, and has for a long time been connected with the music publishing house of S. Brainard's Sons, Cleveland. Among his most popular songs are "Baby Mine," "Don't be Crying, Little Girl," "Down by the Garden Wall," "Echoes," "Little Vacant Chair," "Somebody's Coming when the Dewdrops Fall," and "When My Rover Comes Again." Of his popular piano pieces we may name "First of the Season" galop, "Belles of Virginia Waltzes," "Beta Theta Pi Waltzes," and "Saratoga Life" galop. Mr. Macy has written anthems, hymn tunes, etc., and compiled several collections of music. He frequently writes under the names of "Marion," "Collin Coe" and "Rosabel."

**Main,** SYLVESTER, was born April 18, 1817, at Weston, Conn., and became a teacher of music when only fifteen years old. In 1853 he went to New York, associated himself with I. B. Woodbury in editing music books, and afterwards with W. B. Bradbury. He was teacher, composer and conductor, and for some time editor of the "New York Musical Review." In conjunction with L. H. Biglow he formed the music publishing house of BIGLOW & MAIN, successors to W. B. Bradbury. He edited or assisted in editing more than twenty collections of music, mostly for the church. His death took place October 5, 1873, at Norwalk, Conn.

**Main,** HUBERT PLATT, was born Aug. 17, 1839, at Ridgefield, Conn., and when ten years old was able to readily read music at sight. In 1855 he commenced writing hymn tunes, and afterwards assisted both Bradbury and Woodbury in compiling and editing numerous collections of music. He became connected with the house of Biglow & Main in 1868, since when he has had a general oversight of the business, but devotes some of his time to composition. He has written considerable music for the church, and edited many of the books published by the firm with which he is connected.

**Mann,** ELIAS, American psalmodist, was born in 1750, at Weymouth, Mass. He was for many years a teacher of singing at Northampton, Mass., where he published in 1778 "The Northampton Collection." He also published some music books at Dedham, Mass., and in 1807 "The Massachusetts Collection," issued at Boston. His death took place at Northampton, May 12, 1825.

**Maretzek,** MAX, well-known in this country as an *impresario*, composer and vocal teacher, was born at Brünn, Austria, in June, 1822. After attending school in his native place, he went to Vienna and graduated from the University there. He then took up the study of medicine, which he pursued for two years, at the same time receiving lessons in theory and composition from *kapellmeister* Ritter von Seyfried. Becoming disgusted with medicine, he devoted his whole time to music. He commenced writing operas, among which is "Hamlet" (1843), but finding that it did not prove remunerative, turned his attention to composing dance pieces, which were more profitable. After this he became conductor of an orchestra, with which he successfully visited many of the principal cities of Europe. In 1847 he came to the United States, and engaged in conducting an orchestra. Since that time he has been the manager of many operatic enterprises, meeting with varying success. His schemes, when trying to elevate art, have generally exhibited a wrong balance sheet, but when trying to amuse the masses have proved correspondingly remunerative. Mr. Maretzek, though nearly sixty-four years old, is, as he humorously puts it, "still alive and kicking," being actively engaged in the operatic field.

**Marsh,** SIMEON BULKLEY, was born June 1, 1798, at Sherburne, Chenango Co., N. Y., and sang in a church choir when eight years of age. In 1817 he commenced teaching, and soon after composing. He published at Schenectady, N. Y., three juvenile singing books. He also wrote two cantatas, "The Savior" and "King of the Forest." One alone of his tunes, "Martyn," will perpetuate his name for many years to come. His death occurred in 1875.

**Mason & Hamlin Organ and Piano Company,** BOSTON, MASS. This firm, though not the oldest, ranks among the very foremost of American reed organ manufacturers, a position which it has long held. The business of the firm was founded April 10, 1854, by Henry Mason, a son of Dr. Lowell Mason, and Emmons Hamlin, who had been a workman in the establishment of George A. Prince & Co., of Buffalo, N. Y. These two gentlemen possessed all the qualifications, both musical and mechanical, necessary for producing the best instruments. Of course, at first the business of the firm was quite limited, and during the first year they turned out only 459 melodeons, which, however, was a good number for that time. From this beginning the business rapidly increased. January 28, 1868, the name of the firm was changed to Mason & Hamlin Organ Company, Messrs. Henry Mason and Emmons Hamlin being actively connected with the management of the Company. About this time the firm was strengthened by the admission of Lowell Mason, also a son of Dr. Lowell Mason. Lowell filled the office of president until his death, Oct. 19, 1885. Henry, formerly treasurer, is now president.

Messrs. Mason & Hamlin at first manufactured only melodeons, the melodeon being at that time the chief and best reed instrument. It was in 1847 that Mr. Hamlin of the firm, then in the employment of Prince & Co., made his great improvement in the voicing of the reeds. This consisted in slightly bending and twisting the tongue of the reed in a peculiar manner. The result was that the tone, which before had been thin and sharp, now became more musical. It is no exaggeration to say that this one improvement more than everything else combined has saved the reed organ from falling into oblivion, and made it worthy to rank among other modern musical instruments. This improvement, when applied to melodeons, contributed greatly to their popularity, and was soon adopted by every maker.

In 1861, the firm introduced the first cabinet or parlor organ in its present form. In construction it differed very materially from the melodeon, and had a fuller and more powerful tone. The popularity of the melodeon soon began to wane before this formidable rival. As a name, organ was very wisely chosen, the terms reed, cabinet, or parlor, being used to distinguish it from the pipe organ. The organs at present manufactured by the Mason & Hamlin Organ and Piano Co. are of almost every style and size, and range in price from $22 to $1500. Some of them are fully equal to small pipe organs in power and resource. The present large factories of the firm are located in Cambridgeport, Mass., and were erected about 1875. It is hardly necessary to add that they are built on the most improved plans and with every possible convenience. Machinery of the most perfect kind as well as the most skilled workmen are employed. The result is that the Mason & Hamlin organs combine thorough workmanship, so essential to lasting qualities, with an excellent tone. They are well known in foreign countries, the exports being very large, and the name in this country is almost a household word.

Some time since the Company began experimenting in the manufacture of pianos, resulting in several practical improvements, and in 1882 added the business of piano making to that of organ making. As a preliminary step, the name of the firm was changed to Mason & Hamlin Organ and Piano Company, by an act of the Legislature of Massachusetts. A new building for the accommodation of this branch of the business was erected. Thus far only upright pianos have been manufactured, but they have been received with remarkable favor by musicians and artists throughout the world, and fully sustain the high reputation of the firm. A great improvement recently introduced is a new system of stringing, whereby the liability of the instrument to get out of tune is reduced to a very small minimum.

The home office of the Company is at 154 Tremont street, Boston, and branch offices are located in the following cities : New York, Chicago, London, Vienna, and Melbourne, besides innumerable agencies all over the world.

**Mason,** Dr. Lowell, to whom music in America owes much, was born Jan. 8, 1792, at Medfield, Mass. He early manifested the bent of his nature for music, in which he instructed himself by patient and persevering study. When sixteen years old he took charge of the choir in the village church, and about the same time began teaching, in which capacity he afterwards distinguished himself. In 1812 he went to Savannah, Ga., as a clerk in a bank there, meanwhile continuing to practice, teach, and conduct. With the aid of F. L. Abel he edited a collection of church tunes, mostly arranged from the works of Beethoven, Haydn and Mozart, which was published by the Handel and Haydn Society of Boston in 1822. The work was very successful and greatly aided the society, then in its infancy, but Mason's name was almost entirely suppressed. This led to his removing from Savannah to Boston, in 1827, where he began classes in vocal instruction and became prominently identified with musical affairs. The same year he became president of the society which had published his first work, retaining the position for five years. In 1832 he established the Boston Academy of Music, and had a worthy co-laborer in the person of George James Webb. About this date he became an advocate of the Pestalozzian system and formed classes in it. In 1838 he was granted the power of teaching music in all the public schools of the city, shortly before which he established musical conventions (see CONVENTIONS, MUSICAL), which are now held in all parts of the country. He made his first visit to Europe in 1837, with a view of studying and becoming acquainted with the methods of teaching, particularly in Germany. The impressions received on this tour were collected into a volume and published, under the title of "Musical Letters from Abroad," at New York in 1853. His degree of Doctor of Music, the first one conferred by an American institution of learning and very worthily, too, was bestowed by the New York University in 1835. He was for many years prominently connected with the Public Board of Education of Massachusetts. During the whole of his career his pen was never idle, but he was constantly editing and compiling collections of music suited to every purpose and to every grade of singers. These works, which are numbered by the dozens, had an enormous sale and brought their author a fortune. The latter part of his life was spent at Orange, New Jersey, where his sons resided and where he died, greatly esteemed and regretted,· Aug. 11, 1872.

Dr. Mason ranks foremost among early American musicians. He commenced his work at a time when music was in its infancy here, and soon aroused an interest in it which had been little dreamed of before. How great his influence was can never be ascertained. Suffice it to say that it is still being felt. He was preëminently fitted for a teacher, and his talent in this direction almost amounted to genius. As a composer for the people he was not far behind, so that his precepts were backed by example, thus giving him a power not otherwise obtainable. He was not an educated musician in the sense in which the term is now used, but well fulfilled his mission. His taste for anything concerning music is shown by the care with which he collected his fine library of musical works, best in the country (See MUSICAL LIBRARIES). Of his sons, LOWELL and HENRY were respectively president and treasurer of the Mason & Hamlin Organ and Piano Co., while WILLIAM is a pianist and composer. Lowell recently died. See preceding article.

**Mason,** DR. WILLIAM, third son of the preceding and one of the leading musicians of this country, was born at Boston, Mass., Jan. 24, 1829, not in 1828, as is often stated. His musical inclinations were manifested at a very early age, and when scarcely three years old he would go to the instrument and pick out harmonies (in preference to melodies), those in the minor mode pleasing him best. When seven years old he was allowed, on one occasion, to play the organ at Bowdoin Street Church, Boston, accompanying the choir while they sang the familiar church tune of " Boylston." His father stood behind him and filled in the interludes between the stanzas. At this time he would repeat on the piano any piece which he might have heard on the street or elsewhere. This was gratifying to his father, who, strange as it may seem, took no pains to cultivate or encourage his son's talent. The young man, however, persevered, and carefully studied all the books which came in his way. In 1844 or 1845 he was placed under the care of Rev. Dr. Thayer of Newport for intellectual training. On returning to Boston he became organist of his father's choir, and took piano lessons of Henry Schmidt. His father's wish was that he might enter the ministry, but the parent wisely decided that nature's calling was paramount to his own desires, and in the spring of 1849 the young musician was sent to Germany for a thorough musical education. He first went to Leipsic, where he studied the piano under Moscheles, harmony under Hauptmann, and instrumentation under Richter. Subsequently he studied the piano under Dreyschock at Prague, and finally under Liszt at Weimar. While at Liszt's, during a portion of 1853 and 1854 he had as fellow pupils von Bülow, Pruckner, Klindworth, Hartmann, Schreiber, and others who have since become famous. During his stay abroad he resided for a short period in Hamburg, Dresden, and Frankfort, as well as visited other important German cities. He successfully appeared in public as a player at Prague, Frankfort, and Weimar, and in 1852 made a short visit to London, where he appeared at the "London Harmonic Union Society's" concert at Exeter Hall and played Weber's Concertstück. In July, 1854, he returned home, and shortly after set out on a concert tour, first playing in Boston, then in New York, and then in the larger cities of New England, New York State, Ohio, etc., finally arriving in Chicago. On the return trip the concerts were repeated, always with success. Mr. Mason was entirely unassisted, the programs consisting only of piano pieces. Concert giving, however, was not at all to his taste, and after this tour he settled in New York, where he mainly devoted himself to teaching. In 1855 he established, in conjunction with Carl Bergmann, Theodore Thomas, Joseph Mosenthal and G. Matzka, a series of classical *soirées*, at which instrumental works by the great masters were performed. Many of Robert Schumann's works were thus first introduced in this country. At the end of about a year Bergmann withdrew and was succeeded by F. Bergner. The concerts were continued twelve years, and became widely known as the " Mason and Thomas Soirées of Chamber Music." March 12, 1857, Mr. Mason was married, at Boston, to Miss Mary Isabella Webb, eldest daughter of George

James Webb, for many years his father's able colleague. For several years he was organist of Dr. Alexander's (now Dr. Hall's) church, New York, and has acted in that capacity in the Orange Valley Congregationalist Church, Orange, N. J. He has for about fifteen years been a resident of Orange, and as it is only a short distance from New York, he makes almost daily trips to the city, where he has numerous classes of pupils. His degree of Doctor of Music was bestowed by Yale College, in July, 1872.

Mr. Mason's reputation is not exclusively American, for he is well known in Europe also. It is as a teacher that he is particularly happy, and in which field he is doing a good work. As a composer, however, he takes the foremost rank. His pieces are all characterized by a clear and perfect form, a high polish, and elegance and refinement. They are thoroughly classical, and many of them will not at all suffer in comparison with any pieces of their class ever produced. He has never pandered in the least degree to the popular taste, and his smaller compositions are finished with as much care as his larger ones. To his credit it may be stated that he has not written a single operatic fantasia or a variation on any familiar melody. Though he has composed some polkas, rondos, etc., he delights in the higher forms of piano pieces, in which he is fairly represented by the "Berceuse" and "Reverie." The following is a complete list of his works, and if not large, is one in which every number is worthy of attention:

Op. 1. Deux Romances, sans paroles.
" 2. Les Perles de Rosée. Melodie variée.
" 3. Impromptu.
" 4. Amitié pour Amitié. Morceau de Salon (Also for four hands).
" 5. Valse de Bravoure.
" 6. Silver Spring.
" 7. Trois Valses de Salon.
" 8. Trois Preludes.
" 9. Etude de Concert.
" 10. Lullaby.
" 11. Concert Galop.
" 12. Ballade, in B major.
" 13. Monody. Clavierstück.
" 14. Polka Gracieuse.
" 15. Ballade et Barcarole.
" 16. Danse Rustique.
" 17. Valse Caprice.
" 18. "Bittle-it" Polka.
" 19. Deux Reveries. No. 1. Au Matin; No. 2. Au Soir.
" 20. Spring Dawn. Mazurka Caprice.

" 21. Spring Flower. Impromptu.
" 22. Caprice Grotesque. "Ah! vous dir-ais-je, Maman."
" 23. Deux Humoresques de Bal. No. 1. Polka Caprice. No. 2. Mazurka Caprice.
" 24. Reverie poetique.
" 25. "So-so" Polka.
" 26. Teacher and Pupil. Eight duos for four hands.
" 27. Badinage. Amusement. Four hands.
" 28. Valse Impromptu.
" 29. "Pell-Mell." Galop fantastique.
" 30. Prelude in A minor.
" 31. Scherzo (No. 1), Novelette (No. 2), Two Caprices.
" 32. Romance Etude.
" 33. La Sabotiere. Danse aux Sabots.
" 34. Berceuse.
" 35. Three Characteristic Sketches.
" 36. Dance Caprice.
" 37. Toccata.
" 38. Dance Antique.
" 39. Serenata. Piano and violoncello. Also as piano solo.
" 40. Melody.
" 41. Scherzo.
" 42. Romance—Idyl.
" 43. Minuet.

In addition to the above he has written numerous instrumental and vocal pieces, four-part songs, etc., not included under opus number. His theoretical works consist of "A Method for the Pianoforte" (1867), in the preparation of which he was assisted by E. S. Hoadly; "System for Beginners in the Art of Playing on the Pianoforte" (1871), in the preparation of which he was assisted by E. S. Hoadly; and "Mason's Pianoforte Technics" (1878), in the preparation of which he received assistance from W. S. B. Mathews. The latter is his most important work, an original and distinguishing feature of which is the "Application of Rhythm to Exercises," or the accentual treatment of such exercises as scales, arpeggios, etc. This feature was embodied in the "Method for the Pianoforte" (1867), but only fully presented in the later work. Liszt expressed himself highly pleased with it (Letter of May 26, 1869). It has since been incorporated into many of the later "methods" published in Germany, as well as in this country.

**Massachusetts Compiler.** A collection of church music edited by Oliver Holden and Hans Gram, and published in 1795. It contained a chapter on theory, which, according to the editors, was compiled from some of the best foreign works then published, and one on singing, which advocates a fixed *do*. In the preface, the authors say :

"Many American votaries of sacred music have long expressed their wishes for a compendium of the genuine principles of the science. At the present period it becomes necessary that greater attention be paid to every means for improving that important part of divine worship, as *good musical emigrants* are daily seeking an asylum in this country."

The work seems to have been successful. Its theoretical and practical parts, together with the musical dictionary which it contained, occupy 36 quarto pages, and the selections of music 72 pages.

**Massachusetts Musical Society, The,** was formed in 1807 at Boston, and was in a measure the predecessor of the Handel and Haydn Society. In the spring of that year fifteen persons met together "for the purpose of forming themselves into a society for improving the mode of performing sacred music." A constitution and by-laws were adopted and meetings seem to have been held monthly. The formation of a library was also commenced and the membership increased to about twenty. The society continued to hold its meetings until March 21, 1810, when it was voted to sell the library to liquidate its debts, and on July 6th of the same year it ceased to exist.

**Mathews,** WILLIAM S. B., well-known as a teacher and critic, was born at London, N. H., May 8, 1837. His father was a clergyman but encouraged his son's musical talent, which began to be manifest very early. He eagerly availed himself of every opportunity which came in his way to gain any knowledge of music. When about eleven years old he was placed under the care of a Mr. Folsom of Lowell, with whom he studied some time. He then went to Boston and studied under L. H. Southard, also receiving some advice and encouragement from Dr. Lowell Mason. He commenced his career as a teacher of music by accepting a position in Appleton Academy, Mount Vernon, N. H., in March, 1852, being then not yet fifteen years of age. After this he taught at various places in Massachusetts, New York and Illinois. All the regular instruction he ever received toward a general education was at the district school and a seminary at Sawbornton Bridge, N. H. Being

denied the privilege of a college course, he dilligently applied himself to study, and acquired a knowledge of Latin, Greek, French, German, etc. He is also well-read in metaphysics, *belles-lettres* and theology.

In 1860 he accepted a call as professor of music in a seminary at Macon, Ga., where he received some help from Rev. J. U. Bonnell, its president. Upon the breaking out of the Civil War in 1861, he was forced to resign his position at the seminary, but continued to give private lessons, teaching successively at Macon, Danville, W. Va., and Marion, Ala. This was indeed a gloomy period in his career. During part of the time he is said to have had only two music books, Beethoven's sonatas and Bach's "Well-Tempered Clavier," having been seperated from his library. After the close of the war he returned North, and in January, 1867, became organist of the Centenary M. E. Church, Chicago, a position which he still (1883) holds. In November, 1868, he assumed the duties of editor of the "Musical Independent," published by Lyon & Healy, Chicago, but this paper ceased with the great Chicago fire in October, 1871. He was appointed editor of the "Song Messenger" (Root & Cady, Chicago) in 1872, but it changed hands in 1873, when Mr. Mathews' connection with it ceased. He has for several years been professor of music at Highland Hall, a seminary for young ladies at Evanston, near Chicago. He has also for some time held summer musical institutes.

Mr. Mathews occupies a place among the foremost of piano teachers in this country, and makes a specialty of phrasing and interpretation. He has educated several excellent players. As a writer and critic he is hardly less prominent. He has contributed many articles to the various musical publications of this country, and is not unknown by his pen outside of the circles of music. His writings are all characterized by clearness and force, indicative of a thorough mastery of the subject as well as a logical mode of thinking. At present he is connected with the "Chicago Morning Herald" as musical critic and special editorial writer. He has as yet written no music, but devotes himself exclusively to teaching and writing. The following is a list of his works that have appeared in book form : "Outline of Musical Form," 12 mo., published by Ditson & Co., Boston (1867); "How to Understand Music" (1880), a rather unique work of 225 pages, with which is connected a "Dictionary of Music and Musicians," very handy for reference; "Studies in Phrasing, Memorizing, and Interpretation" (1881); and "How to Teach the Pianoforte" (now in course of preparation). He also assisted in preparing "Emerson Organ Method," by L. O. Emerson, and wrote the letter-press part of "Mason's Pianoforte Technics" (1878).

**Matzka,** GEORGE, was born at Coburg, Germany, in 1825, and at the age of seventeen years became member of the court orchestra of his native city, where he received his musical education. He came to this country in 1852, settled in New York, and became a member of the Philharmonic Society, of which he has been one of the directors for a number of years. Among his compositions are several overtures (that of "Galileo-Galilei" was given by the Philharmonic Society), two string quartets, a sonata for piano and violin, a number of male choruses and songs, etc.

**May Festivals.** These festivals, for musical importance and far-reaching results, it must be admitted by everyone, take the lead of all the festivals in this country. Europe, with all its culture and centuries of musical life, can produce nothing superior if equal to them in artistic excellence and freedom from everything objectionable. It would be difficult to arrange festivals on a plan better calculated to advance the art and elevate the public taste.

The first May Festival was held at Cincinnati, in the Exhibition Hall, May 6th, 7th, 8th, 9th, and 10th, 1873, the year following the last great Peace Jubilee, which probably had considerable influence toward its establishment. (See PEACE JUBILEE). Theodore Thomas was the conductor, assisted by Otto Singer. Mr. Thomas has been conductor at all of the Festivals since and Mr. Singer his assistant until 1882. The chorus numbered 850 voices and the orchestra 107 performers. Among the soloists, some of whom were residents of Cincinnati, were Mrs. Smith, Mrs. Dexter, Miss Cary, and Messrs. M. W. Whitney, and J. F. Rodolphson. The principal works rendered were

| | |
|---|---|
| Dettingen Te Deum, | Handel, |
| Jubilee Overture, | Weber, |
| Suite No. 3, | Bach, |
| Symphony No. 2, | Schumann, |
| Ninth Symphony, | Beethoven, |

with selections from "Tannhäuser"(Wagner), "Midsummer Night's Dream" (Mendelssohn), "Orpheus" (Gluck), "Creation" (Haydn), "Magic Flute" (Mozart), and "Die Meistersinger von Nürnberg" (Wagner). The Festival, despite the high order of the music presented, was a decided success, showing that Americans then knew how to appreciate the best music, and even the "music of the future."

The second Festival was held at Cincinnati, May 11th, 12th, 13th, and 14th, 1875. The general features were the same as those of the first Festival, and the program and its rendition of fully as high order. The soloists were Mrs. Smith, Miss Cary, Miss Whinnery, Miss Emma Cranch, and Messrs. Whitney, Bischoff, Remmertz, and Winch. Chief among the works performed were "Triumphal Hymn" (Braham), Seventh Symphony (Beethoven), "Elijah" (Mendelssohn), Magnificat (Bach), Ninth Symphony (Beethoven), Symphony in C (Schubert), and "Prometheus" (Liszt), with selections from other works. The chorus was 790 strong, and the orchestra of about the same strength as in 1873.

The third Festival, which was held in Cincinnati, May 14th, 15th, 16th, and 17th, 1878, was in many respects more notable than any of the rest. During the three years which had elapsed between this and the preceding Festival, the Cincinnati College of Music had sprung into existence. A building had been erected for its occupation, and it was in the music hall of this that the Festival took place. The great music hall organ, built by Messrs. Hook & Hastings of Boston, one of the very largest and best in America, had just been completed. Indeed, everything seemed to contribute to the success of the Festival, and the enthusiasm of the people of the city was unbounded. Musically, the Festival was fully up to previous standards. The chorus was not quite so large as that of 1873 or of 1875, numbering about 700, but thoroughly drilled. The orchestra was Thomas', and composed exclusively of New York musicians. It numbered 106 pieces. The solo singers were Mrs. Osgood, Mme. Pappenheim, Misses Cary, Cranch, and Rollwagen, and Messrs. Adams, Fritsch, Tagliapietra, Whitney, and Remmertz. Gluck's "Alceste," Beethoven's Eroica Symphony, Handel's "Messiah," Beethoven's Symphony No. 9, in D minor (op. 125), and Liszt's Missa Solennis, were the chief works rendered. The net proceeds of the Festival were about $25,000.

Commencing with 1878, the Cincinnati Festivals have been regularly held every two years. The Festival of 1880 was held May 18th, 19th, 20th, and 21st. The chorus numbered about 600 trained singers, and the orchestra about 156 instrumentalists. Misses Cary and Cranch, and Campanini, Rodolpson, and Whitney, were the principal soloists. The most important works given were Bach's "Ein' Feste Burg," Mozart's "Jupiter" Symphony, Handel's Jubilate, Beethoven's Mass, (op. 123), Schumann's Symphony (op. 120), Beethoven's Fifth Symphony, and Buck's "Golden Legend."

The Festival of 1882, which was held May 16th, 17th, 18th, and 19th, was in no way inferior to any of the previous ones. Mr. Thomas was ably assisted by Arthur Mees, who had charge of the chorus. Both chorus and orchestra were drilled up to a high point of perfection. The first numbered 613 voices and the latter 165 performers. There was, in addition, a boy choir of 100 voices, used in Bach's passion music. The principal soloists were Mme. Materna, Mrs. Osgood, Misses Cary and Cranch, and Messrs. Candidus, Henschel, Toedt, Remmertz, Whitney, and Sullivan. The program, which was fully up to the standard of previous ones, we give in full.

### FIRST DAY.

| | |
|---|---|
| Requiem, - - - - | Mozart. |
| Symphony in F, op. 93, No. 8, | Beethoven. |
| Rec. and Aria from "Fidelio," | Beethoven. |
| Dettingen Te Deum, - - | Handel. |

### SECOND DAY.

#### Matinée.

| | |
|---|---|
| Le Nozze di Figaro (selections), | Mozart. |
| Symphony in A, op. 92, No. 7, | Beethoven. |
| Overture (Genoveva) - | Schumann. |
| Aria, - - - | Bruch. |
| Am Meer, - - | Schubert. |
| Duo, - - - | Mendelssohn. |
| Dramatic Symphony ("Romeo and Juliet"), op. 17, - | Berlioz. |

#### Evening.

| | |
|---|---|
| Passion Music, - - | Bach. |

### THIRD DAY.

#### Matinée.

| | |
|---|---|
| Huldigungs March, selections from "Lohengrin," "Die Meistersinger von Nürnberg," "Das Rheingold," " Die Walküre," and "Götterdämmerung," - | Wagner. |

#### Evening.

| | |
|---|---|
| Symphony in C, No. 9, - | Schubert. |
| Scenes from "Faust," - - | Schumann. |

### FOURTH DAY.

#### Matinée.

| | |
|---|---|
| Euryanthe (selections) - | Weber. |
| Concerto in G, - - - | Bach. |
| Aria, - - - - - | Gluck. |
| "In Questa Tomba," - | Beethoven. |
| Duo, - - - - - | Berlioz. |
| Symphony to Dante's " Divine Comedia," - - - | Liszt. |

#### Evening.

| | |
|---|---|
| Forty-sixth Psalm (Prize composition), - - - - | Gilchrist. |
| Movement to Orchestral Symph, | Rubinstein. |
| Aria from " Oberon," - | Weber. |
| Fall of Troy (selections) - | Berlioz. |

Up to 1880, May Festivals were held only in Cincinnati, but in that year Cleveland organized one, which was held May 13th and 14th. New York was next to follow with a Festival in 1881, Chicago coming last with her first Festival in 1882. These Festivals were all modelled after those of Cincinnati in every important respect. During the year of 1882 there were four May Festivals held, all in the month of May, viz: Cincinnati, New York, Chicago, and Cleveland, all but the last named being under the chief direction of Mr. Thomas. At the New York Festival the chorus varied considerably on different occasions, but averaged about 1800 voices and the orchestra 300 performers. Among the principal works produced were Mozart's Jupiter Symphony, Handel's Utrecht Jubilate, Handel's "Israel in Egypt," and Beethoven's Symphony in C, and his Missa Solennis. The chorus of the Chicago Festival comprised 820 voices, and the orchestra was 172 strong. The program was similar to those of the other Festivals, and the solo singers were, with one or two exceptions, the same as those engaged for the Cincinnati Festival, which may also be said of the New York and Cleveland Festivals. At the Cleveland Festival the chorus numbered 250 voices, and the orchestra 50 performers

The benefit of these Festivals in the advancement of the divine art can not now be measured and may never be fully known, but they are at least worthy of the unreserved support of every lover of music.

**Mechanical Orguinette.** The name of a certain class of mechanical musical instruments, which have lately sprung into existence. They are constructed of every size, from that of a small square box up to that of a diminutive pipe organ, and of many different styles, some resembling reed organs and some pianos. The music is produced automatically, in the smaller sizes by turning a crank and in the larger sizes by pedals, by passing sheets of paper perforated in a certain manner through the instruments, the mechanism being so arranged that whenever a perforation comes in the right place a small lever passes through, opens a valve, and produces the required note. The tone of these instruments, though of course not equaling that of the reed organ, is not bad. They may be of service in some cases where musicians can not be obtained, or where persons are too stupid or too lazy to learn music, but they have no permanent, artistic value.

**Mees,** ARTHUR, was born at Columbus, Ohio, Feb. 13, 1850. While obtaining a good thorough general education, he diligently studied the piano and theory of music. After having graduated from college and spent some time in teaching, he went to Germany, where he studied the piano under Kullak, theory and composition under Weitzmann, and score-playing and chorus training under chapelmaster Dorn. Having remained abroad several years, he returned home and was engaged as one of the teachers in the College of Music, Cincinnati. He soon withdrew, and in conjunction with Schneider and Foley established the CINCINNATI MUSIC SCHOOL. (See article CINCINNATI). In 1882 he was appointed conductor of the Cincinnati May Festival chorus, a position which he still holds. Under his care the large chorus has reached a high degree of excellence, which demonstrates his abilities as a conductor and a musician.

**Melodeon.** From the Greek *melos*, a song, and *odeion*. In this country the melodeon was the direct precursor of the reed organ. As late as 1855 or 1860, it was very popular and almost exclusively manufactured, the reed organ being then unknown. The larger sizes had a case, keyboard, and pedals, like those of the present square piano, and frequently a compass of six octaves. The tone of the instrument was rather sweet and melodious, but lacking in power, and produced from only one set of reeds. When the reed organ was introduced (1860), with its more powerful and varied resources, the melodeon rapidly diminished in favor, and is not now manufactured. Good specimens are frequently to be met with throughout the country.

**Merz,** KARL, the well-known composer and writer on musical topics, was born Sept. 10, 1834, at Bensheim, near Frankfort-on-the-Main, Germany. His early musical instruction was received from his father, who was an excellent violinist and organist of the principal church in that town. Some lessons in harmony were given him by a friend, but these, like the lessons of his father, were rather irregular and desultory, and he gained more by his own unaided study. When not more than eight or nine years old he was able to play the violin in a quartet club which met at the residence of the Baron of Rodenstein, and he frequently played at the musical gatherings at the castle of the count of Schoenberg. On arriving at the age of eleven he assumed his father's duties as organist, which he continued to discharge until leaving home. His literary and general education was received at a seminary and afterwards at college, from which he graduated in 1853. After this he taught school for a year in a small place near Bingen on the Rhine. While on a visit home he met a gentleman from Philadelphia, who invited him to go to the United States. The invitation was accepted, and he arrived here in the autumn of 1854. A position as a clerk in a store in Philadelphia was secured, but he was soon discharged, owing to his lack of knowledge of the English language. While in this strait he met J. H. Bonawitz, who procured him a situation in a band of musicians which played at various places of amusement. He then became organist of the Sixth Presbyterian Church in that city, where he remained a year. He also was engaged as critic on a German musical journal started by Mr. Wolsieffer, and during his stay in Philadelphia he made the acquaintance of the most prominent musicians there.

In 1856 he went to Lancaster County, Pa., where he taught in a seminary, meanwhile studying dilligently. In 1859 he went South and remained there until the breaking out of the Civil War, in April, 1861. Returning to the North, he in September of the same year settled at Oxford, Ohio, and became professor of music in the Oxford Female College. In March, 1868, he began his career as a musical writer by contributing his "musical hints" to "Brainard's Musical World." These were continued in each number, and soon brought their author prominently into notice. He was made assistant editor of the "World," and in 1873 became sole editor, a position which he has most ably filled and which he still (July, 1885) retains. His articles have been widely read, and in a considerable measure influential in advancing the musical interests of the country. They are characterized by an earnest, elevated style, and are, in addition, pleasant to read and logically written. During his residence at Oxford he annually gave a series of two or three concerts, the programs of which were composed of a higher order of pieces than is usual in such cases. Though prevented by the number of his duties from taking the field as a lecturer, he has occasionally appeared in that rôle. The lecture on "Genius," delivered before the Music Teachers' National Association, at Cincinnati, Oxford, and other places in the State of Ohio, has been highly commended. He is not only esteemed as a musician but as a gentleman, and the numerous concerts which he has given for charitable purposes have endeared him to all classes of society. After having been a resident of Oxford for twenty-one years, he in July, 1882, removed to Wooster, Ohio, where he is now professor of music in the Wooster University.

Mr. Merz's works, some of which are very popular, consist of operettas, sacred pieces, choruses, songs, piano solos, waltzes, dances, and pieces in almost every vocal and instrumental form. Among the more important are Trio, for piano, violin, and violoncello, with an arrangement of the andante for the piano; Sonata in C minor, three movements of which are published as "L'Inquietude," "Eloge," and "La Belle Americaine;" "La Tranquilité," andante for piano; Caprice, for two violins and piano; Elegy, for piano and violin; "Bitter Tears," two nocturnes; "Welcome to the Hero," polonaise; "Last Will and Testament," an operetta, first produced at Oxford, O., in 1877; "Katie Dean," an operetta, first produced at Oxford, in 1882; "The Runaway Flirt," an operetta, published in 1868; Gypsy Chorus for Ladies' Voices; "Great and Marvelous," chorus for six voices; "Musical Hints for the Million," containing 434 hints previously published in the "World" (16 mo. 216 pp., 1875); "Modern Method for the Reed Organ" (1878); "Elements of Harmony and Composition" (1881); "Deserted," a song; "The Stranger's Love," a song; Six organ pieces; "To the Golden Rays of Love," quartet; "O Thou who driest the mourner's tears," quartet; "Miriam's Song of Triumph," chorus.

**Millard,** HARRISON, celebrated American song writer, was born Nov. 27, 1830, at Boston. When little more than eight years of age he was admitted into one of the city choirs, and when ten sang in the chorus of the Handel and Hayden Society as alto. His voice changed to a tenor, and on one occasion during the absence of the principal tenor he sang in the oratorio of "Samson." He was then about fifteen years old. In 1851 he went to Europe, and spent three years in studying under the best masters of Italy. After this he spent some time in London, appearing at various musical entertainments as a tenor singer, and traveled with Catherine Hayes in Ireland and Scotland. While abroad he wrote considerable music, and was a frequent contributor to "Dwight's Journal of Music" and other American musical publications. In 1854 he returned to his native country and settled at Boston, giving vocal lessons and singing at concerts. Two years later he removed to New York. In 1859 he produced his first important song, "Viva La America," which had a wonderful success. Upon the breaking out of the Civil War he entered the army and was commissioned as first lieutenant of the 19th New York regiment. After four years of service he was severely wounded at the battle of Chicamauga, rendered unfit for duty, and sent home. Not long after he was offered a position in the custom house, which he still (1881) holds. Mr. Millard has written many popular pieces which have rendered his name familiar all over the country, as is attested by the fact that various musical societies in different states are named after him. His works consist of about 300 songs (among which is the patriotic song of "Flag of the Free") nearly 400 adaptations from French, German, and Italian; many anthems, 4 church services, 4 Te Deums, a grand mass, a vesper, and an Italian opera in 4 acts, entitled "Deborah."

**Miller,** HENRY F., SEN., piano manufacturer, was born at Providence, R. I., in 1825, and died at his summer residence at Beach Bluff, Mass., Aug. 14, 1884. He received in youth a good education at the public and private schools of his native city, and at an early age also commenced the study of music, soon attaining proficiency as a pianist and organist. In the latter capacity he officiated for some time at the church connected with Brown University, Providence. He also, in addition to his musical talent, possessed a decided taste for mechanical studies, and while at school planned and built a hydraulic machine and an electric machine. In 1863, after he had been in the employ of other piano manufacturers for several years, he established in business for himself. Being thoroughly acquainted with the various methods used by others, he was enabled to produce first-class instruments. At the outset the Henry F. Miller pianos were received with favor and soon became popular. From small beginnings the business steadily increased. He accumulated considerable capital, which enabled him to extend the business to all parts of the United States. He manufactured all of the various styles of pianos — grand, square and upright— and also a patented pedal upright piano for the use of organists.

The elegant and commodious building which he occupied at 611 Washington St., Boston, was built for him. He also purchased a fine property at Wakefield, Mass., consisting of land and buildings (said to have originally cost $100,000), which offered the very best facilities for manufacturing. At the time of his death, Mr Miller's business was in a flourishing condition. His sales annually amounted in value to hundreds of thousands of dollars, while his pianos were known and highly esteemed by artists everywhere and the musical world in general. Mr. Miller's family, all of whom survived him, consists of his wife, five sons and two daughters. The sons were all associated with him in his business. He was a man of the strictest integrity, and in all his business relations commanded the respect and confidence of all who knew him. The resolutions passed by the manufacturers and his employees at the time of his death were of unusually high character.

**Miller, Henry F., & Sons Piano Co.,** BOSTON, MASS. This Company, which was organized in 1884 under the laws of the State of Massachusetts with a paid in capital of $ 150,000, succeeded Henry F. Miller, Sr., at the time of his decease. The officers of the Company are his sons, Henry F. Miller, president; James C. Miller, treasurer; Walter H. Miller, manager of warerooms; Edwin C. Miller, assistant superintendent; William F. Miller, clerk, and Joseph H. Gibson, superintendent. The Company manufactures and sells the celebrated Henry F. Miller piano. Their offices and warerooms are at 156.Tremont St., Boston, with a branch wareroom at Philadelphia. They also have agencies in all parts of the United States and Canada. The Miller pianos rank among the very best in the world for durability, tone and finish. Special attention is given by the Company to the manufacture of grand pianos for the concert use of artists.

**Milwaukee Musikverein** (The) MILWAUKEE, WIS. This is one of the oldest as well as the most important musical societies in the West. It was founded in 1849, and is supported by the large German population of the city. The first concert was given May 28, 1850. H. Balatka, F. Abel, A. von Sobolewski, W. Tenzler, A. von Jungsest, R. Schmelz, and A. Mickler, have in turn acted as conductors. Eugene Luening is the present incumbent. The society has not been without its drawbacks and adversities, but notwithstanding these it has exercised a great and elevating influence upon the musical life of the great West. As an epitome of its labors, the following list of works (taken from Dr. Ritter's "Music in America") which it has performed, covering almost the whole field of music, is a creditable one :

| 1st Time. | No. Times. | Work. | Composer. |
|---|---|---|---|
| 1851 | 1 | Messiah (parts), - - - | Handel. |
| 1851 | 5 | Creation, - - - | Haydn. |
| 1851 | 1 | Jesus in Gethsemane (parts), - · | Rossetti. |
| 1851 | 2 | Samson, - - - | Handel. |
| 1852 | 4 | Seasons, - - - - | Haydn. |
| 1852 | 6 | Elijah (choruses), - - | Mendelssohn. |
| 1853 | 6 | Czar and Zimmermann, - - - | Lortzing. |
| 1853 | 5 | Der Wildschütz, - - - | Lortzing. |
| 1854 | 5 | Der Freyschütz, - - - | Weber. |
| 1855 | 6 | Norma, - - - | Bellini. |
| 1855 | 2 | Symphony No. 1, - - - | Beethoven. |
| 1856 | 4 | Alessandro Stradella, - - | Flotow. |
| 1856 | 2 | Symphony No. 6, - - - | Beethoven. |
| 1856 | 1 | Symphony No. 5, - - | Beethoven. |
| 1857 | 2 | Forty-second Psalm, - · | Mendelssohn. |
| 1858 | 2 | Die Zauberflöte, - - - | Mozart. |
| 1858 | 3 | Symphony No. 2, - - - | Beethoven. |
| 1858 | 1 | Nachtlager von Grenada, - | Kreutzer. |
| 1858 | 2 | Stabat Mater, - - - | Rossini. |
| 1859 | 1 | Hymn of Praise, - - - | Mendelssohn. |
| 1859 | 1 | Mohega (drama), - - - | Sobolewski. |
| 1859 | 1 | Song of the Bell, - - | Romberg. |
| 1860 | 1 | Martha, - - - - | Flotow. |
| 1860 | 2 | Requiem Mass, - - - | Mozart. |
| 1860 | 2 | Symphony (E flat major), - - | Mozart. |
| 1861 | 1 | La Traviata, - - - | Verdi. |
| 1861 | 2 | Ninety-fifth Psalm, - - | Mendelssohn. |
| 1861 | 1 | A Night on the Ocean, - - | Tschirch. |
| 1862 | 1 | Symphony (G minor) - - | Gade. |
| 1863 | | Miscellaneous selections. | |
| 1864 | 1 | St. Paul, - - - - | Mendelssohn. |
| 1865 | | Repetition of former works. | |
| 1866 | 1 | Lurline, - - - \ - | Hiller. |
| 1866 | 1 | The Power of Song, · - \ | Brambach. |
| 1866 | 2 | Symphony No. 7, - - - | Beethoven. |
| 1867 | 1 | Symphony No. 1, - - | Haydn. |
| 1868 | 1 | Symphony "Abschied," - - | Haydn. |
| 1868 | 1 | Midsummer Night's Dream (music), - | Mendelssohn. |
| 1869 | 3 | Fra Diavolo, - - - | Auber. |
| 1869 | 1 | Birken und Erlen, - - | Bruch. |
| 1869 | 1 | Symphony (unfinished), - - | Schubert. |
| 1870 | 1 | Mass (C), - | Beethoven. |
| 1871 | 1 | Symphony No. 4, - \ - | Mendelssohn. |
| 1871 | 1 | Symphony "Ocean," - - | Rubinstein. |
| 1872 | 4 | Masaniello, - - - | Auber. |
| 1872 | 1 | Judas Maccabæus (parts), - | Handel. |
| 1872 | 1 | Symphony No. 3 (E flat), - | Haydn. |
| 1872 | 1 | Poëme Symphonique, "Tasso," - | Liszt. |
| 1873 | 1 | Symphony No. 4, - - | Beethoven. |
| 1973 | 1 | Les Préludes, - - - | Liszt. |
| 1873 | 1 | Loreley (finale), - - - | Mendelssohn. |
| 1874 | 1 | Fantasie (piano, orchestra, chorus), - | Beethoven. |
| 1874 | 1 | Sakuntala (overture), - - | Goldmark. |
| 1875 | 2 | Walpurgis Night, - - - | Mendelssohn. |
| 1875 | 1 | Ein Deutsches Requiem, - | Brahms. |
| 1875 | 1 | Lohengrin (introduction and scenes), - | Wagner. |
| 1876 | 1 | Odysseus, - - - | Bruch. |
| 1876 | 1 | Ball Suite, · - - | Lachner. |
| 1877 | 1 | Paradise und die Peri, - - | Schumann. |
| 1877 | 1 | Melusine, - - - | Hoffmann. |
| 1878 | 1 | Symphony No. 1, - - | Brahms. |
| 1878 | 1 | "        " 2, - - | Brahms. |
| 1878 | 1 | "        " 1, - - | Schumann. |
| 1878 | 1 | "        " 9 (choral), - | Beethoven. |
| 1879 | 1 | Symphony (C major), - - | Schubert. |
| 1879 | 1 | Christus, - · - | Kiel. |

| 1st Time. | No. Times. | Works. | | | Composer. |
|---|---|---|---|---|---|
| 1880 | 1 | Der Raub der Sabinerinnen, | - | - | Vierling. |
| 1880 | 1 | Golden Legend, | - | - | Buck. |
| 1880 | 1 | Elijah (in full), | - | - | Mendelssohn. |
| 1880 | 1 | Symphony "Im Wald," | - | - | Raff. |

**Mills,** SEBASTIAN BACH, pianist, was born March 13, 1838, at Leicester, England, where his father was organist, and early showed a decided musical talent. When six or seven years old he appeared in public and was well received. In 1846 he played a brilliant rondo by Czerny, at Drury Lane, with such success that the Queen sent for him to play before her at Buckingham Palace. He frequently assisted at concerts and speedily became a great favorite. In 1847 he went to Germany and studied under Plaidy, Meyer, and Czerny. His progress was rapid, and he was invited to play at various concerts, which he did with great acceptance. After having returned to England he was induced to come to this country, and arrived here in 1856. Being almost a total stranger, he met with a very discouraging reception, and had about decided to return again to his native country when he met Carl Bergmann, who introduced him to musical society. He played Schumann's concerto at a concert given in the city assembly rooms, Broadway, which gained him notice and a place among musicians. His mind was immediately changed and he settled in New York as a teacher of the piano, where he is still (1886) located. He has been very successful, ranking as one of the leading teachers of the country, and has trained many excellent players. From time to time he has appeared as a *virtuoso* at concerts in the principal cities of the United States. His style is clear, sharp, crisp, and bold, making him excell in *bravura* passages, but lacking in grace and feeling. This defect, however, grows less with the advance of age, and some of the boldness and power is profitably exchanged for the finer qualities. Mr. Mills has composed numerous and popular piano pieces, among the most important of which are "Hail Columbia" (concert paraphrase), "Alpine Horn" (transcription), "Barcarolle Venetienne," "Two Tarantellas," "Murmuring Fountain" (caprice), "Recollections of Home," "Caprice Galop," "Fairy Fingers," "Toujours Gai," "Saltarello." "Beautiful Blue Danube," "Barcarolle," "Waltz," etc.

**Mitchell,** NAHUM, was born in 1769, at Bridgewater, Mass. He commenced the study of music and began composing at an early age, but none of his earlier pieces amounted to anything. In conjunction with a Rev. Mr. Buckminster of Boston he compiled a small volume of church music, entitled "Brattle Street Collection," which was published in 1810. In 1812 he brought out "Templi Carmina," a similar collection, which was very successful and in the preparation of which he was assisted by Brown and Holt, two music teachers. It passed through several editions. His music was popular and of a higher order than that produced by a majority of American composers of his day. His principal works besides those already named are a "Grammar of Music" and a series of articles on the "History of Music," published in the Boston "Euterpeiad." Mitchell was at one time member of Congress, and for many years chief justice of the Massachusetts circuit court. He died at Bridgewater, early in September, 1853.

**Mocking Bird,** LISTEN TO THE. One of Sep. Winner's most beautiful and popular ballads. It was composed about 1855, and at once became all the rage. Numberless variations have been written upon it. It is one of the few songs which have gained a national reputation, and it even came to be generally known in England.

**Mollenhauer.** A family of remarkable German musicians, consisting of three brothers.

FREDERIC, the eldest, was born in 1818, at Erfurt. His musical talents were evident from the first, and he formed a strong attachment for the violin. As has often been the case, the parents were displeased with the idea of their son becoming a musician, and he was obliged to surreptitiously pursue his musical studies. He at first took lessons of an old school-teacher, but having soon learned all his master could teach him, continued his studies under a Herr Braum, a pupil of Spohr, making rapid progress. Everything went along all right until a bill for services rendered was presented him by his teacher, which he was totally unable to pay. In this dilemma he was obliged to inform his father of what he had been doing, who graciously forgave him, paid all his debts, and allowed him to continue his studies. For two years he remained with Braum, meanwhile studying harmony and composition with A. Pabst, and the violoncello with E. Methfessel. He also instructed his younger brothers, Henry and Edward. About 1835 he commenced a concert tour which lasted three years and embraced nearly all of Europe. During this period he became acquainted with Spohr (with whom he sometimes played *duos*), Hummel, Schumann, Mendelssohn, and other noted musicians. He was afterwards joined by his brother Edward, and it was Mendelssohn who highly praised the *duo* playing of the two. In 1852 and 1853, during one of their brilliant concert tours, they played in London, and were engaged by Jullien as soloists in his famous orchestral concerts. With him they came to the United States in 1853, and have since resided here. Frederic in 1865 established a "Studio of Music" in Brooklyn, of which he still had charge in 1882. His playing was characterized by boldness, breadth and power. He was favorably known as a composer as well as a teacher and player. He died at Boston, April 14, 1885.

HEINRICH, the second member of the family, was born at Erfurt, Sep. 10, 1825. He early learned to play the piano and violin, receiving instruction from his elder brother, and when but six years old played before the court at Weimar with great success. After having studied the piano and violin some time, he gave them both up for the violoncello, which he studied under Knoppe and on which he soon became proficient. In 1853 he went to Stockholm, where he was engaged as solo violoncellist to the court. At the end of two or three years he resigned this position and traveled in Sweden and Denmark. In 1856 he came to this country, his brothers having preceded him, and made his *début* at one of the New York Philharmonic Society's concerts. He subsequently traveled with Thalberg, Gottschalk and Patti, giving concerts in various parts of the country. Having married he settled in New York, and in 1867 established a conservatory of music in Brooklyn, over which he still (1885) presides. Though busily engaged in teaching, he still frequently appears in public as a solo violoncellist.

EDWARD, violinist, the youngest member of the family, was born at Erfurt in 1827. His first musical instruction was received from his eldest brother, Frederic, under whose care he rapidly progressed, and when only nine years of age frequently appeared in public at concerts. He then visited Berlin, Vienna and St. Petersburg, playing with great success. After leaving his brother he placed himself under the care of Ernst, meanwhile studying harmony and composition. He subsequently became conductor of an orchestra at Hamburg. In order to escape military service he fled to England, where he joined Frederic, and after playing some time with Jullien's orchestra they in 1853 came to the United States. Edward finally settled in New York, where he is still located, highly esteemed as a soloist, teacher, conductor and composer. His opera of "The Corsican Bride" was produced at Winter Palace, New York, in 1862, but undeservedly met with little success. As a composer he is the best known of the three brothers. His works consist of three operas, violin concertos, quartets for strings, songs, duets, etc., many of which remain unpublished.

**Montejo,** ELLA (*née* Senate), a dramatic soprano, is a native of Philadelphia. She studied with Pasquale, Rondinella, François d'Auria, Barili, and other teachers equally well known. In 1880 she made a successful *début* on the concert stage. Soon after she appeared on the lyric boards in her native city in Gilbert and Sullivan's "Pinafore," sustaining the *rôle* of *Josephine* for over 100 nights. The following year she appeared as *Columbia* in an original opera by Giuseppe Operti. For some time thereafter she lived in retirement in consequence of the death of four members of her family—father, mother and two sisters. In 1885 she removed to New York City, and has since re-appeared before the public.

**Moore,** JOHN W., was born at Andover, N. H., April 11, 1807, and was the third son of Dr. Jacob B. Moore, a descendant of a Scotch family and a fair amateur musician.

Of the other two sons, Jacob B. was a partner of Isaac Hill in publishing the "Patriot" and the author of several historical and other works, and Henry E. was a music teacher and the composer of numerous vocal and instrumental pieces. The subject of our sketch learned the printer's trade in the office of the "New Hampshire Patriot." In 1828 he established a weekly paper at Brunswick, Me., called the "Free Press." This he sold in 1831 and returned to Concord, N. H., where in conjunction with his brother Henry he founded the "Concord Advertiser." In 1838 he commenced the publication of the "Bellows Falls Gazette," at Bellows Falls, Vt., which he continued many years. He was also in 1841 appointed postmaster at the place, a position which he retained for more than ten years. In 1863 he removed to Manchester, N. H., where he became editor of the "Daily News" and of "Moore's Musical Record," and where he is still (1885) located. While residing at Bellows Falls, besides many miscellaneous articles for various musical publications, he wrote or edited the following works : "World of Music," "Sacred Minstrel," "Musician's Lexicon," "Musical Library," "Comprehensive Music Teacher," "American Collection of Instrumental Music," and " Star Collection of Instrumental Music." His far most important and useful work, however, is "Moore's Complete Encyclopædia of Music, Elementary, Technical, Historical, Biographical, Vocal and Instrumental" (1 vol. large 8vo. 1000 pages, published by O. Ditson & Co., Boston, 1854), to which he devoted nearly eighteen years' time and labor. The volume contains a great mass of information, not always well digested, and sometimes marred by errors which are the result of the varied sources from which it was drawn. So long a time has elapsed since it was first published that it is now greatly out of date. This defect has been in a measure remedied by an appendix (1875). Mr. Moore is now at work on a second volume, which will soon be issued and will undoubtedly be an improvement upon the first. His "Dictionary of Musical Information" (Boston, O. Ditson & Co., 1876) is a small work, mainly condensed from the encyclopædia, with modifications and corrections to date, and very handy for casual reference.

**Morgan,** GEORGE WASHBOURNE, well known as an organist, was born at Gloucester, England, April 9, 1822. From the age of twelve until twenty years he regularly played twice every day. After holding several positions as organist in his native city, he went to London, and was similarly engaged. He made his first appearance as solo organist at Exeter Hall, and was received with much enthusiasm. In 1853 he came to this country and was appointed organist of St. Thomas' Episcopal Church, New York, where he remained only a year. After this he was organist of Grace Church for thirteen years, of St. Ann's and St. Stephen's Roman Catholic churches for a short time, and of the Brooklyn Tabernacle (Dr. Talmage) for over twelve years. He was the first organist to introduce in this country the organ works of Bach, Hesse and Mendelssohn. His performances at Tremont Temple, Boston, were most highly praised by " Dwight's Journal of Music." In 1876 he repeatedly played at the Centennial Exposition at Philadelphia. His organ recitals at Chickering Hall, New York, for the past six years have steadily increased in favor, and have become one of the established musical features of the metropolis. As an organist Mr. Morgan ranks among the very foremost in this country, possessing a wonderful *technique* and a complete control of his instrument. In the execution of pedal passages he has no superior. He is also a good pianist, and is personally highly esteemed. He now resides at New York. His daughter, MAUD, is an accomplished harpist. She made her *début* in 1876, and has since repeatedly played before large and cultured audiences, always with the greatest success.

**Morgan,** JOHN PAUL, was born Feb. 13, 1841, at Oberlin, Ohio, and began the study of music at an early age. In 1858 he was employed as organist of the Congregational Church, Mt. Vernon, O., but soon after went to New York and studied for three years under J. Huss, meanwhile acting as organist and director of music in the South 5th Street M. E. Church, East Brooklyn. In 1862 he returned to Cleveland, O., where he was organist of the Second Presbyterian Church and taught music. In April, 1863, he went to Germany, and studied theory and composition under Hauptmann, Richter, Reinecke, and

Papperitz; the piano under Wenzel, Plaidy, and Moscheles, and the organ under Richter. After having graduated from the Conservatorium in the spring of 1865, he spent some time with A. G. Ritter at Magdeburg. In August of the same year he returned home and conducted a series of oratorio concerts at Oberlin, O., and at the same time founded the Oberlin Conservatory of Music, which is still in a flourishing condition under the directorship of F. B. Rice. Early in 1866 he again went to New York, and was engaged as organist of the Church of the Messiah, Brooklyn. On Oct. 18th of the same year he was married to Miss Virginia H. Woods, daughter of Rev. W. W. Woods, of Iowa City, Iowa, and in 1867 was appointed organist of Trinity Church, New York. He had charge of five or six musical societies in and around New York; was professor of the organ and theory in the conservatory of William Mason and Theodore Thomas, the New York Conservatory and the conservatory of Carl Anschütz during the brief existence of each, and was active in promoting musical interests in the city. An alarming affection of the throat caused him, in January, 1873, to seek a restoration of health in the South. He returned to New York in the following June, but little better, and in accordance with the advice of physicians almost immediately started for Santa Barbara, Cal. Health was so far restored to him that he became conductor of the Handel and Haydn Society, San Francisco, of the Oakland Harmonic Society, and organist of the First Presbyterian Church, Oakland. In 1877 he founded the "Morgan Conservatory of Music" at Oakland, to which he devoted the most of his time. Disease had been clinging to him, however, and gradually wasted his strength. Nature at last succumbed, and his death took place at Oakland, early in January, 1879. He left a widow and several children.

Mr. Morgan was not only a fine organist but a thorough and conscientious musician. He detested everything superficial and at once impressed those with whom he came in contact with his sincerity and integrity. His works are numerous, and consist of the 86th psalm, a Te Deum, a Benedictus, a Kyrie, a funeral service, a Centennial National Song (words by Bayard Taylor), anthems, songs, and other vocal pieces; a symphony for organ and orchestra; a trio in three movements for piano, violin and violoncello; duets for piano and violin; numerous miscellaneous instrumental compositions, etc.

**Mosenthal,** JOSEPH, was born in December, 1834, at Hesse-Cassel, Germany. He was given a thorough musical education by Spohr, Bott, Kraushaar, and other equally eminent teachers. In 1853 he came to the United States and settled at New York, where in the following year he was engaged as one of the players in Jullien's orchestra, then visiting this country. He afterwards formed one of the string quartet, the others being Bergner, Matzka, and Theodore Thomas, which for twelve years gave performances of chamber music. In 1860 he became organist of Calvary Church, a position which he was still holding in 1878. His time is largely devoted to teaching, and he was for a long time one of New York's most prominent musicians. He is at present (1882) a resident of that city.

**Murray,** JAMES R., was born at Andover, Mass., in 1841, and studied music with Dr. Root, Lowell Mason, Bradbury, Webb, and Eugene Thayer. After serving in the army during the Civil War, he went to Chicago and was for some time editor of the "Song Messenger." In 1871 he returned to his native place, where he has since resided. He is chiefly known as the composer of songs and light vocal pieces and the compiler of various collections for schools and Sunday-schools. "School Chimes" was one of the most popular books of its class. "Pure Diamonds," "Heavenward" and "Royal Gems," for Sunday-schools, have been very successful. Of "Pure Diamonds" alone more than half a million copies were sold.

**Musical Critic and Trade Review.** A semi-monthly publication of 20 pages devoted to musical criticism, news and the music trades. It was established in 1878, and at first known as the *Musical Critic.* Charles Avery Welles is the editor and proprietor. Published at New York. Subscription price, $2 per year. Circulation, about 10,000.

**Musical Courier.** A weekly publication devoted to the interests of music and drama. Published at New York by Blumenberg & Floersheim. Each number contains sixteen or more pages. Subscription price,

$4 per annum. Established in 1880. Circulation, upwards of 5,000.

**Music and Drama.** A weekly review of music in general, formerly issued weekly at New York. It had able correspondents in all parts of this country and in foreign countries, and contained a large amount of information from the musical world in each number. A daily edition of the paper was commenced Nov. 25, 1882, and continued a short time. This is probably the first instance of a regularly established musical daily in the world. It ceased to exist in 1883, but has lately been revived under a new management, and much improved. Amelia Lewis is at present editor.

**Musical glasses.** Glasses resembling the ordinary drinking glasses, from which musical but very peculiar sounds may be produced by rubbing the moistened finger around the rim. They are tuned to the different degrees of the diatonic scale by increasing or diminishing the quantity of water in them. Benjamin Franklin incorporated the glasses into a practical musical instrument. See HARMONICA.

**Musical Herald.** A monthly magazine of forty pages devoted to the advancement of music in all its branches, especially church music. The first number appeared in January, 1880. It is edited by Dr. E. Tourjée, assisted by Louis C. Elson, Stephen A. Emery, W. F. Sherwin and G. E. Whiting. Published by the Musical Herald Co., Boston. Subscription price, $1 per year. Circulation about 10,000. It is one of the most ably conducted journals in this country.

**Musical Magazine, The,** was not strictly a magazine, but a publication consisting mostly of church music, edited and issued by Andrew Law of Newark, N. J. It first appeared about the beginning of the present century, and was undoubtedly the first American periodical devoted exclusively to music. Several numbers were issued, but it seems not to have gained any permanency. It formed a part of Mr. Law's "Art of Singing," the other two parts being "The Musical Primer" and "The Christian Harmony." Sometimes these three parts were bound into one volume. The "Magazine" was printed at Boston, Mass., by E. Lincoln.

**Music Teachers' National Association.** The Music Teachers' National Association was founded in 1876, in Delaware, Ohio, and has for its aim, as specifically stated in its constitution, "mutual improvement by interchange of ideas, and the broadening cf musical culture." From a very modest beginning it has passed through many seasons of discouragement, and for several years it was only kept alive by the self-sacrificing zeal of a few earnest musicians who had faith in its ultimate success. The fact that it was not in a position to take a decided stand on questions of importance to the best interests of musical growth, constituted the chief source of its weakness, and its growth within the last three years may be directly traced to the fact that it has enunciated within that space of time a platform which is broad and liberal. At its annual meetings essays are presented by distinguished musicians, which, with the accompanying discussion, are incorporated, with the other proceedings, in an official report, which is distributed gratuitously. At the meeting in Providence, in 1883, action was taken which resulted in the formation of the AMERICAN COLLEGE OF MUSICIANS the following year at Cleveland. Action was also taken at the Cleveland meeting in the interests of American composers, and the production of works by native composers on a worthy scale has become a leading feature of the annual meetings. At the meeting of 1885 in the Academy of Music, New York, two orchestral concerts were given, at which were produced original orchestral works. This same year the Association took a stand in favor of international copyright, and has consistently agitated the subject in every legitimate manner, and stands pledged to do all in its power to aid this cause. To sum up the work of the Association as briefly as possible, it is an attempt, by legitimate methods, to advance the standards of professional work; to stimulate a thoughtful consideration of all subjects relating to the art of music; and by united effort to make its influence a beneficial one, not only as relating to the profession, but also as a factor in the musical growth of the nation. It is an encouraging sign to note that the recent accessions to the membership of the Association are well-nigh exclusively from the ranks of the best musicians, thus rendering assured the maintenance of a worthy standard. It is to be hoped that the work of this organization may be wisely considered and that it may be an honor to the profession and representative of the best thoughts of American musicians. The officiary for the current year (1885–86) is as follows:

*President,* A. A. Stanley, Providence, R. I.; *Secretary-Treasurer,* Theodore Presser, Philadelphia, Pa.; *Executive Committee,* S. B. Whitney, Boston, Mass., W. F. Heath, Fort Wayne, Ind., Max Leckner, Indianapolis, Ind.; *Program Committee,* Calixa Lavallée, Boston, Mass., A. R. Parsons, New York, F. B. Rice, Oberlin, O.                * *  *

**Musical Record, The.** A weekly paper of sixteen pages devoted to the interests of music in general. It is published at Boston by O. Ditson & Co., and edited by Dexter Smith. It has recently been changed to a 36-page monthly, under the same management and editorship. Subscription price, $1.00 per annum. Established in 1878. Circulation, upwards of 5,000.

**Music Journal, American.** The name of the official paper of the Musical Mutual Protective Union of New York, the largest organized body of professional instrumental musicians in the world. It was established in December, 1884, and issued semi-monthly until Jan. 1, 1886, when it was changed to a weekly. It is published at the office of the Union, No. 64 E. 4th St., New York, under the editorial management of J. Travis Quigg, a well-known journalist and writer on musical affairs. Subscription price, $2.00 per annum.

**Musical Libraries.** Though the United States can not boast of so large and complete musical libraries as Europe, it has several excellent and valuable collections. The most important among them are the following ones, of which a brief description is given:

1.—The library of Harvard Musical Association, which contains about 2500 volumes, selected with care, and the number rapidly increases.

2.—The Boston public library includes a collection of 2000 volumes on the subject of music.

3.—Harvard University has a library containing about the same number of volumes, some of considerable value. Special attention

is given to increasing the number.

4.—The library of Congress contains many musical works and publications, but they consist almost entirely of such as come to it through the copyright law, and consequently of little value. This, however, may be a source of valuable information to the future historian.

5.—The largest and most valuable library in this country is the one collected by Dr. Lowell Mason for his private use, but which now belongs to the theological department of Yale College, being a gift thereto by his widow. The nucleus was the library of C. H. Rinck of Darmstadt, which was purchased by Dr. Mason in 1852, while traveling in Europe. It now contains more than 8,460 seperate publications and 630 manuscripts, and is particularly rich in hymnology, there being no less than 700 volumes relating to this subject alone. There are also some valuable theoretical works of the 16th and 17th centuries. Among the rare works are Riccio's Introitus (Venice, 1589), Andreas Spaeth's Paraphrase of the Psalms (Heidelberg, 1596), de Moncrif's Chansons (Paris, 1755), Kreiger's Musikalische Partien (Nuremberg, 1697), and autograph manuscripts by Dr. Mason, Rinck, A. André, Beczwarzowsky, Fesca, Nageli, G. A. Schneider, N. A. Strungk, etc.

6.—The Yale College library contains a small but valuable collection of musical works, amounting to about 500 volumes.

There are but few private libraries in this country which amount to much. One of them is the library of Karl Merz, Wooster, Ohio, and at present (1886) editor of Brainard's Musical World, which contains between one and two thousand volumes, including some valuable works. Dr. Frédéric L. Ritter, of Poughkeepsie, New York, has a large and valuable library. Geo. P. Upton, of Chicago, translator of "Nohl's Life of Haydn," has a good library, containing nearly a thousand volumes. As we have not been able to examine any of these libraries, we can not give any information regarding their contents in particular.

**Music Publishers' Association.** An association consisting of the principal publishers of music in the United States. Its object is the regulation of the music trade by fixing and sustaining a uniform and standard price for all music published. The Association was once able to regulate the entire trade of the country, but there are now several publishers who are not its members and who regulate their own price for music. Among them are two or three who make a business of publishing for dealers alone, at one-sixth the retail price, whereas the usual discount to dealers is one-half. The dealer may, by ordering a certain amount of music, have his name printed thereon as publisher. But this is usually done only in the case of music not protected by copyright laws and thus has, in a certain sense, become public property. As, however, nearly all foreign music is of this class, the field is both large and profitable.

The Association holds annual meetings, the last one of which occurred April 17th of the present year (1883) at New York, and has the officers usual to such a body. A trademark for sheet-music has been adopted, consisting of a star enclosing a figure, which indicates the number of dimes at which the piece is to be sold. The following firms comprise the Association: Balmer & Weber, St. Louis; S. Brainard's Sons, Cleveland, Ohio; The John Church Co., Cincinnati; O. Ditson & Co., Boston; D. P. Faulds, Louisville, Ky.; F. A. North & Co., Philadelphia; Wm. A. Pond & Co., New York; White, Smith & Co., Boston.

**My country, 'tis of thee.** The first line of a very popular American national hymn of four stanzas, written by Rev. Samuel Francis Smith, D. D., who was born in 1808. It is generally sung to the English tune of "God Save the King," called "America" in this country.

# N.

**Nevada,** EMMA, whose real name is EM-MA WIXON, was born in Nevada (she took her stage name from her native state) about 1860. Her father is Dr. W. W. Wixon, a physician of some reputation. In 1877 she went to Europe and studied for some time with Mme. Marchesi at Vienna. Her first engagement was for Berlin, but sickness compelled her to relinquish it. Under the management of Col. Mapleson, she made her *début* in "Sonnambula," at London, in May, 1880. In September of the same year she sang at Trieste in "Sonnambula" and "Lucia" for several nights. She then sang in Florence, Leghorn, Naples, Genoa and Rome. Verdi heard her at Genoa and assisted her in securing an engagement at La Scala, Milan, where she sang for twenty-one nights. After visiting other Italian cities, she appeared at Prague, and in 1883 made her Parisian *début*. She is the second American lady to sing at the Opéra Comique. Her *répertoire* includes "Sonnambula," "Lucia," "Puritani," "Mignon," "Faust," and other operas.

**New England Psalm Singer, The.** One of the earliest collections of music published in this country. It was edited by William Billings, and issued Oct. 7, 1770. There were 108 pages. Most of the music was original. The work seems to have met with a reception that was very flattering to the author. As a matter of curiosity, the title-page is here given in full:

"The New England Psalm Singer; or American Chorister. Containing a number of Psalm-tunes, Anthems and Canons. In four and five Parts. (Never before published). Composed by William Billings, a Native of Boston, in New England. Matt. 12.16. 'Out of the Mouth of Babes and Sucklings hast thou perfected praise.' James 5.13. 'Is any Merry? Let him sing Psalms.'

O, praise the Lord with one consent,
  And in this grand design
Let Britain and the Colonies
  Unanimously join (jine) !'

Boston: New-England. Printed by Edes & Gill."

Of course, the music in "The New England Psalm Singer" was very crude, and of this fact Billings seems to have become aware, for in his second book, "The Singing Master's Assistant," published in 1778, he says:

"Kind reader, no doubt you remember that about ten years ago I published a book entitled 'The New-England Psalm Singer;' and truly a most masterly performance I then thought it to be. How lavish was I of encomium on this my infant production. 'Welcome, thrice Welcome thou legitimate Offspring of my brain, go forth my little book, go forth and immortalize the name of your Author; may your sale be rapid and may you speedily run through ten thousand Editions:' Said I, 'Thou art my Reuben, my first born; the beginning of my Strength, the Excellency of my Dignity, and the Excellency of my power.' But to my great mortification I soon discovered it was Reuben in the sequel, and Reuben all over; I have discovered that many pieces were never worth my printing or your inspection."

See BILLINGS, WILLIAM.

## New York and Brooklyn.

### NEW YORK.

According to Dr. F. L. Ritter's "Music in America," musical societies were established in New York about the middle of the last century. None of them seem to have secured any permanence, for they appeared and disappeared in rapid succession. At the beginning of the third decade of the present century the principal societies were the *Choral Society*, the *Philharmonic Society* (old), the EUTERPEAN, and a *Handel and Haydn Society*. The latter had a very brief, though brilliant, existence. Ten years later they were the *Musical Fund* (old), the *Euterpean*, and the SACRED-MUSIC SOCIETY. The Musical Fund was the successor of the old Philharmonic Society, and was organized about 1828. Its membership was composed of professional and amateur gentlemen. Monthly rehearsals were given but they were private. The Euterpean and the Sacred-Music Society are noticed in another place. As early as 1845 the German

population of New York had several societies, the principal of which was the *Concordia*,
conducted by Daniel Schlesinger. They have
at present, besides the DEUTSCHE LIEDER-
KRANZ, several Männerchöre, while the resident French have a *Cercle d'Harmonie* in a
flourishing condition. Prominent among the
glee clubs is the *Mendelssohn Glee Club*, of
which Joseph Mosenthal is conductor. There
is also the *Vocal Society*, S. P. Warren, conductor, which devotes itself to the lighter
vocal forms. It has been impossible, in an
article like this, to give a description of or
even mention all the societies of the past or
present, but the following have received more
or less extended notices :

Oratorio Society of New York, Symphony
Society of New York, American Musical
Fund Society, New York Harmonic Society,
Sacred-Music Society, Arion, Choral Society,
Deutsche Liederkranz, Euterpean, Mendels-
sohn Society, Musical Institute, Mason and
Thomas Soirées.          *

ORATORIO SOCIETY OF NEW YORK (The),
was organized in 1873 and incorporated in
June, 1875. The object of its formation is
the promotion and cultivation of choral music,
both sacred and secular, by the study and public performance of works of the highest class.
The Society is governed by a board of fifteen
directors, elected annually from the membership. The first concert was given at Knabe
Hall, Dec. 3, 1883, with a chorus of twenty-
eight. During the last season, that of 1882-
83, it became necessary to limit the membership to five hundred. Qualification for membership is based upon proficiency in sight-
reading, as determined by the conductor by
personal examination. The Society has, in
the ten years of its existence, given ninety-
three public performances and rendered forty-
four works or parts of works. In the spring
of 1881, in connection with the Symphony
Society, it planned and carried out the first
great May Festival held in New York, with
both artistic and financial success. The festival chorus numbered 1200, and the orchestra
287. The average audience for the seven
concerts was 9100 persons. The festival program included the following works : Berlioz's
"Grande Messe des Morts" (Requiem),
Rubinstein's "Tower of Babel," Handel's
"Messiah" and "Dettingen Te Deum,"

Beethoven's 9th Symphony, and Wagner's
"Meistersinger." The first two were new
in America. Most notable among the works
produced by the Society at its regular
concerts are "Requiem," Berlioz; "Pas-
sion Music" (according to St. Matthew),
Bach ; "Requiem," Brahms; "Sulanuth,"
Damrosch; "Samson," "Messiah," "Judas
Maccabæus," "Israel in Egypt," "Alex-
ander's Feast," and "L'Allegro," Handel;
"Creation," "Seasons," and "Tempest,"
Haydn; "Christus," Kiel; "Christus," Liszt;
"Elijah," "St. Paul," and "Walpurgis
Night," Mendelssohn; "Tower of Babel,"
Rubinstein ; "Paradise and Peri," Schumann,
together with a number or lesser works. It
has also assisted the Symphony Society in the
production of "La Damnation de Faust" and
"Romeo and Juliet," Berlioz ; 9th Symphony,
Beethoven ; and selections from the "Meistersinger" and "Parsifal," Wagner. Of these
works, "Messiah" has been given 18 times,
"La Damnation de Faust" 7 times, "Creation"
6 times, "Elijah" 9 times, "Tower of Babel"
5 times, "Requiem" (Berlioz) and "St. Paul"
3 times each. The Society is now in excellent financial condition, is self-sustaining, and
without debt. It has had but one musical
conductor, Dr. Leopold Damrosch, to whom
belongs its inception, and to whose zealous
and tireless efforts is chiefly due its remarkable
progress and unqualified success. His unvary-
ing geniality and courtesy have given him the
affection, and his musical erudition and power
the eminent respect of the chorus.

SYMPHONY SOCIETY OF NEW YORK (The),
was organized in 1878, and chartered April 8,
1879. The object of the Society is the promotion of orchestral music in New York, by
the study and public performance of the different forms of classical music, especially of
symphony. Among its incorporators and
directors the first year were Fr. Beringer,
Wm. H. Draper, August Lewis, Benj. K.
Phelps, Joseph Wiener, Leopold Damrosch,
Stephen M. Knevals, Morris Reno, Chas. F.
Roper, Frederick Zinsser, and Charles C.
Dodge. The first series of concerts was given
during 1878-79. The Society has regularly
given twelve public performances each season, which, together with the special concerts,
gives a total of sixty-four concerts. Eighty-
nine works or parts of works have been ren-

dered, besides those which have been the special work of the soloists. This group numbers twenty-three. Fourteen entirely new works have been produced. Of the orchestral works, the following are the most important: The 2nd, 3rd, 4th, 5th, 6th, 7th, 8th and 9th symphonies of Beethoven, together with his "Egmont," "Leonore No. 3," "Coriolan," and "Consecration of the Home," overtures; Symphony No. 3, Max Bruch (first time); "La Damnation de Faust," "Romeo and Juliet," and "Symphony Fantastique," Berlioz; 1st Symphony (op. 68) and "Academie Festival Overture," Brahms; "Spring," fantasia, Bronsart; "Anakreon," overture, Cherubini; "Festival Overture," Damrosch; "Slavonic Rhapsodie," No. 2 (new), Anton Dvorak; overtures "Sakuntala" and "Penthesilea," Carl Goldmark; Symphony in G (No. 8, Peter's edition), Haydn; Norse Suite, op. 22, A. Hamerik; the symphonic poems, "Tasso," "Les Préludes," "Festklänge," "Mazeppa," and "Die Hunnenschlacht," and the "Hungarian Rhapsodie" No. 2, Liszt; Symphony in G minor and Symphony in C ("Jupiter"), Mozart; "Scotch Symphony" (op. 56), and overtures "Midsummer Night's Dream" and "Fingal's Cave," Mendelssohn; second movement of "Spring Symphony," Joachim Raff; "Ocean Symphony" and "La Russia" (morceau symphonique), Rubinstein; overture, "Olympia," Spontini; Symphony No. 2, A minor (new), Camille Saint-Saëns; Symphony in C and unfinished symphony in B minor, Schubert; Symphony No. 2, in C, and Symphony No. 4, in D minor, Schumann; Suite, op. 43 (new), P. Tschaikowsky; Serenade No. 3, Robert Volkmann; selections from "Tristan and Isolde," "Parsifal," "Siegfried," "Die Walküre," and "Der Meistersinger von Nürnburg," and the "Tannhäuser" and the "Faust" overtures, Wagner; "Euryanthe," overture, Weber. The following list gives the concerts for piano, violin, etc., and orchestra, together with the soloist for each:

Bruch concert, for violin, August Wilhelmj.
Beethoven " for piano, Max Pinner.
Beethoven " for violin, August Wilhelmj.
Chopin " for piano, Madeline Schiller.
Grieg " for piano, Franz Rummel.
Mendls'hn " for violin, Mau. Dengremont.
Raff " for violin, August Wilhelmj.
Saint-Saëns " for piano, Franz Rummel.
Saint-Saëns " for violoncello, A. Fischer.
Saint-Saëns " for piano, Madeline Schiller.
Scharwenka " for piano, Bern. Bökelmann.
Spohr " for violin, Michael Banner.
Volkmann " for contralto, Miss Drasdil.
Wilhelmj " for violin, August Wilhelmj.

The most brilliant of the Society's single productions was that of "La Damnation de Faust," given with the aid of the Oratorio Society of New York (q. v.). The success of the work was remarkable, so much so that six performances were given in four weeks. The greatest work of the Society (also in conjunction with the Oratorio Society) was in the preparation and successful production of the first May Festival given in New York, the general features of which are to be found in the preceding notice (See also the heading, MAY FESTIVALS). Dr. Leopold Damrosch has been conductor of the Society from the first.                                    W. T.

AMERICAN MUSICAL FUND SOCIETY (The). The first movement made in relation to the American Musical Fund Society of New York was begun by the founder of the "American Art Journal," Henry C. Watson, in its predecessor, the "American Musical Times," June 16, 1848. In this article, and in several succeeding, the reasons why such a society should be established were fully developed, and the attention and interest of the profession fully aroused. The melancholy circumstances attending the death of Carl Woehning and of T. Y. Chubb accelerated the movement thus openly set in motion by Mr. Watson, and resulted in a meeting of the German musicians, called together by Mr. David Schaad, for many years secretary of the New York Philharmonic Society. Several meetings took place at No. 26 Delaney street, at which a constitution was formed, Mr. Schneider acting as chairman, Mr. Jos. Frick as treasurer, and Mr. Schaad as secretary pro tem. Then a public call was made for all resident musicians to meet at the Apollo Soloon, on Dec. 23, 1848. Although at these preliminary meetings it was designed to make the Society exclusively German, the public call brought together musicians of all countries, English, Americans, French, Italians, and Germans. Mr. Anthony Reiff was called to the chair, and Mr. Schaad acted a secretary. The principal motion, which settled for the time the character of the Society, was "That the language of the organization should be German." This was lost by an overwhelming majority, although of those present two-thirds were Germans. It was, however, determined that the constitution which the Society might adopt should be translated into the German language. The constitution formed at the preliminary meetings and rendered into English by Mr. John C. Scherpf, Watson's associate on the "Musical Times," was submitted to the musicians present, and, on motion, was referred to a committee for alteration, amendment or revision. The committee chosen and elected by acclamation were Henry C. Watson, Henry C. Timm, D. G. Etienne, M. Rafetti, Thomas Dodworth, and Anthony Reiff. The constitution prepared by this committee, with a German translation of it by Mr. Scherpf, was submitted, and, after discussion, was adopted, Feb. 16, 1849. The charter was obtained April 12th of the same year.                 * * *

PHILHARMONIC SOCIETY. This Society was founded April 5, 1842, for the purpose of cultivating instrumental music. The first concert was given Dec. 7, 1842, at the Apollo Rooms, since when concerts have regularly been given, the 181st of the series occurring April 12, 1879. The Chinese Rooms, Niblo's Garden, Irving Hall, and the Academy of Music have successively been used for the purpose of the Society. The latter was destroyed by fire in 1861, and during the interim of rebuilding Irving Hall was again used. Feb. 17, 1853, the Society was duly incorporated under the laws of the State of New York. The concerts are models in their line, and the programs cover a wide range of the best works, which are instrumental with the exception of numerous vocal solos and an occasional choral piece. The orchestra consists of about 96 performers, each one of whom is an actual member, and among whom the profits of the concerts are divided. The Society is managed by the actual members. Each of these must "be an efficient performer on some instrument, and have been a permanent resident of the city or its vicinity for one year previous to his nomination." An excellent set of rules for admission and government are rigidly enforced, to which fact the Society owes its high reputation. There are four grades of membership, besides the one already specified, as follows: 1. *Associate*, those who are admitted to the public rehearsals and concerts on paying a stipulated sum annually; 2. *Subscribers*, those who are entitled to two tickets for each regular concert, the price being regulated each year by the Society; 3. *Honorary*, a title conferred on eminent artists by the unanimous consent of the actual members; 4. *Honorary Associate*, a title bestowed upon eminent persons not belonging to the musical profession. Among the honorary members are Sir Julius Benedict (1850), and Mme. Parepa-Rosa (1870). The conductors of the Society have been H. C. Timm (1842-45), E. J. Loder (1846-48), U. C. Hill (1849-51), Theodore Eisfeld (1852-60), Carl Bergmann (1861-75), Dr. Leopold Damrosch (1876), Theodore Thomas (1877), Adolph Neuendorff (1878), Theodore Thomas (1879). The Society's headquarters are at Aschenbrodel's Club House, 74 East 4th St., but the library—an excellent one—is kept at 333 East 18th St. The following is a list of instrumental works which it has performed up to 1881:

| 1st Time. | No. Times. | Work. | Composer. |
|---|---|---|---|
| 1842, Dec. 7 | 10 | Symphony (C minor), - - | Beethoven. |
| "    "    7 | 1 | Quintet (D minor), - - | Hummel. |
| "    "    7 | 7 | Overture to "Oberon," | Weber. |
| "    "    7 | 1 | Overture (D), - - | Kalliwoda. |
| 1843, Feb. 18 | 14 | Eroica Symphony, - - | Beethoven. |
| "    "    18 | 2 | Overture to "William Tell," - | Rossini. |
| "    "    18 | 3 | Overture to "Freyschütz," - - | Weber. |
| "    Apr. 22 | 3 | Symphony No. 2, - | Beethoven. |
| "    "    22 | 4 | Overture, "Midsummer Night's Dream," | Mendelssohn. |
| "    "    22 | 1 | Septuor, - - - | Beethoven. |
| "    "    22 | 5 | "Jubilee" Overture, . - | Weber. |
| 1843-44, | 13 | Symphony No. 7, - - | Beethoven. |
| " | 6 | Overture to Zauberflöte, - - | Mozart. |
| " | 6 | "Jupiter" Symphony, - | Mozart. |

| 1st Time. | No. Times. | Work. | Composer. |
|---|---|---|---|
| 1843-44 | 1 | Septuor (two movements) - - | Hummel. |
| " | 1 | Symphony (D minor) - - | Spohr. |
| " | 8 | Overture to "Euryanthe" - - | Weber. |
| " | 4 | Overture, "Beherrscher der Geister" | Weber. |
| 1844-45 | 6 | Symphony No. 8, - - - | Beethoven. |
| " | 2 | Overture, "Hebriden" - - | Mendelssohn. |
| " | 3 | Symphony No. 3, - - - | Haydn. |
| " | 5 | Overture to "Jessonda" - | Spohr. |
| " | 2 | Overture, "Naids" - - | Bennett. |
| " | 1 | Fest-Overture, - - • | Ries. |
| " | 9 | Overture, "Melusine" - - | Mendelssohn. |
| 1845-46 | 6 | Symphony No. 3, - - | Mendelssohn. |
| " | 4 | Overture to "Anacreon" - | Cherubini. |
| " | 1 | Overture to "Jeune Henri" - - | Méhul. |
| " | 2 | Overture, "Marmion" - - | Loder. |
| " | 1 | Concert overture, - - - | Reissiger. |
| ;" | 1 | Symphony No. 1, - - | Kalliwoda. |
| " | 6 | Overture, "Les Francs Juges" - | Berlioz. |
| " | 4 | Symphony (G minor) - - | Mozart. |
| " | 12 | Symphony No. 6, - - - | Beethoven. |
| " | 5 | Choral Symphony (No. 9) - | Beethoven. |
| 1846-47 | 7 | Symphony, "Die Weihe der Töne" - | Spohr. |
| " | 2 | Symphony (E flat major) - | Mozart. |
| " | 5 | Overture to "King Lear" - - | Berlioz. |
| " | 1 | Overture (op. 3) - - - | Bristow. |
| 1847-48 | 1 | Symphony No. 1, - - - | Spohr. |
| " | 5 | Overture to "Egmont" - | Beethoven. |
| " | 1 | Septuor Concertando, - - | Lindpainter. |
| 1848-49 | 4 | Symphony (C major) - - | Gade. |
| " | 1 | Double Symphony, - - | Spohr. |
| " | 1 | Prize Symphony, - - | Lachner. |
| " | 2 | Overture, "Wood Nymph" - - | Bennett. |
| " | 2 | Triomphale, - - - | Ries. |
| " | | Concertstück, - - - | Weber. |
| 1849-50 | 9 | Symphony No. 4, - - | Beethoven. |
| " | 5 | Overture, "Meererstille und Glückliche Fahrt" | Mendelssohn. |
| " | 1 | Overture to "Les Huguenots" - | Meyerbeer. |
| " | 4 | Midsummer Night's Dream music, - | Mendelssohn. |
| " | 1 | Symphony Concertando, - - | Lindpainter. |
| 1850-51 | 9 | Symphony (C major) - - | Schubert. |
| " | 3 | Symphony (B flat major) - | Haydn. |
| " | 1 | Overture, "Vampyr" - | Lindpainter. |
| " | 1 | Overture, "Vestale" - - | Spontini. |
| " | 2 | Overture, "Robespierre" - - | Litolff. |
| " | | Concerto No. 2 (violin) - | F. David. |
| 1851-52 | 6 | Symphony No. 4, - - - | Mendelssohn. |
| " | 1 | Overture, "Joseph" - - | Méhul. |
| " | 2 | Overture to "Faust" - - | Lindpainter. |
| " | | Concerto No. 6 (violin) - | De Beriot. |
| 1852-53 | 6 | Symphony No. 1, - - | Schumann. |
| " | 3 | Overture, "Ossian" - - | Gade. |
| " | 5 | Overture, "Fingal's Cave" - - | Mendelssohn. |
| " | 1 | Overture, "Reiselust" - - | Lobe. |
| " | 3 | Overture, "In the Highlands" - | Gade. |
| " | 9 | Overture, "Leonore" (No. 3) - | Beethoven. |
| 1853-54 | 1 | Symphony, "The Seasons" - - | Spohr. |
| " | 9 | Symphony No. 2 (C) - - | Schumann. |
| " | 1 | Symphony (B flat) - - - | Schneider. |
| " | 2 | Overture, "Vampyr" - - | Marschner. |
| " | 2 | Overture to "Faust" - - | Spohr. |
| 1854-55 | 1 | Overture, "Abraham's Sacrifice" - | Lindpainter. |
| " | 1 | Overture to "Preciosa" - - | Weber. |
| " | 1 | Overture, "Maritana" - - | Wallace. |
| " | 2 | Overture, "Ruy Blas" - - | Mendelssohn. |
| " | 1 | Overture, "Olympia" - - | Spontini. |
| " | 8 | Overture to "Tannhäuser" - - | Wagner. |

| 1st Time. | No. Times. | Work. | Composer. |
|---|---|---|---|
| 1854-55 | | Concerto (E flat—piano) - - | Beethoven. |
| 1855-56 | 1 | Symphony, "Jullien" - - | Bristow. |
| " | 4 | Overture to "Iphigenia" - - | Gluck. |
| " | 1 | Overture, "Hans Heiling" - | Marschner. |
| 1856-57 | 1 | Overture, "Medea" - - | Cherubini. |
| " | 7 | Overture to "Faust" - - | Wagner. |
| " | 1 | Overture, "Uriel Acosta" - - | Schindelmeiss'r |
| " | 1 | Concert Overture, - - | Ries. |
| " | 1 | Overture, "Chant des Belges" - | Litolff. |
| 1857-58 | 1 | Symphony (E) - - | Hiller. |
| " | 4 | Overture to "Manfred" - - | Schumann. |
| " | 1 | Overture, "Merry Wives of Windsor" | Nicolai. |
| " | 4 | Overture, "Coriolan" - - | Beethoven. |
| " | 6 | Overture, Scherzo and Finale, - | Schumann. |
| " | 1 | Symphony-Concerto (piano) - | Litolff. |
| 1858-59 | 1 | Symphony No. 5, - - - | Gade. |
| " | 2 | Symphony No. 2 (D) - - | Haydn. |
| " | 1 | Symphony (F sharp) - - | Bristow. |
| " | 6 | Symphony No. 4, - - | Schumann. |
| " | 1 | Overture to "Siege of Corinth" - | Rossini. |
| " | 1 | Overture, "Fierabras" - - | Schubert. |
| " | | Concerto (A minor—piano) - - | Schumann. |
| 1859-60 | 7 | Tasso, poëme-symphonique, - | Liszt. |
| " | 2 | Overture to "Fidelio" - - | Beethoven. |
| " | 1 | Overture, "Festival" - - | Lachner. |
| 1860-61 | 5 | Symphony No. 3, - - - | Schumann. |
| " | 1 | Overture, "Leonore" (No. 1) - | Beethoven. |
| " | 3 | Overture, "Genoveva" - - | Schumann. |
| " | 1 | Festklänge, poëme-symphonique, - | Liszt. |
| " | 1 | Walpurgis Night, - - - | Mendelssohn. |
| 1861-62 | 2 | Symphony No. 5, - - | Mozart. |
| " | 5 | Les Préludes, poëme-symphonique, - | Liszt. |
| " | 5 | Overture, "Carnaval Romain" - | Berlioz. |
| " | 2 | Overture to "Rienzi" - - | Wagner. |
| " | | Concerto No. 2 (piano) - | Chopin. |
| " | | Concerto for violin, - - | Beethoven. |
| 1862-63 | 1 | Overture, "Traum in der Christnacht" | Hiller. |
| " | 1 | Overture (B flat) - - - | Rubinstein. |
| " | | Fantasie (piano) - | Schubert-Liszt. |
| 1863-64 | 1 | Symphony, "Faust" - - | Liszt. |
| " | 1 | Hymn of Praise, - - | Mendelssohn. |
| " | 2 | Overture to "Flying Dutchman" - | Wagner. |
| " | 1 | Overture, "Scotch" - - | Gade. |
| " | 1 | Concert Overture, - - - | Rietz. |
| 1864-65 | 2 | Symphony (E flat) - - | Haydn. |
| " | 2 | Overture, "Medea" - - | Bargiel. |
| " | 1 | Concerto (violoncello) - - | Ritter. |
| 1865-66 | 4 | Mazeppa, poëme-symphonique, - | Liszt. |
| " | 1 | Symphony No. 1 (D major) - | Mozart. |
| " | 2 | Symphonie Fantastique, - - | Berlioz. |
| " | 3 | Overture, "Prometheus" - | Bargiel. |
| " | 3 | Introduction, "Tristan and Isolde" - | Wagner. |
| 1866-67 | 1 | Symphony (D minor) - - | Volkmann. |
| " | 1 | Romeo and Juliet (two movements) - | Berlioz. |
| " | 1 | Overture, "Nachtlicher Zug" - | Liszt. |
| " | 1 | Overture, "Columbus" - - | Bristow. |
| " | 3 | Introduction to "Lohengrin" - | Wagner. |
| " | 2 | Overture to "Les deux Journées" | Cherubini. |
| 1867-68 | 1 | Overture, "Othello" - - | Ritter. |
| 1868-69 | 1 | Reformation Symphony, - - | Mendelssohn. |
| " | 3 | Symphony (unfinished) - - | Schubert. |
| " | 2 | Music to "Manfred" - - | Schumann. |
| " | 1 | Overture, "Hamlet" - - | Gade. |
| " | 1 | Overture, "Semiramide" - - | Catel. |
| " | 1 | Suite, - - - | Bach. |
| 1869-70 | 2 | Symphony, "Divina Commedia" - | Liszt. |

| *1st Time.* | *No. Times.* | *Work.* | *Composer.* |
|---|---|---|---|
| 1869-70 | 1 | Symphony (C) - - | Raff. |
| " | 4 | Overture, "Sakuntala" - - | Goldmark. |
| " | 2 | Overture, "Leonore" (No. 2) - | Beethoven. |
| 1870-71 | 2 | Symphony, "Ocean" - - | Rubinstein. |
| " | 3 | Music to "Egmont" - - | Beethoven. |
| " | 1 | Overture, "Aladdin" - - | Reinecke. |
| " | 1 | Overture to "Idomeneo" - | Mozart. |
| 1871-72 | 1 | Symphony (G major) - - | Haydn. |
| " | 2 | Symphony, "Im Wald" - - | Raff. |
| " | 1 | Symphony No. 2, - - - | Ritter. |
| " | 1 | Overture, "Julius Cæsar" - | Schumann. |
| " | 3 | Overture to "Meistersinger von Nürnberg" | Wagner. |
| " | 1 | Overture, "Macbeth" - - | Heinefetter. |
| 1872-73 | 1 | Symphony No. 4, - - | Raff. |
| " | 1 | Symphony No. 8, - - - | Gade. |
| " | 1 | Symphony, "Oxford" - - | Haydn. |
| " | 1 | Overture, "Prinzessin Ilse" - - | Erdmansdörfer. |
| " | 2 | Overture, "Consecration of the House" | Beethoven. |
| " | 1 | Overture, "Galilei" - - | Matzka. |
| 1873-74 | 1 | Symphony No. 1, - - | Rubinstein. |
| " | 1 | Symphony, "Arcadian" - - | Bristow. |
| " | 1 | Symphony, "Leonore" - - | Raff. |
| " | 1 | Introduction to "Loreley" - - | Bruch. |
| " | 1 | Overture, "Michel Angelo" - | Gade. |
| " | 1 | Suite, - - - - | Grimm. |
| 1874-75 | 1 | Symphony No. 9, - - | Haydn. |
| " | 1 | Symphony No. 6, - - - | Raff. |
| " | 1 | Symph ny No. 3, - - | Spohr. |
| " | 2 | Symphony No. 1, - - | Mozart. |
| " | 1 | Andante from op. 97, - - | Beethov'n-Liszt |
| " | 1 | Ciaconne, - - - | Bach-Liszt. |
| " | 1 | Overture, "Normannezug" - | Dietrich. |
| " | 1 | Overture (op. 15) - - - | Lassen. |
| " | 1 | Fantasie—Overture, - - | Bennett. |
| 1875-76 | 1 | Symphony No. 1, - - - | Metzdorff. |
| " | 1 | Symphony No. 2, - - | Raff. |
| " | 1 | Overture, "Julius Cæsar" - | Bülow. |
| " | 1 | Overture to "Faniska" - - | Cherubini. |
| " | 1 | Overture, "Romeo and Julia" - | Tschaikowsky |
| 1876-77 | 1 | Symphony, "Ländliche Hochzeit" - | Goldmark. |
| " | 2 | Serenade, - - - | Fuchs. |
| " | 1 | Fantasie, - - - | Beethoven. |
| " | 1 | First act of "Walküre" - - | Wagner. |
| " | 2 | Scena from "Götterdämmerung" - | Wagner. |
| " | | Concerto (piano) - - | Saint-Saëns. |
| " | | Concerto (piano) - - - | Bronsart. |
| 1877-78 | 1 | Symphony No. 1, - - - | Brahms. |
| " | 1 | Symphony No. 2, - - - | Rubinstein. |
| " | 1 | Serenade, - - - | Volkmann. |
| " | 1 | Variations, - - - | Brahms. |
| 1878-79 | 1 | Symphony No. 2, - - | Brahms. |
| " | 1 | Hunnenschlacht, - - - | Liszt. |
| " | 1 | Fantasia, "Francesca di Rimini" - | Tschaikowsky. |
| " | 1 | Symphony No. 3, - - | Tschaikowsky. |
| 1879-80 | 1 | Symphony No. 4, - - | Rubinstein. |
| " | 1 | Walküre Ritt und Siegfrieds Tod, - | Wagner. |
| " | 1 | Third act of "Götterdämmerung" - | Wagner. |
| " | 1 | Concerto (piano) - - - | Tschaikowsky. |

NEW YORK HARMONIC SOCIETY. This Society, which was in a measure the successor of the "Sacred-Music Society," was organized Monday, Sept. 24, 1849. Rehearsals were at once begun under the voluntary direction of H. C. Timm, and soon after Theodore Eisfeld was elected permanent conductor. On the evening of May 10, 1850, the Society gave its first public performance, which consisted of the "Messiah." On the 9th of November following, the oratorio was repeated, Jenny Lind singing the soprano solos. June 28, 1851, Mendelssohn's "Elijah" was given at Tripler Hall. The Society experienced the difficulties which usually beset such an undertaking, and was several times reorganized. In 1863, a number of dissatisfied members instituted a rival society, called "Mendelssohn Society." It continued to hold its own, however, until 1869, when it met the fate of its predecessors, after a useful life of twenty years. Its rival society did not very long survive it. Among the works which it rendered are "Creation," "Judas Maccabæus," "Samson," Neukomm's "David," Mendelssohn's "Hymn of Praise," Bristow's "Praise to God," Ritter's "Forty-Sixth Psalm," and Bach's cantata, "Who believeth and is baptized" (1865). The conductors were H. C. Timm, Theo. Eisfeld, Geo. F. Bristow, Carl Bergmann, Geo. W. Morgan, F. L. Ritter, and J. Peck.

SACRED-MUSIC SOCIETY (The), was organized in 1823. The circumstance which led to its institution seems to have been a dissention between the choir and the vestry of Zion Church, located at the corner of Mott and Cross streets. The choristers petitioned the vestry for an increase of salary or permission to give concerts. This being refused, they finally resolved to withdraw in a body, and for the purpose of continuing the practice of sacred music formed the Sacred-Music Society. The first concert was given at the Presbyterian church, Provost street, Monday evening, March 15, 1824, with a varied program, including numerous selections from Chapple. Wednesday evening, Feb. 28, 1827, the Society gave a concert for the benefit of the Greeks, which netted $590. Malibran assisted. This event gave it a fresh impetus which was very beneficial. It was not until Nov. 18, 1831, at St. Paul's Chapel, that an entire oratorio was performed, which was the "Messiah." The solo singers were Mrs. Austin, Mrs. Singleton, John Jones, A. Kyle, J. Pearson, and Thomas Thornton. The orchestra numbered 38 and the chorus 71 performers. This is said to have been the first performance of an entire oratorio in New York City. It was repeated Jan. 31 and Feb. 2, 1832. From this time the Society devoted itself to a better class of works. Another im-

portant event in its history was the production, Oct. 29, 1838—only two years after its first production at Düsseldorf under the direction of the composer—of Mendelssohn's oratorio, "St. Paul." In 1849, after an existence of twenty-six years, the Society ceased to exist, and was succeeded by the New York Harmonic Society (see preceding). Uriah C. Hill was for many years its conductor.

ARION (The). This society was formed in 1854 by members who seceded from the Deutsche Liederkranz. It is devoted entirely to the cultivation of male choruses, and women are only invited to participate on special occasions. A noteworthy event in the history of the society was the production in 1859 of Wagner's "Tannhäuser," for the first time in America. Six concerts are given each year at its own hall. Its conductors have been Meyerhofer (1854-58), Bergmann (1859), Anschütz (1860-61), F. L. Ritter (1862-66), Bergmann (1867-70), and Dr. Damrosch (1870 to his death in 1884).

NEW YORK CHORAL SOCIETY (The) was in a measure a consolidation of previously existing societies, and was organized in September, 1823. A small army of officers was elected, the president and three vice-presidents all being clergymen. James H. Swindalls acted as first conductor. The constitution required that each active male member pay one dollar into the treasury. Subscribers were required to pay $10 per annum. The first concert of the Society was given at St. George's Chapel, Beekman St., April 20, 1824, the program consisting of selections from Handel, Beethoven, Mozart and Jomelli. The chorus was fifty and the orchestra twenty strong. One of the objects of the Society was to assist with its talents any benevolent institution.

DEUTSCHE LIEDERKRANZ. The beginning of this society dates back to the autumn of 1846, when a call was issued to the Germans of New York. In January, 1847, a constitution was adopted, a board of directors selected, and a conductor appointed. Rehearsals were held at the old Shakspeare Hotel and concerts given at intervals. In 1850, Agricola Paur became conductor, a post which he still retains. Four years later a dissension occurred which resulted in the establishment of the Arion. In 1856 women were admitted as active members—a very wise step, and one which increased the scope of the society as well as insure.l greater permanency. The society has a building of its own, in the hall of which several concerts are given each season. Among the more important works performed are Mozart's "Requiem;" Mendelssohn's "Walpurgisnacht," "Festgesang an die Künstler," "Lobgesang," finale to "Loreley," and "Antigone;" Schumann's "Des Sängersfluch," "Manfred," "Der Rose Pilgerfahrt," "Vom Pagen und der Königstochter," and "Das Paradies und der Peri;" Liszt's "Prometheus;" Gade's "Comala;" Schubert's "Die Verschworenen;" Bruch's "Odysseus," etc.

EUTERPEAN (The) was organized about the beginning of the present century, and was for a long time the oldest musical society in New York City. It was composed of instrumental performers, met every Friday evening during the summer months, and gave but one concert a year. Its artistic influence seems to have been rather small, for the critics of that time found much fault with it. At a concert given at the City Hall, June 30, 1839, the orchestra consisted of 6 first violins, 5 second violins, 4 tenors, 3 violoncellos, 2 contra-basses, 4 flutes, 2 oboes, 2 clarinets, 2 bassoons, 4 horns, 2 trumpets, 3 trombones, kettledrum, drum, and cymbals. The society was, in a measure, the predecessor of the Philharmonic Society, before whose institution in 1842 it ceased to exist.

MUSICAL INSTITUTE. This chorus society was organized about 1844. It brought out in September, 1846, Haydn's "Seasons," and other oratorios afterwards. April 11, 1848, Schumann's "Paradise and the Peri" was performed, and it is said that the composer was very much pleased when he heard of the fact (See "Neue Zeitschrift für Musik.") The society also produced Rossini's "Stabat Mater" for the first time in America. H. C. Timm was its conductor. The chorus numbered 120 and the orchestra 60 performers. About 1850 the society ceased to exist, being merged, along with the Vocal Society and the Sacred-Music Society, into the New York Harmonic Society.

MASON-THOMAS SOIREES. These *soirées* were established in 1855, and were given at the Dodworth rooms on Broadway and Eleventh street. William Mason was pianist, and

Theodore Thomas, Joseph Mosenthal, George Matzka and Carl Bergmann, constituted the string quartet. Bergmann was at the end of a year succeeded by Brannes, and finally by F. Bergner. The works performed were of the highest order and represented both classical and modern composers. The *soirées* merited better patronage than they received. They were discontinued in 1866.

THE APOLLO CLUB, composed exclusively of male voices, is the representative musical society in this city, and, in excellence of *ensemble*, is vocally what the Philharmonic is instrumentally. The Club, now in its fifth season, is as successful financially as it is musically. Three subscription concerts are given during the season under the direction of Mr. Dudley Buck, and are attended by the best musical people in the city. The class of music interpreted, though not particularly elaborate, is usually of a high order. Several of Mr. Buck's most successful works were dedicated to and sung for the first time by the Club. Of these were "The Nun of Nidros," "King Olaf's Christmas," and "Chorus of Spirits and Houris" from Shelley's "Prometheus Unbound." The Club from its inception has steadily increased in reputation, as well as in a financial sense. It originated primarily from the defunct St. Cecilia Society, and was the outcome of a dispute between several prominent members and their conductor, Mr. E. J. Fitzhugh. At a meeting held at the residence of Mr. Chauncey Ives, Nov. 1st, 1877, the Schubert Club was organized, which was afterward changed to that of the Apollo. The first rehearsals were held at Evans' music rooms, 177 Montague Street, and the initial concert, under Mr. Buck's leadership, was given at the Art rooms, Montague Street, March 27th, 1878, with a membership of twenty-four. The expenses were defrayed by each member being assessed a pro rata amount. The success of this first concert led to the organization being placed upon a solid financial basis. A meeting to that end was held June 5th, at the house of the late Dr. Albert E. Sumner, and Mr. Wm. B. Leonard was appointed president. The financial results of the first year showed a modest balance for the Club of four dollars. The present year shows a balance of $2,598 to the bank account of the Club. Subscribing members are limited to three hundred and active members to sixty. From the former party directors are annually elected, in whom is vested the government of the Club. The officers, who remain the same, are Wm. B. Leonard, president; L. S. Burnham, vice-president; William B. Kendall, treasurer; Robert S. Granniss, secretary for board of directors; I. A. Stanwood, chairman active members; Henry S. Brown, secretary, and William B. Rowe, Jr., librarian. In the death of the second vice-president, Dr. Sumner, the Apollo Club lost not only one of the originators, but a valuable counsellor and friend. Rehearsals are held Monday evenings, at Everett Hall, Fulton Street.

THE AMATEUR OPERA ASSOCIATION is probably the most complete organization of its kind in the country. Its members are among the best amateurs of the city, while the performances given are usually of a very creditable order. The Association is now in its eighth year, with an established reputation. From small beginnings the society has grown to be a considerable factor among the several very excellent amateur dramatic and musical associations of the city. The following brief facts will show the progress made by the Association from its inception. It was organized in 1877 from the choir of St. Peter's P. E. Church, by Mr. Henry E. Hutchinson, who became the musical director, a position he retained for three years. The first board of management was composed of Henry E. Hutchinson, James Bogle and James Walter Thompson. To the early efforts of Mr. Bogle the Association owes much of its present success. The first opera given was "Martha," which occurred in 1878 in a hall upon the site of which the Music Hall now stands. The success of this opera was followed by the production of the "Doctor of Alcantara," with Mr. Charles H. Parsons, a well-known amateur, at the head of the management. Performances were given at the Union League Theatre, N. Y., and at the Novelty Theatre in Williamsburg. The "Bohemian Girl," "Fra Diavolo," "Maritana" and the "Pirates of Penzance," followed in quick succession, and were given at the Academy of Music with more or less success. The most ambitious and successful effort yet made by the Association was the performance of the "Chimes of Normandy," which was a revelation even to the most sanguine friends of of the society and fairly placed it upon a solid and artistic basis. The Association is particularly fortunate in the selection of its officers. Mr. Parsons, president, brings to the position real executive ability and hard work, as also do Mr. B. R. Weston, vice-president; Mr. Henry Gorham, secretary; Mr. A. M. Wilder, Jr., treasurer and Signor Rafael-Navarro, musical director. The rooms of the Association are at 179 Montgue Street.

THE AMPHION MUSICAL SOCIETY has its headquarters in the Eastern District, and occupies a handsome suite of club-rooms, including a hall for rehearsals, corner of Clymer Street and Division Avenue. The Society has a two-fold basis — musical and social. It is now in its third year and has experienced a success almost phenomenal. The active membership is limited to sixty and the honorary membership to four hundred. The former is composed of some good material, which, under the able direction of Mr. C. Mortimer Wiske, is welded into a compact body of voices capable of doing some good work. Three invitation concerts are given during the season at the Academy of Music, which are attended by the best people in the Eastern District. The programs provided on these occasions are generally of a light character and comprise mainly German and English part songs. The Society was organized Sept. 5, 1880, and the first rehearsal took place Oct. 5th. The initial concert was given Jan. 24, 1881, in Bedford Avenue Reformed Church, with a chorus of thirty-six voices, directed by their present conductor, Mr. Wiske. The success of this concert stimulated its promoters to greater activity. At the first annual election of officers, held in May, Mr. George Fischer was elected president. The second concert of the second season was given in the Academy of Music, an interesting feature of which was the production by the Society of an ambitious composition, "Frithof." Thomas' orchestra assisted on this occasion. The social element is a strong feature in the work of the Society and well appointed rooms are set apart for social intercourse and recreation. The organization exerts an educating and refining influence in the community to which it especially belongs.

The present officers of the Society are George H. Fisher, president; Messrs. Benjamin Russell and Geo. V. Tompkins, vice–presidents; Wm. M. Seymour, recording secretary; Robert W. Butler, financial secretary; Joseph Applegate, treasurer; Arthur C. Huene, librarian, and C. Mortimer Wiske, musical director.

THE BROOKLYN SÆNGERBUND, the oldest and largest singing society, occupies rooms, temporarily, at 200 Court Street. It was founded on the 5th of July, 1862, by the consolidation of the Thalia and Liederkranz, with forty members, all good voices and music-lovers. At the different national Sænger festivals, in New York, 1865, Philadelphia, 1867, and in Baltimore, 186c, the Bund won prizes and laurels; and again, in Philadelphia, 1882, carried off the second highest prize. The present custom of giving an annual masquerade ball originated in 1866, which was first held at Montague Hall. The annual occurrence of these fancy balls, which take place at the Academy of Music, is an event of considerable interest to the friends of the society and the general public. The society is established upon a solid financial basis and is conspicuous for its benevolent efforts in times of great distress. The present officers and life members are George Rehn, president; John N. Eitel, vice–president; Carl F. Eisenach, secretary; George Dietrick, treasurer; Charles W. Muhlhausen, financial secretary, and William Groschel, musical conductor.

THE DUDLEY BUCK QUARTET CLUB, organized in 1880, enjoys an excellent and extended reputation. The class of music interpreted by this organization is necessarily of a very limited character. The members comprising it are all artists of recognized ability, and, under the personal direction of Mr. Dudley Buck, the eminent composer, are in almost constant practice. In the singing of quartet music the Club is probably without a rival in the State, while the concerts given are among the most elevating and entertaining of their kind listened to.

ACADEMY OF MUSIC (The) was erected in the year 1859. The first public meeting of citizens in promotion of the object was held February 14th of the same year, when it was resolved to erect a suitable building for musical, literary and scientific purposes. To this

end subscriptions were invited. A building committee composed of Messrs. A. A. Law, chairman; A. M. White, treasurer; Luther B. Wyman and S. B. Chittenden, accepted plans submitted by Leopold Erdlitz, architect. The builders were John French and Tappan Reeve and company; decorator, Louis H. Cohn. The building is a plain structure of Philadelphia brick, and occupies a site of ten lots upon Montague street, near Fulton. Its dimensions are 250x100 feet, and it was erected at a cost of $220,000. The interior is of horse-shoe shape and of Moorish design. The general appearance of the building, both as to its exterior and interior, is severely plain and unattractive. The stage is 70x80 feet, with a proscenium 44 feet. The auditorium has a seating capacity of 2300, and is divided into parquet, balcony, dress circle and gallery. The foyer is 40x70 feet, leading from which are two dirctors' rooms. Over these rooms the assembly room, 40x90, with a sixty feet ceiling. This room is used for receptions, musicales, socials, etc. The first public performance occurred Jan. 22, 1861, with Italian opera under the management of Jacob Grau. The initial opera was "Il Giuramento," given by a powerful company, including Mme. Pauline Colson, Miss Isabella Hinckley, Adelaide Phillips, Signors Brignoli, Elena, Ferry, Susini, Steffani, Ipolito and Colletti. Sig. Muzio was musical director. It was the original intention of the promoters of the Academy not to allow the use of the building for other than musical or literary purposes, which, however, proved financially impracticable. The first dramatic performance given in the building was under the management of Henry C. Jarrett, and in it Messrs. J. W. Wallack and E. L. Davenport participated. The Academy is now used for almost any purpose for which it may be engaged, subject, of course, to the decision of the directors. The principal use, however, to which the building is devoted are the Philharmonic, the Apollo and the Amphion concerts, Italian opera, public meetings, and private dramatic entertainments. The shareholders number about 300, and these, with the directors, are entitled to free admission, according to the charter, to all public performances. The present (1884) officers of the Academy are Henry Sanger, president; I. H. Frothingham, treasurer, and C. A. Townsend, secretary.

BROOKLYN PHILHARMONIC SOCIETY was organized and incorporated in 1857, having in view the advancement of music in that city. Membership may be obtained by paying the sum annually fixed by the directors, but the number is limited. The Society is directed by a directory of 25 members, annually chosen, who appoint the government. Five or more concerts are given every season, each preceded by three public rehearsals. These are of high order, and include the best works of every style, some of which have been produced for the first time in America. The orchestra is large, and composed of the best musicians that can be obtained. At first the Brooklyn Athenæum was used for the Society's performances, but since 1862 the Academy of Music, which is capable of accommodating about 3000 persons, has been employed for that purpose. The conductors have been as follows : Theodore Eisfeld (1857–62), Theodore Thomas (1862), Theodore Eisfeld (1863–64), Carl Bergmann (1865), Theodore Thomas (1866–69), Carl Bergmann (1870–72), Theodore Thomas (1873–80). The Society has a library of over 100 orchestral works.

P. J. SMITH.

BROOKLYN CONSERVATORY OF MUSIC. This institution was founded in 1866 by Prof. J. W. Groschel. It was subsequently reorganized and improved by Miss Louise Groschel and Mrs. S. Groschel-Chadick, daughters of the founder, under whose efficient management it still remains. The former lady was for some time a pupil of the Conservatorium at Stuttgart and of Adler at Paris. All the usual branches of music are taught and in addition, when so desired, the French and German languages. A series of four chamber music *soirées* was given during the past season (1883), the programs of which were of high order. The proprietors of the Conservatory have a summer school at Westwood, N. J., which enables the pupils to uninterruptedly continue their studies if they so desire.

**Neuendorff,** ADOLPH, was born June 13, 1843, at Hamburg, and showed a great aptitude for music at an early age. It was not intended, however, that he should follow the profession of a musician, but rather that of his father, a prosperous merchant. A series of reverses led the family to come to the United States, in June, 1855, with the hopes of bettering their prospects. Weinlich, basso of a German opera company playing in New York and a good violinist, became an inmate of the household and kindly consented to give young Adolph some lessons on the violin. After two years' study he secured the position of first violinist in the orchestra of the old Stadt Theatre. About this time he commenced studying the violin under Matzka and theory and composition under Dr. Gustav Schilling. With the latter he remained two years. In the spring of 1859 he made his first appearance as a pianist at a concert given in Dodworth Hall. He accompanied his father on a business trip to Brazil, in 1860, where he remained two years. Returning to New York he resumed his position as first violinist in the Stadt Theatre orchestra. Soon after he received a call to Milwaukee, Wis., as leader of the orchestra of the Stadt Theatre there. About this time he made the acquaintance of Carl Anschütz, with whom he studied theory and composition some time. In the autumn of 1864 he succeeded Mr. Anschütz as conductor of the German opera, having previously been chorus-master. With the company he traveled and gave performances in many of the principal cities of the country. In 1867 he was engaged as conductor of the Stadt Theatre, New York, a post which he held until 1871. In the autumn of the following year he opened the Germania Theatre, of which he was the founder, and with which he is still (Jan., 1884) connected. During 1876 he conducted a series of symphony concerts at his theatre. He was one of the American representatives at the Wagner festival, Bayreuth, in the same year, acting as special correspondent of the New York "Staats Zeitung." Mr. Neuendorff takes a high place among New York's conductors, and is frequently called upon to wield the *bâton* at festivals and concerts. As an *impresario* he has more than once visited Europe to secure artists, and brought over among others Mme. Lichtmay and Theodore Wachtel (1871 and 1874).

**Nielson-Rounsville,** MADAME CHRISTINE, was born Aug. 10, 1845, at Christiansand, Norway. She studied under Haberbier at Leipsic, and in 1871 came to the United States, locating at Chicago, where she still resides as a teacher of the piano. She was married to Dr. Rounsville in 1875.

**Night in Rome, A.** An operetta in two acts. Words and music by Julius Eichberg. First produced at the Museum, Boston, Saturday, Nov. 26, 1864.

**Norton-Gower,** LILIAN, who is also known by her stage name of MLLE. NORDICA, is an American lady but studied in Europe. She made her *début* at the Grand Opéra, Paris, in 1882, as *Marguerite* in "Faust." Soon after she was engaged by Col. Mapleson for Her Majesty's, London, and under his management made her first appearance in this country at the Academy of Music, New York, in November, 1883, in her original *rôle*. During the season she visited the principal cities, and will undoubtedly be heard here often. As *Marguerite* she has few superiors, and whenever she appears in that *rôle* she is sure of a flattering reception.

**Notre Dame de Paris.** An opera composed by W. H. Fry, and first produced at the Academy of Music, Philadelphia, in April, 1864. The libretto is by J. R. Fry, a brother of the composer.

# O.

**Oakley,** WILLIAM H., was born about the beginning of the present century at New York. He was chorister of the old Mulberry Street (now St. Paul's) Methodist Episcopal Church in 1840, and afterwards at other Methodist churches in New York. With the "Alleghanians," of which he was one of the founders, he traveled all over the United States, and became widely known as one of the most prominent Methodist singers and composers. He died at New York, of heart disease, Jan. 7, 1880.

**Oberlin Conservatory of Music.** This well-known school of music was established in 1865 by John P. Morgan and G. W. Steele. Mr. Morgan, who was an alumnus of the Leipzig Conservatorium and later one of the organists of Trinity Church, New York, was its first director. A large proportion of the members of its faculty have been educated at Leipzig, and naturally the school is modeled in no small degree after that institution. Great care is taken to give the students only those compositions for study which may properly be regarded as models, and numerous opportunities are offered for hearing the best compositions of both classic and modern writers. The faculty and officers of government now number eighteen; and the attendance for the past year was 446. The Conservatory is now under the able direction of Prof. F. B. Rice.

**Octave staff.** A system of notation consisting of three groups of lines combined, comprising three octaves of ordinary vocal music; dispensing with flats and sharps, and giving to each note its own position. It was introduced by a Mr. Adams of New Jersey, but never came into use, being of little practical value.

**Old Folks at Home, The,** sometimes called "Suwanee River" from its mention of the river by that name in Florida, is perhaps the most popular of all Stephen Foster's songs. It was written, both words and music, at his old home in Allegheny City in the summer of 1851 after his return from an absence of nearly a year, which fact no doubt inspired the song. Any one having an early copy may be puzzled by the line upon the title page, "Written and composed by Edwin P. Christy." Mr. Christy will be remembered as the manager of the celebrated "Christy Minstrels." It seems that he met Foster on one occasion in New York, and offered him a certain sum for the song in question, provided he was allowed to claim the authorship of it. Foster cared little for fame, and the pressing necessities of poverty must have overruled any objections on his part which would naturally arise. This is only one of the numerous cases in which he was taken advantage of because of his poverty, but it seems the most atrocious of them all. The truth at last became known, and the song is now published with the name of its true composer. Foster entertained a hope that "The Old Folks at Home" might rival in popularity "Home, Sweet Home." It has probably come the nearest to it of any song ever written. The sales have already reached over half a million copies, and there is still a large and steady demand for it. Unlike many songs, its popularity does not seem to be of the transitory kind, and it is more than likely that it will hold its place in song literature for many years to come.

**Oliver,** HENRY KEMBLE, American psalmodist, was born Nov. 24, 1800, at Beverly, Mass. In music he was an amateur and mostly self-taught. He edited and published in conjunction with Dr. Tuckerman, in 1849, the "National Lyre." His other collections are "Oliver's Collection of Church Music" (1860) and "Oliver's Original Sacred Music" (1875). He is well known by his tune of "Federal Street," written in 1832, and still popular. It was performed under his own direction at the Peace Jubilee of 1872 by a chorus of 20,000, the immense audience joining. In 1876 he was residing at Salem, Mass.

**On the Prairies.** The second (American) symphony, op. 15, of Dr. Louis Maas. It is descriptive of a day on the prairies, and is divided into four parts, as follows: 1.—" Morning on the Prairies," 2.—" The Chase" (scherzo) presto, 3.—" An Indian Legend," adagio-andante, 4.—" Evening, Night and Sunrise." The idea of the composition was first suggested to Dr. Maas while he was crossing the boundless prairies of the West. Dedicated to Ex-President Arthur. First performed at the Music Hall, Boston, Dec. 14, 1883, with an orchestra of 100 musicians.

**Opera in America.** Anything like a complete history of the opera in this country is yet to be written. It has existed chiefly in the large cities, such as New York, Boston and New Orleans, and even at best its life has been one of many vicissitudes. It seems, according to J. N. Ireland, author of "Records of the New York Stage," that some of the early English ballads were given in New York more than a century ago. " The Beggar's Opera" was produced in 1751, "Love in a Village" in 1768, "Inkle and Yarico," "The Duenna," and "The Tempest" in 1791, "Guy Mannering" by Bishop in 1816, Davy's "Rob Roy" in 1818, and others at different times. The first season of.Italian opera began in New York, at the Park Theatre, Nov. 26, 1825, with Rossini's "Barber." French opera was first introduced at the same theatre, July 13, 1827, by "Cenerentola." German opera was introduced at Niblo's Garden, Sept. 16, 1856, with "Robert der Teufel," by Meyerbeer. The conductor was Carl Bergmann. The introduction of opera bouffe dates only from Sept. 24, 1867, when "La Grande Duchesse" was produced at the French Theatre, and had the extraordinary run of 158 nights. In Boston the first season of Italian opera began April 23, 1847, at the Howard Athenæum. Some of the most important operas, among them "Aida," "Lohengrin," and "Die Walküre," have been given in New York before presented in either London or Paris. New Orleans is the only city that has supported the opera continuously through the operatic season, but since the Civil War it has been of minor importance in theatrical affairs. The most noted operatic managers whose careers are connected with this country are Seguin, who commenced in 1838, Max Maretzek, whose career dates from 1848, Max and Maurice Strakosch, Carl Rosa, H. L. Bateman, C. D. Hess, etc.

America has not yet produced anything like a distinct operatic school, nor is she likely to for some time to come. The heterogeneous character of the population and the newness of the country forbid. There have been, however, several American operas produced which may lay claim to the name and with success. The principal of them are noticed under their respective headings, but it may be well to state some facts concerning them here. "The Archers; or, The Mountaineers of Switzerland," is probably the first American opera. The music is by Benj. Carr, an Englishman, who came to this country in 1794; the libretto by William Dunlop, and founded on the story of William Tell. It was produced in New York, April 18, 1796. Another American opera is "Edwin and Angelina," produced in New York, Dec. 19, 1798. The libretto, founded on Goldsmith's poem, is by Dr. E. H. Smith, and the music by M. Pellesier, a Frenchman who resided in New York. "Rip Van Winkle," by George F. Bristow, produced at Niblo's Garden, New York, Sep. 27, 1855; "Leonora," by W. H. Fry, produced at the Academy of Music, New York, March 29, 1858; and "Notre Dame de Paris," by the same composer, produced at the Academy of Music, Philadelphia, in April, 1864, are three later and quite successful works. "The Doctor of Alcantara," by Julius Eichberg, produced at the Boston Museum, April 7, 1862, is the most popular American opera ever written. Mr. Eichberg has written three other operas, viz: "The Rose of Tyrol," "A Night in Rome," and "The Two Cadis," which have achieved considerable popularity.

The number of American operas of which notice has been taken by no means indicates the number that has been written, which is very large, but the most of them have been of light, trashy character, modelled after the French opera bouffe, and have sunk into oblivion almost as soon as born. Attempts have been made by American composers at the grand opera, but thus far seemingly without any success. One of the latest productions in this line is "Zenobia," composed by Silas G. Pratt. It was produced at Chicago, though without the proper stage scenery, costumes, etc., in June of the present year (1882), but rather coldly received. That some American composer will yet write a grand opera which will be a success, can not be doubted, but as to whom that person will be remains to be seen.

## Organ, History of in America.

The first American organ was built by Edward Bromfield, Jr., at Boston in 1745. In 1752, Thomas Johnston built an organ for Christ Church, Boston. Part of an instrument built by this maker for the Episcopal church at Salem, Mass., is still in the possession of Messrs. Hook & Hastings. In front there is inscribed in German text, in ivory, the following words: "Thomas Johnston fecit, Boston, Nov. Anglorum, 1754." It was a small affair, having only one manual and six stops. Mr. Johnston died about 1768, and was succeeded by a Dr. Leavitt, who engaged in the business for a number of years. Henry Pratt, of Winchester, N. H., who died in 1849, manufactured about fifty organs during the early part of the century. Meanwhile, notwithstanding their great cost, several foreign organs were imported, chiefly for use in Boston. The first foreign organ erected in this country was the one in the Queen's chapel, Boston, put up in August, 1713, and presented by Thos. Brattle, Esq.

The first American organ builder who became noted as such was William M. Goodrich. Mr. Goodrich was born in 1777, and went to Boston about 1799. In 1805 he commenced the business of organ building, his first organ being one erected in the Catholic church of Bishop Chevereux, in Boston. Shortly after he was engaged to clean and repair several imported organs, from which he received great advantage, being a self-taught artist. So successful was he that, though there was a strong prejudice against American organs, few were imported from abroad. He continued in business until 1833. Ebenezer Goodrich, brother of William, after learning the trade in his manufactory set up in business for himself, and manufactured a number of organs, mostly small ones. In 1807, Thomas Appleton entered the employment of William Goodrich, and after remaining there some years entered into co-partnership with a Mr. Babcock and two gentlemen by the name of Hayts, under the firm name of Hayts, Babcock & Appleton, and commenced the manufacture of pianos and organs. Mr. Goodrich was afterwards induced to join the firm. It was, however, dissolved in 1820, Mr. Appleton continuing business on his own account.

Thus far the art of organ building, though creditable to so young a country, had remained in a rather crude state. In 1827 the manufacture of organs was begun in Boston by Elias and Geo. G. Hook, the oldest of the brothers having learned his trade of Wm. Goodrich, to whom he was apprenticed when only sixteen years old. The Messrs. Hook (afterwards HOOK & HASTINGS, which see), labored hard to produce only good instruments, and with them it may be said commenced a new era in the history of American organ building. They soon took a first position among the makers of this country, which they still hold. Under their care home-made instruments became equal to those imported from abroad, and at the present the art of organ building in America is at fully as high a standard as in any foreign country.

## Organ, reed.

According to some writers, free reeds, that is reeds fastened at one end and left free to vibrate at the other and set in motion by currents of air, are an American invention. As to this, however, there are very grave doubts, though in 1818, Aaron M. Peaseley invented an instrument in which these reeds were used. The patent is signed by James Monroe, President, and John Quincy Adams, Secretary of State, of the United States, and is in the possession of the Mason & Hamlin Organ and Piano Co. The instrument seems not to have amounted to much, and was probably quite imperfect. There is one fact, however, about which there can be no doubt. It is that the free reed was not invented until several years after the beginning of the present century. By whom and just when is a matter of perplexity and will probably remain so, but it would appear from what light we have that the idea had an almost simultaneous birth and working out in several different countries. Thus it will be seen that all instruments constructed with free reeds, such as the accordeon, seraphine, harmonium, etc., are the product of the present century.

In this country the melodeon was the direct precursor of the reed organ. It enjoyed considerable but brief popularity. It was first introduced about the year 1840. In 1845 or 1846, two well-known firms commenced its manufacture, viz : Carhart & Needham and George A. Prince & Co., both of Buffalo, N. Y. The latter firm, which ceased to exist only a few years ago, manufactured the best instruments, many well-preserved specimens of which are still to be met with. The melodeon had far fewer resources and capabilities than the reed organ, and was in every way an inferior instrument (See MELODEON). An instrument closely resembling the reed organ, and which might be called its first cousin, is the harmonium. It differs from the reed organ, however, internally in several important respects, one of which is the fact that the sound is produced by forcing the wind out through the reeds instead of drawing it in, as is the case with the latter instrument.

In the year 1847, Emmons Hamlin, then a workman in the factory of Prince & Co., of Buffalo, but now one of the firm of Mason & Hamlin Organ and Piano Co., discovered that by twisting and bending the tongues of reeds in a certain manner a vast improvement in tone resulted. Previously the tongue had been left flat and straight, and produced a thin, sharp tone. The method of bending the tongues gave a much more mellow tone to the reed, and to it is probably due the popularity of the melodeon, and afterwards of the reed organ. About 1861, the first reed organ was introduced by Messrs. Mason & Hamlin. It was a great advance upon the melodeon. The present form of case was adopted, several sets of reeds and stops employed, and a number of other improvements made. It almost immediately became popular, and soon displaced the melodeon. Improvements have since been made, not only by Mason & Hamlin, but by other makers, and has resulted in a truly musical instrument, which is probably more largely used in this country than any other one instrument, and enjoys considerable popularity in England and other foreign countries. It is sometimes manufactured with not only one, but two and even three manuals and one pedal, and having in all from twenty to thirty stops. In power and resource it can then almost rival the smaller pipe organs. Some fine specimens are made by the Mason & Hamlin Organ and Piano Co., by whom the instrument was originally produced.

**Osgood,** GEORGE L., was born April 3, 1844, and began the practice of music at an early age. He commenced the study of the organ and harmony under John K. Paine, with whom he remained until he entered Harvard College in 1862. Upon graduating in 1866 he went to Germany and studied composition under Haupt and singing under Sieber at Berlin. During this time he became intimately acquainted with the celebrated song writer, Robert Franz, which no doubt influenced him to more closely study German *lieder*. Many of Franz's letters and manuscripts are now in his possession. From Germany he went to Milan and placed himself under Lamperti, of whom he gained a thorough knowledge of the Italian vocal methods. At the expiration of three years he returned to Germany and gave some concerts with good success. On his return to this country he was engaged by Theodore Thomas, with whose orchestra he visited the principal cities. He then settled in Boston, as a teacher of singing, composer, and conductor, where he is now (Jan., 1886) located. His compositions are mostly songs, which are not only of a high order but command a ready sale. As a teacher and conductor he is well known and is doing excellent service to the cause of music.

**Osgood,** MRS. EMMA ALINE, well-known both in the United States and England as an excellent oratorio singer, is a native of Boston (we have been unable to ascertain her early history) and made her *début* at a concert of the Quintet Club in 1873. She was well received and offered an engagement by that organization, with which she made a concert tour in Canada and the States. In 1875 she went to London and studied for some time under Sig. Alberto Randegger. Her first appearance in England was at Crystal Palace, in October of the same year. During 1876 she sang in Manchester, Liverpool, Birmingham, and other English cities. She scored a decided success, and won many praises as *prima donna* in Liszt's oratorio of "St. Elizabeth" during a performance in London. The whole of 1877 was spent in fulfilling engagements at the Brighton, Leeds, and other festivals, and at numerous concerts. In March, 1878, she came to this country and sang at the Cincinnati May Festival and at Thomas' concerts in New York. Returning to England in the autumn she continued her engagements there, singing at Metzler and Chappell's concerts, London; Charles Halle's grand concert, Manchester; Bach choir concerts, St. James' Hall, London; in Sullivan's oratorio, "Light of the World," at Liverpool; etc. In 1880 she paid her second, and in 1881 her third visit to her native country. At the New York, Cincinnati, and Chicago May Festivals of 1882 she was one of the soloists, and came in for a large share of the honors. Her voice is a soprano of great sweetness and sonority, perfect throughout its range, and especially adapted to the singing of oratorios. In rendering some of the popular ballads she has rarely been equaled.

**Ostinelli,** ELIZA. See BISCACCIANTI, MME.

**Ostrolenka.** An opera by Jean Henri Bonawitz—his second—written between 1870 and 1875. It has not yet been produced in a complete form.

# P.

**Paillard, M. J. & Co.,** New York City. The firm of Paillard & Co. is the oldest now existing which manufactures musical boxes. It was founded at Ste. Croix, Switzerland, in 1814, by the great-grandfather of the present members of the New York house. In 1849, of four brothers of the third generation, the two elder remained in Ste. Croix in charge of the factory (then a comparatively small concern), while the two younger came to New York and established themselves in business at No. 80 Nassau street in 1850. One of the latter died soon after, and the surviving brother, M. J. Paillard, continued alone for awhile. He then took a partner, when the firm name became Paillard & Martin, which it remained until 1861, Mr. Martin withdrawing at that time. M. J. Paillard again continued alone until 1865, when he retired from any active part in the business on account of his health. He returned to Switzerland, where he died in December, 1868. Previous to his departure in 1865, he took into partnership his nephew, A. E. Paillard, son of the senior member of the Ste. Croix house, and the firm name was changed to M. J. Paillard & Co., which is still retained. The present members are A. E. Paillard and Geo. A. Paillard, son of the late M. J. Paillard.

When Messrs. Paillard & Co. first began business the facilities for manufacturing were very crude and everything was made by hand, the work often being wrought by the workmen at their homes. Since that time much valuable machinery has been invented, but each instrument still requires a considerable amount of skilled manual labor of the highest order. The firm employs 800 workmen in the factory at Ste. Croix, the machinery of which is run by steam. Every part of the instruments, from the rough castings up, is made in the building, which is done by no other firm, and which results in better and more uniform work. With Messrs. Paillard & Co. have originated nearly all the improvements in music boxes, most of them being due to the inventive genius of the late Amédée Paillard of the Ste. Croix house. A stock ranging in value from $100,000 to $150,000 is constantly on hand at the New York house. There is a branch house in London under the firm name of A. Paillard & Co. The name of Paillard & Co. has a world-wide reputation and is inseparably connected with the history of music boxes.

**Paine,** John Knowles, one of America's leading composers, was born Jan, 9, 1839, at Portland, Maine. His parents were musically inclined and encouraged his talents, which were manifest at an early age. His first teacher in piano and organ playing and composition was Hermann Kotzschmar, a musician of considerable ability residing in his native city. He appeared for the first time in public, June 25, 1857, as an organist, being then eighteen years old, and played a prelude and fugue by Bach with great success. Soon after he became organist of the Haydn Society of Portland, and played the accompaniments to the "Messiah" without any assistance from an orchestra. Feeling the need of better musical instruction than was then afforded by this country, he in 1858 proceeded to Germany. Locating at Berlin he studied the organ, composition, instrumentation, and singing, under Haupt, Wieprecht, and Teschner, making very rapid progress. While there he also gave several organ recitals. In 1861 he returned to the United States, and for some time was engaged in giving concerts, performing the principal organ compositions of Bach, Thiele and other composers, many of which had never been heard in this country before. The proceeds of some of these concerts were given to aid the Union Sanitary Commission. In the following year (1862) he was appointed professor of music at Harvard University, and in this position he has exercised a great and permanent influence in advancing the art. He spent the winter of 1866-67 in visiting Germany, and his mass was performed under his own direction at the Singakademie, Berlin, in February, 1867. Work on his greatest production, the oratorio of "St. Peter," was begun in 1869. The first performance took place at Portland, June 3, 1873, under the direction of the composer. It was performed by the Handel and Haydn Society of Boston, May 9, 1874, and was afterwards added to the regular *répertoire*. His first symphony was performed by Thomas' orchestra at Boston, Jan. 6, 1876. The same year he was made a professor of music in full at Harvard University, being the first occupant of the chair. This position he still (May, 1886) retains. His "Centennial Hymn" was written for the opening of the Exhibition at Philadelphia, in May, 1876. The music is of high order, but adverse criticisms have been passed upon the words (by Whittier) on account of their being ill adapted for musical purposes. All of his orchestral works have been performed in Boston, New York and other cities of this country. Many of his smaller works may frequently be found on the concert programs of various artists. His later works begin with the trio in D minor, op. 22, and show a tendency toward the modern romatic school, both in form and treatment. The following is a list of his published works:

Op. 3. Variations for the Organ—"Austrian Hymn" and "Star Spangled Banner."
" 7. "Christmas Gift." Piano.
" 9. Funeral March. Piano.
" 10. Mass, in D major. Solos, chorus and orchestra.
" 11. Vier Character-Stücke. Piano.
" 12. Romance, C minor. Piano.
" 19. Two preludes. Organ.
" 20. "St. Peter," oratorio.
" 25. Four characteristic pieces. Piano.
" 26. "In the Country." Ten sketches for the piano.
" 27. Centennial Hymn. Words by Whittier.
" 29. Four songs for the soprano voice.

The unpublished works consist of sonatas for the piano, and for the piano and violin; fantasias, variations, and other pieces, for the organ; a string quartet; two piano trios; an overture on "As You Like It;" a symphonie-fantasia on "The Tempest;" a symphony in C minor (op. 23) and one in A (op. 34), entitled "Spring;" a duo concertante for violin, violoncello, and orchestra; songs; motets; and nearly every kind of vocal and instrumental pieces.

**Palmer,** DR. HORATIO RICHMOND, who is well known as a composer of vocal music, was born April 26, 1834, at Sherburne, N. Y. His father, Anson B. Palmer, was a musician of more than ordinary talent, and possessed a very sensitive organization—so sensitive, indeed, that he could scarcely bear the least discord. His mother had a fine voice and was noted for her self-possession. These qualities of his parents he seems to have in a large measure inherited, making him unusually successful as a leader and conductor. His father died in 1868, at Norfolk, Va., whither he had removed after marrying a second time. When nine years old he began to sing alto in his father's choir, and when seventeen became organist and choir-master. Teaching, in which he has been so eminently successful, he took up when fifteen. One of his characteristics was the determination to accomplish whatever he undertook. His musical education has mostly been acquired by hard, unremitting study without the aid of a teacher. One of the earliest positions which he filled was that of professor of music in the Rushford Academy, Rushford, Allegany County, N. Y. In 1861 he removed to Chicago, where, in 1866, he commenced editing and publishing "The Concordia," a musical monthly. The following year he published his first collection of music, "The Song Queen," which reached the enormous sale of 200,000 copies. Of "The Storm King," published in 1871, an equal number of copies has been sold. His "Theory of Music" (1876) clearly and concisely presents the elements of thorough-bass, harmony, composition, and form, and is an invaluable work for the beginner.

During six of the fifteen years of Mr. Palmer's residence in Chicago he was chorister of the second Baptist Church. His reputation was already well established and rapidly growing. Nearly every moment of his time was consumed by various duties, and even the Sabbath could hardly be called a day of rest. Frequently he was obliged to bribe hackmen by an extra fee to drive at the highest legal rate of speed. Sometimes his engagement for one week would be nearly fifteen hundred miles from where it was the previous week. While traveling from one place to another his pockets were generally filled with musical proofs, which must be "read and returned by the first mail." The amount of work which he went through with could hardly have been accomplished by a less systematic and energetic man. His duties still keep him busy, and he has little time for pleasure, except such as is found in labor. During the last fifteen years he has visited nearly every state in the Union as conductor of musical conventions. At his musical institutes, held every summer, many excellent teachers have been educated. In 1874 he removed from Chicago to New York, where he still (May, 1886) resides. He has charge of the Church Choral Union, recently organized in that city. The first season was begun in March, 1881, with 250 singers. At the commencement of the second season (1882) the number had increased to 1600, and at the commencement of the third season (1883) to 4200. Its object is to elevate the standard of music in the churches. Part of the years 1877 and 1878 and of 1881 and 1882 he spent in visiting interesting portions of the Old World. The degree of Doctor of Music was conferred on him by the Alfred University, Alfred Center, N. Y., in June, 1881. Dr. Palmer's music is distinguished for its purity, grace, and melodiousness, and is deservedly popular. The following is a complete list of his works, and they include all of his compositions except, perhaps, some few minor ones :

1. The Song Queen (1867). The sales of this book amounted to upwards of 200,000 copies.
2. Elements of Musical Composition (1867).
3. Rudimental Class Teaching (1867).
4. Sabbath School Songs (1868).
5. The Song Queen, revised (1868).
6. The Normal Collection of Anthems (1870)
7. The Song King (1871). Sales upwards of 200,000 copies.
8. The Standard, with L.O.Emerson (1872).
9. Concert Choruses, consisting mainly of selections from the works of the great masters (1873).
10. Songs of Love for the Bible School (1874)
11. The Leader, assisted by L. O. Emerson (1874).
12. The Song Monarch, assisted by L. O. Emerson (1874).
13. The Song Herald (1876).
14. Theory of Music (1876). 12mo., 168 pp.
15. Book of Anthems (1879).
16. The Sovereign (1879).
17. Rays of Light, for Sunday schools (1882).
18. Concert Gems for Choruses (1883).
19. Book of Threnodies, for funeral occasions (1883).

**Pape,** WILLIAM, BARNESMORE, was born Feb. 27, 1840, (1850?) at Mobile, Ala. He is chiefly known as a brilliant pianist and the author of many showy transcriptions and arrangements of popular airs, which exhibit no special ability. Of his life we have no particulars.

**Parker,** JAMES C. D., well known as a pianist, organist, and composer, was born at Boston, June 2, 1828. He graduated at Harvard College and prepared himself for the profession of law, but his intense love of music conquered everything else. After studying awhile in his native city he proceeded to Leipsic, where he placed himself under the best masters, making rapid progress and attaining great proficiency as a composer and as a performer. He returned to Boston in 1854, and soon took a leading position in her musical affairs. In 1862 he organized an association of amateur vocalists called the "Parker Club," which gave, with piano accompaniment, such works as Gade's "Comala," Mendelssohn's "Walpurgis Night," Berlioz's "Flight into Egypt," Schumann's "Paradise and the Peri," and "Pilgrimage of the Rose," etc. Quietly but surely he has for many years been engaged in elevating the standard of musical taste. He is at present (1886) organist of Trinity Church, and most highly esteemed as a teacher of the organ, piano, and harmony. He has also held the post of organist to the Handel and Haydn Society, and is now professor of the College of Music connected with the Boston University. His "Redemption Hymn" (words from the 51st chapter of Isaiah), composed in 1877, for solo contralto and chorus, with accompaniment, was first given by the Handel and Haydn Society and has since been given by various musical societies all over the country. The "Manual of Harmony" (12mo. 150 pp.) is a good work for beginners. Mr. Parker's other works consist of various sacred pieces, part songs, etc., all of more than ordinary merit.

**Parsons,** ALBERT ROSS, was born at Sandusky, Ohio, Sep. 16, 1847. His American teachers were R. Denton, Buffalo, N.Y., 1854-56, and Dr. F. L. Ritter, New York, 1863-66. He then went to Leipzig, where he studied at the Conservatorium from 1867 to 1869, under Moscheles, Reinecke, Papperitz, Wenzel, Oscar Paul, E. F. Richter and Ferdinand David. In 1870 he was studying at the Pianists' High School, Berlin, having Tausig, Ehlert and Weitzmann as teachers, and in 1871 at the New Academy of Music, under

Kullak. He received much stimulous and inspiration from close personal contact with Wagner, Liszt, Rubinstein and von Bülow. Since 1872 he has been located at New York City as organist, teacher, composer and writer. He is the translator of Wagner's "Beethoven" and the editor of the American edition of Kullak's edition of Chopin. He has lectured on musical topics in various cities and written many articles for the musical press. His compositions consist of songs, vocal quartets, etc., all well written. Besides these he has edited and fingered many piano pieces for instructive purposes. He is highly esteemed and very successful as a teacher, and is an active worker in the Music Teachers' National Association.

**Pattison,** JOHN NELSON, pianist and composer, was born at Niagara Falls, N. Y., Oct. 22, 1843. His talents for music, which were early manifested, were little encouraged by his parents, who considered them a sign of laziness. He was sent to school at Lockport, but managed by hoarding up his spare money to take a term of music lessons and during that time he made extraordinary progress. It was at first intended that he should be a merchant, but this was changed for the profession of medicine, and he went to Buffalo to study. So intense, however, was his love for music, that, sorely against the wishes of his parents, he abandoned everything else and joined a concert company. At this time he was about fifteen years of age. The manager of the company decamped, which left the young man penniless. He started for New York, giving concerts to support himself. While there he heard the celebrated pianist, Thalberg, on whom he called and frankly stated his desires. That musician encouraged him to persevere and go to Europe. He at once made preparations for the trip, and to raise the necessary funds insured his life for a certain sum; which he succeeded in persuading a friend to accept as security for a loan of money. Berlin was the city toward which he bent his steps, though he had not at that time the slightest acquaintance with the German language nor any influential recommendations. His energy and pluck carried him through, and he remained in Germany two years, studying with Hauptmann, Reinecke, Stern, Marx, and von Bülow. He played in Berlin with more than ordinary success. In 1861 he returned to the United States, but in the following year again went to Germany, and studied for some time under Henselt, frequently appearing in concerts. After this he accompanied Thalberg to Italy. Returning to Paris he played at the Pleyel concerts. Since his second return to this country he has repeatedly played in concerts, and accompanied Parepa-Rosa, Kellogg, Ole Bull, Albani, Lucca, and others, on their tours of the States. During 1874 he gave a series of several lectures on music, illustrated by piano recitals, at New York. His recitals will doubtless be remembered by many who attended the Centennial Exhibition in 1876, where he played. From May 10th to Nov. 11 he gave in all 183 performances. He has played at the New York and Brooklyn Philharmonic concerts with great success. His *répertoire* consists of nearly six hundred important works, among which are the most of Beethoven's sonatas, Bach's preludes and fugues, etc., and is largely played from memory. Mr. Pattison is a resident of New York, where he is well known as a pianist, teacher, and composer. His compositions are mostly piano pieces of various kinds, but include some larger works, such as "Concerto Fantasie-romantique," for piano with orchestra; "Niagara," a grand symphony for an orchestra and military band, and "Concert overture for grand orchestra," played in Berlin, Germany, with great success and by Thomas' orchestra in New York.

**Payne,** JOHN HOWARD, was born June 9, 1792, at New York. Very early in life he was taken to Boston, where he made his *début* as an actor at the old Boston Theatre. He became noted in that capacity, both in this country and Europe. In 1841 he was appointed consul at Tunis, and died there April 1, 1852. The remains were buried there but exhumed and brought to this country in the spring of 1883. His monument says that he was born at Boston. This is probably a mistake arising from the fact that he lived there while very young. Payne forever immortalized his name by writing the poem of "Home, Sweet Home." Few pieces have been written which so touch the heart, and it has so often been repeated and is so well known that there is no need of giving it here.

**Peace Jubilees, The.** Two monster festivals of this name have been held in

Boston. The first one occurred in 1869, and surpassed in size anything ever attempted before. At the first performance of "Elijah" Mendelssohn had 700 voices, and at the Crystal Palace, London, in 1862, the chorus numbered 4000, but the chorus of the Peace Jubilee numbered 10,000 and the orchestra 1000, besides bells, anvils, and cannons. A building was erected expressly for the accommodation of the immense audience. The enthusiasm in the city was unbounded, and throughout the country the event was looked upon as one of the greatest events that had taken place in the United States. The success of the first festival led to the planning and holding, in 1872, of a second one, the "World's Peace Jubilee." This entirely eclipsed its vast predecessor. The chorus numbered 20,000, and the orchestra was proportionately large. Everything was on a scale of grandeur never before dreamed of. Several of the famous bands of Europe were present. Among the distinguished foreign musicians in attendance and who were specially engaged were Abt, who directed his own music, Strauss, Bendel, the pianist, Wély, and others. Financially, however, the Jubilee was a failure, resulting in a deficit of over $100,000, which had to be borne by the subscribers.

Both of the festivals were originated by and were under the direction of P. S. Gilmore (See GILMORE, P. S.). It was proposed by Mr. Gilmore to hold the first festival in New York, but not meeting with encouragement there he went to Boston, where he received the needful support. It is hardly necessary to say that Mr. Gilmore, as originator and conductor of the Jubilees, won a reputation and notoriety which he has not yet exhausted. As to the artistic and beneficial musical results, they were disproportionately small when compared with the capital invested. Enthusiasm ran high for awhile, but when it subsided there remained little that was permanent. This, however, was but the natural result of such a festival. While harm may have been done to the steady growth of music by its transient and superficial character, we may with certainty assume that considerable good was done also, some of which was undoubtedly permanent. For a full account of both Jubilees, the reader is referred to Mr. Gilmore's book, "History of the National Peace Jubilee and Great Musical Festival," 1 vol. 758 pp., Boston, Lee & Shepard, 1877.

**Peabody Concerts.** A series of concerts annually given under the care of the Conservatory of Music connected with the Peabody Institute, Baltimore, Md. Since 1865 eight concerts, each of which is preceded by a public rehearsal, have been included in every series. The programs are of high order, and comprise symphonies, suites, concertos, overtures, vocal solos, etc. Everything is rendered in the best manner, and the unusually fine performances of the Conservatory were such as to call forth hearty praise from von Bülow when he was in this country, in 1875-76. Since 1871 the Concerts have been under the able direction of Asger Hamerik, president of the Conservatory, who has given especial attention to the production of works by American, English and Scandinavian composers. The orchestra numbers 50 performers.

**Peak.** There was a numerous family of this name, all more or less musical. Mr. and Mrs. Peak began giving concerts in 1841. In 1854, by which time there were eight members, they introduced bells into their performances, and were thereafter known as bell-ringers. William H. established another company in 1858, Lisetta became noted as a singer, and Alfred Tays was violinist. Until quite recently, Mr. and Mrs. Peak were still giving concerts.

**Pease,** ALFRED H., pianist and composer, was born at Cleveland, O., in 1850. His early love for music was not much encouraged, but he unaided learned to play the piano somewhat. He was sent to school and allowed no musical instruction of any kind. When sixteen years old he entered Gambia College, and so assiduously studied as to impair his health. This led to his going to Europe, where his thirst for music greatly increased. Having finally obtained parental permission to pursue it as a profession, he studied the piano under Kullak and von Bülow, composition under Würst, and scoring under Wieprecht, making very rapid progress. At the end of three years he returned to the United States, but made a short stay, going back again to Europe, where he studied for three years more under the best masters. After returning to this country for the second time he made an extended concert tour. Previous to his death he played in most of the important cities and towns. As a pianist he was graceful and brilliant and had few superiors. His works are marked by originality, close study, and careful writing. They consist of songs, piano pieces, some orchestral compositions, etc. The songs number about 100, the earliest of which is ''Break! Break! Break!'' composed in 1864. They are sung by Mme. Nilsson and Antoinette Sterling, Milles, Albani, Drasdil, and Beebe, Clara Louise Kellogg, Myron W. Whitney, and other equally eminent singers. Among the piano pieces ''Antoinette Polka Mazurka,'' ''Caprice Espagnol'' and ''Delta Kappa Epsilon March'' are very popular. In this class are to be included a score of arrangements for four hands, from the operas of ''Lohengrin,'' ''Faust,'' ''Aida,'' ''Crispino,'' ''Les Huguenots,'' etc. Of the orchestral compositions the ''Reverie and Andante,'' ''Andante and Scherzo,'' and ''Romanze,'' have been performed by Thomas' orchestra in New York and other cities. The ''Concerto,'' written in 1875, has also been given by Mr. Thomas with great success.

The death of Mr. Pease was particularly sad. For several months previous no trace of him could be found, though rewards were offered for any information which would lead to a knowledge of his whereabouts. He was at last discovered in St. Louis, Mo., by a newspaper reporter, but it was too late, and he died in that city, Thursday, July 13, 1882, of congestion of the brain, undoubtedly brought on by excesses. He had a bright future before him, and, being a young man, might have taken a leading position among American musicians. His parents, to whom his death was a severe blow, now reside at Buffalo.

**Penfield,** SMITH NEWHALL, organist and composer, was born at Oberlin, Ohio, April 4, 1837. He became organist while very young. His earlier musical studies were pursued in New York. He subsequently went to Leipzig and studied the piano with Moscheles, Papperitz and Reinecke, the organ with Richter, counterpoint and fugue with Richter and Hauptmann, and composition with Reinecke. He also studied at Paris with Delioux. For some time after his return he resided at Rochester, N. Y. He then removed to Savannah,

Ga., where he established the Savannah Conservatory of Music and the Mozart Club. For a number of years he has resided at New York City. He has given organ recitals at the Church of the Pilgrims, Brooklyn, at St. George's Church, New York, and more recently at Chickering Hall. In 1883 he was made Doctor of Music by the University of New York, and in 1884 elected president of the M. T. N. A. In the autumn of 1885 he founded the New York Harmonic Society. Dr. Penfield's compositions consist of organ and piano music, songs, anthems, glees, a string quintet, an overture for full orchestra, and a cantata—the 18th Psalm—for soli, chorus and orchestra.

**Perabo,** ERNST, well-known in this country as a pianist, composer and teacher, was born Nov. 14, 1845, at Wiesbaden, Germany. He was the youngest of ten children, all of whom became musicians, and the only child by his father's second marriage. When five years old his musical instruction was begun by his father, and his precocity and rapid progress may be inferred from the fact that when eight he could play Bach's ''Well-tempered Clavier'' by heart—a feat worthy of an accomplished musician and almost unparalleled for one so young. In 1852 his parents came to the United States, landing at New York. During the residence of the family there he first appeared in public as a player, and with gratifying success. From New York the family removed to Dover, N. H., from there to Boston, and thence to Chicago, all in three years, two of which were spent in Dover. While in Boston he again appeared in public as a player at a concert under the direction of Carl Zerrahn. His father was unable to send him abroad to complete his musical education, but finally some men of means were interested in his behalf, prominent among whom was Mr. Scharfenberg (of the firm of Scharfenberg & Lewis, music dealers), who had become acquainted with the family while in New York. He was accordingly sent to Germany, leaving this country Sep. 1, 1858, and settled at Hamburg, where he not only studied music but literature also. Oct. 22, 1862, after a residence of four years at Hamburg, he entered the Conservatorium at Leipzig, receiving instruction on the piano from Moscheles and Wenzel, in harmony from Papperitz, Hauptmann, and Richter, and in composition from Reinecke. At the public examination of May, 1865, he played a part of Burgmüller's concerto in F sharp minor, then heard for the first time in Leipzig.

Having completed his studies at the Conservatorium, Mr. Perabo, in November, 1865, returned to this country. He first visited his parents, then living in Sandusky, O., and also gave some concerts in Chicago and Cleveland. After some hesitation, he in March, 1866, settled in Boston. He was invited to play at the last concert of the season given by the Harvard Musical Association, which occurred April 21st. Since then he has regularly appeared at one or more concerts of this society. He has also given every season a series of recitals and *matinées* of his own, which are of the very highest order. Among other things he has played the whole of Schubert's piano sonatas in public. His *répertoire* includes the best works, and he is particularly happy as an interpreter of Beethoven. As a teacher of the piano he is surpassed by few, and he always has a large number of pupils. His compositions, mostly for the piano, and published both in this country and Germany, are quite numerous and of great merit. Among them are a Scherzo (op. 2), 3 Studies (op. 9), and an Introduction and Andante (op. 45). He has published some collections of pieces for the use of pupils, and made concert arrangements of Rubinstein's "Ocean Symphony" and "Dimitri Dunskoi." Occasionally he employs his pen as a musical writer, though not so often as might be wished.

**Perkins,** COL. ORSON, was born Dec. 17, 1802, at Hartland, Windsor Co., Vt. He inherited considerable musical talent and a good voice, and when twenty years of age had attained some notoriety as a singer. Soon after he commenced the career in which he was so eminently successful—that of a singing-master. He married Hannah Rust, a soprano singer of Rochester, Vt., by whom he had eight children. Six of them grew to maturity, as follows: William Oscar, Henry Southwick, Azro Orson, Edwin Hazen, Ellen Froncilia, and Jules Edson. The first two are widely known as teachers, composers and conductors, and the last was ( before his death) a very fine bass singer. The fourth son is also a teacher, and the daughter (now Mrs. George S. Cheney of Boston) possesses good vocal talents. Mr. Perkins was a man of great purity and strength of character. His voice, a baritone of extended compass and pure quality, he retained up to the close of life. After leading a long and actively devoted career, he passed away at Taftsville, Vt., at the ripe age of nearly eighty, April 19, 1882.

**Perkins,** HENRY SOUTHWICK, second son of the preceding, was born at Stockbridge, Windsor Co., Vt., March 20, 1833. His early life was spent in working on a farm, and his knowledge of music was such as could be gained during leisure hours. In 1849 a family removed to Woodstock, Vt. Having arrived at age and being his own master, he visited Boston. From there he went to Lowell, where he engaged in the show business. The venture was not successful, however, and he next became a member of the "Mendelssohn Quartet Concert Company," with which he traveled in New Hampshire, Pennsylvania, New York, New Jersey, and Vermont. He now fully decided that music should be his life-work, and accordingly entered the Boston Music School, Boston, graduating therefrom in 1861. After this he commenced holding musical conventions and institutes, making Chicago (to which he had removed in 1857) his permanent home. In 1867 he was appointed professor of music in the Iowa State University at Iowa City, and also director of the State Academy of Music, located in the same city. The first post he held two years and the second one five years. He also held the position of president of the Kansas State Academy of Music for five years, commencing with 1869. It has always been his aim to introduce the best class of music by bringing forward such works as Haydn's "Creation," Handel's "Messiah," Mendelssohn's "Elijah," Mozart's "12th mass," etc. On account of impaired health he made a trip abroad in the summer of 1875, successively visiting England, France, Switzerland, Belgium, Germany, Austria, Italy, and Egypt. At both Paris and Florence he spent considerable time in perfecting himself in the different branches of his profession.

Mr. Perkins edited his first work, "The Nightingale," for public schools, in 1860, being assisted by his brother. He has edited in all, either alone or in conjunction with others, twenty-five books, the most prominent among which are the "Song Echo," "The Advance," "New Century," "Perkins' Glee and Chorus Book," and "Model Class Book." The following is a complete list of his books :

1. Nightingale (1860). Public schools.
2. Sabbath School Trumpet (1864).
3. Church Bell (1867).
4. College Hymn and Tune Book (1868).
5. Perkins' Vocal Method (1868). 2 vols.
6. Song Echo (1871).
7. Advance (1872). Church music.
8. River of Life (1873). Sunday schools.
9. Headlight (1873). Public schools.
10. Convention Choruses (1874).
11. Sunnyside (1875). Sunday schools.
12. Shining River (1875). Sunday schools.
13. New Century (1876). Choirs, classes, etc.
14. Glee and Chorus Book (1876).
15. Graded Music Reader, 1 and 2 b'ks (1877).
16. Graded Music Reader, 3 book (1878).
17. Glorious Tidings (1878). Sunday schools.
18. Perkins' Class and Choir (1879).
19. Perkins' Graded Anthems (1880).
20. Palms of Victory (1880). Sunday schools.
21. Model Class Book (1881).
22. Good Templar (1881). Temperance.
23. Song Wave (1882). Public schools.
24. The Wavelet (1882). Public schools.
25. The Choir (1883). Choirs, classes, etc.

He has also written numerous popular songs and quartets, among which are "Make Your Home Beautiful," "Maist Onie Day," "Dear Happy Home," "Alone," "Let Me Die by the Sea," "Tender and True," "Sweet and Low," and "Sleep in Peace."

**Perkins,** Dr. WILLIAM OSCAR, eldest son of Col. Orson Perkins and brother of the preceding, was born at Stockbridge, Windsor Co., Vt., May 23, 1831. He received his literary education at Kimball Academy, Meriden, N. H., and after graduating taught for some time at New Brunswick, N. J. He then went to Boston, where he began teaching music in 1858. Having studied with the best American musicians, he went to Europe, taking voice-lessons of J. Q. Wetherbee, London, a fellow of the Royal Academy of Music, and G. Perini, Milan. Ever since his return to the United States he has been busily engaged as teacher, conductor, and composer. He has held over 200 musical conventions in the Northern States and Canada, conducted ten summer "Normals" of from four to six weeks each, besides local societies, concerts, etc. During a portion of 1871 and 1872 he traveled in Europe for the purpose of study and observation. The degree of Doctor of Music was conferred on him by the Hamilton (N. Y.) College in 1879.

Mr. Perkins is a musician of more than ordinary ability and favorably known throughout the country. The following is a list of his music books, which contain the most of his compositions :

1. Choral Harmony. For the church. 1859
2. Nightingale. Day schools. - 1860
3. Union Star Glee Book. - 1861
4. Atlantic Glee Book. - : 1861
5. Tabernacle. For the church. 1862
6. Golden Robin. Day schools. - 1863
7. Sabbath School Trumpet. - 1864
8. Church Bell. - - 1867
9. Starry Crown. Sunday schools. 1869
10. Dominion Songster. (For Canada). 1870
11. Laurel Wreath. High schools. 1870
12. Chorister. For the church. - 1870
13. Mocking Bird. Day schools. 1871
14. Orphean. Boys' schools and colleges 1871
15. Church Welcome. - 1872
16. Seminary Album. Ladies' schools. 1873
17. Perkins' Anthem Book. For choirs. 1874
18. Shining River. Sunday schools. 1875
19. Zion. For the church. 1875
20. Perkins' Singing School. For classes 1875
21. Whippoorwill. Day schools. - 1876
22. Male Voice Glee Book. - 1876
23. American Glee Book. (Mixed voices)1877
24. Herald. For the church. - 1877
25. Requiem. Funeral occasions. 1878
26. Crystal Fountain. Temperance. 1878
27. Singers' Class Book. - 1878
28. Tree of Life. Sunday schools. 1878
29. Temple, The. Church and conv'ntion 1879
30. Anthem Harp, The. For choirs. 1880
31. Vocal Echoes. (Female voices). 1881
32. Choral Choir. Choir and convention 1882
33. Peerless, The. For classes. - 1882

**Perkins,** JULE EDSON, youngest son of Col. Orson Perkins, was born at Stockbridge, Windsor Co., Vt., March 19, 1845. When ten years of age he sang alto in a church choir and also appeared in public as a pianist. His systematic musical studies were begun in Boston when he was about fourteen. There he continued until 1867. In that year, after some hesitation between the ministry and the stage, he went to Paris, where he studied one year under M. Delle Sedie. From Paris he went to Italy, studying under the best Italian masters at Milan and Florence for five years. During this period he filled engagements at Padua, Pisa, Genoa, Rome, Milan, and one of several months at Warsaw, Poland. He made his regular operatic *début* in 1869 with great success. By 1873 his fame had reached

England, and in that year he with other candidates for operatic engagements appeared at La Scala, Milan, before numerous *impresarii*, agents and critics. An incident occurred at this time which shows the sharpness of some operatic managers. He had sung one selection, which was listened to with profound attention, and was requested to sing another by Col. J. H. Mapleson. While this was being done, that worthy gentleman "begged his friends to excuse him a moment," when he hastened behind the scenes, captured the young basso and took him to a *café*, and had a six years' engagement signed before the other agents were aware of it. Upon learning of this a Constantinople *impresario* offered Col. Mapleson £4000 ( nearly $20,000 ) for his bargain.

Mr. Perkins made his *début* as a concert singer in Haydn's "Creation," at Royal Albert Hall, London, Jan. 13, 1874, before an audience of 10,000. His success was instantaneous and complete, and almost amounted to an ovation. The praise and compliments showered upon him during his operatic tour of the English provinces have seldom or never been given to any other artist of less than world-wide reputation. His *répertoire* was extensive, including "La Favorita," "Don Giovanni," "Il Flauto Magico," "Zauberflöte," "Norma," "Faust," and other operas. *Mephistopheles* in "Faust" and *Sarastro* in "Il Flauto Magico" were the *rôles* in which he created the greatest impression. He was equally at home in the oratorio or opera, and in both had rare success. July 23, 1874, he was married to Mlle. Marie Roze (see ROZE), the well-known *prima donna*, who was a member of the same company. With her he visited this country for the last time during the same summer. Previous to this he had made two visits, viz: 1869 and 1871, usually singing in the summer institutes of his brother, H. S. Perkins. He died at Manchester, Eng., Feb. 25, 1875. By his death not only America but the whole musical world lost an artist of rare promise. His voice was a bass of great compass, depth and fine quality, and excellently cultivated.

**Perry,** EMORY, American singer, was born July 25, 1759, at Holiston, Mass. When seventeen years old he was appointed chorister, and received $30 a year for his services

—a fair salary at that time. In 1818 he removed to Milford, where he received $100, and in 1821 to Worcester, where he received $300. He was very successful as a teacher of singing, and taught upwards of 20,000 pupils. His voice was a remarkable one, having a compass extending from two octaves below middle C to one octave above it. Its quality was very uniform, being rich and pleasing, though somewhat reedy in the extreme lowest register. The date of his death we have not learned.

**Peter, St.** An oratorio by John K. Paine, op. 20. First produced, under the direction of the composer, at Portland, Me., June 3, 1873. Given by the Handel and Haydn Society of Boston, May 9, 1874.

**Petersilea,** CARLYLE, one of America's most prominent pianists and teachers, was born at Boston, Jan. 18, 1844. His mother, Mary Ann Carew, was an English lady, and his father, Franz Petersilea, was a native of Oldesleben in the Grand Duchy of Saxe-weimar, Germany. Franz was destined for the ministry, and in consequence received an excellent classical education, but his passion for music could not be resisted. He devoted his life to the art, and will be remembered as an able and scholarly musician by many persons still living. He died at Mattapan, near Boston, Sep. 22, 1878. Carlyle was early and systematically instructed in music by his father. By the time he was seven years of age he was already giving lessons, and when twelve performed such compositions as Hummel's "Rondeau Brilliant" in public. In order to complete his studies he in 1862, being then sixteen, went to Germany and entered the Conservatorium at Leipzig. There for three years he studied under Plaidy, Wenzel, and Moscheles, with whom he became a great favorite. At the Grand Prüfungen, held in the gewandhaus of the Conservatorium, he triumphantly performed the "Henselt Concerto" (Moscheles conducting), which had never before been played in Leipzig except by von Bülow. He graduated with the highest honors, being awarded the prize of the Helbig fund. He then made a professional tour of the principal German cities and was everywhere received with enthusiasm. Upon returning to this country he was most cordially received at New York, as he also was at Boston, where he first appeared at a concert given in the Music Hall, playing Chopin's F minor concerto and Liszt's arrangement of Schumann's "Erl King." He soon settled in the latter city and became highly successful as a teacher and soloist. Feeling the necessity of more room for the rapidly increasing number of his pupils, he in 1871 founded the conservatory now known as "The Petersilea Academy of Music, Elocution and Languages," located on Columbus Avenue.

Early in life Mr. Petersilea astonished musicians by the extent of his *répertoire*, which now covers nearly the whole field of piano literature. Three qualities which he possesses to a great degree are reading at sight, *technique*, and a ready and unfailing memory. Between January 20 and May 29, 1874, he gave a series of ten recitals at which he played from memory the whole of Beethoven's 32 sonatas, a feat accomplished before only by Charles Halle of London. His powers of sight reading were evidenced by his playing, on one occasion, Chopin's E minor concerto with Theodore Thomas' orchestra after only a few hours' notice, in the place of Josefy. Since 1875 he has been pianist of the Boylston Club of Boston, a position for which he is admirably fitted. Notwithstanding his duties as a teacher, he occasionally appears as a soloist at the Philharmonic, Boylston Club, and Harvard Symphony concerts. Quite recently he made a tour of the West with Mrs. Annie Louise Cary-Raymond. As a pianist, he possesses the power, depth and breadth necessary to interpret Beethoven's music, and the delicacy and poetic fancy so essential in rendering Chopin's works. As a teacher, he has few superiors, as is attested by the number of excellent players which he has educated. Thus far Mr. Petersilea has given little attention to composing, but it is hoped that he may give more in the future.

**Philadelphia** takes a prominent place among the cities of this country for the number of its musical societies and its "vigorous musical life." There are sixty-five of the societies, the oldest of which is the Musical Fund Society, established Feb. 29, 1820. The Society built a hall for its use in 1823, and about 1830 opened an academy for instruction in music. It has liberally aided its professional members and their families. For fif-

teen years the funds have been gradually accumulating, and with the sum thus obtained it is designed to establish a school of music. The Society has quite a large library of music in score. The members number fifty, of whom fourteen are professional musicians. Of the other societies the Orpheus Club was organized in August, 1872, and has 30 active and 300 associate members. The Cecilian Society has about 400 active members, and was founded May 25, 1875. The Beethoven Society was organized in 1869, and the other societies at various times.

The University of Pennsylvania, which is located in Philadelphia, has a course of study in music. Degrees are bestowed upon students who pass an examination in harmony, counterpoint, and composition. The professor of music is Hugh A. Clarke, who has an orchestra and a glee club composed of undergraduates. Among the private institutions for musical instruction is the Philadelphia Musical Academy, presided over by Mme. Emma Seiler, which has a regular attendance of over 100 pupils.

The following is a list of the musical societies in Philadelphia, with the name of the conductor, and in some cases the year when organized:

|  |  |
|---|---|
| Abt Society, | Hugh A Clarke. |
| Allemania, | F. W. Künsel. |
| Amphion Society, | - |
| Arbeiter Sängerbund, | - |
| Arion, | J. Schaaf. |
| Arion (Germantown), | - |
| Aurora, | - |
| Beethoven Liederkranz, | F. W. Künsel. |
| Beethoven Männerchor, | L. Gröbl. |
| Cæcilia, | - |
| Cecilian (1875), | M. H. Cross. |
| Cecilian Musical Beneficial Association, | B. G. S. Wilks (Pres.) |
| Columbia Gesangverein, | W. Winter. |
| Columbia Burschenschaft, | L. Ockenlander. |
| Concordia Gesangverein, | E. Gastel. |
| Concordia Quartet Club, | L. Engelke. |
| Eintracht, | H. Peters. |
| Eintracht Quartet Club, | |
| Fidelio Gesangverein, | G. Wilke. |
| Fidelio Männerchor, | |
| Gambrinus Sängerkranz, | F. Stadler (Sec). |
| Germania Liederkranz, | G. Wilke. |
| Germania Männerchor, | C. M. Schmitz. |
| Handel and Haydn Society, | C. Sentz. |
| Harmonie, | F. W. Künsel. |
| Harmonie Quartet Club, | - |
| Kreuznacher Sängerbund, | W. Winter. |
| Liederkranz, | Dr. Römermann. |
| Liedertafel, | J. W. Jost. |

Liedertafel d. D. F. Gemeinde,    P. Jost.
Lotus Club,    -    C. M. Schmitz.
La Lyre,    -    -    F. M. A. Perrot.
Lyric Club,    -    -    H. Keely.
Manayunk Choral Society,   W. A. Newland.
Männerchor,    -    -    E. Gastel.
Marburger Liedertafel,    -    G. Fölker.
Mendelssohn Club,    -    W. W. Gilchrist.
Mozart Harmonie,    -    -    -
Mozart Männerchor,    -    J. G. Dickel.
Mozart Quartet Club,    -    -
Musical Fund Society (1820), Dr. Dunglison.
Orchester der D. F. Gemeinde, C. Heinemann
Orpheus Club (1872),    -    M. H. Cross.
Philadelphia Amateur Orchestra,   J. Brophy.
Philadelphia Musical Association, L. Engelke.
Philadelphia Opera Verein,    -    F. Wink.
Philharmonia Männerchor,    -    -    -
Quartet Club,    -    -    H. Peters.
Rothmanner Gesangverein,    H. Peters.
Sängerbund,    -    -    C. Gärtner.
Schiller Liedertafel,    -    J. Schaaf.
Schiller Quartet Club,    -    -    -
Schwabischer Liederkranz,    -
Schweitzer Männerchor,    -    J. Brenner.
Southwark Sängerbund,    -    -
Southwark Liederkranz,    -    -
Teutonia Männerchor,    -    -
Teutonia Sängerbund,    -    H. Peters.
Tischler Männerchor,    -    J. Brenner.
Turner Gesang Section,    -    J. W. Jost.
Union Sängerbund,    -    -
West Phila. Choral Society, W. W. Gilchrist.
West Philadelphia Harmonie,   -   A. Faas.
West Philadelphia Männerchbr,    -
Young Männerchor,    -    R. Gräuer.

UNIVERSITY OF PENNSYLVANIA. The musical department of this University is under the charge of Prof. Hugh A. Clarke. Two years of three terms each cover the course, the first being devoted to harmony and the second to counterpoint and composition. Pupils of both sexes are admitted, provided they have a good rudimental knowledge of music and the ability to play some instrument. Diplomas or certificates are conferred on the judgment of the professor at the conclusion of the course. Students may at any subsequent time receive the degree of Bachelor of Music upon the following conditions: 1. By passing an examination in harmony, counterpoint and composition, by three examiners appointed by the professor, subject to the approval of the provost; the examination to be oral or written, or both, at the option of the examiners. 2. They must submit to the examiners an original composition in the form of a cantata for solos and chorus, with accompaniment of at least a quintet of string instruments. 3. This composition must be of such length as to require at least

twenty minutes for its performance; it must contain a four-part fugue, and the accompaniment must be independent, except in the fugue. 4. The composition must be accompanied by a written statement that it is the student's own unaided effort. A series of lectures on harmony, counterpoint and composition are given each term by the professor, the fee for which is $10.

PHILADELPHIA MUSICAL ACADEMY. This institution was founded in 1870, by John F. Himmelsbach, Rudolph Hennig and Wenzel Kopta. Two years later Kopta returned to Europe, and the Academy passed under the control of Messrs. Himmelsbach and Hennig. At the end of five years, Mr. Himmelsbach became sole proprietor and director. In 1877 he also returned to Europe and was succeeded by Richard Zeckwer, under whose able direction it has since been. Mr. Zeckwer is a graduate of the Leipzig Conservatorium, where he studied under Moscheles, Hauptmann, Richter and Reinecke. He came to America in 1869, and has been connected with the Academy from its inception. The methods of imparting instruction are largely modeled after those employed in European conservatories. All branches of music are taught and the principal modern languages. The number of pupils in attendance upon the Academy during the year 1884-85 was 755. Among the more noted of the teachers are Richard Zeckwer, Rudolph Hennig, F. Grischow, F. E. Cresson, David Wood, Pasquale Rondinella and W. W. Gilchrist.

**Philharmonic Societies.** See BOSTON and NEW YORK AND BROOKLYN.

**Phillips,** ADELAIDE, one of America's greatest contralto singers, was born at Bristol, England, in 1833. She came to the United States (by the way of Canada) with her parents when seven years old. Her vocal powers were early manifested, and she made her first public appearance at the Tremont Theatre, Boston, Jan. 12, 1842, when she personated several characters in a little comedy. The following year she appeared at the Boston Museum, also dancing between plays. Thus far she had been instructed by Thomas Comer of Boston, but when she sang before Jenny Lind in 1850 that lady was so pleased that she advised her to go to Europe to complete her education. The necessary funds were raised by subscription and a benefit concert. She arrived in London in March, 1852, where she studied the voice with Sig. E. Garcia and piano and harmony with W. Chalmers. After a year and a half, the additional means having been furnished by Jonas Chickering, the celebrated piano manufacturer, she went to Italy and placed herself under the best masters there. Her professional *début* was made at Milan, Dec. 17, 1854, as *Rosina* in "The Barber of Seville." She returned with her father to this country in 1855. In 1861 she visited England, France, and other European countries, singing in the principal cities, and meeting with a warm welcome. At home she made repeated tours and won a permanent place in the hearts of the people. She joined the Boston Ideal Opera Company in 1879, in which she was often heard. *Azucena* in Verdi's "Il Trovatore" was her favorite *rôle*. Her sphere was by no means confined to the opera, for she frequently sang in oratorio at the concerts of the Boston Handel and Haydn Society with scarcely less success. She appeared in Boston for the last time at the Museum, in November, 1880, at Mary Beebe's benefit, and her last appearance on any stage was at Cincinnati, in December, 1881. Failing health compelled a rest, but it was too late, and she died in September, 1882, in the southern part of France, whither she had gone seeking relief. Miss Phillip's voice was a pure, rich contralto with a compass of 2½ octaves, ranging up to B flat in *alt*. She was not only a fine artist, but a kind-hearted, noble woman, and her death was lamented by a very large circle of friends. Her mother died in 1855, the year of her return from Europe, and her father, Alfred Phillips, at Marshfield, Mass., Oct. 16, 1870.

**Phillips,** PHILIP, was born Aug. 13, 1834, at Jamestown, Chautauqua Co., N. Y., and began music teaching when he was nineteen years of age. He settled in Cincinnati, but in 1866 removed to New York, where he has since resided. In the United States and England he is quite widely known as a very pleasing singer of songs, mostly sacred. He has composed a great number of hymn tunes and religious pieces, and edited several collections of such music, among which are the "Singing Pilgrim," "Musical Leaves," "Hallowed Songs," "Centenary Singer," "Song Ser-

mons," and a Hymnal (1871) for the Methodist Episcopal Church.

**Piano in America, The.** Anything like a complete, or even a partial, history of the development of piano making in this country is yet to be written. The piano was being manufactured in Europe when this nation was born, yet American inventive genius has done as much toward perfecting the instrument as that of all other nations combined. The first piano produced in this country was made by Benjamin Crehore, at Milton, a rural village about fifteen miles from Boston, as early as the beginning of this century. The house where he worked is still standing, and it is to be regretted that the first piano does not also remain. From the business of Crehore grew that of Babcock, Appleton & Babcock. In the workshop of the latter named firm John Osborne learned his trade, and he taught Jonas Chickering, the "father of the American piano." In 1823 Mr. Chickering set up in business for himself, and exercised his ingenuity in improving the piano. To him in a large measure is due the rapid perfection of the American piano, which enabled it to successfully compete with the best foreign makes. It may be added that during the early part of his career Mr. Chickering had a partner by the name of Mackay, a sea captain, through whose efforts he built up quite a trade in South America. Many of his instruments are still to be found in Buenos Ayres. Mr. Mackay died in 1841, or was lost with his ship at sea. Some further idea of the growth and development of piano making in the United States may be gained by consulting the histories of CHICKERING & SONS, STEINWAY & SONS, and other leading piano firms.

**Pinner,** MAX, pianist, was born April 14, 1851, at New York. In 1865 he went to Leipzig and entered the Conservatorium there. Three years later he placed himself under Tausig and Weitzmann at Berlin for the study of the piano and harmony. In 1873 he was studying with Liszt, and afterwards met with success as a pianist at Berlin, Leipzig, Vienna and other cities. He returned to New York in 1878 and settled there as a teacher. On account of ill health he has lately seldom appeared in public as a performer.

**Pilgrim's Progress, The.** A cantata in three parts. The libretto is founded on and taken from Bunyan's "Pilgrim's Progress;" music by J. C. Beckel. Published in 1882.

**Pitch.** In Europe, efforts have been made to establish a uniform pitch, and with partial success. The matter has been agitated in this country, but without producing anything very tangible in the way of results. Some impetus was given to the movement by a meeting of musicians and musical instrument manufacturers, held at the New England Conservatory of Music, Nov. 18, 1882. The following preambles and resolution was adopted :

*Whereas,* there is no fixed standard of pitch to which leaders and manufacturers are compelled to conform ; and

*Whereas,* this state of things has led to the widest diversity in tuning instruments and orchestras ; and

*Whereas,* the pitch has gone up nearly a tone and a half since Handel's time, and a quarter of a tone during the past year in Boston ;

*Resolved,* that we, in this meeting assembled, express it as our conviction that, first, there ought to be a fixed standard pitch ; second, that the prevailing pitch ought to be lowered ; third, that we unite upon 260.2 vibrations per second for the middle C, as being the pitch best calculated to lead to the most desirable result, and that we will use our endeavors to make this movement universal.

The report was prepared by a committee consisting of Carl Zerrahn, Dr. Louis Maas, J. C. D. Parker, A. Kielblock, L. W. Wheeler, Edgar A. Buck, and Otto Bendix. Letters from B. J. Lang, Theodore Thomas, Mason & Hamlin Organ and Piano Co., Hook & Hastings, Hutchings, Plaisted & Co., warmly endorsing the movement were read. It is to be sincerely hoped that the reforms attempted by this meeting will receive public encouragement and eventually be adopted. As will readily be seen, the pitch recommended by the meeting is very nearly the same as that which is fixed by law in France. That it is the best one which could have been fixed upon, however, is far from certain. A standard which makes middle C=256 would be better, as it disposes of any fractions in the octaves and almost exactly agrees with the classical pitch. The matter is still being agitated, and must, in time, lead to beneficial results.

**Plain and Easy Instruction.** Probably the first practical instruction book on singing published in America. The full title is "A very Plain and Easy Instruction to the Art of Singing Psalm tunes;" and the balance of the title-page reads, "with the Cantos or Trebles of twenty-eight Psalm tunes, contrived in such a manner that the Learner may attain the Skill of singing them with the greatest ease and speed imaginable." The work was issued about 1712, and was prepared by Rev. John Tufts, pastor of the Second Church, Newbury, Mass. Some two or three years later he issued a new and greatly improved book, containing thirty-seven tunes harmonized in three parts. In it he attempts to teach the learner to sing by using letters in the place of notes. Many editions were printed and sold, which would seem to indicate a great popularity.

**Pond,** SYLVANUS BILLINGS, was born in Worcester County, Mass., in 1792. While still quite young he went to Albany, N. Y., where his fondness of music led him to engage in the musical instrument business. He was at first alone but afterwards associated himself with a Mr. Meacham, under the firm name of Meacham & Pond. In 1832, upon invitation, he went to New York and joined Firth & Hall, and the name was changed to Firth, Hall & Pond. He remained with the firm many years (See POND, W. A. & Co.) Mr. Pond took a great interest in Sunday schools, and soon after going to New York connected himself with the Brick Church (Presbyterian), of which Rev. Dr. Spring was so long pastor. He was for some time leader of the choir, and at this time wrote his first Sunday school singing book, "Union Melodies," which was very successful. Another one of his works was the "United States Psalmody," for choirs and singing societies, which also had a large sale. He was at one time director of the New York Academy of Music, and afterwards of the New York Sacred-Music Society. His music is almost exclusively sacred, and includes several popular hymn tunes, among which are "Armenia" (1835) and "Franklin Square" (1850). In 1850 he retired from active business, and died in Brooklyn in 1871, respected by all who knew him.

**Pond, William A. & Co.,** NEW YORK. About 1815 a young Englishman named John Firth commenced business at 8 Warren St., New York, as a manufacturer of flutes and fifes. He learned his trade with Edward Riley, also an Englishman, who began business about 1812. William Hall, another of Riley's pupils, set up in business about 1820, in Wooster street. Between him and Firth there existed a warm friendship (they married sisters, daughters of their former employer), which resulted, in 1821, in their forming a copartnership as Firth & Hall and establishing themselves at 362 Pearl street. They were prospered and steadily built up a very desirable trade. In 1830 they added to their other business that of making pianos, and about the same time commenced to publish music on a small scale. Late in 1832 they were, by invitation, joined by S. B. Pond, who was in the musical instrument business at Albany, N. Y. (See Pond, S. B.) The firm then became Firth, Hall & Pond, and the establishment was removed to 1 Franklin Square, which, by the way, was the first presidential mansion, and is still known as "Washington's House." Mr. Pond, after entering the firm, took charge of the piano department. This seems not to have been very profitable, and after twenty years it was disposed of. The factory was at this time located at Williamsburg. He also for a long time wrote much of the music which they published. In 1847 the firm of Firth, Hall & Pond was dissolved. Gen. Hall, withdrew, and with his son, James F. Hall, commenced business on Broadway as William Hall & Son. The son subsequently joined the federal army, and the father after a few years retired from business. He died in 1873 (See Hall). After Gen. Hall's withdrawal the firm became Firth, Pond & Co., the company consisting of William Pond (for many years head of the house) and John Mayell, brother-in law of the elder Pond. In 1850, S. B. Pond retired from business, and in 1856 the firm removed to 547 Broadway. The name was again changed in 1863, Mr. Firth withdrawing, who, with his son, established the house of Firth, Son & Co., bought out in 1867 by C. H. Ditson & Co. It then became William A. Pond & Co., which has been retained to the present day. The firm, until very recently, consisted of Col. William A. Pond and his son, William A. Pond, Jr. It is not only an extensive dealer, but publishes very largely, and ranks among the leading houses of the United States. For

Boosey & Co., the English publishers, and other foreign firms, it is the accredited agent in this country. In 1878 its immense business was removed from 547 Broadway to 25 Union Square. The head of the house, Col. Wm. A Pond, very recently (Dec., 1885) died.

**Ponte,** LORENZO DA, poet, was born March 10, 1749, at Ceneda, in the Venetian States. His parents were very poor, but at the age of fourteen he entered the seminary of his native town, and after studying five years went to Venice to seek his fortune. There he had a number of amorous difficulties, and being compelled to leave went to Treviso. From Treviso (which he was also forced to leave) he went to Vienna, becoming court poet in the place of Metastasio, who had lately died. While holding this post he wrote the librettos of Mozart's three operas, "Figaro," "Don Giovanni," and "Cosi fan tutte." Leaving Vienna after the Emperor's (Joseph II) death he went to Trieste, where he married an English lady, and thence in 1792 to Paris. London was his next stopping place, and there he was engaged as poet of the Italian opera. On account of financial trouble he set sail for the United States, and landed at Philadelphia, May 30, 1803. He proceeded to New York, and was successful as a teacher of Italian. In 1811 he went to Sunbury, Pa., to manufacture liquors, but this, like his other business ventures, proved a failure, and he returned to New York. His last bright day was on the arrival of the Garcia family, when "Don Giovanni" was given. He died at New York, Aug. 17, 1839, in abject misery, the natural result of the life which he led. It was chiefly through his exertions that the fine opera house at the corner of Church and Leonard streets was erected. The building was opened Nov. 18. 1833, and destroyed by fire Sep. 23. 1839.

**Praise to God.** An oratorio by Geo. F. Bristow—one of his most important works. It was produced in 1860, and thrice performed —the third time by the New York Harmonic Society at the Academy of Music, Brooklyn, for the benefit of the Old Ladies' Home, and netted $2000.

**Pratt,** SILAS G., was born Aug. 13, 1846, at Addison, Vt. At a very early age his parents removed West, locating on a farm near Plainfield, Ill. While still young his talents manifested themselves in a decided manner.

In 1857, on account of his father's financial troubles, he went to Chicago and became a clerk in the house of H. M. Higgins. He subsequently, after serving a year with Root & Cady, was engaged by Lyon & Healy as their chief clerk. He took up the practice of the piano, at which he dilligently labored. His first composition, "Lorena Schottisch," was written at the age of fourteen. By exercising the greatest economy, he was enabled, in 1868, at the age of twenty-two, to realize the long-cherished desire of going abroad to secure a good musical education. Under the care of Bendel at Berlin, and afterwards of Kullak, he made rapid progress. Full of enthusiasm for art, it was but natural that he should overdo, and as a consequence he lost the use of his right wrist. This was a severe blow and destroyed his hopes of becoming a *virtuoso*, but he soon found a consolation in composing. Incessant study and work at last forced him to take a tour for the benefit of his health, during which he visited Leipsic, Eisenach, Coburg, Nuremberg, Regensburg and Munich. At the latter place he made the acquaintance of Gung'l, the celebrated waltz composer. While there he also began his opera of "Antonio," which was not finished until 1874. Upon returning to Berlin he placed himself under F. Kiel for the study of counterpoint, and during the winter his first symphony was completed. The ensuing summer was spent at the baths of Gastein and in a trip through Switzerland. With the winter he again returned to Berlin, and soon after sailed for his native country. His first public appearance here was at Chicago, in April, 1872, when he gave a concert chiefly composed of his own piano and vocal works. The great fire of the October before had made the city a poor place for an artist, and he was forced to accept the clerkship which he had relinquished four years before. He attended the second great "Peace Jubilee" at Boston, having charge of the Chicago musicians. The first movement of his symphony was performed and well received. Soon after he organized the Apollo Club. During the winter of 1873–74 he made a short concert tour, after which he took up teaching. In the summer he re-wrote or completed the opera of "Antonio," which was successfully produced under the direction of Hans Balatka. Early in 1875

he again went to Europe for the purpose of study and observation. After attending the rehearsals of Wagner's trilogy at Bayreuth, in the fall of the same year, he went to Weimar and gave a recital before Liszt and other distinguished musicians. His "Anniversary Overture" was performed at Berlin, July 4, 1876, and soon after at Weimar. Owing to financial troubles he accepted the position of consular clerk, but continued his labors as a composer. Having achieved several triumphs he left Berlin for Paris, and thence proceeded to London, where some of his compositions were performed. He returned to the United States in 1877, and has since resided at Chicago as teacher and composer. His latest large work is the opera of "Zenobia" (see ZENOBIA), which was produced upon the stage at McVicker's Theatre, Chicago, and fairly well received. The following is a list of Mr. Pratt's works, with the year of production :

| | |
|---|---|
| Lorena Schottisch, | 1861 |
| Eclipse Waltz, | 1862 |
| Matinée Polka, | 1865 |
| Shakesperian Grand March, | 1866 |
| The Sigh. Nocturne. | 1866 |
| The Smile. Polka. | 1866 |
| Grand March Heroique, | 1867 |
| Orchestra Galop, | 1867 |
| Ola. Serenade impromptu. | 1867 |
| The Carousal. Paraphrase on "We won't go home till morning." | 1867 |
| Goodbye, | 1868 |
| Reve d'esprit. Valse characteristic. | 1868 |
| Primeur Nocturne, Berlin, | 1869 |
| Orb of Night. Waltz. " | 1870 |
| Gone. Impromptu. " | 1870 |
| Shadow Thoughts. 3 impromptus. " | 1870 |
|    1. Hidden Whispers, | |
|    2. Silent Complaint, | |
|    3. Mazurka. | |
| Symphonie sketch, "Magdalena's Lament." For orchestra (Ms.) " | 1870 |
| Oh, Let Me Love Thee. Song. " | 1870 |
| Antonio. Opera. (1st sketch, Ms.) " | 1870 |
| La Douleur Mazurka, " | 1871 |
| Mazurka Caprice, " | 1871 |
| First Grand Symphony (Ms.) " | 1871 |
| Dream Wanderings. Paraphrase on "The Old Folks at Home." " | 1871 |
| The Smile. Song. " | 1871 |
| Rainy Day. Vocal quartet. | 1872 |
| Dream Visions. Vocal. | 1872 |
| Wanderer's Song, | 1872 |
| Soul Longings. Strings and piano. | 1873 |
| Retrospection. Song. | 1873 |
| Homage to Chicago. March. | 1873 |
| Fantasie Caprice, | 1874 |
| First grand polonaise, | 1874 |

Opera of "Antonio" (completion), 1874
Grand Valse Etude, 1875
Fantasie Impromptu, 1875
Two Romanzas. Piano. Berlin, 1876
Opera of "Antonio" (scoring), Weimar, 1876
Pansy and the Maid. Ballad. " 1876
My Own Ideal, " 1876
Anniversary Overture (orch., Ms.) " 1876
Prodigal Son. Symphony. " 1876
Winds of the Night. Male cho. Berlin, 1877
Long Ago. Song. London, 1877
Still dwells my Heart with Thee, " 1877
Variations, "Sweet bye and bye," 1877
Canon. String orchestra. (Ms.) 1877
Never Again. Song. Chicago, 1878
Zenobia (commenced), " 1878
Second grand polonaise. (Ms.) " 1878
Stay at Home. Song. " 1878
Sunset Impromptu. (Ms.) Columbus, Ky. 1878
Mazurka Andante, Chicago, 1878
Mazurka Minuet, 1878
Pastoral for organ. (Ms.) 1879
Inca's Downfall. Cantata for solos and
  chorus. (Ms.) 1879
Nocturne Impromptu, 1879
Caprice Fantastique. (Ms.) 1879
My Only Own. Song. 1879
Love in Spring. Song. 1879
Serenade for string orchestra, 1879
Wedding Polonaise, 1879
Baladine. (Ms.; op. 40). 1880
Waltz Graciuse, 1880
Zenobia (scoring and completion) op. 41, 1880
Waltz Semplice, 1880
Antique minuet and pastoral, 1880
Meditation Religeuse. Piano (op. 42), 1881
In Venice. Barcarolle. Piano. 1881
Overture, "Zenobia," 1881
Hymn to Night. Song. 1882
Court Minuet, 1882
"The sail auf Wielerschen." Song. 1882

**Presser,** THEODORE, was born of German parents at Pittsburgh, Pa., July 3, 1848. He early evinced a great love of music, which was duly encouraged. In 1864 he became a music clerk in a store in his native city, of which he rose to be manager in four years. While obtaining a collegiate education he dilligently studied music. He began his career as teacher at Ada, O., in 1869. Being unsatisfied with both his surroundings and his attainments, he went to Xenia, O., and entered a conservatory there. After three years more of teaching, during which time he had charge of the musical department in a female seminary, he went to Boston and studied under the best teachers there. In 1876 he took charge of the musical department of the Ohio Wesleyan University. He subsequently went to Europe, where he faithfully studied for two years. On his return he was appointed pro-

fessor of music in Hollins Institute, Virginia. In 1883 he established at Lynchburgh, Va., The Etude, a monthly publication for teachers and students of the piano. The following year he removed to Philadelphia, where The Etude is now published and where he resides, devoting much time to teaching. We must not forget to add that to Mr. Presser is due the inception of the Music Teachers' National Association, and its safe passage through the critical period of its existence is mainly the result of his untiring energy and ability. As a teacher he is remarkably successful, having a rare faculty both of interesting the pupils and imparting instruction. He has some sixty *études* in manuscript which he has for years used in private teaching, while his published piano studies are received with favor by teachers everywhere. He is the translator and publisher of Urbach's Prize Pianoforte Method, and has rendered available to American students other important works. Mr. Presser is one of the most indefatigable of our musical workers and for this alone deserves honorable mention. As he is yet comparatively young, he will probably live to accomplish much more for his chosen art.

**Prévost,** EUGENE, was born Aug. 23, 1809, at Paris, and studied at the Conservatoire. He obtained the "Prix de Rome," and after his return from Italy produced the 2-act opera of "Cosimo" at the Opéra Comique with considerable success. After his marriage with Eléonore Colon he went to Havre as conductor of the theatre there. In 1838 he went to New Orleans, where he was unusually successful as singing master, also holding the post of conductor of the French theatre. In this capacity he produced several dramatic pieces of his own, among them "Esmeralda," which contains some striking music. During 1842 he was leader of the orchestra at Niblo's Garden, New York. When the Civil War broke out Prévost went to Paris, and was director of the concerts of the Champs Elysées. He was recalled to New Orleans by his son, Léon, in 1867, and died there in July, 1872. Besides his dramatic pieces he wrote considerable sacred music. He was given the cross of the Order of Charles III by the Queen of Spain.

**Prince, George A. & Co.,** BUFFALO, N. Y. This firm of melodeon and reed organ manufacturers was established about 1840, by George A. Prince. In 1846 Mr. Prince took out patents for several improvements in melodeons, and was at this time employing 150 men and turning out 75 instruments per week. In 1847 Emmons Hamlin (then a workman in the manufactory of Prince & Co.) discovered that the tone of the reeds of a melodeon was greatly improved by slightly bending and twisting the tongues. This gave a renewed impetus to their manufacture. Mr. Hamlin became a member of the firm of Mason & Hamlin in 1854. After the production of the reed organ, about 1861, Prince & Co. began to make them in connection with their melodeons. All their instruments, of which they manufactured nearly 60,000, are characterized by a fine tone and great lasting qualities. The writer has often played upon one of their earliest melodeons (now 40 years old) and the tone, though not powerful, of course, there being only one set of reeds, is very sweet and mellow. As far as musical capacity is concerned, the instrument is just as good as when first made. The firm, one of the leading ones in this country, became embarrassed during the financial crisis which has just passed, and about 1875 was forced into bankruptcy.

# Q.

**Quigg,** J. Travis, the well-known musical writer and editor of the American Music Journal, is a native of Philadelphia, where he began his career as a journalist. He has been identified with many musical enterprises, notably the inauguration of the Thomas orchestral concerts in 1876 at the Forrest Mansion Garden, Philadelphia. He has also written several popular songs and light compositions for the piano. At various times he has been engaged as musical editor upon the St. Louis Critic, the Kansas City Times, the Chicago Herald, and Freund's Music and Drama, besides contributing for leading papers in his native city.

# R.

**Read,** DANIEL, one of the early American psalmodists, was born in Connecticut (presumably at or near New Haven, where he was long a resident) in 1757. His first work was the "American Singing book, or a New and Easy Guide to the art of Psalmody," issued in 1771. In 1793 he published the "Columbian Harmony," consisting entirely of church music, and in 1806 the " Litchfield Collection," containing 112 pages of similar music, much of which was original. Read's music may be classed with that of Billings and Holden, and though it contains some crudities, it is full of life and vigor. Some of his tunes are in general use at the present day and are likely to live for a long time to come. "Windham," " Sherburne," " Russia," " Stafford," and "Lisbon," are known to almost every church singer. He died at New Haven in 1836. At a concert of ancient music given at New Haven in May, 1853, the pitch-pipe originally belonging to Read was used, and much of the music rendered was of his composing.

**Records of the New York Stage.** The title of a valuable work comprising a history of the New York stage from 1750 to 1860, giving the date, and in most cases the cast, of all dramatic works produced thereon. It was edited by Joseph N. Ireland, now (1886) a resident of Bridgeport, Conn., and issued to subscribers at $15 for the 8vo. and $25 for the 4to. The first volume appeared in December, 1866, and the second one in April or May, 1867. Part of the edition, which numbered only 200 copies, was sold to non-subscribers at $25 and $40. The work has now become rare and commands quite a premium. Could there be a sufficient demand, a second edition, bringing events down to the present time, would probably be issued. It is to be regretted that the work is not more accessible, and that similar histories of the stage in the principal cities of the United States have not been written.

**Redemption Hymn,** in E flat, for contralto solo, chorus and accompaniment, by J. C. D. Parker. Words from the 51st chapter of Isaiah. Composed in 1877, and given by the Handel and Haydn Society of Boston. Since performed by musical societies all over the country.

**Reeves,** DAVID WALLIS, was born Feb. 14, 1838, at Oswego, N. Y. His early musical advantages were few, but when fifteen years old he was apprenticed to Thomas Canham, a band instructor, with whom he dilligently studied the violin and the cornet. At the age of nineteen he became leader of a circus band. Soon after he went to New York, joining Dodworth's Orchestra, and subsequently Rumsey and Newcomb's Minstrels. With the latter company he went to England, where he was presented with a fine cornet by Henry Distin. In 1862 he became a member of Dodworth's Band in New York, and was the first to perform Levy's celebrated "Whirlwind Polka" in America, astonishing everyone by his triple tongueing, the secret of which he learned in London. In February, 1866, he accepted the position of leader of the American Band, Providence, R. I., which he still (1885) retains. He has brought the organization up to a high standard. Mr. Reeves has frequently appeared in Boston, New York and other cities as soloist, being an exceptionally fine player. His compositions are mostly for military bands. They exhibit many musicianly qualities, and some of them have obtained a wide popularity.

**Remmertz,** FRANZ, bass singer, is a native of Düsseldorff, Germany, where he was born probably about 1845. It was designed that he should be an architect, but music proved the greater attraction, and he removed to Munich to cultivate his talents. He made his *début* as an operatic singer, but has confined himself mostly to the concert room. In 1869 he came to New York, where he has since resided. He sang at the New York, Cincinnati and Chicago May Festivals of 1882, and has filled engagements in nearly every part of the country, earning a national reputation. His voice is of rugged, sonorous quality, and his singing characterized by energy and force.

**Richardson,** NATHAN, was born at South Reading, Mass., in 1823.* He studied music for several years with Dreyschock at Prague. After his return to the United States he prepared and published his "Modern School for the Pianoforte," which was little more than a transcript of his lessons with his teacher. The criticisms which it evoked led him to prepare his "New Method for the Pianoforte" (Boston, O. Ditson & Co.), which has had a popularity equaled by no other musical instruction book. The sales have thus far footed up to over 500,000 copies, and still amount to about 20,000 copies annually. He was one of the founders of the firm of Russell & Richardson, music dealers, Boston. John W. Moore, in his "Dictionary of Musical Information," states that Richardson died in Paris (whither he had gone on account of failing health), Nov. 19, 1855, but W. S. B. Mathews in "How to Understand Music" gives the year as 1858. This is probably nearer correct, as the "New Method" was not published until 1859.

**Rice,** FENELON B., Doctor of Music, was born at Green, Ohio, Jan. 2, 1841. He was educated at Hillsdale College, Mich., after which he entered the Boston Music School, graduating therefrom in 1863. In 1867 he went to Germany and entered the Conservatorium at Leipzig. After two years of study there he returned to the United States, and was, in 1871, appointed professor of music in Oberlin College, Oberlin, O., and director of the Conservatory connected with that institution. He is still (June, 1886) located at Oberlin, where he has done much to elevate the standard of music. His time is entirely devoted to teaching and looking after the interests of the large school which is in his charge. The degree of Doctor of Music was conferred on him by Hillsdale (O.) College, and that of A. M. by Oberlin College.

**Richings-Bernard,** MME. CAROLINE, was born in England in 1827, and came to the United States when very young. She made her *début* as a pianist at Philadelphia, Nov.

*One account says he was born at Gloucester about 1830.*

30, 1847, and in 1852 sang for the first time in "La Fille du Regiment." She sang in English and Italian opera throughout the country with much success until 1867, when she married a tenor singer, P. Bernard, in consequence of whose managerial and financial inability she soon lost what money she had previously earned. In 1873 she organized an "Old Folks Concert Company," which proved a failure. After this she taught at Baltimore and Richmond. She was the principal singer of the "Mozart Association" at the latter place, which annually produces a number of operatic works. Her last public appearance was in August, 1881, when she sang in an operetta of her own, "The Duchess," at Baltimore. Her voice was a fine one and supplemented by good acting. She died of small-pox at Richmond, Jan. 14, 1882, lamented by all who knew her.

**Rip Van Winkle.** An American romantic opera. The libretto is by J. H. Wainwright; the music by George F. Bristow. First produced at Niblo's Garden, New York, Sep. 27, 1855, by the Pyne-Harrison English opera company, after which it was performed for 30 consecutive nights. It was translated into Italian, provided with new scenery, costumes, etc., and was on the eve of a revival with Miss Clara Louise Kellogg as the heroine, when the Academy of Music was destroyed by fire in 1865. With the exception, perhaps, of Eichberg's "Doctor of Alcantara," it achieved a success equaled by no other American work, and deserves more recognition at the hands of our *impresarii.*

**Ritter,** DR. FREDERIC LOUIS, was born at Strassburg in 1834. His father was of Spanish extraction, and the family name was originally Caballero. He commenced his studies at an early age with Hauser and H. M. Schletterer, and when sixteen was sent to Paris, where they were continued under the care of his cousin, Georges Kastner. Soon after he went to Germany, and made diligent use of his time while there. In 1852, being then eighteen, he returned to Lorraine, where he was appointed professor of music in the Protestant seminary of Fénéstrange. Such were the representations made by some of the family who had settled in the United States, he was induced to come to this country. For several years he resided in Cincinnati, contributing much to the musical life and advancement of taste in that city by his enthusiasm. He formed the "Cecilia" (choral) and "Philharmonic" (orchestral) societies, which produced for the first time in America a number of important works. In 1862 he went to New York, where he became conductor of the Sacred Harmonic Society—a post which he retained for eight years—and of the Arion Choral Society (male voices). He organized and conducted, in 1867, the first musical festival held in the city, and during the same year received the appointment of professor of music and director of the musical department of Vassar College, Poughkeepsie, N. Y., whither he removed in 1874. He still (May, 1886) holds the position. The degree of Doctor of Music was conferred on him by the University of New York in 1874.

Dr. Ritter's literary labors include articles on musical topics, printed in French, German, and English periodicals, and several books. His most important work is "A History of Music in the Form of Lectures," published at Boston (Ditson & Co.); vol. 1, 1870; vol. 2, 1874. A second and much enlarged edition has appeared in London (W. Reeves). He edited the English edition of "Das Reich der Töne"—The Realm of Tones (Schuberth & Co., New York, 1883)—and wrote the Appendix, containing short biographies of American musicians. His new books, "Music in England" and "Music in America" (Chas. Scribner's Sons, New York) were issued in Nov., 1883. As a composer, he may be classed with the modern Franco-German school. The following is a list of his works :

Op.  1. "Hafis," cyclus of Persian songs.
 "   2. Preambule Scherzo.   Piano.
 "   3. Ten children's songs.
 "   4. Fairy Love.
 "   5. Eight piano pieces.
 "   6. Six songs.
 "   7. Five choruses.   Male voices.
 "   8. Psalm 23rd.   Female voices.
 "  10. Five songs.
 "  11. Organ fantasia and fugue.
 "  12. Voices of the Night.   Piano.
 "  13. Dirge for Two Veterans.   Poem by Walt Whitman, with melodramatic music for the piano.
 "  14. The 95th Psalm.   For female voices, with organ accompaniment.
 "  15. Six songs.
 "  16. Suite for Pianoforte.
 "  17. The 4th Psalm.   For baritone solo, chorus, and orchestra.

Ten Irish melodies with piano accompaniment; "A Practical Method for the Instruction of Chorus Classes," in 2 parts ; "O Salutaris," baritone solo and organ; "Ave Maria," mezzo-soprano solo and organ ; "Parting," song for mezzo-soprano voice; ]] 3 symphonies, A, E minor and E flat ; "Stella," poëme-symphonique d'après Victor Hugo; overture, "Othello ;" concerto for violoncello and orchestra; concerto for piano and orchestra; fantasia for bass clarinet and orchestra ; Septette-serenade, for flute, horn and string quintet; string quintet; several string quartets; the 46th Psalm, for soprano solo, chorus and orchestra, first performed at the New York festival of 1867.

All works to the sign, ]], have been published ; the rest still remain in manuscript. Many of the larger ones have also been rendered by the Philharmonic societies of New York and Brooklyn.

FANNY RAYMOND-RITTER, wife of the preceding, is well known as the author or translator of several musical works. She has brought out translations of Ehlert's "Letters on Music" (Ditson & Co.) and of Schumann's essays and criticisms, "Music and Musicians;" and written two pamphlets, "Some Famous Songs," an art historical sketch, and "Woman as a Musician." The latter three are published by Schuberth & Co.

**Rivé-King** (pronounced *ree-vay*) JULIE, generally conceded to be one of the first pianists in America and equaled by few of her sex in the world, was born Oct. 31, 1857, at Cincinnati, O. Her genius for music was inherited from her mother, Mme. Caroline Rivé, an eminent teacher (See succeeding sketch), and became evident when she was little more than an infant. Her mother, therefore, carefully instructed her in the art from the first, and to this fact much of her present success may be attributed. So rapid was her progress that before attaining the age of eight years she appeared in public at one of her mother's concerts, playing Thalberg's "Transcription of Themes from 'Don Juan.' " Soon after she went with her mother to New York, where she studied under Wm. Mason, S. B. Mills, Francis De Korbay, and Pruckner. In order to complete her education she, at the age of fifteen years, went to Europe, receiving instructions from Reinecke at Leipzig, Blassman and Rischpieter of Dresden, and, finally, from Liszt at Weimar. She made her professional *début*, under Reinecke's direction, at one of the Euterpe concerts, Leipzig, having attained her seventeenth year, before a highly cultured audience. On this occasion she played Beethoven's third concerto and Liszt's second rhapsodie, and was received with such enthusiasm as to almost create a *furore*. Seldom has so young an artist gained such a signal victory upon first appearance. Just as she was about arranging for a tour of Europe she was suddenly recalled to the United States by the death of her father, who was killed in a railroad accident. Her American reputation dates from her first appearance in Cincinnati, during the winter of 1873-74. It was greatly increased by her appearing at a concert of the Philharmonic Society, New York, in the spring of 1875, when she played Liszt's concerto in E flat and Schumann's "Faschingsschwank" (op. 26), a very severe task for any player. The following winter she played Beethoven's 5th concerto at the Philharmonic concerts, and was received with every possible token of appreciation. Her first appearance in Chicago was during the second season of the Apollo Club, at the Methodist Episcopal Church. There her triumph was even more decided than it had been at any other place. During the last twelve years she has performed at upwards of 1800 concerts and recitals. Nearly every important musical society in this country and Canada has engaged her one or more times as soloist, and she has played in all the principal cities. For some time after leaving Cincinnati she made Chicago her home, but now (May, 1886) resides at New York, where she holds a distinguished position. Nine years ago she was married to Mr. Frank H. King, who is well-known in musical circles.

Mme. Rivé-King can hardly be overrated as a player. She possesses a wonderful command of her instrument and a consummate *technique*, which enables her to perform the most difficult pieces with ease. Constant practice from earliest childhood has given her great wrist and digital power, and there is no perceptible diminution of the force and clearness of her touch, even during the performance of the heaviest compositions. Slow playing has developed the full, round tone which is one of the characteristics of all her interpretations. She at once enters into the spirit of the work, and strives to bring out and make apparent the intention of the composer. Her programs are models of good taste, in which both the classical and the romantic schools are fairly represented. One thing greatly in her favor as a player is her fredom from nervousness when appearing before an audience ; indeed, the presence of an audience seems rather to inspire her. Mme. Rivé-King is not alone a great pianist, but has displayed considerable talent as a composer. The following is a list of her compositions and transcriptions, all piano solos :

Andante und Allegro (Mendelssohn, op. 64).
Ballade et Polonaise de Concert (Vieux.—38).
Bubbling Spring. Tone poem characteristic.
"Carmen" (Bizet). Grand fantasia.
Concert sonata in A major (Scarlatti). Revised and fingered.
Gems of Scotland. Caprice de concert, introducing the airs of "Kathleen," "Annie Laurie," and "Blue Bells of Scotland."
Hand in Hand. Polka caprice.
La ci Darem la Mano (Chopin, op. 2).
March of the Goblins. Also for 4 hands.
Mazurka des Graces. Morceau de salon.
Old Hundred. Paraphrase de concert.
On Blooming Meadows. Concert waltz. Also arranged for 4 hands.
Pensées Dansantes (Thoughts of the Dance). Valse brilliante. Also for 4 hands.
Polonaise Heroique. Morceau de concert. Also for 4 hands. Dedicated to Liszt.
Prelude and Fugue (Haberbier-Guilmant).
Rhapsodie Hongroise, No. 2 (Liszt).
Wiener Bonbons (Strauss).
"Tabs from the Vienna Woods."
Impromptu in A flat.
"Nearer, My God, to Thee."
"Home, Sweet Home."
Supplication.

**Rivé,** CAROLINE, *née* Staub, mother of the preceding, was born in France, in the year 1822. She had a fine soprano voice, and took lessons from Garcia, who advised her to adopt the lyric stage as a profession. This she did not do, but married a young French artist named Rivé. Together they came to the United States, landing at New Orleans, then the great musical center. During a severe cholera epidemic they lost three children. They then removed to Baton Rouge, La., thence to Louisville, Ky., and finally, about 1854, to Cincinnati, O. There she was very successful as a teacher, and had a large number of pupils. Feeling that her health was failing, she went to reside with her daughter in New York, and died there Oct. 31, 1882. Her husband died about nine years previous. Mme. Rivé was not only most highly esteemed as a teacher, but equally so as a woman. For many years she lived a true Christian life, and was beloved by all who knew her for her sympathy, kindness, and charity.

**Root,** DR. GEORGE FREDERICK, one of America's most popular composers of vocal music, was born Aug. 30, 1820, at Sheffield, Berkshire Co., Mass., and is the eldest of a family of eight children. His youthful years were spent in working on his father's farm, but his soul was full of music, and he learned, unaided, to play several musical instruments. By the time he had arrived at the age of eighteen, life on the farm had grown to be irksome. Knowing that his calling lay in .the line of music, he was anxious to be about it. Accordingly, in 1838, having obtained the consent of his parents, he went to Boston to enter upon the career for which nature so admirably fitted him. For some time after arriving in the city no opening to his taste presented itself. While still undecided what to do, A. N. Johnson, then a popular and successful organist and teacher in Boston, took him into his music school on trial. The result was so satisfactory that Mr. Johnson gave him a permanent position as a teacher and admitted him to his own home. A year later a partnership was formed between the two. About the same time he became director of music at Winter Street and Park Street churches. In 1844 he was induced by Jacob Abbott, whose name is familiar in literary circles, to remove to New York and become instructor of music in Abbott's Institute. He had not long been there before he found his time fully occupied in teaching in various private institutions. He was also given charge of the music in the old Presbyterian Church, Mercer street, now well-known as the "Church of Strangers," under Dr. Deems. About the time of his removal from Boston, or soon after, he was married to Miss Mary Olive Woodman, a most estimable young lady, who proved a great helpmeet to him.

In 1850 he went to Paris, where he spent a year in diligent study. Shortly after his return home he determined to try his ability as a composer, and the result was his famous song of "Hazel Dell." It was published by Wm. Hall & Son of New York, became one of the most popular songs of the day, and even now has a steady and quite large sale. The publishers immediately made arrangements to issue all of his compositions for three years. Fearful of failure he had used the German equivalent of Root, "Wurzel," for a signature, and many of his later pieces bear the same name. "Hazel Dell" was followed by the cantata of "The Flower Queen" (1851), words by Fanny J. Crosby. It was first produced in New York City, with great success. Desiring to devote more time to composition, he retired to "Willow Farm" at North Reading, a home erected by himself and brother for the comfort of their parents. There he remained several years, only leaving his seclusion when called upon to conduct musical conventions. In the summer of 1852 the first Normal Musical Institute (See INSTITUTES OF MUSIC, NORMAL), was held in New York, the faculty consisting of Dr. Lowell Mason, Thos. Hastings, Wm. B. Bradbury, and Dr. Root. The idea and scheme originated with Dr. Root, and has been productive of much good. He still takes the lead with his "Normals," though they are now held by other teachers. He is also one of the leading convention conductors (See CONVENTIONS, MUSICAL), having been engaged in the work for the last forty years, the earlier part of this period in conjunction with Dr. Mason, W. B. Bradbury, and others. In 1860 Dr. Root went to Chicago and became one of the firm of Root & Cady, music-publishers. They were very successful, and one of his books alone, the "Triumph" (1868) paid a profit of about $50,000. Through the great Chicago fire of October, 1871, they lost all their stock, valued at about $200,000. Soon after the firm was dissolved, Mr. Cady going to New York. Dr. Root still (May, 1886) resides in Chicago, and is still busy in editing various works, composing, and conducting. Some years ago he transferred his services to John Church & Co. of Cincinnati, who are now his publishers. The degree of Doctor of Music was bestowed upon him in 1881 by the University of Chicago.

Dr. Root occupies an important place in the musical history of this country. It was Lowell

Mason who lifted music from almost nothing and gave it an impetus, but he left no better follower than Dr. Root to carry on his work. It is as a composer of songs and other vocal pieces that Dr. Root excels. While they are within the comprehension of the masses they have an elevating influence and are admirably adapted for raising the standard of music, which has been the one great object of his life. Of course, in time many of them will pass into oblivion, but this is nothing against their past or present value. Among the songs which have gained a national popularity may be mentioned "Hazel Dell" (1851); "Rosalie, the Prairie Flower" (1852–53); "Battle Cry of Fredom," written in answer to T. F. Seward's famous "Rally 'round the Flag, Boys," and sung by the Hutchinson Family at the great mass meeting at Union Square, New York, in 1861; "Tramp, Tramp, Tramp, the Boys are Marching," which has been heard in every shape from one end of the land to the other; "Just Before the Battle, Mother;" "Vacant Chair," all of which, except the first two, belong to the war period; "The Old Folks are Gone," "A Hundred Years Ago," and "Old Patomac Shore." "There's Music in the Air" is a fine quartet, and for many years held its place as a standard piece for serenading purposes. "Shining Shore" has long been a great favorite in Sunday schools. All of the cantatas are popular, and some of them contain many gems. Among the books are "Sabbath Bell," "Diapason," "Triumph" "Silver Lute," "Choir and Congregation," "Chorus Castle," "Realm of Song," and "Musical Cirriculum." The latter is a most excellent and comprehensive work for the piano. Space will not permit us to name any more, but the following is a list of Dr. Root's principal works, with year of publication:

1. Academy Vocalist. Ladies' voices.   1848
2. Flower Queen. Cantata. Words by Fanny J. Crosby. First produced in New York City.   1851
3. Daniel. Cantata. First produced in New York City.   1852
4. Pilgrim Fathers. Cantata. First produced in New York City.   1854
5. Belshazzar's Feast. Cantata. First produced in New York City.   1855
6. Festival Glee Book.   1856
7. Haymakers. Cantata. First produced in New York City.   1856
8. Sabbath Bell. Church music.   1856
9. Diapason. Church music.   1860
10. Cabinet Organ School.   1863
11. Musical Cirriculum. For the piano.   1864
12. Silver Lute. Day schools.   1865
13. Coronet. Glees, etc.   1867
14. Triumph. Church music.   1868
15. Prize. Sunday schools.   1870
16. Forest Choir. Day schools.   1871
17. Model Organ Method.   1872
18. Glory. Church music.   1872
19. Choir and Congregation. Church.   1875
20. First Years in Song Land. Day schools 1879
21. Palace of Song. Classes and conventions.   1879
22. Song Tournament. Cantata.   1879
23. Chorus Castle. Choral societies.   1880
24. Under the Palms. Sunday school cantata.   1880
25. David, the Shepherd Boy. Sunday school cantata.   1881
26. Realm of Song (The). Classes and conventions.   1882
27. Choicest Gift (The). Sunday school cantata.   1883
28. Pure Delight. Sunday schools.   1883

Dr. Root's two daughters, NELLIE and MAY, are respectively contralto and mezzo-soprano singers.

**Root,** FREDERICK W., son of the preceding, was born at Boston, June 13, 1846. His musical instruction was begun when he was five years old by his father, and when about fourteen he was placed under the care of B. C. Blodgett, who took great pains to advance his pupil. He subsequently studied with Wm. Mason, Robert Goldbeck, and Jas. Flint, an organist of some repute. After the removal of the family to Chicago, in 1860, he frequently assisted his father in conducting conventions, also taking voice lessons from Carlo Bassini of New York at intervals. In 1869 he went to Europe and spent several years in study and travel. On returning to the United States he resumed his studies with Wm. Mason and Carlo Bassini. He has since mainly devoted himself to teaching, conducting, and composing, and now (May, 1886) resides at Chicago. As a teacher of vocal music he is very successful and takes a leading position. In 1866 Mr. Root was employed by Root & Cady, for whom he did a great deal of arranging and composing of music, having the popular taste in mind. Some of his pieces, however, were of true artistic finish, notably the song, "Beyond," which is worthy of attention. He remained with the firm until the fire of October, 1871. Mr. Root's works consist of a cantata, composed for the Beethoven Society; a vocal method;

a burlesque operetta; a class singing book; songs, glees, choruses, etc. "The Landing of the Pilgrims" (to Mrs. Heman's words) is a particularly fine piece of choral writing. For several years he was editor of the "Song Messenger," and still contributes occasional articles to the musical press.

**Rose of Tyrol.** An operetta in two acts. Words from the French; music by Julius Eichberg. Produced at the Museum, Boston, Monday, April 6, 1868.

**Rudersdorff,** HERMINE or ERMINIA, was born at Ivanowsky in the Ukraine, Russia, Dec, 12, 1822, her father being a distinguished violinist there at the time. She studied singing at Paris with Bordogni and at Milan with de Micherout. After this she appeared at various concerts in Germany, and sang in Mendelssohn's "Lobgesang," June 5, 1840, at Leipzig. In 1844 she married, at Frankfort, Dr. Küchenmeister, a professor of mathematics. From 1852 to 1854 she sang in light French and new German operas with great success at Berlin, having previously appeared in the principal German cities. May 23, 1854, she made her first appearance in England, at Drury Lane, London, as *Donna Anna* in "Don Giovanni," and was well received. She was engaged at Covent Garden and other London theatres for several years, and during the intervals between the seasons visited the English provinces, Germany, Holland and Paris. It was, however, as a concert singer that she excelled, and consequently she was frequently called upon to sing at the principal festivals. Her rendition of some oratorio parts was magnificent and produced a wonderful effect. In 1871 she was induced to come to the United States by the Handel and Haydn Society of Boston, and such was her reception that she was prevailed upon to make this country her permanent home. She sang at the Peace Jubilee of 1872, but mainly devoted herself to teaching, in which she was very successful; indeed, so great was her success that she soon took a leading position in the profession and was compelled to accept only such pupils as gave evidence of a special talent. Among the vocalists she trained may be mentioned Anna Drasdil, Emma Thursby, Isabel Fasset, Emily Winant, Fannie Kellogg, Helen Billings, Eugénie Pappenheim, Carlotta Patti, Minnie Hauck, etc.

Mme. Rudersdorff was not only a teacher and singer, but occasionally appeared in the *rôle* of a composer. She also contributed musical articles to various publications, and in 1873 furnished the libretto of Randegger's cantata of "Fridolin," produced at the Birmingham (Eng.) festival. Having accumulated considerable money, she bought an estate of 84 acres in a quiet rural town near Boston, where she spent the summer months in agricultural recreations. After a year's painful illness, death released her from suffering, Sunday morning, Feb. 26, 1882. She was conscious to the last moment, and gave full directions for the disposition of her property. Her name was well known on both continents, and her death produced a feeling of gloom in musical circles throughout the country. She will not soon be forgotten as a most estimable musician and woman.

**Rudolphsen,** JOHN FREDERICK, singer, actor, and teacher, was born March 19, 1827, at Hamburg, Germany. He early received instruction on the violin, also in theory and composition. At the age of sixteen he entered the orchestra, playing under Karl Krebs and Richard Wagner. Oct. 6, 1848, he arrived in New York City as a member of Gung'l's famous band. After Gung'l's return to Europe, he was engaged for four or five years as a member of the orchestra of the Italian Opera, New York, then conducted by Max Maretzek. During a portion of this period he studied singing, and made his *début* as an operatic singer at Niblo's Garden, New York, in Mme. Anna Bishop's English Opera Company in 1853. Having sung for a number of years in opera, he traveled extensively throughout the country as a concert singer. In 1862 he was called to Boston by the Handel and Haydn Society to sing in the "Messiah." He located there and was for a long time a prominent teacher and singer. About the year 1875 he again took up his travels, accompanying Mme. Camilla Urso in her tours of this country. In November, 1879, he was called to Cincinnati as professor of singing in the then newly established College of Music. This position he still (May, 1883) retains. His abilities as a teacher are of high order, and he is particularly well versed in everything that pertains to the vocal art. He has composed a number of songs, that of "Break, Break" being particularly fine, and a Te Deum in B flat.

**Ryder,** THOMAS PHILANDER, was born at Copasset, Mass., June 29, 1836. He early manifested a great love for music, but his tastes received no encouragement previous to his fourteenth year, when he was given some instruction upon the piano by a friend. His progress was very rapid, and he soon began composing little pieces. While still young he was thrown upon his own resources by the death of his father, but he managed to obtain time to practice music. When nineteen he began studying with Gustav Satter, and also took some lessons in organ playing and harmony. After holding various positions as organist, the first of which was at Nyannis, Mass., he became organist at Tremont Temple, Boston, a position which he held for nearly ten years. His skill as an accompanist is equaled by few. He still resides in Boston, and numbers among his pupils many talented musicians. His compositions are mostly for the piano. The first one to attract general attention was the "Chanson des Alpes," published in 1880 by White, Smith & Co. Among his other popular pieces are "Old Oaken Bucket," "Nearer, My God, to Thee," "A Dainty Morsel," "Lida," "Rustic Maiden," "Sounds from the Glen," etc. He is also acknowledged to be a choral conductor of unusual skill, and has filled many important positions in this capacity.

**Ryder, George H., & Co.,** BOSTON. This house, which manufactures church organs, was established Nov. 1, 1870, by Geo. H. Ryder, who is at present sole proprietor. About two organs per month are turned out, the total number thus far constructed is 112, varying in price from $600 to $6000 or more. Mr. Ryder, who was born May 9, 1838, has had twenty-five years' experience in the business, and is, besides, an excellent organist, having officiated in several of the Boston churches. A selected force of workmen is employed in the factory, which is located at Reading, Mass. Mr. Ryder has built many organs for use in and around Boston, as well as various ones throughout the country, among which are 1st Baptist Church, Chelsea, Mass., and 1st M. E. Church, Cleveland, Ohio.

# S.

**Schilling,** Dr. Gustav, well-known as a musical writer, was born Nov. 3, 1805, at Schweigershausen, Hanover, where his father was a clergyman. He was educated at Göttingen and Halle, and in 1830 became director of Stöpel's Music School at Stuttgart. In 1857, on account of financial difficulties, he was compelled to leave his native country and came to the United States, landing at New York. Two years later (1859) he was also compelled to flee from thence. He then spent several years in wandering throughout Canada, and probably at one time resided in Montreal. In 1871 he settled at Burlington, Iowa, as a teacher, also contributing articles to various German-American publications, under the *noms de plume* of "The Deceased" and "The Hermit of Iowa." Seemingly impelled by some restless spirit, perhaps also hoping to better his financial condition, he removed from Burlington to the State of Nebraska, where he died in June (?), 1880.* He left a daughter, but whether or not any other children we have been unable to ascertain. At one period of his residence in the West he had a music school. Dr. Schilling wrote "Æsthetics of Music," in 2 volumes; "Polyphonomos," a book relating to harmony; "The Musical Europe," a collection of biographical sketches; a "Dictionary of Musical Words; a work on acoustics, one on harmony, etc. He also rewrote Philip Emanuel Bach's piano school. But the work by which he will longest be remembered is the "Encyclopädie der gesammten musikalischen Wissenschaften, oder Universal Lexikon der Tonkunst" (Encyclopædia of General Musical Knowledge, or Universal Lexicon of Music), 7 vols., 8vo., Stuttgart, 1835-40; published in this country by Schuberth & Co., New York. It is thought he left in manuscript a work entitled "Art of Touch," which he is known to have written. Many of his works have been severely criticised, and perhaps justly so, though they contain much that is good. Schilling's life was one of unusual adversity and change. How much of this was due to himself we will not undertake to say. His light, which rose so brightly in Germany fifty years ago, suffered extinction in the New World, far from his native country.

**Schlesinger,** Daniel, was born at Hamburg, Dec. 15, 1799. His study of the piano began when he was five years old, and later he took some lessons on the organ. For some time he was employed in a counting house, but music held the chief place in his devotions. While in London on one occasion he happened to hear Ferdinand Ries, and at once became a pupil of that musician, making rapid progress. He also took lessons of Moscheles. He was elected a member of the Philharmonic Society, London, and played in several concerts of the society, producing several of his own compositions. In 1832 he made a professional tour, visiting Hamburg, Leipzig, Vienna, Paris, and other cities. At the suggestion of one of his brothers he in 1836 came to the United States, landing at New York, and making his *début* as a pianist at the National Theatre, without, however, meeting with a very good reception. In the following year, at a second appearance, he played Hummel's A flat concerto and was applauded. His time was mostly devoted to teaching, but from time to time he came before the public as a player. He died at New York, Jan. 8, 1838.

**Schœnfeld,** Henry, was born at Milwaukee, Wis., Oct. 4, 1856, and educated at the Leipzig Conservatorium and under Lassen at Weimar. We have few particulars of his life, but his compositions evince more than ordinary

---

*Grove's "Dictionary of Music and Musicians" states that he is still living in Montreal, in which it probably follows Mendel's "Dictionary." This, however, is a mistake, arising, perhaps, from his having once lived in the place named. It is certain that he died as above stated, though the exact date and place have not as yet been determined. Right here I would acknowledge my indebtedness to Mr. Karl Merz, editor of "Brainard's Musical World," (who corresponded with Schilling for several years) for the facts of his life during his residence in America.*

talent as a composer. Among them is an "Easter Idyll;" a cantata, for solos, chorus and orchestra; several sonatas, piano pieces, songs, etc.

**Schultze,** EDWARD, was born in Germany about 1828. He was one of the members of the Germania Orchestra (See that heading), and came to this country with that organization in 1848. When it disbanded (1855) he located in Boston, where he for a long time resided, esteemed as a teacher and player. In 1877 he became director of the musical department of the Syracuse University, which conferred on him the degree of Doctor of Music.

**Seguin,** ARTHUR EDWARD SHELDON, was born at London, April 7, 1809, and received his musical training at the Royal Academy of Music. In 1828 he made his *début* as a singer at a concert and was well received. During 1833 and 1834 he was engaged at Covent Garden, and from 1835 to 1837 at Drury Lane, singing, meanwhile, in various festivals and concerts. He came to the United States in 1838, and on Oct. 15th of that year appeared at the National Theatre, New York, as the *Count* in Rooke's "Amilie." Subsequently he organized an opera company called the "Seguin Troupe," which gave performances in many of the towns and cities of this country and Canada. He died at New York, Dec. 9, 1852. His voice was a bass of peculiar depth and richness. It is said that he was elected a chief by one of the Indian tribes and given a name meaning "The man with the deep, mellow voice."

**Seguin,** ANN, *née* Childe, wife of the preceding, was also a pupil at the Royal Academy of Music, and made her *début* at the same time and place as her husband. Some time after, they were married, and she came with him to this country. She sang with him in operas until his death, in 1852, when she retired from the stage and settled at New York. She was still living there in 1882.

**Seiler,** MME. EMMA, was born Feb. 23, 1821, at Würzburg, Bavaria, where her father occupied a high social position. The most prominent artists and scientists were numbered among the friends of the family, which fact had a marked influence upon the education of the children. At the age of twenty-one years she married a Swiss physician, and went to

reside with him near the village of Langenthal, Canton Berne, where she remained nine years. In 1851 she had the misfortune to lose her husband, and was left with two little children without any means of support. Having been well trained in singing and possessing a fine voice, she resolved to become a teacher of the art. She soon found, however, that she was far from fitted to do this. Not only was she destitute of any starting point from which she could proceed, but also, of any method. This led her to study the various vocal works published and at the same time take lessons of the most celebrated teachers, but from them she learned little new. Each teacher had a different system, and these systems were arranged with little regard for logic or the structure of the throat. Mme. Seiler rightly came to the conclusion that ignorance could work more harm in the teaching of vocal than in any other branch of music. And this fact she was destined to have illustrated in her own experience, for while studying under the care of an eminent teacher she entirely lost her voice. After this calamity she studied the piano under Frederic Weick at Dresden, with a view of becoming a teacher of that instrument. While devoting herself to this department of teaching she heard of numerous cases where persons had lost their voice through injudicious methods of training, and this, combined with the loss of her own voice, made her determine to obtain such knowledge as was necessary to a natural and healthy development of the powers of the human voice. With this object in view she embraced every opportunity to hear the greatest singers, and even went to Italy, but there, as later in France, she found the same ignorance and superficiality.

On her return she sought the counsel of Prof. Helmholtz, at that time residing at Heidelburg. Through the assistance of that distinguished scientist she became familiar with all the new discoveries in acoustics, learned the properties of true musical tones, and finally succeeded in producing them with her own voice. She then brought into requisition the laryngoscope (then just invented) to observe the physiological processes which go on in the larynx during the production of such tones. The constant strain broke down her health, and for a year she was compelled to desist from labor. Soon after resuming her investigations she published the results in a little book, "Altes und henesuber die hensbildung der Stimme, von E. Seiler," at Leipzig, where she was then staying. As may be imagined, the work at once created a decided sensation, though no one suspected its being written by a woman. One of the special features was the description of a pair of cartilages which she discovered in her investigations, and of which anatomists had previously been ignorant.

In consequence of an article written by herself and printed in the Leipzig "Musik Zeitung," she was offered and accepted a position at Vienna. She was prevented from fulfilling her engagement, however, by the war of 1866 between Germany and Austria, which immediately broke out. This made it impossible for her to support herself by teaching in Berlin, where she had been residing for some time, and she accepted the invitation of some friends in the United States to come to this country. She landed at Philadelphia, provided with letters of introduction from Prof. Helmholtz, Du Bois Ramant, and other scientists of Europe, which gained her admission to many of the first families of the city. There she continued her studies in the physiology of the voice, and as a result published, in 1869, "Voice in Singing," which was received with such favor, both by scientists and by musicians, that a second edition was soon called for. In recognition of her labors, she was elected a member of the American Philosophical Society, an honor seldom or never before conferred upon a woman in America. Shortly after the publication of the work she opened a school of vocal art, in which she employed her method. In 1875 she was led, on account of the many persons who applied to her for vocal culture in speaking, to publish a third work, "The Voice in Speaking," in the preparation of which she had the assistance of her son, Dr. Carl Seiler.

Mme. Seiler recently gave up her school, and now devotes all her time to private teaching and the preparation of a new edition of her German book. With the exception of Manuel Garcia of London, she is, perhaps, the only vocal teacher who has, to any great extent, cultivated a scientific knowledge of the voice, and it is gratifying to know that her labors are appreciated in a measure at least. To students of voice-culture her works are a great boon, and they may always be consulted with profit.

**Seward,** THEODORE FRELINGHUYSEN, was born at Florida, Orange Co., N. Y., Jan. 25, 1835. He early devoted himself to music, and has been very successful as a teacher of piano, organ, voice, and theory. He is the editor, either wholly or in part, of the following works, which contain much of his music: "Sunnyside Glee Book," "Temple Choir," "The Singer," "Coronation," "Vineyard of Song," "Glee Circle," "Pestalozzian Music Teacher," and "Tonic Sol-fa Music Reader." At different periods he has been editor of the "New York Musical Pioneer" and the "New York Musical Gazette," and now has charge of the "Tonic Sol-fa Advocate." He is one of the chief champions of the tonic sol-fa system in America, to the spreading of which he devotes much of his time. His present residence is Orange, N. J.

**Sharland,** JOHN B., was born of English parents at Halifax, N. S., in 1837. Early in life he went to Boston, where he learned the trade of a piano maker in Jonas Chickering's establishment. The numerous artists whom he heard, however, led him to abandon the piano business and take to music as a profession. He soon became a successful pianist and teacher, and rapidly acquired a leading position among Boston's musicians. Mr. Sharland has been connected with the following musical societies: (1.) The "Cecilia Club," as pianist. (2.) The "Lurline Club," so-called from Wallace's opera of "Lurline," as conductor. After giving a few concerts it was discontinued, owing to the breaking out of the Civil War. (3.) The "Foster Club," as conductor. This society received its name from its patron, George Foster, Esq., and produced Schumann's "Gypsy Life" and other works of that class. On the death of Mr. Foster it was merged into the "Cecilia" (not the society previously referred to). Mr. Sharland's connection with it covers a period of four years, and he was succeeded by John Howard. (4.) The "Boylston Club," as conductor, from the autumn of 1872 to April, 1875. Much of the musical proficiency of the Club is due to his efforts. He was succeeded by Geo. L. Osgood. (5.) The "Thomas Choral

Society," so-called in compliment to Theodore Thomas, as conductor. It consisted of 300 voices, and the following are some of the works given during its existence of several years: "Song of Destiny" (3 times), Brahms; "Prometheus," Liszt; 9th Symphony (3), Beethoven; "Faust," (4), Berlioz; "Orpheus" (3), Gluck. The society was supported by Mr. Thomas' orchestra. Mr. Sharland was for two years organist and director of Mr. Alger's choir of 40 voices, which gave concerts at the Music Hall every Sunday. He was also one of the music committee and organist with Dr. Willcox at the great Peace Jubilee, and had the training of the 10,000 children's voices. At the present he is director of the "Newport Choral Society," founded six years ago; the "Brockton Choral Union," now two years old; the "Belmont Choral Union," also two years old; the "Boston Glee and Madrigal Society;" and instructor of music in the public schools of Boston. The latter position he has uninterruptedly held for the last eighteen years.

**Sherwin,** WILLIAM FISK, was born at Ashfield, Franklin Co., Mass., March 14, 1826, and has gained considerable reputation as a teacher, composer, and conductor of conventions. He has edited, in conjunction with others, several collections of music, and written a large number of songs, anthems and other vocal pieces. He now (April, 1886) resides at Boston and is connected with the New England Conservatory of Music.

**Sherwood,** WILLIAM HALL, one of America's most celebrated pianists, was born at Lyons, N. Y., Jan. 31, 1854. His father, Rev. L. H. Sherwood, M. A., a fine musician, was founder of the LYONS MUSICAL ACADEMY (See that heading). At a very early age his musical talents began to manifest themselves, and to his father's careful training he probably owes much of his subsequent success. Such was his progress that between the ages of nine and eleven years he appeared in concerts in New York, Pennsylvania and Canada. The ensuing six years were mostly spent in obtaining a general education, though he frequently gave lessons at his father's institution. Having fully determined upon music as a profession, he in the summer of 1871 placed himself under the care of Dr. William Mason, who was then holding a normal institute at Binghamton, N. Y. Upon the advice of that musician he went to Berlin in the autumn of the same year and became a pupil of Kullak. After seven months of study he was one of those selected to play at Kullak's annual concert at the Singakademie, and performed Chopin's fantasia in F minor, op. 49, receiving great applause. His health becoming somewhat impaired, he left Berlin and went to Stuttgart, where he remained several months, studying composition under Doppler. He then returned to Berlin and continued his studies under Kullak and Weitzmann. Several piano pieces which he now completed were very favorably commented upon, and a capriccio, op. 4, was published by Breitkopf & Härtel some time later. Also five piano pieces, ops. 1, 2 and 3, by M. Behr of Berlin, and taught by Theodore Kullak in his advanced classes. During his second winter in Berlin, he played Beethoven's "Emperor Concerto" several times, once at the Beethoven festival (Wuerst, conductor), when he was compelled to bow to the applause and recalled no less than *eight times!*

The flattering beginning would have turned the head of more than one young artist, but not so with Mr. Sherwood. He began to feel dissatisfied with his *technique* and touch, and spent more than a year in developing the facility of his fingers and wrists, studying for a period to excellent advantage with Deppe. In February, 1875, he repaired to Leipzig and placed himself under Richter for the study of counterpoint and composition. He did not, however, long remain there, for on the arrival of Liszt at Weimar he went to that place, accompanied by his wife, formerly Miss Mary Fay, a talented pianist, whom he married in the autumn of 1874. Liszt received them warmly, showing them many kindnesses, and even consented to become godfather to their first child. At Liszt's last *matinée* of the season, Mr. Sherwood played twice, before a distinguished audience. He then proceeded to Hamburg and played Grieg's A minor concerto at a philharmonic concert. During his stay of two weeks he made six public appearances, and was received each time with great applause. At the Singakademie, Berlin, Feb. 18, 1876, he gave his own concert, assisted by his wife, which was a great success and unanimously praised by the German press.

In May, 1876, after having been abroad nearly five years, Mr. Sherwood returned to the United States. He played at Boston, New York, Philadelphia, Pittsburgh, Cincinnati, St. Louis, Chicago, Detroit, Buffalo, and many other cities east and west, fully establishing a reputation as one of the finest of modern pianists. During the Centennial Exhibition he frequently appeared at the Philadelphia Academy of Music before immense audiences, arousing great enthusiasm. In the autumn of 1876 he settled at Boston, and soon came to be in great demand as a soloist and teacher. For two or three seasons he taught at the New England Conservatory of Music, but becoming dissatisfied with some things about the conservatory system, particularly the short time allowed for lessons, he discontinued this work, and has since given only private instruction. He gave two recitals at the opening of Hershey Music Hall, Chicago, Jan. 23 and 25, 1877, which materially added to his fame in the West. In the summer of 1878 he held a very successful normal at his native place, which was followed by two at Canandaigua, N. Y. He has also given numerous recitals and lectures at the annual meetings of the Music Teachers' National Association. During May and June, 1879, he made a tour of the Northern and Western States, which embraced the following places: Boston (3), Providence, R. I., Portland, Me., Cambridge, Andover, Bradford, Taunton, and Lowell, Mass., Oberlin, O. (3), Pittsburgh, Pa., Lexington, Ky., Cincinnati (2), Chicago (6), St. Louis (4), Milwaukee, Wis. (2), St. Paul, Minn. (2), Cedar Rapids (2), Burlington, Dubuque, and Burlington, Ia., Owatomca and Minneapolis, Minn., Evanston, Ill., Detroit, Mich., Buffalo, Auburn, and Syracuse, N. Y. He has also made repeated similar tours. Among Mr. Sherwood's later recitals may be mentioned the series given in the hall of the Academy of Arts, Philadelphia, during the week commencing Dec. 4, 1882. The programs were especially comprehensive, and included a number of pieces by American composers. He has made a feature of short lecture analysis of the works performed at many of his recitals.

As a pianist Mr. Sherwood possesses many excellent qualities. A perfect *technique* is united to great delicacy as well as depth of expression. The works of the great masters are rarely so well rendered as when in his hands, while he enters into the spirit of the modern school's productions; indeed, he may justly be classed with the most eminent of living players. So fully has his time been occupied in teaching and other duties, he has had little opportunity for composition. His works probably do not number over 15 or 20. We have already mentioned the five piano pieces and capriccio, ops. 1, 2, 3 and 4. Of the others may be named a Scherzo in E major, op. 7; an Idyll in A major, op. 5, No. 2; a Mazurka in A minor, op. 6, No. 2; a "Scherzo Symphonique" in G sharp minor; Allegro Patetico and Medea, ops. 12 and 13, and a set of six pieces, op. 14.

**Sherwood,** Mrs. WILLIAM H., *née* Miss Mary Neilson Fay, was born at Williamsburg, N. Y., about 1855. She studied under Wm. Mason, Richard Hoffman, Gustav Satter, and for a short time with Rubinstein during his stay in this country. Upon advice of the latter she went to Berlin and placed herself under the instruction of Kullak. After her marriage with Mr. Sherwood in the autumn of 1874, she accompanied him on his travels, and assisted him at his last concert in Berlin. Since returning to the United States, she has frequently taken a part in her husband's recitals, and is well-known everywhere. Besides being one of the finest lady pianists of our time, she is very successful as a teacher.

**Sherwood,** EDGAR H., teacher, pianist, and composer, was born at Lyons, N. Y., in 1845, and is brother of L. H. Sherwood, principal of the Lyons Musical Academy. His father, Hon. Lyman Sherwood, was a prominent lawyer of his day. He was able to play the violin when four years old, but his musical talents were not encouraged. The practice of medicine was the profession chosen for him, and he entered the office of a local physician for study. In 1862 he enlisted and served through the war. At its close he returned North and chose music as a profession, studying and practicing diligently. He commenced his career as a teacher, in which he has been remarkably successful, in a seminary at Dansville, N. Y. He now resides at Rochester, N. Y. He has written numerous songs and piano pieces. Many of the latter are used by musicians generally for concert and teaching purposes. Of them we may specify "Grand Menuet" (A flat), "Polonaise" (A minor) and "Anemone" (rondeau) as being particularly fine.

**Shumway,** NEHEMIAH, an early American psalmodist, published at Philadelphia in 1801, THE AMERICAN HARMONY, a book of 220 pages, including a singer's manual. Many of the tunes and anthems were of his composition. As to his birth or death or any other particulars of his life we are ignorant.

**Silver Threads Among the Gold.** A popular song and chorus, written about ten years ago (1872). The words are by Eben E. Rexford; the music by H. P. Danks. For some time after its appearance it was all the rage, being everywhere sung both in private and public, and achieved a success only paralleled by a few of Winner's, Foster's and Hays' songs. The sales were several hundred thousand copies.

**Singer,** OTTO, was born July 26, 1833, at Sora, Saxony. In 1851 he entered the Conservatorium at Leipsic, where he remained until 1855, studying under Richter, Moscheles, and Hauptmann. He went to Dresden in 1859, and for two years at intervals studied with Liszt, of whom he was a devout admirer and follower. Upon being offered a position as teacher in the new conservatory of Theodore Thomas and Wm. Mason, he came to New York in 1867. Early in 1873, the conservatory having previously come to an end, and at the instance of Mr. Thomas, he went to Cincinnati and took charge of the chorus of the first Cincinnati May Festival. To his zeal and ability much of the success of the Festival was due, and at the same time he secured to himself no little fame. Becoming in great demand as a teacher and conductor, he settled in Cincinnati. He had the training of the choral forces at the May Festivals of 1875 and 1878, but in 1880 was succeeded by Mr. Brand. At the Festival of 1878 he conducted Liszt's "Graner" mass, and his own "Ode," composed expressly for the opening and dedication of the Music Hall. Upon the organization of the College of Music in 1878 he was engaged as one of the instructors, and is now (May, 1884) professor of the piano and theory and one of the lecturers on music. In this capacity he has done good work, and very materially assisted in advancing the interests and reputation of the College. In 1880 he was one of the committee of three appointed to pass judgment upon the compositions offered in competition for the prize of $1000 offered by the Festival Association. He is highly esteemed in Cincinnati and elsewhere, and takes a prominent place among American musicians. Mr. Singer's compositions are numerous, though few of them have been published. In all of them he shows a decided leaning toward the modern school represented by Liszt. They consist of "The Landing of the Pilgrim Fathers" (1876) cantata, and "Festival Ode," cantata, composed for the dedication of the Music Hall, Cincinnati, in 1878; several symphonies; two concertos for piano and orchestra; variations for two pianos, op. 1; fantasia for piano and orchestra, op. 2; duo for piano and violin, op. 3; a rhapsodie in C; and a number of piano pieces.

**Smith,** DEXTER, was born at Peabody, Mass., Nov. 14, 1839, and has gained considerable reputation in musical circles. He has written several songs, and numerous poems. For a long time he was editor and publisher of "Dexter Smith's Paper," which ceased to exist a number of years ago. He now has editorial charge of "The Musical Record," published by O. Ditson & Co., Boston.

**Smith,** WILSON GEORGE, was born in Elyria, Lorain Co., O., Aug. 19, 1855. His predilection for music was early manifested, but received no encouragement. He was unable, from poor health, to pursue a collegiate course, and after graduating from the public schools of Cleveland, held a responsible position in a prominent wholesale mercantile house for several years. The permission of his parents to follow music as a profession having at last been obtained, he went to Cincinnati and studied for some time with Otto Singer. A number of compositions written about this time were favorably commented upon by several eminent musicians and encouraged him to persevere. In 1880 he went to Berlin, where he remained two years, studying the piano with Xavier Scharwenka, Oscar Raif and Moritz Moszkowski, and theory and composition with F. Kiel, Phillipp Scharwenka and Franz Neumann, with all of whom he was a favorite. During his stay in Berlin, he was several times compelled to suspend study and practice entirely on account of nervous prostration. Returning to America, he located at Cleveland, where he still resides. Soon after, a number of his compositions—a set of characteristic piano pieces dedicated to Edward Grieg—were published by A. P. Schmidt & Co., of Boston. They called forth a flattering letter from that musician. Several of his pieces were performed by Calixa Laval-lée at his first American recital before the M. T. N. A., and were received with marked favor. His name is now to be found on the concert programs of many distinguished artists. Mr. Smith is the editor of the Modern Classic and Encore Series published by S. Brainard's Sons, which display his musicianly abilities. He is also acquiring considerable reputation as a musical writer and critic, being connected with some of the best musical journals in the country. If his life is spared, he will undoubtedly take the front rank in the musical profession. Previous to op. 10 his compositions comprise such as were written before he went abroad. The following list of his works does not include many later fugitive and stray pieces:

Op. 10. Two songs.
" 11. Mazurka Hongroise.
" 12. Valse Melodique.
" 13. Moment Musicale.
" 14. Two piano pieces.
" 15. Serenade for piano.
" 16. Theme and variations (Ms.)
" 17. Petite Valse de Concert.
" 18. Homage a Grieg (5 piano pieces).
" 19. Two songs.
" 20. Three songs.
" 21. Echoes of Ye Olden Time (4 piano pieces).
" 22. Two songs.
" 23. Swedish Dance.
" 24. Menuet and Danse Arabesque.
" 25. Gavotte and Mazurka.
" 26. Valse Sentimental and Mazurka.
" 27. Pensée d'Amour (Romance for piano)
" 28. Characteristic sketches for piano; transcriptions. 1. Norwegian Dance (Grieg), 2. Courante (Handel), 3. Two Songs (Franz).

**Southard,** L. H., born about 1826, is well known in this country as an organist, composer, and teacher. He has edited several collections of music, and written two or three operas. His "New Course in Harmony" was published in 1855, and "Elements of Thorough-Bass and Harmony" (16mo 100 pp) in 1867. He resides at Boston.

**Stanley,** W. H., a tenor singer of some repute, was born in England, and came to this country in 1871. Since coming here he has sung in the principal cities in concerts, oratorios and operas. For some time he resided at Boston, but now resides at New York. His *répertoire* includes "Bohemian Girl," "Martha," "Patience," "Mascott," "Messiah," "Samson," "Elijah," "Creation," "Judas Maccabæus," "St. Paul," "Joshua," and other well-known works.

**Star Spangled Banner.** One of the most beautiful and popular of American national songs. The words were written by Francis Scott Key, Esq., (died in 1846) during our second struggle with England, in 1812, and according to an eminent writer under the following circumstances: "A gentleman had left Baltimore with a flag of truce, for the purpose of getting released from the British fleet a friend of his who had been captured at Marlborough. He went as far as the mouth of the Patuxent, and was not permitted to return, lest the intended attack on Baltimore should be disclosed. He was, therefore, brought up the bay to the mouth of the Patapsco, where the flag vessel was kept under the guns of a frigate; and he was compelled to witness the bombardment of Fort McHenry, which the admiral had boasted he would carry in a few hours, and that the city must fall. He watched the flag of the fort through the whole day, with an anxiety that can be better felt than described, until the night prevented him from seeing it. In the night he watched the bombshells, and at early dawn his eye was again greeted by the proudly waving flag of his country." It was while watching the progress of the battle that night that Key wrote the words which have now become immortal. The flag which was the source of his inspiration was made by a Mrs. Sanderson, then a girl only fifteen years old, and presented to Col. George Armistead, commander of the fort, just before the British ships came up the bay. After the war it was given back to Mrs. Sanderson, in whose family it has since remained. The State of Maryland has repeatedly tried to purchase the valuable relic, but always without success. Mrs. Sanderson died at New York City, in 1882, at the age of eighty-five years.

The words of the Star Spangled Banner were adapted to English music by F. Durang and first sung by him in a house near the Holiday Theatre, Baltimore. The song was first printed by B. Ides of the same city. The four stanzas written by Key are as follows, to which is added a fifth stanza by Dr. O. W. Holmes:

1. O say, can you see by the dawn's early light,
What so proudly we hailed at the twilight's last gleaming,
Whose stripes and bright bars, through the perilous fight,
O'er the ramparts we watched, were so gallantly streaming?
And the rocket's red glare, the bombs bursting in the air,
Gave proof through the night that our flag was still there.

2. On the shore, dimly seen through the mist of the deep,
Where the foe's haughty host in dread silence reposes,
What is that which the breeze, o'er the towering steep,
As it fitfully blows, half conceals, half discloses?
Now it catches the gleam of the morning's first beam,
In full glory reflected, now shines in the stream.

3. And where is that band which so vauntingly swore,
'Mid the havoc of war and the battle's confusion,
A home and a country they'd leave us no more?
Their blood has washed out their foul footstep's pollution.
No refuge could save the hireling and slave
From the terror of flight or the gloom of the grave.

4. Oh, thus be it ever when freeman shall stand
Between their loved home and war's desolation;
Blest with victory and peace, may the heaven-rescued land,
Praise the Power that hath made and preserved us a nation.
Then conquer we must, when our cause it is just,
And this be our motto, "In God is our trust."

5. When our land is illumed with liberty's smile,
If a foe from within strike a blow at her glory,
Down, down with the traitor that dares to defile
The flag of her stars and the page of her story!
By the millions unchained who our birthright have gained,
We will keep her bright blazon forever unstained!

*Chorus—1st verse.*

O say, does that star spangled banner still wave
O'er the land of the free and the home of the brave?

*2nd verse.*

'Tis the star spangled banner, O long may it wave
O'er the land of the free and the home of the brave.

*Last verses.*

And the star spangled banner in triumph shall wave
While the land of the free is the home of the brave.

The following is the melody as first written, and as it is now sung:

*As originally written.*

**CHORUS.**

*As now sung.*

**CHORUS.**

**Steck, George & Co.,** New York City. This American piano manufacturing firm was established in 1857, by the present senior partner, George A. Steck, who had previously worked at the trade for a number of years. Mr. Steck and his partners have been very successful, and their instruments are known for their good tone and durable workmanship all over Europe and America. Mr. Steck has taken out several patents, one in 1870 for an improvement in the upright piano frame.

**Steiniger-Clark,** Anna, pianist and teacher, was born in Magdeburg, Prussia. Her father, an officer in the Prussian artillery, removed to Berlin, but died soon after, when she was about eight years old. Her musical talents were plainly evident when she was little more than an infant. A year after her father's death, she began her studies under the direction of Agthe, with whom she remained some time. After taking a few lessons of Ehrlich, she became a pupil of Kullak. While under Agthe's care she had made her *début*, when sixteen years old, at a concert in the Royal Opera House, Berlin, taking part in Mozart's concerto for three pianos. She continued her studies after this, but all the while became more and more dissatisfied with the systems of instruction used by her teachers. Some time after, Ludwig Deppe arrived in Berlin, of whom she at once became an ardent pupil. In 1878, accompanied by Mme. Aafke Kuypers, she made a successful tour of Holland, receiving distinctions from the Queen of Holland. Other tours followed until her reputation had spread over the greater part of Europe. During the winter of 1882-83 she made a tour of Germany. About this time she met in Berlin a young American musician, Frederick Clark, an excellent pianist, whom she soon after married. With him she came to the United States in 1885, and made her first appearance at a concert of the Boston Symphony Orchestra, under Gericke's direction, in the Music Hall, Boston, playing Beethoven's concerto in G minor. She now resides at Boston, and devotes much of her time to teaching. She locates the source of power in playing in the shoulder region, and bases her system accordingly. Frau Steiniger-Clark's playing proclaims her to be a true artist and one of the first pianists of our time. During the past season (January and February, 1886) she gave a series of six Beethoven concerts in Chickering Hall, Boston. She played the ten sonatas of Beethoven for piano and violin, thus given for the first time in America, the Eroica variations, sonatas ops. 110 and 111, and 7, 10 and 3, etc., for piano solo. After this she was engaged by Herr Gericke as piano soloist of the Boston Symphony Orchestra during its western tour in April, when she played in Cincinnati, Chicago, Cleveland and other cities.

**Steinway,** HENRY ENGELHARD, well-known as founder of the piano house bearing his name, was born at Wolfshagen, Duchy of Brunswick, Germany, Feb. 15, 1797. His particular genius made itself manifest in early boyhood by the manufacturing of various musical instruments for his own use. While still young he entered a factory and learned the business of organ making. In 1849 he sent his son, Charles, to this country to report upon the prospects of piano manufacturing, and in 1850 followed with the rest of the fam-

ily, establishing the house of Steinway & Sons (see succeeding article). He remained at the head of the firm until his death at New York, Feb. 7, 1871. Of his sons, Henry, Jr., died at New York, March 11, 1865; Charles, at Brunswick, during a European tour, March 31, 1865; and Albert, at New York, May 14, 1877, the latter two of typhoid fever. The business is now conducted by C. F. Theodore and William Steinway, assisted by the younger members of the family.

**Steinway & Sons,** NEW YORK CITY. Henry E. Steinway (originally *Steinweg*, but anglicised to Steinway), founder of this celebrated piano making house, was born in 1797, at Wolfshagen in the Duchy of Brunswick. At the age of fifteen he was, through wars and accidents, the sole survivor of the family, which originally consisted of twelve persons. When seventeen, he entered the army, from which he was honorably discharged on becoming of age. It was then his desire to become a cabinet maker, but the guilds required five years' apprenticeship and five years' service as a journeyman before he could become his own master. This he would not submit to, and after working one year as a cabinet maker under an irregular master, he turned his attention to organ making and settled at Seesen, a city of about 3000 inhabitants at the foot of the Hartz mountains. In February, 1825, he was married, and on Nov. 25th of the same year his eldest son, C. F. Theodore, was born. Mr. Steinway soon commenced making pianos on a small scale, and as early as August, 1839, he exhibited one grand, one grand square (3 strings), and one square at the state fair of Brunswick. The business had reached large proportions when it was seriously crippled by the Prussian "Zollverein" in 1845, and totally destroyed by the Revolution of 1848. The remote thought of some time emigrating to America now became an ever present one, and in April, 1849, Charles, his second son, was sent over to inspect the ground. So favorable were the reports made that the next year the whole family, with the exception of Theodore, who remained behind to complete unfinished work, came to the United States, landing at New York, June 5, 1850. On their arrival the family consisted of, besides the father and mother, four sons (not counting Theodore), Charles, Henry, William and Albert, and three daughters. For three years the father and eldest sons worked in various manufactories that they might become thoroughly familiar with the American trade. In March, 1853, they united and formed the firm of Steinway & Sons. Their headquarters were at first on Varick street, but increase of business necessitated one removal after another. In 1855 they exhibited a square piano, the iron frame of which combined the overstrung scale with the single casting. In 1858 they purchased the plot of ground bounded by Fourth and Lexington avenues and 52nd and 53rd streets, on which their present factory was erected. The fine marble building on East 14th St. was built in 1863, and three years later the well-known Steinway Hall, located on the same lot, was opened to the public. To such an extent did their business increase that in 1870 and 1871 they bought several hundred acres of land at Astoria, L. I. (opposite 100 to 120th sts.), on which a steam saw-mill, iron and brass foundries, etc., were erected. Henry, the third son, died March 11, 1865, and Charles, the second son, March 31 of the same year, in Brunswick, while on a European tour. In consequence, Theodore gave up his business in Brunswick and became a partner of the New York firm. Henry, the father, died at New York, Feb. 7, 1871. The firm now (1886) consists of C. F. Theodore Steinway, William Steinway, Henry W. T. Steinway, Charles H. Steinway, Frederick T. Steinway, Henry Ziegler, and George A. Steinway. In 1875 they opened warerooms at 15 Lower Seymour street, London, with a concert hall attached, and in 1880 a branch establishment was opened at No. 20-24 Neue Rosenstrasse, Hamburg, Germany. They have, besides, agencies all over the world. It is hardly necessary to add anything in praise of their pianos, for they are known and esteemed all over the world, having invariably taken first prizes wherever exhibited.

**Sterling,** ANTOINETTE, was born, according to Grove's "Dictionary of Music and Musicians," at Sterlingville, N. Y., Jan. 23, 1850. In 1867 she went to New York and placed herself under the care of Sig. Abella. She then went to Europe and studied with Mme. Marchesi at Cologne, Pauline Viardot at Baden-Baden, and Manuel Garcia at Lon-

don. On returning to the United States, in 1871, she was well received as a concert singer. May 13, 1873, she gave a farewell concert at Irving Hall, Boston, and then went to England, where she made her first appearance at the Promenade Concerts, Covent Garden, Nov. 5th. She soon became very popular, and in 1875 was married to John MacKinlay, since when she has resided at London. Her voice is a contralto of great richness, volume and compass.

**Stickney,** JOHN, one of the early American psalmodists, was born at Stoughton, Mass., in 1742. He traveled from place to place throughout the New England States, and became well-known as a teacher, composer, and publisher of music. In 1774 he issued "The Gentlemen and Lady's Musical Companion," printed by Daniel Bailey of Newburyport. It is a small collection of psalms, anthems, etc., with rules for learning to sing. He finally settled at South Hadley, and died in 1826. His wife was also a good singer and teacher.

**St. Louis.** The first musical society to attain any degree of permanence and general popularity in this city was the

PHILHARMONIC.

It was organized in 1860, and for ten years exercised a most healthful influence in the growth of local musical art. Charles Balmer was the president and the leading spirit of the organization, and the conductors were Edward Sobolewski and Egmont Frölich, the latter during the last three seasons. Both choral and orchestral works were performed at public concerts, with frequent semi-public *soirées* for the rendition of smaller compositions.

There are a large number of singing societies among the German population, the most prominent of which are the

LIEDERKRANZ and ARION.

Both of these societies have sung with honor at the great sängerfests held in various parts of the country.

THE HAYDN ORCHESTRA

flourished a few seasons, but succumbed, like its predecessor,

THE PHILHARMONIC,

to financial troubles. Numerous choral societies for the production of oratorios, cantatas and light operas, have been organized from time to time, but only to attain a brief existence.

Three or four years ago, however, a musical revival set in, and one of the first expressions was the formation of the

### ST. LOUIS CHORAL SOCIETY.

Good performances of the "Messiah," "Dettingen Te Deum," "Elijah," and other large works, have been given by this society, under the direction of Joseph Otten, and the public interest seems to warrant expectations of permanence.

The present season (1883) has been signalized by another organization, which has called itself

### THE SHAW MUSICAL SOCIETY,

in honor of Henry Shaw, Esq., one of the most philanthropic and distinguished citizens of St. Louis.

A few seasons ago the

### ST. LOUIS MUSICAL UNION

was founded for the purpose of producing good orchestral works. It is a complete orchestra of 55 instrumentalists, and their work, under the leadership of August Waldauer, is exerting an excellent influence. A series of six concerts are given by subscription during the winter.

Various efforts to found and maintain chamber concerts have been made at different times, and now St. Louis is the possessor of two string quintets, known respectively as

THE PHILHARMONIC and THE MENDELSSOHN. Both have good metal, and the first-named has given a series of excellent concerts every season for the last three or four years. The latter is a recent organization.

For chamber concerts St. Louis has one of the most charming and suitable halls in the world, viz.: the Memorial Hall attached to the Art Museum. For larger concerts the Mercantile Library, Philharmonic, and Temple halls have long done unsatisfactory duty. The city is now on the eve of coming into possession of a grand Exposition and Music Hall, which will equal or surpass any effort of the kind thus far made in this country. The plans call for a grand hall to seat 4000 spectators, with stage room for a colossal organ and 1000 persons, and a smaller hall to seat 1200 persons. The stock is all subscribed for, and the autumn of 1884 will witness the St. Louis Music Hall an accomplished fact.

Of conservatories and schools of music, St. Louis has its quota. Besides the BEETHOVEN CONSERVATORY, mentioned under its own heading, there are a College of Music conducted by M. J. and A. J. Epstein, and a small institution called the Haydn Conservatory. Musical talent is abundant, and the members of the musical profession are, as a class, thoroughly respectable and competent, numbering among their ranks several individuals of marked ability and extended reputation.

For several years considerable encouragement has been given by the churches toward the development of good church music, and there are now several choirs which will compare favorably with the best in sister cities. The Second Baptist Church takes the lead in this direction, with E. M. Bowman as its director and organist. Of the other churches noted for their good music are the Messiah, St. George's, First and Second Presbyterian, Pilgrim, St. Xavier's, St. John's (Catholic), and Shaare Emeth.         * * *

**Stoughton Musical Society** (The), STOUGHTON, MASS. This is the oldest existing musical society in America, and seems to have sprung from the labors of William Billings. It was organized Nov. 7, 1786, after the close of the Revolutionary war. Its first president and leader was Elijah Dunbar, Esq. The annual meeting of the members takes place on Christmas day, and in the evening a concert and supper is given. The membership is now five hundred, drawn from Stoughton and surrounding towns. It was exclusively male until a few years ago, when ladies were admitted, though they had long sung in the chorus. The Society published in 1828 a compilation of church music, and in 1878 the "Stoughton Musical Society's Collection of Sacred Music," a volume containing many pieces by early American composers, which are thus saved from being lost. The present president of the Society is Mr. Winslow Battles.

**Strakosch,** MAURICE, was born at Lemberg, Galicia, in 1825. His father, who was wealthy, removed to Germany in 1828, and there the young man had every opportunity of gratifying his passion for music. He became a fine pianist, and after completing his education traveled from Denmark to Russia. At St. Petersburg he was received with especial favor. Returning to Paris, he spent three years in traveling in France, Spain and Italy, being everywhere well received. In 1848 he came to the United States, and has since made it his permanent home at New York. He married Amalia Patti. His reputation is now almost exclusively that of an *impresario*, in which capacity he has acted for 30 years, having organized his first company in 1855.

**Strakosch,** MAX, brother of the preceding, was born in 1834. He is finely educated, and is said to fluently speak several languages. He came to this country and was at first associated with his brother as business manager. When Maurice went to Europe in 1859 with his sister-in-law, Amalia Patti, he became general manager. Among the famous artists which have traveled under the management of the brothers are Thalberg, Mme. Parodi, E. Mollenhauer, Mme. la Grange, Mme. d'Angri, Mme. Frezzolini, Karl Formes, Brignoli, Amadio, Barili, Mme. Gazzinga, Adelina Patti, Natali, Gottschalk, Carlotta Patti, Carlo Patti, Wehle, Errani, Mancusi, Mme. Parepa-Rosa, Miss Kellogg, Mlle. Nilsson, Miss Cary, Vieuxtemps, Capaul, Mario, Mlle. Torriani, Campanini, del Puente, Mlle. Lucca, Mlle. di Murska, Mlle. Albani, Mlle. Heilbron, Carpi, de Bassini, Tagliapietra, Mme. Tietjens, Mme. Goddard, Mme. Carreno, Tom Karl, Mme. Roze, Mlle. Litta, C. R. Adams, and Lazzarini.

**Sudds,** WILLIAM F., was born at London, England, March 5, 1843. When seven years of age, his parents came to the United States and located on a farm near Gouverneur, St. Lawrence Co., N. Y. His musical tastes manifested themselves at an early period, so that by the time he was fifteen he could play the violin, guitar, flute, cornet, and violoncello. A year or two later he was permitted to practice on the piano of a friend, and most eagerly did he avail himself of the opportunity, walking three miles after the day's work for that purpose. Soon after the commencement of the Civil War he entered the army, and it was while a convalescent soldier at the hospital, New Orleans, in 1864, that he took his first regular music lessons of a French professor. Nine years later he was a pupil at the Boston Conservatory of Music, where he studied the organ under Eugene Thayer,

and the violin and composition under Julius Eichberg. Mr. Sudds is located at Gouverneur, where he keeps a fine music store, adjoining which is a studio. He is organist of the First Baptist Church, and until recently had charge of the musical department of Gouverneur Seminary. On account of the growing demands of his publishers, he has to reject many applications for instruction in music. In appearance he is tall and well proportioned, walks in a vigorous, energetic manner, and is quite near-sighted, but does not wear glasses in the street, hence he often passes his friends without recognition. Mr. Sudds' music comprises nearly every kind of composition, both vocal and instrumental. Some of his pieces have become very popular and all of them find a ready sale, as may be inferred from the fact that his income from his musical works alone is several thousand dollars per annum. Of his pieces of higher order may be mentioned "Sky Lark," "Slumber Song," "Trust her not," etc. His numbered works run up to 140, besides which he has written a large quantity of fugitive and unnumbered pieces. The following is a list of his more important productions :

BOOKS.—Anthem Gems, vol. 1 ; Anthem Gems, vol. 2; National School for the Pianoforte, 1881, an excellent work which has been highly commended ; National School for the Pianoforte, abridged ; National Guide to Reed Organ Playing ; Parlor Organ Treasury ; Part Song Galaxy ; Quartet Choir Collection.

SONGS AND PART SONGS —Douglass Tender and True, Guess Who, What Lack the Valleys? What Cares the World for Me ? Slumber Song, The Sky Lark, I Love My Love, Twilight on the Sea, Honor the Brave, What Care I how fair She be ?

INSTRUMENTAL.—Sounds at Day Dawn ; 1st Grand Valse Brilliante, 2nd do, 3rd do ; American Triumphal March ; Message of Love, polka ; Message of Love, waltz ; Bells of Shandon, morceau ; Elfin Dances, 3 nos., op. 87 ; Evening Hour, op. 84 ; Enchantment, polonaise, op. 91 ; Le Sou Doux, reverie, op. 102 ; Realms of Fancy, morceau, op. 114 ; Loire d'Elite, waltz brilliante, op. 115 ; As Twilight Falls, nocturne, op. 120 ; Shepherd Girl, morceau, op. 121 ; Bon Ton, galop, op. 127 ; Dance of the Fairies, waltz brilliante, op. 128; Days that are Gone, reverie, op. 136.

**Suffern,** J. WILLIAM, was born at Suf-
ferns, N. Y., Nov. 1, 1829. He commenced
teaching music at the age of twenty years, and
has held several positions as organist. He is
well-known throughout the Western States as
a conductor of musical conventions, in which
work he has been much engaged. He has
compiled and edited several collections of
music, and composed numerous pieces. His
residence is at New York City.

**Swan,** TIMOTHY, one of the early Amer-
ican psalmodists, was of Scottish descent, and
was born at Worcester, Mass., July 23, 1758.
He began to teach music at the age of seven-
teen years, and in 1801, while residing at
Sheffield, published THE NEW ENGLAND HAR-
MONY. It was printed at Northampton, by
Andrew Wright, and contained 104 pages.

A copy of the book was presented to the Harvard Musical Association, by the author, Oct.
26, 1841. After publishing his book he removed to Vermont, but finally returned and
settled at Northfield, Mass., where he died
July 23, 1842, respected and beloved by all
who knew him. Some of his tunes still hold
their place in books of psalmody, among
which are "China," "Pownal" and "Poland."

**Sweet Bye and Bye.** A simple melody and refrain, composed by J. P. Webster,
an American composer, but of whom little is
known. It is one of the most popular religious tunes ever written, and is sung in every
civilized country of the world. The melody
has formed the theme of variations by different composers. The words are by S. F.
Bennett.

# T.

**Tale of the Viking, The.** A cantata founded on the old legend of the same name, by George E. Whiting. For solos, chorus and orchestra. Written about 1875. Published by Schirmer of New York.

**Taylor,** SAMUEL PRIESTLY, organist, was born at London, England, in 1779, and was able to play the organ when only seven years old. In 1806 he came to the United States and settled in Brooklyn, holding several positions as organist there and in New York, and giving instruction on the organ, piano, violin, violoncello, and clarinet. He entered one of the bands during the war of 1812, and was president of the old Philharmonic Society. In 1819 he removed to Boston, and was organist of the Handel and Haydn Society for two years. While there he compiled a popular organ instruction book. He returned to Brooklyn in 1826, where he continued to teach until 1864, and to play the organ up to the advanced age of ninety-two years. He was still living in 1874.

**Thayer,** ALEXANDER WHEELOCK, U. S. Consul at Trieste, Germany, was born at South Natick, Mass., Oct. 17, 1817. He is a frequent contributor to the American musical press and the author of numerous articles in Grove's "Dictionary of Music and Musicians," but he calls for mention here on account of his " Life of Beethoven" (Ludwig von Beethoven's Leben," a work which far surpasses all others in accuracy and extent of research. The first volume was published at Berlin in 1866, the second in 1872, and the third has just appeared.

**Thayer,** DR. EUGENE, one of America's most celebrated organists, was born at Mendon, Mass., Dec. 11, 1838. He early manifested a love for music, but did not begin the study of the organ until the age of fourteen. In 1862 he was called to Boston by the inauguration of the great organ in the Music Hall, being one of the performers on that occasion. His reception was cordial and secured him a high place in Boston musical affairs, which he con-

tinued to hold for nearly twenty years. In 1865 and 1866 he was in Europe, studying with Haupt, Wieprecht and other masters, and afterwards visited and played upon all the famous organs of the Old World. For many years he held the highest positions in Boston, having been organist of the Music Hall, editor of the "Organist's Journal" and of the "Choir Journal," director of the "Boston Choral Union," of the "New England Church Music Association," and of many other societies. He is virtually the originator of free organ recitals in this country, having given the first one April 10, 1869, in the old Hollis Street Church, Boston. Since that time he has given many hundreds elsewhere and has performed over three thousand times in public in the leading cities of America and Europe. These recitals have exercised no little influence in raising the standard of musical taste. He has delivered many lectures, and is a contributor of acknowledged ability to various magazines and journals. On all matters pertaining to the organ he is one of the first authorities. In 1881 he accepted a call to the Fifth Avenue Presbyterian Church (Rev. Dr. John Hall's), New York, and has since resided in that city, devoting his time to church composition, teaching and invention. He is the inventor of several valuable patents. His degree of Doctor of Music was earned by passing the Oxford test, his composition being a cantata for soli and chorus, in eight real parts, with full orchestral accompaniment. He has also written other compositions, both published and unpublished.

**The Corsican Bride.** An opera by Edward Mollenhauer. It was produced at Winter Garden, New York, in 1862. Artistically it was a success but financially a failure, owing to the unsettled condition of the country at that time. Could it have been produced under favorable circumstances, it would probably have met with the success which it deserved.

**Thomas,** THEODORE, one of America's

foremost conductors, was born at Ostfriesland, Hanover, Oct. 11, 1835. When ten years of age (1845) he came to this country with his parents. He had been taught the violin by his father, a good violinist, and after arriving here was for some time engaged as orchestral player in theatres, minstrel troupes, and opera and concert companies. In 1853 he joined the Philharmonic Society, having previously tried his hand at conducting both German and Italian opera, but resigned his membership in 1858. The same year he commenced, in conjunction with William Mason, Carl Bergmann, J. Mosenthal, and George Matzka, a series of *soirées* of classical music, which were continued two or three seasons. Soon after he began the organization of his orchestra, and in 1864 commenced his symphony concerts at Irving Hall. These concerts met with considerable opposition at first, but soon came to be recognized as one of New York's chief musical institutions. They were continued until 1878. In 1866 Mr. Thomas originated the "Summer-Night Concerts" at Central Park Garden. In order to keep his orchestra together, he began traveling with it during the winter season, but this undertaking did not prove a financial success and had to be abandoned. In 1878 he accepted the position of director of the newly-established College of Music, Cincinnati, but resigned the post in 1881 and returned to New York, where he now resides and holds various positions as conductor.

Mr. Thomas has conducted all of the Cincinnati May Festivals thus far, beginning with 1873, and those of New York and Chicago of 1882. At the most of them his orchestra was engaged. During the present summer (1883) his tour with his orchestra includes the principal cities from New York to San Francisco. At Chicago he gives six weeks of "Summer-Night Concerts." It is almost solely as a conductor that he has achieved his present high position. While he possesses many social qualities, he wields the *bâton* with a firm hand, and in consequence his orchestra has reached a degree of proficiency rarely attained by any similar organization, either in this country or Europe. His programs are of the highest order, on which the old and new masters are fairly represented. It is not too much to say that he has done as much as almost any other person in raising the standard of music in this country. Thus far he has not appeared in the *rôle* of a composer.

**Thomas,** John R., song writer, was born at Newport, South Wales, in 1830, and came to the United States at an early age. For some time he was connected with a minstrel troupe on Broadway, and later with the Seguin English opera company, assuming the *rôle* of *Count* in the "Bohemian Girl" and various other characters. He finally permanently settled at New York, where he still (June, 1885) resides with his wife and family. Mr. Thomas is chiefly noted for his songs, both sacred and secular, some of which have become very popular. Among his best known and most important productions are "Annie of the Vale," "Cottage by the Sea," "'Tis but a Little Faded Flower," "Mother Kissed me in my Dreams," "Beautiful Isle of the Sea," "The Owl," "Fishes in the Sea," "Sweet be thy Repose," "Against the Stream," "Janette," "Angel Voices," "Land of Dreams," "The Hand that Rocks the World." "The Voice of Effie Moore," "Eileen Alanna," "Seek and ye shall find" (sacred), "No Crown without the Cross" (sacred), "The Mother's Prayer," "Flag of the Free" (patriotic), "May God Protect Columbia," etc.

**Thompson,** Will L., was born at East Liverpool, Ohio, Nov. 7, 1849. He commenced the study of music when eight years of age, and at seventeen went to Boston and took a regular course under the best teachers there. He afterward went to Leipzig and received private lessons for some time. Mr. Thompson's ambition was to become a writer of songs for the masses, and in this he has been eminently successful. In 1874, while spending a season at the seashore, he wrote the popular songs, "Gathering Shells from the Sea-Shore" and "Drifting with the Tide," which he offered to a well-known music-publisher for $25 each. Fortunately for him, his offer was not accepted, and he determined to go into the publishing business himself. Accordingly he opened an establishment at East Liverpool, his native place, and his songs at once sprung into popularity. "Gathering Shells" alone reached the enormous sale of 265,000 copies. He has written about fifty songs, all of which have been successful. "Come Where the Lilies Bloom" is perhaps his most popular quartet. Few American composers have gained a greater reputation in writing popular music for the masses than Mr. Thompson.

**Thursby,** EMMA C., was born at Brooklyn, N. Y., Nov. 17, 1857. Her father was of English descent and her mother came of one of the old Knickerbocker families. She first studied with Julius Meyer of her native city, and subsequently with Sig. Errani of New York and Mme. Rudersdorff of Boston. She then went to Italy and studied for some time under Lamperti and San Giovanni. On her return to this country she appeared in concerts and oratorios, but did not attempt any operatic *rôles*. Her first concert was given at Plymouth Church, and proved to be a great success. In 1875 she was engaged by P. S. Gilmore for his popular summer-night concerts, and when he afterwards traveled with his military band she accompanied him as the leading vocalist. In consequence, her reputation soon became a national one, and she was offered and accepted an engagement as singer in Dr. Taylor's church, New York, at a salary of $3000 per year. She was subsequently engaged by Maurice Strakosch, and under his management went to Europe, singing in concerts at London, Liverpool, Paris, Cologne, and other places. In England especially she was very warmly received and made many friends. During the season of 1879-80 she traveled throughout the United States, and became a general favorite. Since that time she has frequently sung both in this country and Europe. Miss Thursby occupies a leading position among America's concert singers.

**Timm,** HENRY C., was born at Hamburg, Germany, July 11, 1811, and studied under Methfessel and Jacob Schmitt. In 1835 he came to the United States, and made his first appearance as a pianist at the old Park Theatre, New York, playing Hummel's Rondo Brilliant, in A. He accepted the post of second horn player in the orchestra of the same theatre, and occasionally played piano solos between the acts. Later on he traveled as director with a sort of operatic company which gave performances in the Southern States. He has held positions as organist in various New York churches, was one of the founders of the New York Philharmonic Society, and for many years its president. He

also occasionally officiated as conductor, and for several years was the piano accompanist. Latterly his time has mostly been devoted to teaching. He has composed numerous works, but few of them have been published. For nearly half a century he has labored in the best interest of musical art, and may justly be considered one of its pioneers in this country. Of a kind, amiable disposition, he is highly respected by all who know him.

**Toedt,** THEODORE J., was born in New York about thirty-five years ago. His musical education was mostly gained from his sister, a good solo violinist. He is a member of the choir of St. Bartholomew's Church, and has frequently appeared as a concert and oratorio singer in the principal cities of the Union, with a fair amount of success. He sang in the New York May Festival of 1882. His voice is a tenor of pleasing quality but limited power.

**Tomlins,** WILLIAM L., conductor and teacher, was born in England about 1844. He studied music in the tonic sol-fa schools, and with G. A. Macfarren and Edourd Silas. In 1869 he came to New York, and from thence went to Chicago, where he still (July, 1885) resides as conductor and teacher of vocal music.

**Tourjée,** DR. EBEN, who must be reckoned among the leading American educators, and who is well-known as the founder and head of the New England Conservatory of Music, was born at Warwick, R. I., June 1, 1834, and is one of the descendants of the French Huguenots who fled to this country soon after the Edict of Nantes and settled in Narragansett. When only eight years old he was working in a factory at East Greenwich, and being compelled to struggle with poverty he found little opportunity to gratify his musical inclinations, which even then began to be manifested. By rigid economy he managed to attend the Academy at East Greenwich for some time, and at eleven became the chorister in the Methodist church in Phenix. The choir was at that time one of the best in the country. Soon after he became a pupil of Henry Eastcot of Providence, and speedily received the appointment of church organist. By the time he had reached the age of seventeen he was a clerk in a Providence music store, and two years later became a dealer himself at Fall River. He also taught music in the public schools, and edited "The Key Note," which was afterward merged into the "Massachusetts Musical Journal," under his care. During this time he dilligently studied under the best Boston teachers. In 1856 he went to Newport, R. I., as organist of Trinity Church, and was an instructor in music, conductor of choral societies, etc. As early as 1853 he introduced and used the class or conservatory system of teaching, with over 500 pupils. Several years later he founded a music school at East Greenwich (chartered by the State in 1859), which gave him greater opportunity to carry out his plans. In order to gain a thorough knowledge of the work, he went to Europe, where he remained until 1864, visiting the best foreign conservatories and entering himself as a pupil. On his return, he went to Providence, and there founded the first conservatory in America—that is, which was called by that name, for his school at East Greenwich was really one. Its prosperity was such that in 1867 a removal to Boston was deemed advisable. In 1870 it was incorporated by the Massachusetts Legislature, under the name of NEW ENGLAND CONSERVATORY OF MUSIC (A full description of it is given under the heading, BOSTON). Dr. Tourjée is still at its head. When a College of Music was instituted in the Boston University, in 1872, he was elected Dean, and still occupies that position.

Dr. Tourjée is a man of varied and brilliant talents, which he fortunately uses for the advancement of that which is pure and noble. As a musical educator and organizer, he holds rank among the very first in this country, but his activity is not confined to the sphere of music alone. For several years he was president of the Y. M. C. A., and whatever tends to benefit mankind in any way receives his hearty commendation and support. He has compiled several collections, among which are the "Chorus Choir," the "Tribute of Praise," and the M. E. Church Hymnal.

**Trajetta,** PHILIPO, was born January 8 (?), 1777, at Venice. After having become well grounded in the rudiments of music, he studied under Feneroli and Perillo, and subsequently under Piccini at Naples. On the outbreak of the revolution he joined the patriot army, and was in consequence confined in a dungeon, but at the end of eight months was released and shipped on board an American vessel, arriving at Boston in the winter of 1799. After a short stay in Boston he went to New York. He then traveled extensively in the South, resided for some time in Virginia, and finally died at Philadelphia, Jan. 9, 1854. He was a thorough contrapuntist, a fine singer and a good performer on various instruments. Among his works are the cantatas of "The Christian's Joy," "Prophecy," "The Nativity" and "The Day of Rest;" the oratorios of "Jerusalem in Affliction" and "Daughter of Zion;" and the opera of "The Venetian Masker's."

**Tracy,** JAMES M., was born at Bath, N. H., in 1839. His musical talents were early manifest, and at the age of eleven years he was sent to Lowell, Mass., where he received his first regular music lessons of a Mrs. Fulsome. Some time after, his father having removed to Concord, N. H., he continued his lessons under John Jackson of that place. He then went to Boston and studied the organ and harmony with L. H. Southard and the piano with Carl Hause. After remaining in Boston about two years he accepted an engagement as organist and director of music of the Unitarian Church, Bangor, Me. In 1858 he went to Leipzig, Germany, and entered the Conservatorium there, also privately studying with Plaidy, Richter, and Knorr. At the end of two years he proceeded to Weimar, where he was a pupil of Liszt for one year. Returning to the United States in 1861, he settled at Rochester, N. Y., as a pianist and teacher. Five years later he removed to Boston, where he now (July, 1886) resides. For the past twelve years he has been engaged as one of the principal teachers in the Boston Conservatory of Music. He is the author of the "Boston Conservatory Method for the Piano, Theory, and Harmony," several books of technical studies, and of various articles in musical publications. He has also given eight series of piano recitals, playing at the last series all of Beethoven's sonatas.

# U.

**Upton,** GEORGE P., was born Oct. 25, 1834, at Roxbury, Mass. He was educated at Brown University, Providence, R. I., from which he graduated in 1854. The following year, being then of age, he went to Chicago, and immediately entered upon newspaper work, writing his first article for the "Native Citizen." In 1856 he became city editor of the "Chicago Evening Journal," retaining the post until 1862. While connected with this journal he first employed his pen in musical work, his being the first criticisms written in that city. In 1862 he became city editor of the "Chicago Tribune," in 1863 war correspondent, in 1864 night editor, in 1867 news editor, and in 1868 literary, dramatic and art editor. Since 1871 he has occupied a place upon the regular staff. He was its music critic until 1882, when he resigned the position. Mr. Upton's musical works consist of, besides innumerable short articles on various topics, "Woman in Music," 1 vol., 1882, published by Osgood & Co., Boston; "The Standard Operas," and translations of "Nohl's Life of Haydn," "Life of Liszt" and "Life of Wagner," which are issued by Jansen, McClurg & Co. of Chicago, and are valuable additions to our musical literature. He has a fine musical library, containing over 1000 volumes.

**Urania.** "Urania, or A Choice Collection of Psalm-Tunes, Anthems and Hymns. From the most approv'd Authors, with some entirely new : In Two, Three and Four Parts. The whole peculiarly adapted to the use of Churches and Private Families. To which are prefix'd the Plainest and most Necessary Rules of Psalmody. By James Lyon, A. B., Hen. Dawkins, fecit. 1761. Price 15s." This work was printed at Philadelphia, from handsomely engraved plates, and contains twelve pages of musical instruction. It was dedicated "To the Clergy of every Denomination in America," and contains the names of 142 subscribers. It contained a number of original pieces, but was mostly compiled from English sources. Lyon is said to have been financially ruined by the venture.

# V.

**Van Zandt,** MARIE, was born in 1861, in the state of Texas, and is of Dutch extraction, as is indicated by her name. Her happy childhood days were spent on her father's large farm. She learned to sing almost as soon as to talk, her mother being an excellent vocalist. The Civil War depriving her father of his fortune, it was proposed that the young singer's talents should be utilized in assisting to support the family. She sought employment in one of the Eastern cities and then went to London, where she met and was greatly encouraged by Patti. She entered a convent school as boarder, studying with great energy. After leaving the convent she studied, among other teachers, with Lamperti at Milan for a short time. She then sang in many of the cities of Northern Europe, and having gained considerable reputation, was offered and accepted an engagement at the Opéra Comique, Paris, appearing in the *rôle* of *Mignon*.

Miss Van Zandt, though young, is an unusually fine singer, of whom much may be expected in the future. Her countenance is an expressive one, indicating both refinement and depth of thought. She also possesses a rare but none the less commendable trait—that of sound common sense, which was manifested in her refusing to Italianize her name. During her earlier life she learned many healthful and practical accomplishments. Though having many rich jewels, she rarely ever displays them, and her simple tastes are evident from the furnishing of her apartments. America has produced some of the most celebrated singers of the world, and Miss Van Zandt certainly deserves a high place among them.

**Vintage, The.** One of the earliest of American operas. The libretto is by William Dunlop; the music by Victor Pellisier, a French resident of New York. Produced at New York in 1799, with good success.

**Voice, The.** A 20-page monthly, founded in January, 1879, by the present editor and proprietor, Edgar S. Werner, and published at 48 University Place, New York. It is an international review of the speaking and singing voice, is the organ of the vocal and elocutionary professions, and makes a specialty of the cure of vocal defects and voice culture. Subscription price, $1.50. Issued monthly.

# W.

**Walter,** Rev. Thomas, was born at Roxbury, Mass., in 1696, and published in 1721 "The Grounds and Rules of Musick Explained : or an Introduction to the Art of Singing by Note : Fitted to the Meanest Capacities. Let everything that hath breath praise the Lord." The work passed through several editions, the last of which was published in 1764. Most of the tunes, twenty-four in number, were taken from Ainsworth's Psalms or Ravenscroft's collection. Walter died in 1728.

**Warren,** George William, was born at Albany, N. Y., Aug. 17, 1828. He early devoted himself to music, and removed to New York City, becoming known as an organist, composer and teacher. Many of his piano pieces, songs, etc., have gained considerable popularity. He still resides at New York.

**Warren,** Samuel P., one of the leading American organists, was born at Montreal, Canada, Feb. 18, 1841. As his father was an extensive organ manufacturer, he early became thoroughly familiar with the usual details of construction. Having passed through college and evincing more than usual musical talent, it was decided that he should visit Europe to pursue his studies. In 1861 he went to Berlin, where he received instruction from Haupt (organ), G. Schumann (piano), and Wieprecht (instrumentation). He especially devoted himself to his favorite instrument, and after completing the usual four years' course, returned to Montreal. The following year (1865) he removed to New York, where he is still (May, 1885) residing. For two years he was organist of Dr. Bellow's church, next of Grace Church, and then of Trinity Church, after which he returned to his old post at Grace Church. Mr. Warren, strange to say, has as yet published nothing for his instrument, and his printed compositions are confined to some sacred music and songs. His organ concerts have done much to render familiar the best grade of organ music.

**Warren,** Alfred E., was born about 1834, at a small town of England called Edmonton. His father was a prominent piano manufacturer of London, and at one time maker to Her Majesty the Queen. When about eighteen years old he resolved to follow music as a profession, and placed himself under the best teachers of London, where he obtained the most of his musical education. He then received and accepted a tempting offer to go to Calcutta, India, where he remained several years, meeting with much success. Failure of health compelled him to seek a different climate, and he came to this country, arriving here in 1861. Boston has ever since been his place of residence, and he has achieved a national reputation as a pianist, composer and teacher. Mr. Warren did not appear in the *rôle* of a composer until after coming to this country, his first published composition being "Valse de Favorita," issued by Ditson & Co. in 1861. His "Inman Line," march, dedicated to William Inman, Esq., became very popular. It was composed for the World's Peace Jubilee of 1872, and performed there, Saturday, June 22. His "Strauss Autograph Waltzes" were also very popular, and as no name was at first attached to them, it was for some time supposed that they were by Strauss himself. The following are the best known and most important of his works :

Inman Line. March.
March de Syrious.
Strauss Autograph Waltzes.
Strauss Engagement Waltzes.
Life in the Tropic Waltzes.
Thoughts of Love. Mazurka.
Rays of Hope. Mazurka.
Army and Navy. March. Written for the dedication of the monument on Boston Common. A manuscript copy of the piece and a photograph of the composer was placed in the box under the base.

Songs.—Silent Evermore, Life of a Sailor Free, The Fisherman's Wife, Under the Leaves that Fall, Good bye, my dearest, good bye, Sleep On, Sad Tears are Falling, Farewell.

**Webb,** GEORGE JAMES, was born in Wiltshire, England, June 24, 1803. He was intended for the church, but gave much of his time to the study of music, which he subsequently adopted as a profession. In 1830 he came to the United States and settled at Boston, becoming an earnest and efficient co-laborer of Dr. Lowell Mason. He was one of the founders in 1836 of the Boston Academy of Music (see the heading, BOSTON), and one of the earliest conductors of symphony and oratorio performances in Boston. For many years he held a leading position as teacher of singing and the piano. In 1870 he removed to Orange, N. J., teaching in New York City. His compositions mostly consist of church tunes and pieces, some of which have come into general use. He was residing in New York in 1881, and still active.

**Weber,** ALBERT, celebrated as a piano manufacturer, was born in Bavaria, but early came to the United States and settled in New York in 1845. He worked at his trade during the day and gave music lessons at night, being a practical musician. For some time he occupied a position as organist at one of the churches. Through economy and hard labor he managed to save a considerable sum of money, and in 1852 founded the present extensive house of Weber. He continued to manage the business to the time of his death in 1879, when he was succeeded by his son, Albert Weber, Jr. (See succeeding article.)

**Weber, Albert,** NEW YORK. The Weber piano manufacturing house, one of the leading in the United States, was founded in 1852, by the father of the present proprietor. His early struggles were of a nature to discourage an ordinary person, but by indomitable pluck and energy he succeeded in establishing the business on a sound footing, and winning his way against all opposition. The erection of the present factory was begun in 1867, but the business did not begin to assume its present proportions until four years later, when 750 instruments were turned out in a year. In 1878, two years after the Centennial, the production was 1650, and in 1879, 1900 instruments. The elder Weber died in 1879, and was succeeded by his son, Albert Weber, Jr., (born in September, 1858) who has since successfully carried on the immense business. Branch houses were established at Chicago and Boston in 1880. About sixty pianos are now finished at the factory every week.

**Webster,** JOSEPH P., was born about 1830, at Manchester, N. H. He became known in New England as the director of a quartet company called "Euterpeans." He subsequently went West, and for some time resided at New Albany, Ind. In 1868 he published, at Chicago, "The Signet Ring," a collection of music for Sabbath schools. He wrote some songs, a cantata, and some other music, but will longest be remembered for his famous melody of "Sweet Bye and Bye." His death occurred some eight or ten years ago in Wisconsin. He left a daughter, Miss May, we think, who has considerable talent as a musician.

**Wels,** KARL, was born at Prague in 1830, and while yet a young man came to this country, settling at New York, where he is esteemed as a pianist, composer and teacher. He published in 1864 a collection of church music, but is chiefly known for his piano compositions, among which are three transcriptions, "Sleep well, sweet Angel," "Good Night, Farewell," and "Little Mendicant."

**Werrenrath,** GEORGE, tenor singer, was born at Copenhagen, Denmark, about 1840. His musical career began at Hamburg, Germany, where he studied under Canthal, the composer. After appearing in concerts and operas in the minor cities of Germany, he accepted a three years' engagement at the Royal Opera, Wiesbaden, sustaining *rôles* in "Faust," "L'Africaine," "Lohengrin," "Magic Flute," "Stradella," "Martha," "Der Freischütz," and "Belisario." At the end of this time he went to Paris to continue his studies. From there he proceeded to London, successfully appearing in English opera and concerts. During his stay he became acquainted with Gounod, with whom he traveled in concert tours of Belgium. Upon the advice of Gounod he went to Milan and studied a year under Lamperti. Returning to England he filled various engagements until 1876, when he came to the United States. His first appearances at New York and Boston were at the symphony concerts given by Theodore Thomas. He was engaged as one of the principal singers upon organization of the Wagner Opera Festival, and his rendition of *Lohengrin* showed him to be an actor of more than ordinary ability. His success in the oratorio, particularly the "Messiah," "Creation," and "Samson," is nearly as marked as in the opera. He was the first to give in America a series of song recitals, introducing this style of concert in Chicago, in February, 1879, when in four evenings he sang seventy-five classical songs. In 1881 he gave two series of song recitals in Brooklyn, which were highly praised. During his residence of six years and a half in America, Mr. Werrenrath has been engaged as solo tenor of Plymouth (H. W. Beecher's). Church. Last summer (1882), while on a visit to his native city, he had the honor of singing before the royal family of Denmark. He is a fine linguist as well as a finished musician, speaking with almost equal ease the Danish, Swedish, German, French, Italian and English languages.

**Westendorf,** THOMAS P., was born at Bowling Green, Caroline Co., Ky., Feb. 23, 1847. His father was of German birth and his mother a native of Virginia. When he was twelve years old the family removed to Chicago, where he received his musical education, studying the piano under Louis Staab and the violin under Henry Declerque. For some time he taught brass bands, and subsequently in a State institution at Plainfield, Ind. During the past eight years he has been engaged in teaching at the Louisville House of Refuge, Louisville, Ky., where his wife is also employed. Mr. Westendorf has written about 300 vocal and nearly as many instrumental pieces. Of his songs, "Our Little Darling's Grave," "I'll take you Home again, Kathleen," "Toddlin Down the Brea," "From Jerusalem to Jerico," "Don't Forget the Old Folks, Tom," and many others, have attained no little popularity. Among his popular instrumental pieces are "Gingham Quickstep," "In Life's Fair Morning Waltz," "Innocence," "Sounds from Fairyland," "Harvest Morn," "Love's Greeting," etc. His little daughter, Jennie, has often figured in his songs, and is the prime cause of many of them. He has recently completed an opera on which he has been engaged for three years, which will probably be produced soon.

**Wetmore,** DR. TRUMAN S., born at Winchester, Conn., Aug. 12, 1774, was a contemporary of Stephen Jenks, and one of the early American psalmodists. His music was popular in his day, and a few of his tunes are still to be found in church collections. He died at his native place, July 21, 1861.

**What is Home Without a Mother?** The title of one of Sep. Winner's most popular songs. It is the second one which he wrote, and was composed, both words and music, in 1851. In a short time it became all the rage, being sung, played and whistled everywhere, and the sales were enormously large for the time. Its popularity was subsequently dimmed by the production of "Listen to the Mocking Bird."

**Wheeler,** J. HARRY, was born Oct. 5, 1842, at Lynn, Mass. His father and mother, both of whom are living (1886), were highly musical, his father having directed musical societies and choirs for more than forty years. He was placed under the private teaching of the best masters of his native city, and while yet attending school at the age af fifteen he began teaching large classes in vocal music. At this time he was offered and accepted the directorship of a large chorus organization. But the home musical culture was only as an accomplishment, it being the intention of his parents that he should lead a mercantile life. He was therefore placed in a prominent Boston business house. In that city he was constantly under the influence of music and musicians, and after a few years abandoned the business for music. After this he received musical instruction from the best teachers in Boston, singing in public with success. Some time later he traveled in the West and South, holding musical conventions with success. He enlisted during the war and was sergeant-major of a western regiment. After this he went to Europe, studying voice culture with Garcia, San Giovanni, Trivulsi, Bruni, Lamperti, and other celebrated teachers, and thoroughly preparing himself for that branch of the profession. On his return to the United States he was engaged as a teacher of the voice and singing at the New England Conservatory of Music, Boston, a position which he still retains. Many of his pupils have become eminent as opera, concert and church singers and teachers. As a teacher he is equaled by few, having had a vast experience. He has written much upon vocal culture. His work entitled "Vocal Physiology" has met with a very large sale, and is said to be one of the most practical works on this subject ever written. He is also director of the Boston Normal Musical Institute, which is held every summer.

**Whiting,** GEORGE ELBRIDGE, was born at Holliston, Mass., Sep. 14, 1842. At the age of five years he began the study of music with his brother, Amos, then organist of a church at Springfield. He soon relinquished the piano for the organ, and when thirteen made his first public appearance as a player. Two years later he went to Hartford, Conn., and soon after became organist of one of the churches there, succeeding Dudley Buck. While there he founded the Beethoven Society. In 1862 he removed to Boston. Having studied with Mr. Morgan of New York, he went to Liverpool, Eng., where for a year he was a pupil of the famous English organ player, Best. On returning home he was engaged as organist of St. Joseph's Church, Albany, N.Y. Being unsatisfied with his attainments, he spent some time at Berlin, finishing under Radecke. After three years service at Albany, he accepted a call to King's Chapel, Boston, and retained the position five years. In 1874, having meanwhile filled various engagements, he became organist of the Music Hall. He was also for some time at the head of the organ department of the New England Conservatory of Music. In May, 1878, he removed to Cincinnati as one of the principal organ instructors in the then newly established College of Music, and took charge of the great organ in the Music Hall, on which he has played at several of the May Festivals. After fulfilling his contract at Cincinnati (for three years) he returned to his old position at the head of the organ department of the N. E. Conservatory of Music, Boston, where he now (May, 1886) is. Mr. Whiting is one of the leading organists of this country, and ranks very high as a composer. The following is a list of his works: "The Organist," containing 12 pieces for the organ; 3 preludes for the organ, in C and D minor; "The First Six Months on the Organ," consisting of 25 studies; 20 preludes for the organ, in 2 books; mass in C minor, for four solo voices, chorus, orchestra and organ, performed in 1872; mass in F minor, for chorus, orchestra and organ, written for the opening of the cathedral at Boston in 1874; prologue to Longfellow's "Golden Legend," for chorus and orchestra, performed in 1873; "Dream Pictures," cantata, performed in 1877; "The Tale of the Viking," cantata, for solos, chorus and orchestra (Schirmer, N. Y.); a set of figured vespers; "Lenora," contata, for 4 solo voices, chorus and orchestra, libretto by Burger (in Ms.); concerto in D minor, for piano; allegro brilliant, for orchestra; fantasia and fugue in E minor; sonata in A minor; fantasia in F; 3 concert *études,* A minor, F, and B flat; suite for violoncello and piano; concert overture, "The Princess;" about 50 songs for various voices; a number of part songs; several morning and evening services; miscellaneous organ pieces.

**Whitney,** MYRON W., one of America's most celebrated bass singers, was born at Ashbury, Mass., Sep. 5, 1836. At the age of sixteen he went to Boston and studied with E. H. Frost, making his first public appearance at a Christmas performance of the "Messiah" given by the Handel and Haydn Society at Tremont Temple in 1858. Feeling dissatisfied with his attainments after ten years of concert singing, he went to Florence and studied with Luigi Vennucini for some time. Proceeding to London he took lessons of Randegger in oratorio singing. He filled various engagements, one of which was a tour of England, Ireland and Scotland, and greatly increased his reputation by a masterly rendition of the part of *Elijah* at the Birmingham Festival. He also appeared at Oxford University in Handel's "Acis and Galatea," as *Polyphemus,* singing the music as originally written. Since 1876 he has refused all offers from abroad and remained in his native country. He has sung in nearly all of the May Festivals (especially those of Cincinnati), and at festivals in Boston, New York, Chicago, Pittsburgh, Cleveland, Indianapolis, and other cities. His *répertoire* includes "Messiah," "Samson," "Joshua," "Jephtha," "Israel in Egypt," "Elijah," "St. Paul," "Son and Stranger," "Last Judgment," Bach's Passion Music, "Eli," "Twelfth Night," "Fridolin," "Creation," "Seasons," and other works of high order. As an oratorio singer he has few equals. He is in every way a great artist, and possesses a magnificent bass voice of nearly three octaves compass, extending from B flat below the bass staff upwards.

**Whitney,** SAMUEL BRENTON, was born at Woodstock, Vermont, June 4, 1842. His early musical education was received from Carl Wels of New York. For four years he was organist of Christ Church, Montpelier, Vt., then of St. Peter's, Albany, and subsequently of St. Paul's, Burlington. In 1870 he went to Cambridge, Mass., where he continued his studies under J. K. Paine, playing for him at the Appleton Chapel, Harvard College. The following year he was appointed organist of the Church of the Advent, Boston, and afterwards director of the music, both of which posts he still (May, 1886) holds. He is also professor of the organ and lecturer in the Boston University and the New England Conservatory of Music. In all matters pertaining to church music he is considered one of the best authorities in this country, and his articles are always clear and forcible. As an organist he excels in interpreting the works of Bach. He has organized and conducted numerous choir festivals in Boston and various towns of Vermont. Among Mr. Whitney's compositions are a piano trio, several church services for full choir, a few pieces for the organ, and some piano pieces and songs, all of which show originality and purity of form. He has, besides, made transcriptions of various classical and modern works. He is a prominent member of some of Boston's best musical organizations, and conducts various singing societies, besides being one of the organ examiners of the American College of Musicians, and one of its two vice-presidents.

**White,** CHARLES ALBERT, was born at Taunton, Mass., March 20, 1832. His early life was spent on a farm, but his love of music evinced itself at an early age, and with a "fiddle" made out of shingles and barrel hoops he experienced all the delights of a Paganini ! In a few years he became quite proficient on the violin, led an orchestra, and even composed some dance and ballet music. While professor in the Naval School at Newport he commenced his career as a song writer, in which he has been so successful. The favor with which his productions were received led him to conceive the idea of becoming his own publisher, and on Sep. 1, 1868, he founded the music-publishing house of WHITE, SMITH & Co., which has rapidly risen to an important position among those of this country.

All the details of the business are under his personal supervision. Among Mr. White's most popular vocal productions are "Against the Tide," "Blue and Gray," "Come, Silver Moon," "Hesitation," "Moonlight on the Lake," "When 'Tis Moonlight," "My Love's a Rover," "Sweet to the Milkmaid the Plowboy Sang," and "When the Leaves begin to Fall."

**White, Smith & Co.,** BOSTON. This music-publishing house was founded Sep. 1, 1868. The principal partners are C. A. White, well known as a composer, and W. F. Smith. Their catalogue comprises nearly 10,000 publications, and is rapidly being added to. They have recently put into operation a large lithographic press, and now compete in this respect with foreign publishers. A branch house has been established in Chicago, and they now rank among the leading music firms of the country. They publish a great number of popular pieces, and issue the "Folio," a 32-page monthly magazine devoted to musical matters.

**Wilcox & White,** MERIDEN, CONN. This firm of organ manufacturers was formed in 1876, by a number of wealthy residents of Meriden, who opposed their money to the practical skill and experience of the Messrs. White, who for a number of years held leading positions with J. Estey & Co., Brattleboro, Vt., and who were accompanied by a number of Estey & Co.'s workmen. A four-story brick building, 200 feet long, with two wings 100 feet long, was erected and provided with the best modern appliances. The business rapidly grew to such an extent that another building, five stories high and 110 feet long, was necessitated. The Wilcox & White organs are favorably known the world over, and the demand for them large, as is evidenced by the fact that about 5000 instruments are manufactured yearly. The officers of the Company are as follows: H. C. Wilcox, president; J. H. White, secretary and treasurer; and H. K. White, manufacturing superintendent. The warerooms are located at 25 Union Square, New York.

**Wilcox,** DR. JOHN HENRY, was born Oct. 6, 1827, at Savannah, Ga. Of his early life we have no particulars. He graduated at Trinity College, Hartford, Conn., Aug. 2, 1849. The following year he took up his residence in Boston, and soon after became organist of St. Paul's (Episcopal) Church, succeeding Dr. S. P. Tucherman. Upon the establishment of the Church of the Immaculate Conception, he was appointed organist thereof, and retained the post until July, 1874. The degree of Doctor of Music was conferred on him by the Georgetown College, "Trigesina Juni MDCCCLXIV" (June 3, 1864). For some years previous to his death he perceptibly failed, both in body and mind. He died at Boston, June 20, 1875. During his residence in Boston he was at different times connected with Hook & Hastings, George Simmons, and Hutchings, Plaisted & Co., organ builders, and there was no part of the organ with which he was not familiar. It is said that he could remember the size, number and location of draw-stops, etc., of every organ he had ever seen. As an organist he had no little ability, but he mostly confined himself to the lighter and more popular class of music. He composed much music for the Catholic Church, some of which has been published, but most of which is in manuscript.

**Winant,** EMILY, contralto singer, was born about 1860, and studied with the late Mme. Rudersdorff, from whom she acquired an excellent method. Her first public appearance was at one of Remenyi's concerts, New York, in November, 1878. She has frequently sung at the Philharmonic and symphonic concerts, and was one of the soloists at the New York May Festival of 1882. At present she holds a position in the choir of St. Thomas' Church.

**Winner,** SEPTIMUS, one of America's most celebrated song writers, was born at Philadelphia, May 11, 1827. His early days were spent much the same as those of other boys. Having come into possession of an old violin, he managed, by dilligent practice, to become a very fair player in the course of a year. After this he for a short time took lessons of Leopold Meignen, then a well-known teacher. The violin remained his favorite instrument, but after attaining considerable proficiency upon this he took up the study of the organ, piano, and various stringed instruments, on all of which he became a fair player. By the time he had arrived at the age of twenty he was a successful music teacher. For five years he was leader of the Philadel-

phia Band, and in 1853 he opened a music store in his native city. The panic of 1857 greatly demoralized trade, and the following year he removed his establishment to Williamsport. At the end of a year, however, he returned to Philadelphia. He now has a branch store in Germantown (a part of Philadelphia), where he has for a long time resided. Mr. Winner was married in 1848 to Miss Hannah J. Guyer, by whom he has had several children, and who is still living. Five of the children are also living. Septimus, Jr., is in partnership with his father, and Joseph has gained considerable reputation as a song writer under the name of "Joseph Eastburn."

Mr. Winner's songs, with which he has been so successful, number several hundred, the words to all of them being by himself. His first song, as well as his first composition, was "How Sweet are the Roses," published by Lee & Walker, Philadelphia, in 1850. It appeared under the *nom de plume* of "Alice Hawthorne," an arrangement of his mother's maiden name, and was shortly followed by "What is Home Without a Mother," which constitutes the first of what afterwards came to be known as the "Hawthorne Ballads." Its popularity, though almost phenomenal, was eclipsed by that of "Listen to the Mocking Bird," which has probably been heard in some shape by everyone who knows anything at all about music. It is said that the idea of writing this song was suggested to Mr. Winner by the performances of a colored individual, Richard Milburn, commonly called "Whistling Dick," who was noted for his imitations of the mocking bird. It would be impossible, in an article like this, to specify all of Mr. Winner's songs, but others that may be mentioned are "The Love of one fond Heart," "Pet of the Cradle," "Whispering Hope," "Our Good Old Friends," "Dreaming of the Loved Ones," "Just as of Old," "Lost Isabel," "Wherefore," "Side by Side," "Song of the Farmers," "Days Gone By," "What Care I," "Love once gone, is gone forever," "Farewell song of Enoch Arden; or, I'll sail the seas over" (suggested by Tennyson's beautiful poem), "Yes, I would the war were over," "Give us back our old Commander," "Aunt Jemima's Plaster," and "Ten Little Injuns." He has composed quite a number of instrumental pieces, but is chiefly known in this field for his arrangements for various instruments, which number upwards of 1500. His series of easy guides or methods has become very popular. It includes the following instruments : Piano, reed organ, guitar, violin, flute, violoncello, accordeon and flutina, German accordeon, banjo, concertina, fife, clarinet, flageolet, and cornet. For the most of them he has also edited collections of music. Mr. Winner has written under the names of "Percy Guyer," "Mark Mason," and "Paul Stenton," as well as his own name and that of "Alice Hawthorne."

**Wolfsohn,** CARL, pianist and composer, was born at Alzey, Reinhessen, Germany, Dec. 14, 1834. His musical talent early showed itself, and at the age of twelve he was placed under the care of Aloys Schmitt of Frankfort, with whom he remained two years, his studies at the end of that time being interrupted by the revolution of 1848. About this time he commenced composing, and wrote some patriotic songs. In December, 1848, he made his *début* as a pianist at Mozart Hall, Frankfort, playing the piano part of Beethoven's Quintet. From Frankfort he went to Mannheim, where he studied with Mme. Heinfelter and Vincenz Lachner. In 1851 he made a concert tour in Rhenish Bavaria, with the celebrated violinist, Therese Milanolo, and in 1852 went to London, remaining there two years. He then (1854) came to the United States, and soon after took up his residence at Philadelphia, where he held a leading position in musical circles. In 1856 he made a concert tour throughout the States with Theodore Thomas, in conjunction with whom he for several years conducted a series of chamber concerts in Philadelphia. His first public appearance in New York was early in 1865, when he achieved a great success and was received with more than ordinary favor. He organized the Beethoven Society of Philadelphia in 1869, which is still flourishing, and on the occasion of the Beethoven Centennial Festival, Dec. 17, 1870, made his *début* as an orchestral conductor. After giving two seasons of symphony concerts he was obliged to suspend them on account of insufficient support. In the fall of 1873, upon invitation, he removed to Chicago, which has since been his place of residence. Shortly after his removal he organized a Beethoven Society similar to the one in Philadel-

phia, which has given excellent performances of important works.

Mr. Wolfsohn ranks among the leading artists of this country, having a fine *technique* and at once entering into the spirit of the work, which he impresses upon each person of his audience. He is especially happy as an interpreter of Beethoven's sonatas, the entire series of which (33 in number) he has thrice played in public. He has also given numerous recitals from the works of Chopin, Schumann, and other great composers. As a composer he has not been very active. His productions consist of a transcription of airs from "Faust," a "Valse de Concert," numerous melodies for the violin, several concertos for piano and strings, and some songs and piano pieces, in all of which the hand of the musician may be traced.

**Wollenhaupt,** HERMANN ADOLPH, pianist and composer, was born Sep. 27, 1827, at Schkeuditz, Saxony. He studied under Julius Knorr and Hauptmann, and in 1845 came to the United States, locating at New York. On various occasions he appeared as pianist at the Philharmonic and other concerts, and came to be highly esteemed both as a teacher and as a composer. His compositions are chiefly for the piano, and being written with more than usual care and taste have proved useful for teaching purposes. Many of them have been republished in Europe, making his name respected wherever known. He died at New York, Sep. 18, 1863. The following is a partial list of his works :

Whispering Winds ; Souvenir et Salut, andante and étude (op. 7); Belinda-Polka and Iris-Polka, 2 nos. (op. 8); Warrior's Joy March, impromptu (op. 9); Polka di Bravura (op. 10); La Rose and La Violet, two polkas (op. 14); Nocturne (op. 15); La Campanella, étude de concert (op. 16); Morceau en forme d'étude (op. 22); Deux polkas de *salon*, No. 1, L'Hirondelle, No. 2, La Gazelle (op. 23); Galop di Bravura (op. 24); Le Ruisseau, valse étude (op. 25); Hélene, valse brilliant (op. 26); Deux morceaux de *salon*, No. 1, Mazurka, No. 2, Valse Styrienne (op. 27); Mazeppa, galop de concert, also arranged for 4 hands (op. 43); Andante élégique (op. 45); Fantasia, "Il Trovatore" (op. 46); Grand Valse Styrienne (op. 47); Stories of Nocomis, four morceaux caractéristiques, for 4 hands (op. 48); A Bord de l'Arago, valse brilliant (op. 33); Sweetest Smile, polka (op. 49); Sparkling Diamonds, mazourka fantastique (op. 53); Song of the Syrens, valse brilliant (op. 54); Star Spangled Banner, paraphrase brilliant (op. 60); German March; Fleurs de Paradis, morceau de *salon*; Deceitful Birds, soprano or alto voice; Wanderer's Musings, soprano or alto.

**Woodbury,** ISAAC BAKER, was born Oct. 18, 1819, at Beverly, Mass. At an early age he was apprenticed to the blacksmith's trade at Boston, learning music in his spare moments. In 1839 he joined a traveling vocal company, the "Bay State Glee Club," which gave performances in various New England towns. In 1851 he visited Europe for the purpose of study, and after his return settled at New York, becoming actively engaged in composing and in editing various collections of church and Sabbath school music. He was also well-known as a conductor of conventions, and was connected with several musical papers as editor or contributor. His music is fresh and sparkling, and was quite popular in its day. Many of his church tunes are now in general use, among which are "Rakem," "Eucharist," "Salena," "Tamar," "Ozrem," and "Siloam." He died at Columbia, S. C., Oct. 26, 1858, at the age of thirty-nine.

**Work,** HENRY C., composer of popular songs, was born Oct. 1, 1832, at Middletown, Conn., and was of Scottish descent. When he was but an infant his father removed to Illinois, where his early years were spent. To his attendance upon the primitive camp-meetings "out West" his first musical impressions are due. When he had arrived at the age of fourteen years, the family returned to Connecticut, and it was decided that Henry must learn some trade. He was accordingly apprenticed to the printing business. During every spare moment he busied himself in studying such works on harmony as it was possible for him to secure, and finally he ventured to compose a song, which he called "We are Coming, Sister Mary." This he submitted to Edwin P. Christy, of minstrel fame, who was so well pleased with it that he sang it at his concerts. It was afterwards published by Firth, Pond & Co. of New York.

He wrote some other songs, but becoming dissatisfied with his own productions, he ceased to compose for several years. In 1861 appeared "Brave Boys are They," the first of a series of war songs, which includes "Kingdom Coming," "Wake, Nicodemus," "Grafted into the Army," "Babylon is Fallen," "Song of a Thousand Years," "God Save the Nation," and "Marching Through Georgia." The last named, written during the winter of 1864-65, is alone sufficient to perpetuate the name of its author, and is fast becoming a national melody. In 1865 he took a trip to Europe, and after his return bought, with his brother, several hundred acres of land at Vineland, N. J., with a view of establishing a fruit farm, but the investment proved an unprofitable one. His songs, among which must be mentioned the famous temperance one, "Come Home, Father," were principally published by Root & Cady, Chicago, but his contract with them was dissolved by the great Chicago fire of October, 1871. For several years more he ceased to write, and then came before the public again with "The Magic Veil," "Sweet Echo Dell," "Grandfather's Clock," and equally popular songs. "Grandfather's Clock" was first sung by Sam Lucas in New Haven, and has had a circulation attained by few pieces. Among his other songs, which number nearly four score, may be mentioned "Shadows on the Floor," "Mac O'Macorkity," "California Bird Song," (Pity me, Loo!), "King Bibler's Army," "The Fire Bells are Ringing," and "Used-up Joe" (comic). Mr. Work was not a professional musician, and hence did not develope his talents as he might otherwise have done. While composing he generally sought a quiet, retired place somewhere in the country. He died at Hartford, Conn., June 8, 1884.

**Wyman,** ADDISON P., was born at Cornish, N. H., June 23, 1832. He early learned the violin, and taught both vocal and instrumental music. In 1859 he was employed at Wheeling, W. Va., and in 1867 opened a music school at Claremont, N. H. He became widely known as a teacher and composer. His death occurred at Washington, Pa., April 15, 1872, and the remains were interred at his native place. Anne E., his wife, who died at Boston, Sep. 24, 1871, was a fair soprano singer. Mr. Wyman's compositions are chiefly for the piano, and some of them attained a wonderful popularity, which is not yet exhausted. Among them may be mentioned "Silvery Waves," "Woodland Echoes," "Music Among the Pines," "Wedding Bells March," "Fairy Visions," "Song of the Skylark," "Evening Parade March," "Moonlight Musings," and others. It is said that "Silvery Waves," which has already sold to the extent of nearly 1,000,000 copies, was retained by Messrs. S. Brainard's Sons, the music-publishers, for two years before it was issued, so fearful were they that it would not prove profitable!

# Y.

**Yankee Doodle.** An American national melody written, curious as it may seem, by an Englishman. The circumstances of its origin are as follows : In the summer of 1775 the British army, under the command of Abercrombie, lay encamped on the east bank of the Hudson, a little south of Albany, awaiting reinforcements of militia from the Eastern States, before beginning the campaign against the French. As company after company of the raw levies poured into camp during the month of June, each man differently armed and dressed from his neighbor, the scene was one to excite the mirth of a deacon. Their appearance was never equaled, except, perhaps, by the famous regiment of Sir John Falstaff. Among the British was a certain Dr. Shackburg or Shamburg, a surgeon, who, it seems, was also somewhat of a musician. He arranged the tune of Yankee Doodle to words of his own writing and dedicated it to the new comers. The joke took immensely and the tune thus passed to a permanent place in history.

Yankee Doodle was not original with Dr. Shackburg. John W. Moore, in his "Encyclopædia of Music" (article "Song"), says that the tune can be traced back to the time of Charles I. There are two or three more ancient melodies closely resembling it, and undoubtedly Dr. Shackburg did nothing more than arrange it to suit his own purpose. During its somewhat extended existence, it has been fitted with many different sets of words. In England one set of words began with— "The Roundheads and Cavaliers," and another with "Nankee Doodle came to town." In the United States there was a set which started off like this: "Lucy Locket lost her pocket." At a later period the tories had one, of which the first line was—"Yankee Doodle came to town." Francis Hopkinson of Philadelphia also wrote a set entitled "Battle of the Kegs." While the British ships were stationed in the Delaware river, in December, 1777, David Bushnell prepared a large number of kegs of powder so arranged that they would explode on reaching the fleet. They were, however, dispersed by the ice and prematurely exploded. But the British were effectually aroused, and for many hours kept up a firing at every dark object in the river. We herewith give the melody and the words of Dr. Shackburg :

REFRAIN.

1. Father and I went down to camp,
     Along with Captain Goodwin,
   And there we saw the men and boys
     As thick as hasty pudding.

*Refrain or Chorus—*
     Yankee Doodle keep it up,
     Yankee Doodle dandy ;
     Mind the music and the step,
     And with the girls be handy.

2.   And there was Captain Washington
       Upon a slapping stallion ;
     And giving orders to his men,
       I guess there was a million.

3.   And then the feathers on his hat,
       They looked so tarnal finey,
     I wanted peskily to get
       And give to my Jemima.

4.   And there they had a swamping gun
       As big as a log of maple,
     On a deuced little car ,
       A load for father's cattle.

5.   And every time they fired it off
       It took a horn of powder ;
     It made a noise like father's gun,
       Only a nation louder.

6.   I went as near to it myself
       As Jacob's underpinnin',
     And father went as near again—
       I thought the deuce was in him.

7.   (It scared me so I ran the streets,
       Nor stopped, as I remember,
     Till I got home, and safely locked
       In granny's little chamber.)

8.   And there I see a little keg,
       Its heads were made of leather,
     They knocked upon't with little sticks,
       To call the folks together.

9.   And there they'd fife away like fun,
       And play on corn-stalk fiddles :
     And some had ribbons red as blood
       All bound around their middles.

10.  The troopers, too, would gallop up,
       And fire right in our faces ;
     It scared me almost half to death
       To see them run such races.

11.  Uncle Sam came there to change
       Some pancakes and some onions
     For 'lasses cakes to carry home
       To give his wife and young ones.

12.  But I can't tell you half I see,
       They kept up such a smother ;
     So I took my hat off, made a bow,
       And scampered home to mother.

# Z.

**Zenobia.** A grand opera in four acts. Both the libretto, the themes of which are taken from Ware's well-known work, and the music are by Silas G. Pratt. It was begun in 1878, and first produced, in concert form, at Chicago, June 15 and 16, 1882. Its first production on the stage was at McVicker's Theatre, Chicago, March 26, 1883, with Miss Dora Henninges in the title *rôle*. In spite of several drawbacks, one of which was the illness of the soprano, it was fairly well received, and more interest manifested in it than in any similar American work. After a week's representation it was withdrawn. The opera contains several very fine numbers.

**Zerrahn,** CARL, was born at Malchow, Mecklenburg-Schwerin, Germany, July 28, 1826. He began the study of music at an early age under the care of a teacher of his native town. From 1841 to 1845 he studied with I. F. Weber of Rostoch, in 1846 at Hanover, and during 1846 and 1847 at Berlin. In 1848 he came to the United States with the famous Germania Orchestra (see GERMANIA ORCHESTRA), of which he remained a member until its dissolution in 1854. He conducted a series of six subscription concerts in 1855, with an orchestra of fifty-four players. Two years later he began the Philharmonic concerts, the programs of which were of unusually high order, and which were continued until 1863. In 1866 the Harvard Musical Association resolved to take up the work thus dropped, and Mr. Zerrahn was appointed conductor of the symphony concerts, a post which he ably filled and which he retained during the sixteen years they were continued. In 1882 he became leader of the Philharmonic Orchestra, then a recent organization. Besides his duties as conductor in Boston, he also conducts several societies in various cities and towns of Massachusetts. Much of the musical success of the two great Peace Jubilees held in Boston was due to his energy and ability. In 1877 he was called to San Francisco to take charge of the musical festival held there during that year, which made his reputation a thoroughly national one. Mr. Zerrahn is a good musician, and as a conductor deservedly occupies the foremost rank. For many years he has been a resident of Boston, where his efforts for the advancement of music are fully appreciated. As a gentleman he is highly esteemed by all who know him.

**Zeuner,** CHARLES, organist and composer, was born at Eisleben, near Gotha, Saxony, Sept. 20, 1795, and baptised as HEINRICH CHRISTOPHER ZEUNER, but seems to have changed his given name on coming to the United States, which he did in 1824. He took up his residence at Boston, where he came to be highly esteemed. In 1839 he published "The American Harp," containing 400 pages. His oratorio of "Feast of Tabernacles" was published in 1832, at which time he was organist of Park Street Church, president of the Musical Professional Society, and organist of the Handel and Haydn Society. The latter position he held from 1830 to 1837. His second important book, "Ancient Lyre," contained 364 pages and was published in 1848. Besides preparing several works himself, he wrote much music for the publications of other authors. In 1854 he removed from Boston to Philadelphia, where he was first organist of St. Andrew's Episcopal Church, and subsequently of the Arch Street Presbyterian Church. For several years he exhibited symptoms of insanity, but they were not thought to be serious. On Saturday, Nov. 7, 1857, he left his boarding place and proceeded to West Philadelphia. The same day his body was found in Smith's woods with the head shattered by a gun. It was evident that he had committed suicide. Mr. Zeuner was an excellent musician and respected by all who knew him.

**Ziegfeld,** DR. FLORENS, one of America's most prominent musical educators, was born at Jever, near the sea coast in the Grand Duchy of Oldenburg, Germany, June 10, 1841. His father, an official in the court of the grand duke, was passionately fond of music, and in him this same passion early developed. When six years of age he took his first piano lessons. Under the care of the best teachers he made very rapid progress, and at the age of ten played in both public and private concerts. Through excessive study his health became undermined, and at the age of fifteen he came to New York to visit a brother there. In 1859 he returned to Germany to finish his musical education. He entered the Conservatorium at Leipzig, where for several years he studied under Moscheles, Richter, Plaidy, Wenzel, David, Papperitz, and others. In 1863 he received a flattering offer to go to Russia and take charge of a large conservatory there, but declined, having already decided to make the United States his future home. He arrived here for the second time in 1863, and in November settled in Chicago as teacher of music. In 1867, under the name of the Chicago Academy of Music, he laid the foundation of the Chicago Musical College (see article CHICAGO). In 1868 he gave his first concert with his pupils in Crosby's Opera House, with great success. Such was the success of the school that in the fall of 1871 it occupied the entire building at No. 253 Wabash Avenue. The great fire of that year swept away everything. Within two months, however, the indomitable Doctor had re-opened the school under its present name. Dr. Ziegfeld went to Europe in the interests of the Peace Jubilee, and his acquaintance with eminent musicians abroad enabled him to secure many attractions. With Liszt, Wagner, and others, he maintained a correspondence more or less extensive. Since settling in Chicago, he has visited Europe eleven times, occasionally accompanied by some of his pupils. Dr. Ziegfeld is a true artist and musician, and one of which this country may well be proud. As he is yet in the prime of life, he will probably live to accomplish much more for his chosen art.

**Zundel,** JOHN, was born in 1815, at Hochdorf, near Stuttgart, Germany, and received his first musical education at the Royal Academy of Esslingen, Wurtemburg, where he remained from 1829 to 1831. In 1833 he received the appointment of teacher of music in a seminary at Esslingen, at the same time studying the vio-

lin under a pupil of Molique. Upon the advice of E. F. Walcker, the organ builder, he relinquished that instrument for the organ, taking lessons first of J. G. French and subsequently of H. Rinck at Darmstadt. In 1840 he went to St. Petersburg for the purpose of giving a concert on one of Walcker's organs. Circumstances led him to temporarily take up his residence at St. Petersburg as organist and teacher. Through the representations of several Americans who resided at the Russian capital, he was induced to come to the United States, and landed at New York in October, 1847. At first he met with no success and, discouraged, was about to return to Russia, when he was persuaded to remain by Scharfenberg & Louis, music-publishers of New York. In 1848 he was engaged as organist of the Unitarian Church (Dr. Farnley's), Brooklyn, and in 1850 of Plymouth Church. The latter position he held until 1865, excepting the years 1856 and 1857, when he was organist of Dr. Tyng's church and for the second time of Dr. Farnley's, Brooklyn. In 1865 he went to Europe, seeking restoration of his wife's health, and remained abroad two years. On returning he resumed his duties at Plymouth Church, which he continued to discharge until 1878, when he again went to Europe. He died (according to David Baptie) at Cannstadt, Germany, in July, 1882. Before departing he was presented with a substantial token in recognition of his long and valuable services, by the members of the church.

Mr. Zundel's principal works are as follows :

1.  250 Voluntaries and Interludes.
2.  A melodeon instructor.
3.  The Amateur Organist, a collection of voluntaries, etc.
4.  Concert Variations, for the organ.
5.  Six Voluntaries.
6.  444 Interludes and Voluntaries.
7.  The First Year at the Organ.
8.  Grand Festival March.
9.  Christian Heart Songs. Original tunes and anthems.
10. Introitas Anthem.
11. The School Harmonist.
12. Grand Te Deum Laudamus.
13. Beyond the Smiling. Solo and quartet.
14. Be Still, O Heart. Mezzo-soprano and quartet.
15. Treatise on Harmony and Modulation.